WALKING

ON

FIRE

WALKING

ON

FIRE

A Novel

Kathryn Crawley

SHE WRITES PRESS

Published 2023
Printed in the United States of America
Print ISBN: 978-1-64742-438-1
E-ISBN: 978-1-64742-439-8
Library of Congress Control Number: 2022920602

For information, address:
She Writes Press
1569 Solano Ave #546
Berkeley, CA 94707

Book Design by Stacey Aaronson

She Writes Press is a division of SparkPoint Studio, LLC.

To friends in Greece who became my family.

To the city of Thessaloniki which became my home.

one 🌿

Words buzzed past like angry bees. On the edge of her chair and listening intently, Kate tried to grab a familiar Greek word amid the scramble of sounds. Announcements from the Olympic Airline loudspeaker in New York's Kennedy Airport waiting area came in a steady stream, first in Greek, then English, then French. Despite working the past three months to learn the Greek language, Kate could make out only *Kalispera* or "Good evening."

She glanced down at the dark-blue textbook open on her lap. *Conversational Greek.* Worry spun circles inside her chest. With effort, Kate could read sentences about Peter attending classes at the university or Mary going for lunch. But neither those words, nor the memory of her tutor's slow-paced voice, were anything like what surrounded her now. She closed the book.

At twenty-five years of age, this was Kate's first time in New York. It was September 1974. Here, people walked too quickly and spoke too fast. They didn't smile or offer an "excuse me" after bumping into her. The sheer number of people was overwhelming, in stark contrast to her early morning start in Texas. After the hour drive from her hometown to Lubbock, she was comfortable in the airport with cowboys in wide-brimmed hats and women whose teased hair reached skyward. At Love Field in Dallas, the men wore business suits and women's hairstyles were more fashionable, but most everyone was friendly, or at least polite. New York was full of unwelcoming strangers with eyes fastened straight ahead.

Kate used her dollars—too many dollars—for a sandwich and a Coke. She had an hour until boarding the late evening flight. Kate threw away her trash and crammed herself and her carry-on bag into a phone booth. Hands shaking, she slipped a dime into the slot for a collect call to her parents in their small West Texas town. As they accepted the charges, she imagined them joined together and sharing the earpiece of the kitchen phone, her father's balding head against her mother's always perfect hairdo.

Working to keep her voice steady, she started out. "So far so good."

As they greeted her, the sound of their voices made her breath catch in her throat. *What have I done?* She was on her way to a distant country where she wouldn't know a soul.

"I'm glad we got that return ticket with an open date," Kate continued, comforted by the knowledge she could come back home soon if things didn't work out. For a fleeting moment, Kate wished she was back in her parents' kitchen, in her chair between the two of them, finishing dinner before heading to the TV room. Her finger traced the slots for nickels, dimes, and quarters on the pay phone.

Earlier in the summer, Kate had been thrilled with the offer of a speech therapy position in a center for Greek cerebral palsied children in the northern port city of Thessaloniki. She had resigned from her job in Colorado, packed boxes, and piled clothes into her orange Karmann Ghia for the drive back home to Texas, ready for an exciting overseas adventure.

Her giddy anticipation came to an abrupt halt one morning several weeks before she was scheduled to leave in mid-September. Kate stepped off her parents' porch into the already blinding sun for the rolled-up Lubbock newspaper. Sliding the rubber band off the paper, she was shocked by the photograph on the front page. Angry protesters in Athens gathered around a burning American flag, flames shooting into the air. Kate couldn't believe what she read next: "American tourists' cameras were smashed to the ground in Thessaloniki."

Thessaloniki. In a very short time, Greece and Thessaloniki had migrated to the center of her universe. Her destination for a job and a new home had now become a danger zone.

Propped against pillows on her bed, Kate read accounts in *Time* magazine that anti-American sentiment was rampant after the collapse of the Greek dictatorship in July. Greece and Turkey were at war over Cyprus.

"But why blame all of this on us—on America?" she said aloud to Schatzi, the dachshund nestled beside her. His brown eyes looked up at her expectantly. He had no answer.

At supper in early September, Kate and her parents had sat around the dining table, ice cubes melting in their tall glasses of sweet tea. Her dad cleared his throat and repositioned his glasses on his face.

"Katie, I called the State Department today."

Her head spun in his direction. "You what?" Her voice was almost a shriek.

She couldn't believe he hadn't consulted her. The process of becoming independent from her parents had been lengthy. But now that Kate had lived on her own for the past two years, she was accustomed to making decisions for herself. She gritted her teeth. The conversation was yanking her backward in time.

He shrugged his shoulders. "I just thought I'd find out if there were any advisories against Americans traveling to Greece." The air conditioner whirred in the background.

Seeing his furrowed brow and eyes squinting with concern, Kate softened. "What did they say?"

"They said they couldn't stop you from going over there." He waited. "But they also said you shouldn't appear to be an American." He raised his eyebrows with skepticism, mirroring her own thought of that improbability. With Kate's brownish-blond hair, cheerleader smile, and turned-up nose, there seemed little chance she could pass for someone other than an American.

"That's easy, then. I'll just pretend to be Canadian." She didn't try hiding her sarcasm.

Her mother refolded her napkin and put it next to her plate, smoothing the contours of her hair, although nothing was out of place, even in this heat. Kate knew it was all her mother could do not to scream, "Stop all this nonsense and stay home where it's safe!" Instead, her mother reached for the pitcher of tea and refilled their glasses.

Kate broke the silence. "I don't care. I'm going. Mrs. Stylianou said there was nothing to be afraid of." She had written her contact at the therapy center in Thessaloniki asking if it would be safe for an American to come to Greece right now. Unfolding the letter next to her plate, Kate again read words to them in a voice louder than necessary . . . words encouraging her to come.

"When we read your letter to our friends, they all laughed at my question. You have no reason to worry."

Kate turned the letter in their direction as if to emphasize the message. "She even said she'd be wearing a skirt with the colors of the American flag when she meets me at the airport." Kate slid the letter back in the envelope. "If I don't do this now, who knows when I'll get another chance?"

Her father moved the tines of his fork across the remnants of chicken fried steak on his plate. He seemed to choose his words carefully. "We don't want to stop you, Katie. We just want to make sure you'll be safe." Her mother was silent and began stacking their dishes to move to the sink.

Kate sipped the sweetness gathered at the bottom of her glass, then forced a smile across the table to her parents. "It's gonna be okay." Her words were meant for herself as well as them. "It's all gonna be okay," she repeated.

The air conditioner hummed, and the ice cubes continued melting. Her father stood and put his hands lightly on Kate's shoulders before heading to the TV room. The sound of running water and the clatter of plates came from the kitchen. Their lives together had resumed a normal routine, at least temporarily.

Now, a few weeks later, Kate was momentarily surprised to remember where she was . . . in a phone booth in New York. Her eyes scanned the teal polyester pantsuit and patterned rayon blouse she and her mother decided would be best for traveling. Posing with a broad smile in front of the trifold mirror at Hemphill-Wells Department Store in Lubbock, hands on her hips, she had imagined herself stepping off the plane in Greece. *What happened to all of my excitement?* Kate turned back to the phone and focused on the black circle with numbers in white surrounding the dial.

"Oh, sugar. You're gonna do just fine." Her mother's voice was higher pitched than usual.

"Now don't forget to keep your Canadian disguise on." Her father attempted humor.

"Don't worry—it's all in place." Kate patted her hair, remembering when she had styled it many hours before in the bathroom mirror at home.

"Well, guess I'd better go." She strained to keep her voice even. "I'll find a way to let you know I got there okay." Kate worked to mask her reluctance. After saying goodbye multiple times, she placed the phone back on the hook and watched the traffic stream past the glass plates of the phone booth.

Kate stood and pulled opened the bifold door, hoisting her carry-on bag on her shoulder. She returned to the Olympic Airlines pre-boarding area and found an unoccupied hard plastic chair near the gate.

And waited.

two 🌿

Kate clicked her seatbelt. She watched the shadows of men loading baggage onto the Olympic flight bound for Athens. *It's really happening.* She was here and couldn't run off the plane at the last minute, as a tiny part of her fantasized. Lights blinked into the darkness of the night sky while the steady vibration of engines hummed.

The intercom called for attention. An attractive stewardess with almond-shaped eyes was dressed in a blue suit with a pillbox hat fastened to her dark, wavy hair. As Kate watched her acting out the instructions, a momentary fear took hold. She would be flying all the way across the Atlantic Ocean, over hundreds of miles of deep, dark water. A shiver ran through her body. Kate squeezed her eyes shut for a brief moment as the plane taxied down the runway.

Half an hour into the flight, Kate watched the stewardess approach, now with a fitted apron and a blue-and-white scarf knotted to one side of her neck. Her eyes skipped past Kate as she slid a tray her way. *What is this? Dinner? And a small bottle of wine?* Kate unfolded a cloth napkin, aware of yet another step she was taking into a new world.

Until now she had only flown between Texas and Colorado or Wyoming. After fumbling with the salad dressing container, she struggled to spread butter onto a hard roll, then ate the beef tips and rice in silence. Kate sipped the last of the wine and returned her tray to the stewardess. She glanced at her fellow passengers who were getting comfortable with the pillows and small blankets passed to them. Following suit, she eventually dozed off.

Suddenly, Kate jerked awake. Her watch said 2:00 a.m., but red light slivered from beneath the plastic window shade. She raised it and saw the dawn sky shimmering dramatically on snow-covered peaks. Her heart jumped, this time with delight. *Are these the Alps?* Kate wanted to ask someone, but the man in the adjacent seat was asleep. She gazed and gazed, stunned by the grandeur of the sight.

Kate stretched her legs as far as she could under the seat in front of her. She continued staring out the window at the brightness, speeding toward a new life she never could have imagined. Only four years before, she had walked down a church aisle in a confection-spun wedding dress of satin and tulle, floating in a fantasy. Jim waited in front at the altar, smiling and handsome in a black tux. Kate was thrilled to be handed off from her father's arm to the arm of her future husband. Her father had always taken care of her, and now she would be secure with Jim. It was a dream she'd had since a little girl, when she would painstakingly cut out elaborate dresses for her paper doll brides.

The words from the minister and the rest of the marriage ceremony were a blur. When the organ sounded a triumphant recessional, they hurried down the aisle, out the church doors, and into their happy new life together. Jim would finish law school and she would complete graduate school, and then "real life" would start.

The once promising future, however, was stopped cold. Surely, whatever was waiting at the other end of this airplane ride couldn't be as difficult as losing the man of her dreams. Like most of her sorority sisters at their Southern Baptist university, Kate's plan after college was to become a wife and mother, imitating the lives of her parents and grandparents, a continuous series of happy stories. A life which had seemed on track until a rainy Sunday afternoon in Waco, two years into the marriage, vanished.

Hearing his tread on the stairs leading to their second-floor apartment, Kate wiped her hands on her apron and headed to greet him. Jim was returning from studying at the law library. He kept his back to her after shutting the door and paused before turning around.

"Hey, darlin'," Kate said as she reached out to him. Jim was the golden-haired, golden-voiced, broad-shouldered person who could easily unlock the meaning of an Emily Dickinson poem for her English literature paper. He always knew what he was talking about. He always made the decisions for them.

"Hey," he murmured, as he shook the rain off his jacket. His embrace was brief before moving to his usual chair, the green velour Barcalounger they'd picked out at the furniture store. She perched on the arm of the couch nearby, facing him. It was then she realized something was wrong. His face was a mask. Kate watched him avoid her eyes. *What's happening? Did a job offer fall through?* She waited for him to start, just like she always did.

"Listen," he finally began, "there's something I gotta talk to you about."

"Sure, Bunky." She used the pet name they'd had for each other since their earliest days together.

"We're coming up to a decision time," Jim continued.

Kate assumed she had guessed right, and it had something to do with where they'd move in the fall after their studies ended. His job, of course, would take precedence, but she'd already started the hunt for speech therapy positions in their target areas. "I know. I've already been researching jobs in Fort Worth and Tyler—"

"I'm not sure that's the best thing." Jim still would not look at her. His voice was curt. His briefcase remained in his lap. He slid his fingers over the handle back and forth, back and forth. He stopped and took a deep breath. "This marriage thing just isn't working out for me." His eyes stayed focused on his hands. Jim's voice, his beautiful voice that could soar in a solo at the Baptist church, was barely audible. "There's a big world out there." He paused. "I don't think I can see it with you."

The air went out of Kate's chest like she'd been punched. She stared at him in disbelief. The room spun. There was nothing to hold onto. "What on earth are you talking about? You can't mean that!" she yelled into the living room they had carefully decorated with wedding gifts.

Finally, he faced her. "I'm sorry. I didn't mean for it to happen this way." Despite the harsh message he had just delivered, there was a softness in his eyes.

Kate fell back onto the couch, clenching her fists and covering her face. Her breath came in short bursts. Any power she might have had seemed to be slipping away. "No! No! No!" Her words died in her throat as she ran into the bedroom and fell on the bed. She clawed the bedspread, sobbing and searching desperately for words she could use to make Jim understand how wrong this all was. But Kate had never been good at making him change his mind. And, as she gradually calmed, she knew this time would be no different.

One month later, Kate sat in the bedroom watching her older

brother stretch masking tape over the last of the boxes. "Nothing else from here, Katie?" Her father stood in the doorway, slipping off his work gloves and wiping his brow with a handkerchief.

"That's it, Dad. Thanks." Kate surveyed the room one last time, sighing as her eyes lingered on the cherrywood bedroom suite they'd found in an antique store. It would be staying with Jim. She made herself walk into the living room where she could see the orange and black U-Haul from the second-floor picture window. Her brother and parents were congregated around the trailer, one of them occasionally glancing in her direction. Kate bit her lip, trying to chase away the memories of the reverse process when she and Jim had first moved in two summers ago.

Her divorce had been a fiery crash of dreams onto the hard black asphalt of reality. The next part of her life felt like she was driving in thick fog with only one headlight. A former college roommate invited her to Wyoming, where Kate found a speech therapy job with the Casper school system. Venturing into an unimagined and unwanted life as a single person, Kate sat alone in a different apartment on a different couch, knees scrunched to her chest, arms folded around them, trying not to fall into an abyss.

Months crippled past. At Christmas, her younger brother shoved *The Female Eunuch* into her hands. "Maybe you should read this."

A new word—"feminism"—was in the air. She read the book. Then she read other books and consumed page after page of *Ms.* magazine. Gradually, life as a single person became easier to navigate.

At the end of the school year in Wyoming, Kate was ready to take a leap. She found a more challenging job at a rehabilitation center in a larger city, Colorado Springs. Later that year, Kate spotted an advertisement in a professional journal for another job. In Greece. In a place called Thessaloniki.

Now Kate was on an airplane moving away from everything familiar and heading to Greece. She reached into the seat pocket and pulled out *Conversational Greek*. Mary and Peter were going for lunch near the university.

"Pou einai to kainourio estiatorio?" They were asking for directions to a new restaurant. That much, at least, she understood.

three ✤

Stepping into the Athens airport, Kate was immediately over-whelmed by a kaleidoscope of vibrant colors, alongside boom-ing noises and bustling activity. Travelers and employees rushed to their destinations. New York had been hectic, but at least she had been in America. Not any longer. Since planes from other countries were landing at the same time, she was surrounded by a multitude of languages and sights. African women wore scarves piled on their heads, men appeared with capes and loose trousers, and the acrid scent of underarms pervaded.

Momentarily stunned, Kate searched for an unoccupied space and moved toward a wall. After a few seconds, she steadied herself. A sign in English, NON-GREEK CITIZENS, directed her toward a long line. She shifted her travel bag on her shoulder and headed there. As she waited, Kate tried calming herself by reading signs in the cavernous room. The bright red letters *EXOTHOS* meant "exit," which she related to the word "exodus." *ELLINIKON* referred to "Hellenic," which she had learned was what Greeks called them-selves. Kate distracted herself by reading other Greek words, pre-tending she was inside a giant puzzle and seeking solace amid the chaos.

Alerts sounded like oversized doorbells, announcing incoming and outgoing flights over the PA system in Greek, followed by a stilted form of English, then French. Kate inched forward in line, searching for another word to dissect while fingering the edges of her passport.

When it was her turn, she shakily presented her passport to the officer at the booth. He wore a light-blue, well-pressed shirt with buttoned epaulets on the shoulders. Kate studied the waves of his dark, well-oiled hair while his eyes remained on her passport. Methodically, he flipped through the blank pages. She recalled the words from the newspaper article: "American tourists' cameras were ripped from their necks and smashed to the ground." It was clearly impossible not to appear to be an American with United States of America emblazoned in gold on the front of her passport. The officer raised deep brown eyes to stare at her, matching face with picture in her booklet. He kept a serious expression as he lifted a rubber stamp and ground it onto the blank page. Pushing her passport back, he motioned for the next person in line.

"*Efharisto,*" she said, thanking him. It was her first time to speak Greek in Greece after hours of practicing at home. He nodded his head in response but didn't make eye contact.

Kate followed signs to the luggage retrieval area. Her yellow suitcase traveled on a conveyor belt, the only one of its color. It now seemed a lifetime ago when the sunshine-bright suitcase was new and waiting on her bedspread. Kate reached out to grab her bag, excusing herself with "*Sygnomee*" to a man in front, another of the words she'd practiced repeatedly in front of the bathroom mirror. *I'm really here!*

Chimes of announcements and the babble of languages crowded around her as she followed the flow of passengers. Finally, Thessaloniki appeared on a sign. She read the curving letters in Greek as well as English. Relief flooded inside. The end of her journey was in sight. Right there. Straight ahead in both languages.

"You made it!" she whispered to herself and rushed forward with renewed purpose.

Kate approached the ticket counter and smiled at the young woman wearing a light-blue blouse and blue-and-white patterned neck scarf. Glancing at the ticket in Kate's hand, the woman motioned to the board behind her. The word "canceled" in English was below a Greek word obviously giving the same message. It took Kate a few seconds to comprehend what she was reading. "But . . . but you see, I need. . . " she stammered.

"I am sorry, Miss. There are no airplanes to Thessaloniki today. It is a national strike." Kate tried to ask what she could do but was met with, "It is not in our control. I am sorry."

The woman resumed a conversation with her colleagues in rapid-fire Greek. Kate was stunned. *This can't be happening.*

With effort, she moved away from the ticket counter and scanned her surroundings. Her eyes fell on a coffee bar across the corridor. Kate pulled her suitcase over to a small table and chair, heart racing toward panic. *No flight. What am I going to do now? I need to call Mrs. Stylianou and tell her.* Kate knew Thessaloniki was in northern Greece, a distance away from Athens on a map, but she had no idea how far away. Kate chewed on her bottom lip, desperate to find a solution.

Down the wide hallway on the right was a bank of pay telephones. *And how do I even make a phone call in Greece?* Kate pulled the envelope from Mrs. Stylianou's last letter with the return address on Aristotelous Street. A memory flashed of her excitement seeing the address when the letter had come.

"Even their streets are named after philosophers!" she'd joked to her mother. That day seemed so long ago.

Kate surveyed the coffee bar. A man in a white shirt and black bowtie poured steaming water into a cup. Patrons at tables enjoyed their coffee and conversation. She needed to ask for help, but what if the person she chose hated Americans?

"Pardon me." Kate jumped in surprise at the voice coming from behind. "Forgive me. I did not intend to frighten you." The kind words came from a short, middle-aged man speaking to her in English. His blue shirt had epaulets on the shoulders, and the pair of wings on his nametag possibly indicated he was a pilot. "I think you are having a problem?"

Heartened by the sincere expression on his face, Kate hesitated only briefly before responding. "I am, but I'm afraid you can't help me. I was scheduled—"

"Yes. Yes. The airline strike. This country, now that it's free, has some kind of strike every week," he said with a touch of exasperation yet humor in his voice.

She wasn't sure what he meant by free, but now was not the time for such a question. "I was supposed to meet someone at the airport in Thessaloniki." Kate held Mrs. Stylianou's letter up to him.

"I see." He scanned the letter. "I am Petros. In English, it is Peter." Kate shook the hand outstretched to her, half-smiling with the thought she was finally meeting Peter from her textbook.

"Um, I'm sorry. Right now, I can't remember how to say 'Happy to meet you' in Greek."

"You can say *hairo polee* but 'pleased to meet you' is fine." His warm smile helped Kate relax a bit.

"*Hairo polee,*" Kate echoed.

"We can together try to find the name in the telephone book." He pointed in the direction of the phones and picked up her suitcase. "I am certain this is not the welcome you expected in Greece," he said as they walked together. Kate forced a smile. He continued. "Also, there are trains from Athens to Thessaloniki."

Approaching an open booth with an old-fashioned phone attached to a wall, Petros put her suitcase down and lifted a large book attached with a chain. He thumbed through several pages. Kate watched him scan the names on the thin pages, waiting and hoping to see some kind of recognition on his face. She guessed the answer before he said anything. "I am sorry. There is no Stylianou on Aristotelous."

"I think she said it was her husband's store?" His finger went down the list more slowly this time.

"There is no Stylianou on Aristotelous Street." His smile was apologetic. "The train?" Kate's head started to spin. "Of course, your friends will know there is a strike. Greece is a small country."

Kate struggled to keep her emotions in check. "I'm afraid that if I take a train, I'll end up in this same situation with nobody to call." Her lips quivered with this last word.

At that moment, a broad smile spread across Petros's face. Kate followed his gaze. A line was forming in front of the ticket counter for flights to Thessaloniki.

"Quick, quick!" He pulled her suitcase down the hallway and made a place for her in what could only loosely be called a line. Kate had already noticed Greeks' tendency to spread out in front of where they were trying to go next. The idea of standing orderly in front or back of someone else didn't seem to be a custom here.

Petros waited with Kate, lifted her suitcase for processing, and made sure she had her boarding pass. Sticking her hand out to him, Kate began, "You have no idea how much I appreciate your help today."

Clasping her hand, Petros smiled. "Please say a good word to your President Ford for the poor small country of Greece when you return to America. That is, if you ever go back there after the beautiful Greece."

Kate thanked him again and watched as he disappeared into the crowd. A broad grin spread on her face. This was the first full-faced smile she had since . . . and then she realized she had completely lost track of time. Her watch showed it was nighttime back home. Yet it seemed like she'd been gone weeks instead of hours.

A chime and an announcement signaled her flight. Kate didn't know several kinds of gods were smiling on her. This would be the very last flight to Thessaloniki before the strike began in earnest.

four ✿

The airplane to Thessaloniki was a small one with two seats per row, every seat occupied. Once in the air, Kate pulled out the thin blue letter from Mrs. Stylianou. She ran her finger around the small squares of red-and-blue border design, recalling when it had first arrived.

Opening the mailbox in the lobby of her apartment complex in Colorado Springs, she had gasped. Her name and address were on the distinctive envelope. Stamps featured colorful drawings of women in native costumes and *Hellas,* a word she assumed meant "Greece." Inside her apartment, Kate sank down in her beanbag chair with the unopened letter and stopped to stare at Pike's Peak outside her window. It rose toward the sky, just as it had for eons.

Kate hesitated, hands shaking with anticipation. It was June, and she had given up hope of hearing back from the Hellenic Center for Cerebral Palsied Children. The advertisement in a professional journal appeared in March. She'd responded on a whim. The job description read, "Greek language background preferred but not required." Kate was seeking a new adventure somewhere—anywhere.

Steadying her hands, Kate let out a long breath and slid her finger carefully under the fold to open the envelope. She held the onionskin blue pages and marveled at the neatly spaced words. The lines spreading down the page were almost mechanically perfect, each English letter precisely formed. Her breathing stopped as she worked to comprehend the meaning of the words on the paper.

"Please excuse me that I answer you after such a long period of time." Mrs. Stylianou, the center's representative, explained she had to wait for the nine board members to meet and discuss the position.

Kate's heart quickened as she continued reading.

"We decided to ask you to work in our center, and we hope that after you spend two or three months here, you will be able to speak the language enough to help our children."

Kate let out a yell and held the letter to her chest, wiping away tears with the back of her hand. A new door was opening in her life, into a life beyond her wildest dreams.

Mrs. Stylianou explained the salary would be small but that it was almost twice what was paid to the physiotherapists, since there was no training for speech therapists in Greece. She suggested there was an opportunity for private practice work in the afternoons after the clinic closed.

"There will be many patients begging for your help," the letter continued. "We are sorry that we are unable to pay for your airfare, but we will provide for you once you arrive."

It didn't matter. The money she'd been saving for a trip to Europe with her brother was waiting in her bank account.

Kate jumped up and rushed to her bedroom to call her parents in Texas. She knew her mother would be in the kitchen starting supper. Grabbing the receiver of the phone in her bedroom, she pulled on the long cord so she could walk while she talked.

"Mother!" she screamed. "You'll never believe it! They want me in Greece!" Her voice had broken with the last word.

To get ready for her adventure, Kate was surprised to find an album, *Learning Modern Greek in Record Time,* in a Colorado Springs bookstore. Listening as the calm male voice guided her into the mystery of this new language, she cracked the code of the alphabet and soon could read words. A Greek tutor in Denver introduced her to the book *Conversational Greek* and helped with grammar rules and short conversations. Kate quit her job at the end of July and headed back home to Texas.

Now, in the sky over Greece, she closed her eyes and imagined a scene she'd witnessed many times of her mother in the kitchen talking to their two dachshunds. She drifted off to sleep.

Kate was jolted awake by an intercom announcement and a shift of altitude. The plane broke through the clouds. Her breath caught in her throat. Down below, a city with rows of multistory buildings curved around a body of water. Sunlight sparkled as it bounced off waves. Kate had studied Thessaloniki in the *World Book Encyclopedia* at home and knew the Gulf of Salonika was at one edge of the Aegean Sea. And now part of that same Aegean Sea was directly below. Her heart danced with excitement. Kate fluffed her hair and peeked at her makeup in the small circle mirror of her compact.

Craning her head to look out again, she saw a building at one end of the runway, covered by a brown-and-green camouflage net. Military planes were parked nearby. Was this connected to Greece's war with Turkey over Cyprus that she'd read about? And what about the anti-Americanism she'd been warned of? Her thrill switched to unease.

Kate glanced around again at the faces of her fellow passengers. Many of them showed some similarity of dark hair, olive complexions, and prominent noses. There had been a few glances of curiosity in her direction. Her brownish-blond hair and upturned nose didn't match anyone else on the plane. No one had tried to start a conver-

21

sation, and she had been safe in her anonymity. Kate folded and refolded her hands as she waited for the bump of landing.

They taxied toward a modest two-story building, with the word "Thessaloniki" atop in both Greek and English. As the plane grounded to a halt, the space around her erupted with a cascade of Greek words, as passengers gathered their belongings and pushed toward the exit. Kate followed the crowd as they descended a shaky metal stairway onto the tarmac. Suddenly, she was on Greek land. A rush of warm air hit as she joined the group walking toward the building. *Even in September it feels like summer.* Something about the warmth nudged optimistic feelings to switch back on. Kate smiled tentatively. *Maybe this is a good idea after all?*

Once inside the airport, Kate searched for Mrs. Lena Stylianou. She scanned the crowd waiting in a cordoned-off area. No one was waving at her. No one wore the colors of the American flag, as promised in her letter. Men in open-necked shirts and slacks and with briefcases rushed past on their way to the glass doorways at the other end of the large room. A few grandmothers in black dresses with pocketbooks on their arms waited, holding the hands of small children anxious to run and meet parents from the flight. Kate moved closer to a conveyor belt disgorging luggage. She took turns monitoring the glass doors and the suitcases making their rounds. At last, her yellow suitcase, now with black marks and smudges, appeared. The space had quickly emptied, with only a few people milling about in the sudden quiet.

An older man, an Olympic employee in a gray uniform, approached. "Help with suitcase for bus? To Thessaloniki?"

"No, efharisto," using her much practiced "thank you." "I am waiting to be picked up."

He shook his head. "No stay here. All passengers go to city. Olympic terminal in city." His eyes were kind but there was an insistence in his voice.

Kate had neither the willpower nor the words to protest. Reluctantly, she followed him and her suitcase through the glass doors and to a waiting bus. Gasoline vapors surrounded her as she watched her suitcase hoisted into the luggage hold. Kate summoned the energy to pull herself up the stairs and drop into an empty seat on the first row. Up to this point, she had not cried. Mrs. Lena Stylianou had said she would meet her at the airport, but she was not here. And now Kate was heading into the city. *What will I do there? No phone number. Only a street address. Nothing else.* She let go. Tears slipped down her cheeks.

Kate stared straight ahead, listening to the engine rev and watching the driver's hand grab the black ball of the gear shift. And then he paused. He noticed something. Kate did too. Running toward the bus was a slim woman in a white blouse and a long skirt in the colors of red, white, and blue.

Shooting up from her seat, Kate stumbled down the stairs and into the waiting arms of Mrs. Lena Stylianou.

"I am very sorry, Kate," she greeted in perfect English as their embrace ended. "We heard on the radio that the strike was delayed. Let us find your luggage."

Kate pointed to the yellow suitcase and the driver set it on the sidewalk. Mrs. Stylianou's smile was warm. "Welcome to Greece. We are very happy to have you with us."

"Efharisto, Mrs. Stylianou." Kate wanted to show she had learned some Greek.

"Please. I am Lena. Let us go, shall we?"

23

Still shaking, Kate reached for the handle of her suitcase, finding Lena's hand already there. This lovely woman beamed at her. Kate smiled back, feeling the turmoil of her journey melt away. Together they lifted the suitcase.

At last, I think I may have finally arrived.

five ✦

Kate worked to match Lena's stride as they lugged her suitcase past rows of small cars, sneaking glances at her companion as they walked along together. With her light-olive complexion and shiny dark-brown hair pulled back with a clip, Lena was beautiful. Really beautiful. Kate realized she hadn't thought much about what Mrs. Stylianou would be like. Lena was much younger than she'd anticipated, probably just a few years older than Kate. And she exuded kindness.

Walking along, Kate thought for a moment she'd landed in a miniaturized world, as the cars seemed shrunken in comparison to American models. Nothing here resembled the collection of Buicks, Chevrolets, and pickup trucks in the parking lot of the Lubbock airport when she started her trip under a wide, blue Texas sky. The sky here was also bright but with a slight haziness.

Kate's energy began to fade. She had no idea if her departure had been one day ago or two. She'd lost track of time. The sunlight showed it was probably early afternoon in Greece. Slightly dizzy, she was grateful when Lena stopped behind a car of a foreign make she didn't recognize. Kate took the chance to lean onto it and breathe in the thick, warm air.

"We are here." Lena's voice was calm and had a musical quality. She unlocked the trunk of a small, boxy white car.

Feeling a bit self-conscious about her oversized luggage, Kate wondered what Lena thought as they struggled to fit it into the limited trunk space. With a final push, the yellow suitcase was in place. Kate slipped off her jacket before settling in the front seat.

"I hope that your trip was not too difficult." Lena smiled cordially at Kate as they shut their doors.

"It was scary when I found out about the strike, but a very nice man at the airport in Athens came to my rescue." Kate let out a long breath as she recalled Petros and his kindness. For the first time since her trip began, she felt safe. Lena started the car, and they were off.

They eased out of the parking lot, past the surprising sight of palm trees lining the exit and onto a busy highway. "Your English— you speak so beautifully." Kate was asking a question with her comment.

Lena nodded her head to one side. "I was fortunate to attend a private English-speaking high school. And that is where I met my husband, Yiannis." Her smile broadened. "You will meet him soon at our home, which is half an hour from Thessaloniki. Our boys are staying with my mother in the city for the night. You will meet them tomorrow."

The mention of the boys crushed the lightness Kate was just beginning to feel. In one of her letters, Lena had mentioned that she had a child with cerebral palsy. With all the airport adventures, Kate had temporarily forgotten the reason for her trip. She was here to do a job. Mrs. Stylianou, this lovely Lena, had brought her here to help her son speak better. In Greek. A language eluding her so mightily that she couldn't fathom carrying on a conversation, let alone do her job.

"I'm really happy to be here. But I'm worried about the language."

"Please do not worry. Because there are no speech therapists trained in Greece, you have techniques we do not have in this country. We will help you, and you will help our children." Lena's confidence tamped down Kate's fears, at least temporarily. Soon they turned onto a smaller road, heading away from what appeared to be a city.

"Thessaloniki?" Kate asked, pointing behind them.

"Bravo. Yes. Some people call it Saloniki or Salonika or Thessalonika—so you have many choices." She glanced at Kate. "Our city was named for a sister of Alexander the Great, Princess Thessalonike of Macedon. Their father was King Philip of Macedonia."

Kate watched the city fade into the landscape as the names Alexander the Great and Macedonia swirled in her head. She knew Alexander the Great from history classes and Macedonia from Baptist Sunday School lessons, but she had never expected to actually be in this ancient land. Here was the Thessaloniki on maps, in the newspapers, mispronounced by her friends when she told them where she was headed. And now she was finally here. Kate's fatigue gradually took over, as she stifled a yawn with her hand. Her arms and legs rested heavily in the seat.

There was a haze in the air as they drove along. It made the scene seem almost dream-like, with whitewashed churches and rows of tall, thin cypress trees scattered on the horizon. Buses and trucks whizzed by on the narrow two-lane road, passing Lena's slower-moving car. Their horns honked as they signaled going by, blaring a series of musical notes. Kate contrasted it to driving to the Lubbock airport in her parents' car at the start of her trip, where orderly four-lane highways skirted past rows of cotton fields, and pickup trucks trailed streams of dust in the distance. A world away. Literally.

"I hope your family is well," Lena said, keeping her eyes on the road ahead. "We invite you to call them from our home to let them know you arrived safely."

Kate checked her watch, still set on Texas time. "Thank you. But I'm afraid it's still early morning for them." She imagined daylight creeping into the darkness surrounding her parents' two-story home and the quiet in their bedroom as they slept. A twinge of homesickness struck. Turning her face toward the window and away from Lena, she squeezed back unexpected tears. "Maybe I can call them later."

They passed through what she assumed was a village. Men sat outside a coffee shop on one side of the road. An empty restaurant with small tables and chairs was on the other, unlit strands of light bulbs crisscrossing over the patio. Atop the building Kate saw a sign with rambling shapes that she couldn't read. *Greek letters in script?* Her lessons in Greek hadn't gone beyond upper- and lowercase block letters. Currents of fear circled inside at this new reminder of the complexity of the language. *How will I ever do this?* Something akin to dread began creeping inside. She watched the landscape change to fields with an occasional house or building.

They drove in silence until Kate heard the click of a blinker signal. Lena slowed and they left the road, passing through a green metal gate between white stucco walls. A curving lane ran alongside trees standing in ordered rows and reaching toward the horizon. The afternoon sun traced their shadows on the brown earth.

"Yiannis is very proud of his trees—olives, almonds, and pistachios."

Kate heard the delight in Lena's voice.

"We moved here only a few months ago, but he started the farm a few years before then. It was another child for him. You can see he is a very good father!"

Kate smiled at this playful remark, glad for the relief from her unease. They drove on toward a large two-story stone house with red geraniums in window boxes. Trumpet vines spilled over a wall on the left. Kate smiled as she recognized small peach and apricot trees on the right, familiar from her grandmother's yard. Ahead, a carport was attached to the house, with another car parked there.

"We will leave your suitcase. Yiannis will get it later."

Walking across a flagstone patio, Kate was surprised to see three sheep grazing on the grass nearby. Just beyond, she glimpsed a garden with multicolored zinnias and vegetables. A faint smell of animals scented the air. She stopped on hearing a strange honking noise coming from behind the house.

Lena laughed. "Yes, it is a funny sound. 'Peacocks,' I think in English. We have many animals here."

The front door was intricately carved with vines and flowers, making Kate wonder if she were entering into a fairy tale. Lena pulled open the heavy door, and they were inside an entryway with low light filtering through a row of small windows. A wooden stairway led upstairs. Lena stopped to remove her shoes and put on slippers.

"If you do not mind, we remove our shoes inside the house. Please take any pair you would like." A row of many shoes lined one wall. "My husband's father owns a shoe factory. We are not without shoes!" Lena laughed again.

Kate sat on a small, caned chair and unbuckled the Mary Jane pumps she'd been wearing for almost two days, choosing a pair of slippers. The fur lining and soft leather felt luxurious against her nylon stockinged feet, and she welcomed this unusual practice of removing shoes when entering a house.

"Yianni—we are here!" Lena yelled upward.

Their footsteps echoed off the stone walls of the lower entry and the wooden steps of the stairway, which led to a highly polished floor at the top. To the left was a kitchen with a brightly colored oilcloth on the table and four ladderback chairs. To the right, windows and a door opened onto a balcony. Straight ahead, a large living room with white stucco walls revealed a stone fireplace and wall-to-ceiling bookshelves.

Kate heard music. To her surprise, it was the jazz standard "Autumn Leaves" sung in heavily accented English. She flashed on a scene less than one week before at Furr's Cafeteria in Lubbock, a silver-haired woman playing this song on a grand piano. West Texas farmers and shoppers carried trays to Formica tables accompanied by this "touch of class." Her parents, aunt and uncle, and cousins had gathered at Furr's for a farewell dinner before Kate left for Greece. Dining at Furr's Cafeteria had been a part of her life since a little girl. Now, hearing the familiar tune "Autumn Leaves" in this magnificent Greek home only reinforced the surreal sense of what she was experiencing.

Entering the room, Kate found the source of the music was a small black-and-white television with snowy reception in one corner. Next, her eyes were drawn to a series of striking black-and-white photographs hung on one wall of the living room.

A set of windows brought in late-afternoon light. In the center of the room, three large, overstuffed chairs were arranged around a low table with magazines and an open newspaper. The scent of a cigarette and a cloud of smoke rose from one of the chairs. Kate followed Lena farther into the room. Someone was seated, a cigarette poised between his fingers.

"And this is my husband, Yiannis." Lena encouraged Kate in his direction. The man balanced his cigarette on the edge of an ashtray and slowly rose to greet her.

He was smallish, with a somber expression, and wore a baggy, gray sweater. Kate was taken aback by a thin line of scars running from his eyebrow to his mouth on one side, creating a slight asymmetry to his face. He had dark-rimmed glasses and a bushy black mustache. Kate hesitated. Nothing about him seemed welcoming.

Kate reached her hand out to him. *"Fimai ee Katina,"* she spouted the introduction she had practiced with her tutor but hadn't yet had the chance to use. Her embrace of Lena, when she'd stumbled down the steps of the bus, had taken the place of any formal greeting.

Yiannis's hand met hers. He stared at her for a few moments with eyes steely and cold. Suddenly, his face broke open with a large smile and his eyes softened.

He responded in perfect but accented English. "Hello, Katina. I am Yiannis." He motioned to a chair. "Please sit, Katina."

She followed his invitation and perched on the edge of the chair.

"Kate," Lena said. "The name 'Katina' is very old-fashioned. You could be called 'Kaitie' or 'Katerina' instead."

Yiannis interrupted his wife. "No, no, Lena." Yiannis grinned at her and then at Kate. "I think we should call her 'Katina.' It will fit in just the right way. *Yemize to stoma,*" he said, accompanying these Greek words with a hand gesture opening and closing.

"He says it fills up the mouth," Lena translated.

Kate took this for something good, judging by the way Lena smiled at the idea.

With mock seriousness, Yiannis intoned, "I baptize you Katina."

Kate attempted to smile. She didn't know anything about Greek baptisms or the importance in Greek culture of bestowing a name.

All Kate knew was she needed to rest. And hopefully, very soon, to sleep.

six ✿

When she awoke, it took Kate a moment to remember where she was. The room was bright and sunny. Her yellow suitcase was open on the other twin bed; her pantsuit draped over a chair. Car horns sounded from the road in one direction and farm animals from the other. Greece. The Stylianou farm. She checked her watch, now set on Greek time. Eleven o'clock.

Kate tied the belt of her bathrobe and peeked out the door, listening for voices or movement in the house before venturing down the hall to the bathroom. She washed her face, then wished herself a "good morning" with her new name.

"Kalimera, Katina," she said to the mirror.

Through open windows in the hallway, she heard a high-pitched female voice speaking rapidly, followed by responses from a voice she recognized as Lena's. Moving to get a better view, Kate saw Lena and a woman of small stature, both bent over as they gathered bounty from the garden out front. The day dazzled with sunlight.

Kate made her way into the kitchen. A plate was set out on the table, alongside a rounded loaf of bread, knife, slices of feta cheese, and two ripe figs. A jar of Nescafe coffee and spoon sat next to a cup. Just as she was trying to figure out how she would heat water for coffee, Kate heard footsteps on the outside stairway. The kitchen door swung open.

"Kalimera!" Lena's voice sung out.

Even in an oversized work shirt and skirt with grass stains, Lena had a radiance about her. Kate had temporarily forgotten how magical Mrs. Stylianou had turned out to be.

"Kalimera," Kate answered back.

"I hope that you slept well," Lena smiled, washing her hands. "May I make your first morning coffee in Greece?"

"Yes, efharisto," Kate thanked her and tried sawing through the crusty loaf, ending up with a crooked piece of bread.

Kate watched Lena boil water in a small, long-handled pot with a pouring lip, and then spoon coffee into the cup.

"Milk?" Lena asked. "It is from our sheep."

Milk from their own sheep? Kate had never had such a thing.

"Parakalo," Kate answered. "Please" was another of her much-practiced Greek words.

Lena stirred hot water into the coffee crystals and added the milk. "Later today we will go into Thessaloniki and meet my children: Aris, and Soto—the one with cerebral palsy."

With that announcement, anxiety flooded in. Soto. Her job. To improve this boy's speech in a language which spun around her in a whirlwind of chaos. Even in the best of circumstances, it would be a challenge to do therapy in a foreign language. But she couldn't understand regular Greek, much less the distorted words of someone with cerebral palsy.

"Kala." Kate nodded her head and used another of the words she knew . . . "good."

Kate's previous delight just a few moments earlier had now evaporated. With two hands for steadiness, she brought the cup of steaming coffee to her mouth. She tried recalling the few cerebral palsied children she'd helped during her two years of working and others from her summer job as a counselor in a camp for disabled children. What would Soto be like? How severe was his cerebral palsy? Would he like her? What Greek words could she say to him and his brother? And, ultimately, could she help him?

Neither the tanginess of the feta, nor the sweetness of the figs could steer her mind away from her apprehension. Although she'd had some specialized training in working with these children, Kate was not yet a seasoned therapist.

Lena interrupted her thoughts. "I must go to a nearby village for a few hours. I will leave lunch for you and come back later. You may walk around the farm or get more rest. I hope that is not a problem?" Lena asked.

"Thank you, Lena. I'll be fine," Kate answered, relieved she could put off the inevitable meeting with Soto a bit longer.

Lena excused herself and left the room. Kate finished her breakfast and washed the dishes. In the bathroom, she stepped into a low tub and fussed with an unusual handheld sprayer to wash the trip off her body. She put on slacks and a dressy blouse, fixed her hair and makeup.

"*Yeia sas. Hairo polee pou sas gnorizo.*" She addressed the mirror, practicing again the words from drills with her tutor of, "Hello. Very happy to know you." Kate ventured out onto the balcony, bringing *Conversational Greek* with her. She leaned against the railing. Sheep munched grass, a peacock stepped daintily around the edge of the vegetable garden, and a man trudged through the orchard in the distance. Kate sat in a cushioned wicker chair and tried studying.

After the lunch of homemade cheese pie and a salad of tomatoes and olives Lena had set out, Kate went back to the bedroom to finish getting ready. Hearing Lena's car approach, she headed downstairs.

Her shoes waited in the entryway where she'd left them the day before. Kate hesitated momentarily while fastening the second buckle, reluctant for the next set of challenges. Forcing herself to stand, she pulled open the heavy wooden door. Once outside, the farm aromas and the warm sunlight surrounded her as she met Lena at the car. "Thank you very much for your hospitality. I had no idea that I'd be so lucky to be in such a beautiful place."

"We are the ones who thank you for coming to help us—Katina." Lena smiled as she emphasized the new name Yiannis had given her.

Once on the road, Kate watched the countryside unfold behind the windshield. She was again amazed by the small cars and the speed with which they raced by. Up ahead, a group of buildings, surrounded by trees and rows of crops, emerged on the left.

"This is the American Farm School where we got our eggs and fresh vegetables before we moved to our farm."

"American?"

"Yes. After the Second World War, America helped Greece very much." Lena smiled. "There have not always been—hostil—?"

"Hostilities?"

"Yes, *hostilities* between our two countries."

There it was. Her other fear. She was an American. Lena and Yiannis had been a wonderful surprise, fully embracing her and making her feel welcomed. But she wasn't sure how they viewed her country. What about the stories she'd read of those who had burned the American flag and stomped on the cameras of tourists? Who were these people and where were they?

After several minutes of silence, Lena turned to the right in the direction of the city. On both sides of the highway were small low-slung structures with land between them. To the left, sparkling water played peek-a-boo beyond stands of trees and tops of buildings, which now became two- and three-story structures. The sight of the sea had a slightly calming effect. But the yoyo of emotions bounced inside, just as they had since the very beginning of her adventure.

"The Gulf of Salonika?" Kate asked as she viewed the water. "Is this near Metamorphosis, where one of your letters was from?"

Metamorphosis. The beautiful Greek word that worked its way into the English language and was the title of a Kafka story she'd read in college.

"That is the Bay of Salonika, connected to the Gulf. Metamorphosis is a few hours away, where my family has a summer home. There are beaches outside of Thessaloniki, and we have a lovely sea walk that travels the length of the city. I am sure you will enjoy it. Since ancient times, the Greeks have made our lives near to water." Scenes from Kate's hometown in Texas came to mind, landlocked with miles of treeless prairies. How far away all of that seemed now.

The landscape gradually changed to a more urban terrain of larger buildings. An older three-story mansion appeared ahead, with a sweeping staircase and tall windows framed with baroque ornamentation. It was surrounded by a low fence, small trees, and gardens. "That's such a beautiful building," Kate marveled.

"This entire street—I think it is called a 'boulevard'—was once filled with homes like this. It is Vasilisis Olga or Queen Olga Street. She was one of our royals long ago."

The fairy-tale villa was surrounded on either side by newer multistoried concrete structures, many with signs for commercial businesses on the ground floor. Kate guessed there were residences above the stores, as women on upper floor balconies watered plants and shook sheets to air them. *Just like in the movies.*

As the traffic grew heavier, large, blue buses made frequent stops on both sides of the road. Groups of people exited and entered buses, with everyone in a hurry. Traveling farther, the buildings grew taller and more modern. Kate had read Thessaloniki was the second largest city in Greece. She'd never lived in a place this large before.

Kate was distracted by the urban scenery until Lena slowed and signaled with her blinker. Fear and insecurity rushed back in. She was heading to meet Soto.

They entered an expansive gravel parking lot between two multistory buildings. Kate was surprised at the small amusement park toward the back of the lot, with a Ferris wheel, children's rides, and a rink of some kind.

"That is Luna Park. My boys love to spend time there." Lena grabbed bags from the back seat. "Come, Katina, and meet my family."

Kate took a deep breath and reluctantly got out of the car, with no choice but to follow Lena through a glass door marked 84-B. They crossed a marble-tiled lobby and entered an elevator with a mirror covering the rear portion of the small space. With the noises of gears engaging and the faint fragrance of freshly picked vegetables from Lena's bag, Kate had a sensation of unreality. Like a character in a movie, she was being transported upward to yet another scene. The elevator bumped to a stop on the fourth floor. They walked down a narrow light-filled hall, and Lena pressed a doorbell.

The door opened. An older woman, short and rounded with facial features hinting at an older version of Lena's beauty, welcomed them with a greeting in Greek. She hugged Kate warmly. "This is Mary, my mother," Lena explained in English. Dark eyes sparkling, moving her head from side to side, Mary reached out to Kate's cheek and stroked it affectionately.

"And this is my Aunt Sophia." Lena introduced a taller woman with curly brown hair, younger than Lena's mother. Continuing the warm greetings, Sophia kissed her on each cheek. "Welcome to Greece. We are very honored to have you with us." Sophia's English was perfect, and her ready smile was broad and engaging.

This home was smaller than either of Kate's apartments in Wyoming or Colorado. There was a sitting room with a couch and chairs, and a kitchen was off to one side. Through lace curtains, glimpses of sunlight glinted off the bay. "Please, Kate, sit and tell us about your trip," Aunt Sophia offered.

"Umm . . . a very long *taxithi*," remembering the word for "trip," which was easy to recall because of its association with "taxi." Just then, noise from another part of the apartment interrupted them.

"Lena, the boys?" Aunt Sophia eyed her niece.

Kate knew it was finally time to meet the Stylianou children and her reason for being in this apartment, this city, this exotic land. Lena had told Kate the youngest boy, Aristotle, known as Aris, was eight years old and Sotiris, or Soto, was ten. Aris was the first to bound into the living room. A handsome, bright-eyed boy with close-cropped brown hair, he regarded Kate with curiosity before shyly glancing to the side while shaking her hand.

Then came Soto, whose shiny black bangs and sides framed a

handsome face. He made his way into the room on feet slightly un-balanced in stride, a stiffened torso, one arm postured straight down while the other was held at an angle. His head was cocked to one side, lips pursed together tightly. His eyes tried to look directly at Kate but kept being pulled away by the tension in his body. Abruptly, an arm shot forward to greet her. With an obvious inten-tion of having something to communicate, Soto's head bobbed, and his lips were tugged even farther to the side. Finally, it came.

"Hel-lo!" he said in English, before laughing. His face spread with joy at his accomplishment. The notes in his laugh were wide-ranging.

Kate recognized Soto's type of cerebral palsy was a combina-tion of spasticity and also athetosis, characterized by wavelike movements. At least she now understood some of the challenges for therapy with him. He would have to learn a strategy for a more re-laxed body and to retrain the way he formed his words.

"Hello to you!" Kate reached for his hand to shake it, then smiled at both boys. Soto's effort to use English, not to mention his tremendous struggle to speak, touched her heart deeply. *This dear, dear boy.* How she hoped she could help him.

Both boys gawked at her a few moments with curiosity before returning to their play in another room. Kate sank down on the couch, feeling lightheaded. The enormity of her task ahead, and her folly in thinking she could pull this off, suddenly struck. Her spontaneous smile now required a conscious effort to stay on her face.

seven 🌿

"*E*fharisto." Kate smiled at Lena's mother and aunt, as she thanked them for the refreshments they brought her way. First came a tray with a small bowl and tiny spoon, with something resembling fruit preserves. It was centered on a crocheted doily.

"Kala," was the only compliment she could think of after eating the sugary offering. The next tray featured a plate with a tyropita, similar to the one she'd had at lunch but quite different from the bland cheese pie she had eaten at the only Greek restaurant in her university city.

"*Polee kala!*" Kate added an enthusiastic "very" to her previous compliment, as she crunched through layers of flaky homemade dough. When offered coffee, she was glad to remember the phrase, "*Nero, parakalo,*" asking for "Water, please" instead. Kate took her time sipping from the tall glass, also presented on its own tray. Although she had experienced a modified form of this hospitality at her Greek tutor's home in Denver, it was uncomfortable being treated so royally.

"Yiannis will be here shortly," Lena explained, gathering the plates and glass to take to the kitchen.

Settling back onto the couch, Kate heard a quiet buzz of conversation from the kitchen and wondered if it had anything to do with her. *What do they really think of me?*

Kate heard the sound of a key in the lock followed by a voice booming "Katina!" through an opening door. Yiannis approached her with a mock bow and *"Thespinis,"* a word she knew meant "Miss." Kate smiled broadly, grateful for his playfulness. She was again newly taken aback and curious about the scars on his face. Under his arm he carried a newspaper. After kissing his mother-in-law on both cheeks, he opened the newspaper and showed something to Lena, as Aunt Sophia peered over his shoulder. Their discussion in Greek was impossible to follow. Yiannis checked his watch, Lena glanced at Kate, and Aunt Sophia shook her head. The conversation continued. The rapid words and vigorous gestures reminded Kate of airplanes coming into an airport from many directions and taking off again. Kate sensed something was about to happen.

"Katina," Yiannis addressed her. "We are taking you to evening entertainment. We are going to the cinema!"

She stood. *"Einai kala!"* Kate used a phrase indicating, "That is good." *At least I can relax in the dark.* She yearned for a refuge from conversation. Her head ached from listening intently for familiar words.

Kate followed as Lena, Yiannis, and Aunt Sophia headed toward the door. Lena's mother joined them, smiling as she wiped her hands on a dish towel. She kissed Kate on both cheeks, then said something in Greek and wagged her head back and forth. Lena translated, "She says you will be a new member of the family."

"Efharisto polee." Kate thanked her very much but wondered how Soto's grandmother would feel if the speech therapy didn't help as much as they all hoped. Now that she had met Soto, Kate was astounded by the enormity of her task ahead. They walked down the hallway and crowded into the elevator.

On busy Queen Olga Street, the daylight had been replaced with bright lights and busy sidewalks. Cars and buses careened along the roadway. "This way," Yiannis shouted to Kate over the noise, his smile now a wide grin. Aunt Sophia cast a worried glance in her direction, only to be appeased, apparently, by an explanation from Lena.

The movie theater was a short walk away. Lena took Kate's elbow to keep her close in the crush of people rushing by. On the outside, the theater reminded Kate of movie houses back home, except the upcoming movie attractions on posters were in Greek, French, and Italian rather than English. Yiannis paid for the tickets, and they crossed through a lobby, entering an auditorium with rows of moviegoers already in place. Lights danced from the projector in the balcony onto a large screen in front. Some of the chaos from the street seemed to have come inside. Young boys peddled soft drinks from metal buckets, calling out "Coca Cola!" amid a scramble of Greek words, their voices competing with music and announcements of coming movies.

Sitting down next to Lena, Kate noticed Aunt Sophia was missing. Just as the movie was about to begin, she reappeared with a white cardboard box, which was passed hand by hand to Kate. Opening it, she selected one of the delicate pastries inside and sent the box back down the row. Kate began eating just as the movie started. She felt a wave of relief seeing the title in English. *In the Year of the Pig.* At least she could understand the language of the movie.

The screen went black. Helicopter sounds filled the darkness. Words appeared. It was a quote from 1776 about the ideals of American independence, followed by photographs of Civil War statues. Kate's momentary pride in her country's history was soon replaced by uncertainty. American soldiers were tramping through the jungles of Vietnam. *What kind of movie is this?*

At the first sight of the larger-than-life head of Lyndon Johnson on the screen, raucous catcalls broke out in the audience. Lyndon Johnson, her fellow Texan. She had seen him in person one afternoon when driving past his ranch in Johnson City and even snapped a Kodak photo of him. Kate pushed back in her seat, bracing for what might come next.

Her conservative college had only a few anti-war demonstrations. There were none of the huge events happening across the country to demand an end to the Vietnam War. Kate was among the many Americans who watched names of the dead appearing on nightly television and had concluded it was a senseless war. Now, at this moment, Vietnam loomed large on the screen in front of her. Her body remained on high alert. She quickly realized the film was a documentary tracing the history of French then American involvement in Vietnam. Finally, came a full-throated indictment of America's war in southeast Asia. Greek subtitles ran across the bottom of the screen like ants at a picnic.

With each passing frame, the sweet pastry in her hand became nauseating in her mouth. The audience around her was not sitting quietly. The sound of hissing to LBJ, Nixon, and Henry Kissinger grew like a garden of snakes. Greek words were thrown at the screen. They were being hurled at her also. If these people only knew there was an enemy in their midst. She froze.

From the corner of her eye, Kate saw Lena turn her head away from the screen. Reaching across the armrest, Lena touched Kate on the forearm and kept her hand there for a few moments. The gesture was protective and welcomed. Kate wrapped the remaining bits of pastry in a napkin and wiped her fingers as best she could. She settled into the darkness of the theater as images flooded the screen and bled into her mind, until it was finally over. When the lights came on, Kate shakily stood and filed out of the row with her companions, avoiding their glances.

Back in the warm night air under the bright lights of the movie marquee and amid noise and commotion from the sidewalk, Kate stood with Lena, Yiannis, and Aunt Sophia, who spoke first.

"Kate, we apologize for this movie. We hope it was not uncomfortable for you." Her eyes conveyed concern.

Lena spoke up. "We did not know it would be so harsh against your country."

Kate glanced at the crowd. "Well, it was a surprise. I didn't know that people outside of America had such strong feelings about the war."

Yiannis spoke next. "Katina, your country is a big power. They can make problems for people all over the world. They—"

"Yianni, we will have this discussion another time. It is late. We must pick up the boys and go back to the farm," Lena said. She put her hand on Kate's back to guide her toward the apartment building. Kate heard the murmuring of what sounded like a heated conversation between Aunt Sophia and Yiannis, but she concentrated on weaving her way through the crowd with Lena.

At the entryway to the building, Aunt Sophia kissed her on both cheeks. "We again apologize for the movie. You came from very far away to help us, and we are grateful. Sleep well tonight."

Aunt Sophia and Lena went inside. Yiannis unlocked the car for Kate and stood outside smoking a cigarette, waiting for Lena and the boys. An employee from his factory had driven Lena's car back to the farm for them.

In the back seat on their trip home, Kate was sandwiched between Soto and Aris. Lena pivoted in her seat to address Kate. "Katina, we are sorry for your discomfort at the cinema."

Soto had fallen asleep and slumped in Kate's direction. Lena reached over to reposition him. "During the dictatorship, we were not allowed to have any movies like this. Anything political or critical of the government or its allies was forbidden. Now we are like young children. We take the opportunity to see whatever we can."

Glancing at her through the rearview mirror, Yiannis took over the conversation. "That is why we are hungry for things like this—what is the word for more than hungry—starts with some kind of bird?" Yiannis asked.

"Raven something?" Lena asked.

"Ravenous," Kate told them.

"Yes. That is it. We took a chance in taking you to this movie. You passed the test—you are not asking us to take you back to the airport!" Lena joked.

Kate was relieved the banter with Lena and Yiannis was playful, but her disquiet lingered. "Okay. But you may still be on probation," she tried to joke back, hoping they understood this word and her own attempt at humor.

Soto had shifted again. His arm now rested on her lap, his small hand open. Kate put her hand on top of his. The warmth of his hand provided a small measure of comfort to help combat the fear still trapped inside her from the movie theater.

eight

Propped against a pillow in bed the next morning, Kate heard the clamor below her window of Yiannis loading the boys into his car. A shudder ran through her body as she recalled her fear at the movie theater. Just as quickly, though, she remembered her conversation with Yiannis when they'd returned to the farm. Standing in the kitchen, Yiannis and Kate had watched Lena escort a sleepy and unsteady Soto to bed. "Katina, you will find that Greeks have great affection for Americans—but not your government."

"I'm trying to understand. I'd worried about what I might run into here in Greece. But I wasn't ready just yet to see it firsthand. It was scary."

"Please do not worry." Yiannis raised his arms, mimicking a body builder showing off his muscles. "We protect our Katina!" he said with mock fierceness.

"I'm sure I'll sleep much safer knowing that," Katina bantered back. *"Kalinixta."* She had wished him a "goodnight," her sense of relief combining with an immense fatigue. She had fallen asleep easily and slept until morning.

When she came to the breakfast table, Lena was heating sheep's milk in a pan. "I am making it safe to drink and to make yogurt," she explained as she wrapped part of her apron around the handle to move the pot off the flame.

Homemade yogurt? Kate continued to be amazed.

"Yiannis drove the boys to school, and later we will go to ELEPAAP."

ELEPAAP. Kate had initially been surprised to hear the therapy center referred to by its initials. It sounded like a snack food. "I have kept the American secret long enough from the staff," Lena joked.

Lena's words triggered a sense of dread. The little she'd been around Soto, she could barely understand anything he said, even simple words. Kate had realized fairly quickly the reason Lena recruited her—to help Soto learn to speak more clearly. He was obviously a bright child, but he struggled considerably to make his thoughts known to others. At ELEPAAP there was an entire group of children waiting for therapy, some with speech problems and others with eating and drinking difficulties. She was here to help them in Greek, a language far beyond her reach. *Oh, Kate. Why are you here?*

She hurriedly finished breakfast.

Dressed in her traveling pantsuit and a fresh blouse, Kate stood in front of the bathroom mirror applying mascara and lipstick. She again practiced the greetings she had learned from her tutor. She would use the second person plural verb form for politeness with each person and say it was a pleasure to meet them. Kate fluffed her hair, practicing one last time.

Too soon, it was time to go.

As they approached the city, Kate recognized a few familiar landmarks. Instead of continuing down busy Queen Olga Street, however, Lena turned right onto a smaller street with a timeworn three-story house on one corner and a new apartment building on the other. On the bottom floor of the building, women carried fresh loaves of bread from a store. The aroma traveled across the street as Lena pulled in near an older two-story villa fronted by a sagging fence of white stucco with iron railings.

"This is ELEPAAP."

There was a hint of pride in her voice. Lena had helped found this center in Thessaloniki, a branch of an organization in Athens dedicated to providing therapy to cerebral palsied children.

A row of towering palm trees lined the front yard. The door of a white van opened. Along a walkway from the building, two women in light-blue smocks waited with wheelchairs. Children scrambled out of the van. Soto was already at school and part of the welcoming committee. Spying his mother and Kate, he waved an arm in their direction but continued waiting for his friends.

A small, dark-haired boy with bright eyes jumped from the van to bring one of the wheelchairs to an older boy with wriggling arms and legs, who was then lifted into the chair. Soto and the other boy headed back to the building, both pushing the wheelchair. Kate watched as more children made their way out, many wearing school uniforms of dark blue with white collars.

Finally, a woman emerged with a boy in her arms, someone who seemed too old to be carried. His arms and legs were flexed like a pretzel, but his smile was dazzling. A broad grin showed he was missing two front teeth. Kate smiled at the boy and his mother, who returned a sweet, tender smile of her own. This was why Kate was here. She had developed an affection for physically disabled children ever since her summer as a counselor at the Texas Lions Camp. It was the formative experience for her career as a speech therapist.

Kate followed Lena down the walkway toward the building.

Lena said, "We are now qualified by the government for a school with two special teachers. It is very exciting for the children and their parents." They passed by a grassy space in front of the building, which might have been a formal garden before the space was a therapy center. "The children play here and in the back, where we have a ramp for the wheelchairs." Two doors decorated with rusted iron filigree were propped open. Inside, Kate was met by a winding marble staircase. She took a deep breath, and they headed up to the second floor. She was finally here.

The staircase, tall ceilings, and large windows gave the sense this building was once a grand home. Reaching the top floor, a hubbub of activity greeted them. To the right, a woman in an office waved at them as she talked excitedly on the phone, glasses atop her short dark hair.

"Kuria Argero is our social worker in charge of admissions, therapy schedules, and transportation."

Kate knew the word *Kuria* was "Mrs." She thought back, with a brief twinge of sadness, to the social worker at the rehabilitation center in Colorado Springs who had been her friend.

Trailing Lena past mothers holding small children on their laps as they waited outside Kuria Argero's office, Kate sensed their eyes tracking her with curiosity. Excited young voices reverberated from down another hallway, punctuated by instructions of adult females trying to exert control.

They walked ahead to an expansive office, a place of quiet in comparison to the rest of the building. Seated behind an oversized desk was an older gentleman with a bald head, round nose and cheeks, and clear glasses. Lena introduced her in Greek to *Kurios* Garefilo, Mr. Garefilo, the director of the center. Kate smiled. He spoke a few French words until she indicated she didn't speak French.

"Sorry. Not English," he said.

Lena directed him, in a respectful and polite manner, to sign the papers in front of him. Kurios Garefilo then gave Kate documents to sign.

He smiled and offered, "Café?"

Following Lena's cue, she nodded. This kind of ritual certainly hadn't been the way she signed contracts for her previous jobs in America.

Coffee was brought into the room by Kuria Anastasia, a large, dark-complexioned woman with deep brown eyes. Her salt-and-pepper hair was tied back with a scarf, and she wore a gray apron. The rest of her clothing was black.

Lena whispered to Kate in English, "She wears *mavro*—'black'—because she is a widow. Many women never again wear colored clothing after a husband dies." This explained the prevalence of black-clad women Kate had noticed at the airport and on the streets.

Lena commented on the coffee in demitasse cups brought in on a tray. "This is *Elliniko café* or 'Greek coffee'—sometimes called *Turkiko* after our rivals the Turks."

Turkey. Last summer's war between Greece and Turkey. Anti-Americanism. What do all of these people think about an American working with them? Do some of them hate my country? Kate's apprehension about meeting the staff was now joined by the specter of politics. She was edging across a shaky tightrope.

Kuria Anastasia smiled broadly, bowing her head slightly as she offered the coffee, in an obvious deference to Kate. This unsettled

Kate, who had always been taught to respect elders, not the other way around.

"Steen ygeia sas," Lena said raising her cup. "That is our tradition, toasting to health—*ygeia*. Your English word 'hygiene' comes from this. We say *sas* for 'your' and *mas* for 'our.'"

Kate imitated the phrase and sipped the muddy liquid. It tasted like watery coffee, followed by an ooze of thick sediment, reminding her of mud at the bottom of a lake. She was relieved to return the cup to its saucer.

Touring the center, Kate wondered how she would be accepted by the staff. In one room, a lovely dark-haired woman—a physical therapist—sang to a young boy lying on a therapy mat. She glanced up at Kate as she moved his legs back and forth. The scene reminded her of physical therapists she had worked with in Colorado.

"Yeia sas," was all Kate could get out, the simplest form of "hello." All the words from the chapter in her textbook on introductions were suddenly missing. She tried again. "Eimai ee Katina," she introduced herself using Yiannis's name for her.

"Maybe Katerina would be a better name," Lena offered.

Kate forced a smile, remembering what Lena had said about Katina being old-fashioned.

The physical therapist welcomed her briefly before continuing her exercises with the child. Similar incidents played out when she met another physical therapist, and an occupational therapist. Their greetings to her were polite, but Kate found herself unable to contribute anything meaningful to the conversations.

Her dry mouth made her few words even harder to articulate. She detected a skepticism, certain the staff members noticed her practically nonexistent Greek. Since Lena had said there were no speech therapists trained in Greece, Kate knew she must be a valued resource, even with her limited language skills. She had said her salary would be higher than the other therapists because of this. Did they know this and resent her already? The insecurity she had long struggled with had accompanied her to Greece, after all.

At that moment, Kate had an overwhelming urge to run. *I should ask Lena to take me to the airport before I have the chance to fail. How can I do speech therapy in a language I can't even speak?* Beads of sweat trickled underneath her blouse.

Making her way back down the curving marble steps, even Kate's feet were out of place with her knee-high hose and Mary Jane pumps. She was the only one wearing stockings on this warm September day. But the absence of sandals, like everyone else had on, was the least of her problems.

nine 🌿

"Katina, you should have come with us last night." Yiannis tapped the ashes from his cigarette onto a saucer. They sipped coffee on the balcony overlooking the garden as morning light hit the tops of almond trees. Sheep grazed lazily on the grass.

Kate had declined the invitation to join Yiannis and Lena for dinner Saturday night in the city. Instead, she had opted to stay at the farm to study her Greek textbook, propelled by a new urgency to learn the language that continued eluding her.

"We saw Melina Mercouri. She was in Thessaloniki for a film festival." Kate knew of the actress's role in the popular movie *Never On Sunday*, as well as its lively song.

"Really? *Krima*," Kate responded with the word for "pity." It would have been fun to see her, writing home to her parents and friends about it. But the need to cram as much Greek into her head as possible was her goal right now. Kate had sat at the desk in the bedroom, saying aloud the words in each sentence, reading longer and longer paragraphs. The structure of the language was getting clearer when she read it, but spoken words were lost in a swarm of sounds.

The few moments of silence between Kate and Yiannis were broken by a tinny motor noise coming from a small tractor. The farmhand drove toward the highway outside the gate.

"Christos is going to the village to sing at church," Yiannis said.

Kate smiled, remembering her visit to a Greek Orthodox Church in Denver with her tutor. The scent of incense, the glow of candles, the chanting male voices, and the art of stylized Byzantine iconography were strikingly different from the Baptist church of her youth. As the clatter of the tractor faded, she wondered about the role of religion in the lives of people like Christos. And to the Stylianou family.

The day before, Kate had met the farm helper, his wife Vangelio, and their two boys, who lived in an apartment below the Stylianou home. Both Christos and Vangelio were small in stature but muscular. His green eyes made Kate wonder about his original ancestry, since he didn't resemble any other Greeks she'd met. Vangelio had a plump face, black hair with sprigs of gray, and eyes squinting behind round cheeks. They had been returning from chores in the field. Their greetings to her were friendly, although Kate couldn't understand a word Vangelio said. Her words mushed together, probably because she was missing all of her teeth. Vangelio mimed drinking from a cup and pointed beyond the screen door to her kitchen. She was offering an invitation for coffee. Greek hospitality was everywhere.

Now, Yiannis stubbed his cigarette. "Come, Katina. Let me give you a grand tour."

Kate followed him down the wooden stairway outside the kitchen door. The air was sweet and fresh. Surveying the landscape, she was amazed at the natural wonderland he had created.

"I have installed an irrigation system for my trees." They trekked over mounds of soft dirt amid rows of his olive, pistachio, and almond trees. Peacocks roamed freely, honking and occasionally quivering their tailfeathers. "And here are my feathered and furry friends." Pigeons cooed from their wire enclosures, alongside cages of various species of ducks and hutches with rabbits. A system of waterways ran in cement troughs throughout the area. Nearby, a large henhouse and area for pecking were enclosed by wire, and in the distance, a fat pig grunted and wandered inside his pen. They walked past stacks of blue boxes housing bees.

"Gosh, this is amazing! Just like a zoo."

"Do you know, Katina, the Greek origin of the word you just said?" Yiannis stopped and grinned at her. "*Zoee* means 'life' and *zoa* means 'animal' and our word *zoologia* is 'zoology'—the study of animals." He adjusted his cap with a mock show of pride, and they continued their tour. Kate was struck anew by all she was learning.

When it was time for midday dinner, Kate hesitated at the kitchen doorway. A large platter on the table bore the main dish— rabbit. The sight of the headless torso of a small animal on the plat- ter, even though it was covered in tomato sauce with vegetables, made her stomach flip. She'd admired the rabbits on her tour with Yiannis but never imagined one as lunch. Kate managed to choke down a little, primarily eating the vegetables and leaving most of the meat to the side. After the meal, it was time for the Greek tradi- tion of an afternoon siesta and Kate's opportunity for more study- ing. She was determined to keep going with her lessons.

On Sunday night with the boys in bed, Kate watched Lena pre- pare the following day's meal. She sliced tops off green peppers and hollowed out the insides, while ground meat and onions sizzled in a pan. Lulled by Lena's voice, she listened to stories of growing up in Thessaloniki. Lena had met Yiannis at a private English-speaking high school. After they married, their son was born with cerebral palsy.

Lena sighed and her voice softened. "Raising such a child was not easy. Usually, these children were hidden away. Some thought it would be better if he did not survive." Her words hit Kate unexpectedly hard.

Not survive? Sweet Soto?

Lena brought the pan to the table and spooned the meat and rice mixture into the peppers. Throughout the conversation, Lena slowed her speech, using both English and Greek words, ensuring Kate understood what she was saying. With patience, she corrected any Greek questions or comments Kate attempted.

A knock on the kitchen door interrupted them. It was Christos bringing in a full bucket of milk, which he hefted onto the counter. He said something to Kate she didn't understand. Lena translated. "He says he hopes you bring something good to Greece from your President Ford."

Kate nodded her head and said, *"Nai,"* the word for "yes," thinking she could at least pretend to have a direct line to Washington. When he had gone, Kate told Lena, "I can't believe everyone here is so interested in America." She watched Lena strain the sheep's milk into a pan.

Grabbing a broom from behind the door, Kate swept the tiled floor. She had adopted this task in an effort to be helpful. Lena's next words, however, surprised Kate, as they carried a hint of accusation.

"Katina, you must know that your country has very much power, especially in our small country."

Hoping to provide a reasonable explanation about America, Kate responded. "Yes, well I'm sorry my country isn't able to help Greece more, but we already have so many obligations around the world." There. She had made an attempt to defend America.

Lena set the pan on the stove and turned on the burner to slowly bring the milk to a boil. Although not cruel, her voice was firm and the expression on her face was serious. "Katina. I believe you do not understand. Who do you think brought the dictatorship to Greece? You saw the crowd at the movie. Even here in Thessaloniki, they have burned your flag."

Kate's broom stopped mid-stroke under a chair. She was immobilized. Since arriving in Greece, Kate had trusted Lena implicitly with every detail of her life. How could she doubt her now? But how could what she was saying be true? America brought the dictatorship to Greece? Her chest tightened, words squeezing out. "I—I don't know about politics, Lena. I know that my country has critics all around the world, and I think everybody is probably jealous of us." As soon as the words were out of her mouth, Kate wondered how foolish she must sound. She read the skepticism on Lena's face.

Lena adjusted the flame of the burner before resuming the conversation. Her expression was tender and sympathetic. "Katina, there will be time for all of this to be figured out. Your country has many good things to share." Lena wiped her hands, then reached out to touch her gently on the cheek. "And one of them is you."

Shaken by this possibility of America's complicity in the dictatorship, Kate brushed the dust and crumbs into the dustpan and emptied them in the trash. She put the broom in its place, bid Lena a hasty goodnight, and strode hurriedly down the hallway. Back in her room, she opened *Conversational Greek* and put her trembling finger on the first sentence on the page to make herself focus. Learning Greek and helping children, like Soto who was sleeping down the hallway, was even more a priority to her now. She wanted to bring something good to Greece, something good from America.

After switching off the light and slipping into bed, Kate moved away from her worries about politics and her upcoming job at ELEPAAP. Instead, she reflected on her other reason for being here. Hadn't she jumped into this adventure partly to run away from a life in America and her shattered dreams? Even squeezing her eyes shut as tightly as she could, it was impossible to block out the pictures in her mind: her white wedding dress as she and Jim bounded out of the church, the door of the ugly orange-and-black U-Haul slamming shut in the parking lot of her Waco apartment, and the boxes of wedding gifts packed away in her parents' house.

Kate bit her knuckle to silence her sobs. Was this trip to Greece going to become a fool's errand in another of the unexpected twists and turns that was now her life? She reached her arms around her shoulders and rocked herself gently until she fell asleep.

ten 🌿

The sound of crowing roosters pulled Kate up from sleep and away from her dream. She had been an adult, sitting cross-legged in her grandmother's long-ago backyard in Texas, creating intricate designs in the dirt with yellow chinaberries. Jiggling the remaining berries in her hand while contemplating the pattern, Kate heard the sudden whine of the screen door. She expected to see her grandmother whom she adored, the gray-haired and always bustling family matriarch. A true remnant of the Old West, her grandmother had delighted in riding horses and shooting rattlesnakes, while writing poetry and keeping her fingernails polished.

Kate's eyes strained to see the figure at the threshold. Just as the face came into view, everything abruptly disappeared. She woke. The dream and the backyard were gone. Kate was in Greece in a room filled with bright light and fluttering curtains. Roosters called from a distance. Kate desperately wished to go back to her dream or at least be back home.

A soft tapping on the bedroom door was followed by the tune of a song from her youth, "The Yellow Rose of Texas." Lena poked her head into the room and sang the chorus, throwing a playful smile in Kate's direction.

"Lena, how do you know that song?" Kate sat up in bed.

"Many years ago, my high school choir sang to Vice President and Ladybird Johnson when they visited Thessaloniki. And now I have a Texan in my house!"

Kate grinned, imagining her larger-than-life Texas counterparts in Thessaloniki. She shifted her pillow behind her and hesitated, before saying what could no longer be postponed. "Lena, I guess it's time for me to start work and move to the city, right?" Like ripping off a Band-Aid, Kate knew the best way forward was to do it quickly—ask the question and get started with what would be next.

Lena sat on the other twin bed beside Kate's open yellow suitcase. "That is what I was thinking also." She smoothed imaginary wrinkles from her apron. "Do you remember the building where my mother lives? One floor above her is our old apartment, which is furnished. Yiannis and I decided it would be good for you to live there. My mother will be nearby for anything you need."

Hesitating, Lena pushed a strand of hair behind her ear. "The workers at ELEPAAP do not like that you will be paid a higher salary than theirs. If you live in our apartment free, we can make your salary equal to the other workers." With a hint of apology in her voice, she continued. "I know this is different from our original agreement, but I did not know there would be difficulties from the staff." She stopped again. "We will assist if you do not have enough money. Do not worry, please?"

It took Kate a minute to process what Lena said. She chewed the nail of her left thumb. Difficulties with the staff? Maybe what she suspected about their resentment toward her was true. What else was going on behind the scenes about her position at ELEPAAP, and what did everyone, including Lena, really think of her? What had been said? Did any of this have to do with Kate's being an American? A wave of apprehension washed over her.

Finally, Kate spoke. "I—I guess that sounds okay." She bit harder into her nail. There were so many details she hadn't even considered, like whether apartments in Greece came furnished or not. And then her work. Bringing her hand down, she laced her fingers together to steady them. "Do you think there's going to be a problem with the staff?"

"I do not believe so. But if you accept this arrangement with the apartment and salary, that will help."

Kate nodded her head in agreement, slightly queasy as if she'd just stepped off a spinning carnival ride. She hoped Lena was right.

Lena rose and pushed open the curtains to let the sun come into the room more fully. Dust motes played in the streams of sunlight. "We will stop by ELEPAAP to see your therapy room and then go to the apartment. Our new Greek American agreement," Lena joked. "Please do not worry, Yellow Rose." She left the room humming.

As the door shut, Kate eyed her suitcase. How long ago had it been since the suitcase was fresh and new on her bed in Texas? Not even one week. It seemed like much longer. She had always been the little girl who wanted to stay home with her mother instead of going to kindergarten, and then the new wife who loved ironing the organdy curtains for the bedroom with Jim. These past few days she had already begun to make a new nest in this sunny room at the farm, but now it was time to leave. Kate willed her feet to touch the floor and get started.

eleven

Lena helped Kate haul her suitcase down the back stairway from the kitchen. Together they pushed it into the car's small trunk, reminding Kate of that first afternoon at the airport. Once in the car, her apprehension joined as a passenger. The sheltered days at Lena's had ended.

Passing trees on their way out, Kate thought of the walks with Lena over the past few days, the luscious figs they'd plucked and eaten while strolling. She had never seen a pomegranate tree before, but quickly learned how to dig out the pulpy red-purple seeds and eat blissfully.

"Katina, you will come here on weekends. This will also be your home." Lena seemed to be reading her mind.

Kate glanced at Lena. In a short time, her position of sitting in the front seat beside this beautiful, gracious woman had become natural. They drove past Christos standing in the garden, weeds in one hand, vigorously waving goodbye with the other, as the car headed toward the green metal gate.

The road was becoming familiar, with landmarks of the coffee shop and whitewashed church in the nearby village, the American Farm School, and turning right toward Thessaloniki. Traffic and activity multiplied as they approached the city. Leaving Queen Olga Street, Kate read the street sign, Christovasilis.

"Christ King?" Kate asked, translating it.

"Bravo," Lena nodded affirmatively, as she pulled into a space near ELEPAAP. Once inside the building, they followed voices and peeked into a large room on the ground floor. The staff and children were seated around a rotund man in a black robe, brimless black cap, beard, and long braid down his back. He moved his arms dramatically as he spoke.

Lena put her index finger to her lips for quiet until they moved into a room to the left of the doorway. "The priest is blessing the school for the start of the new year," she said in a low voice. "The government gives us the classroom and teachers, so the church must be part of our school." In response to Kate's puzzled expression, Lena said, "The church and the government always work together. It is how things are done."

Kate couldn't imagine something like this back home. She recalled the phrase "separation of church and state." Instantly, Kate remembered Mr. Lauderdale standing at the blackboard in her high school civics class as he wrote this phrase with chalk, oblivious to spit wads flying from the back of the room. The concept of government being independent from religion was something she'd never thought much about, something she'd taken for granted. She was now witnessing the marriage of the two in Greece. Kate wondered what else she would find that set her country apart from Greece.

As she glanced around the large room where they stood, Kate was surprised to hear Lena announce, "And this will be your room. It was where Pat worked when she was here." Kate was taken aback by the emptiness of the space as well as the mention of Pat. Lena had told her about a Greek American speech therapist who had worked at ELEPAAP a few years earlier. Trickles of insecurity seeped into Kate's mind. What if she couldn't measure up to what the previous therapist had done? This therapist, unlike her, had come with Greek language skills intact.

The almost vacant room was expansive, with its only window bringing in light from the front garden next to the street. A large mirror, probably installed for therapy sessions, was attached to the wall. A stack of furniture was piled in a corner. Her offices in her two previous jobs were small cubicles with a desk, children's table and chairs, and a cupboard full of materials. Here she would be designing her own workspace and therapy programs. In a foreign language. The prospect was overwhelming.

"Come." Lena motioned. "Before the blessing is over."

Walking to the car, Kate worried about creating a welcoming place for the children, given the room's emptiness and lack of bright colors. Slowly, she lowered herself into the passenger seat and glanced back at ELEPAAP. Where was the spark of enthusiasm that had ignited this whole adventure? Kate knew she had to find it again. But how?

They drove back to Queen Olga Street, their silence in contrast to the honking of car horns and screeching brakes of buses. "You can take the bus, or you can walk to work. The apartment is several blocks down this street." Lena waited at a traffic light as pedestrians scurried across the street.

Kate decided it would be easier to walk. She didn't yet feel ready to negotiate the bus system alone. Studying the sidewalks, she worked to identify stores and buildings for landmarks.

Farther ahead, they crossed a busy intersection. "This is the first large street to remember. The Twenty-Fifth of March or just

Martiou. It was liberation day from the Turks," Lena said. They traveled a few blocks to the next intersection. "Here is Markos Botsaris, named for a hero of our War for Independence. Your bus stop is Salamina, which was a battle at sea. But you can learn that history later." Lena shook her head and smiled. "Sorry. Too much history and too many names."

Lena was again reading her mind. *How can I possibly remember all this?* Soon they were back in the gravel lot and parked in front of the door marked 84-B.

Kate struggled to keep her voice steady. "Tomorrow, I can go set up and get acquainted, right?" Having seen her room now, the reality of actually starting therapy with the children set in. *What were you thinking, Kate?* This phrase was becoming well-worn in her mind. She tried to swallow, but her throat was dry.

"There is no national emergency," Lena teased. "Please do not hurry. We have waited this long for you."

"And how do you think I should start?" She heard her own voice faltering. *What if none of this works? What if I can't help any of the children? What then?*

"Would you like to begin by helping mothers feed their children, until your Greek improves?"

Lena had told Kate about her trips to Switzerland with Soto to learn techniques to practice with him at home. She had watched Lena assist her son whenever he wanted a drink, holding his head in the crook of her elbow to steady it, making it easier for him to sip. This technique was something Kate had learned in a course at the Colorado Springs rehab center for working with cerebral palsied children, who often had feeding difficulties. Her graduate school program hadn't taught this area of expertise, but Kate's desire to specialize with disabled children made her seek extra training. It was ELEPAAP's job description of a cerebral palsied population that had initially drawn her to apply.

"That sounds good," Kate said, relaxing slightly. She grabbed onto this advice and believed it would be a way forward for her with the children. She could use gestures and pantomime with the mothers. As her Greek skills progressed, she could work with the children with language difficulties. "Can I start with Soto, since I know him?"

"If you like. Now for the next part. Your new home." Lena got out to open the trunk of the car.

Kate sat a few seconds longer. The voice of her grandmother charged in. "Now you just get up and get going, darlin'." There was no other choice but to follow that command.

twelve ✦

A gain, Lena and Kate carried the suitcase, this time across the parking lot. Lena unlocked the heavy glass door at the entrance marked 84-B, and they made their way over the polished marble tiles of the lobby. Crowding into the small elevator with the mirror behind them, Lena pushed the button for the fifth floor. The sound of elevator gears accompanied them upward.

The elevator bumped to a stop. They exited into a hallway, with the apartment of Lena's mother visible down the open stairwell one floor below. A brass plate on the door read, Stylianou. Lena slid her key into the lock. "We keep this apartment if we need to stay overnight in the city."

Lena switched on a light in the entryway where they placed her suitcase. Kate followed Lena to the left and through a set of glass doors into a spacious room with walls of bookshelves.

"Yiannis is proud of his library. Many books in English for you." At the far end of the room, Lena unlatched another set of glass doors, then pulled a cord to raise a slatted wooden window shade, letting in a stream of sunshine. They moved out onto a balcony. Outside, Queen Olga Street was to the right and the amusement park to the left. Beyond the park was the glittering blue of the Bay of Salonika.

"Those mountains there?" Lena pointed out in the distance. "The tallest one is Mount Olympus."

The peak rising beyond the water reminded Kate of *The Iliad* from her high school freshman English class and stories of the gods who supposedly had lived there.

Lena brushed dust off a small metal table on the balcony. "They say that on top you can see the outline of the face of God."

At once, Kate's worries were eclipsed by her amazement at where she stood. Mount Olympus. Face of God. A balcony of her very own. A smile spread across her face.

Back into the hallway, Kate trailed Lena to a room on the right. There was a certain mustiness, the scent of an unoccupied space. Lena opened glass doors, then the slatted wooden window shades, flooding the room with light and revealing a bedroom with a double bed and an armoire. Kate walked around the bed to look out. Three other apartment complexes formed a quadrangle, something she'd only seen in the movies, like Hitchcock's *Rear Window*. *So exciting–this is my new home!*

Back in the hall, Kate walked past a gray telephone sitting on a doily on a low table. "Yiannis can explain making a call to America," Lena said in passing.

Kate didn't know how expensive overseas calls were, but it was comforting she could pick up the phone to call her parents, if necessary. She had spoken to them once, on her first day at the farm, to let them know she'd arrived safely.

Lena motioned to the next room. "And here is the *kouzina*." They moved into a small room with cabinets, a tiny refrigerator, and a portable stovetop with two gas burners. "Do you know how this works?"

"I have no idea," Kate said. Lena twisted a knob on a small propane tank and struck a match. A circle of blue flame on the

69

burner came to life. "Okay, let me try it." Kate fumbled coordinating the lit match and switching on the gas, not getting it until the third try.

Marveling at this relic, she flashed to the avocado-green stove in the apartment kitchen in Waco. That had been the first home of her own. With Jim. Suddenly, she was back there, in a flowered apron, busily following a recipe from the Betty Crocker cookbook on the counter. She let out the breath stuck in her chest and made herself return to the red linoleum of the kitchen underneath her feet.

"Here is the balcony for your kouzina," Lena said, opening a single glass door.

Kate followed her onto a concrete rectangle with iron railings. They faced the stacks of apartments on all three sides. Someone was hanging laundry, another watering flowers, and across the way a woman sweeping a balcony. *Is this really my life?*

Leaving the kitchen, they passed a bathroom and headed toward the end of the hallway into what had obviously been the boys' room with bunk beds, a bookcase, and a desk. Doors opened onto another balcony with the view of Olympus in the distance.

This is it. Kate knew instantly this would be her bedroom. She would happily forgo the luxury of a full bed for the chance to have this balcony outside her door. The face of God would be waiting for her every morning. Kate no longer thought of God as a kindly grandfather with a flowing white beard watching over her, but she had to believe there was something out there. What place did God have in her life now, here in Greece?

As they moved back into the hallway and toward the front door, Kate struggled to keep her emotions in check. Soon she would be here alone. "The apartment is wonderful. Thanks so much."

"Ah, Katina," Lena shook her head in mock scolding. "Do not get too comfortable. You never know when the four of us will come through the door to spend the night in the city with you." Lena smiled and pulled a bundle from her bag. Wrapped in foil were several pieces of homemade *prasopita,* leek and feta pie. "*Kalo riziko.* That means . . . oh, I am forgetting. What does a plant have that goes down?"

"Roots?"

"Yes. We say, 'good roots' when someone moves to a new home." Lena gave her a kiss on each cheek. "We thank you for coming to Greece to help us." Then the door shut, and she was gone.

Evening came. Kate's first night by herself in Greece. Sitting on the balcony, she watched the circling lights from the Ferris wheel in the amusement park and the dancing waves of the Bay of Salonika beyond. A plate with crumbs from the prasopita sat on a small table. *Conversational Greek* rested on her lap with a half-finished letter to her parents as a bookmark.

Kate thought back to other first nights. Alone in a strange apartment in Wyoming, sliding the chain lock into place and wedging a chair against the door. It had been the first time she'd ever lived by herself. A year later she had sat on another couch in Colorado Springs, not knowing anyone, wondering who to call if there were a problem.

The painful days that followed those frightening first nights had eventually led her into the next chapters of this new life that was now hers. Kate had learned to live by herself and made new circles of friends. Even though Greece was a foreign country, she already had the makings of a family with the Stylianous, and Lena's mother was only one flight of stairs away.

For the first time in days, a crack in the steep wall of apprehension appeared. A tentative sense of well-being spread from her head down to her feet that rested on the balcony railing.

thirteen 🌿

*M*orning arrived. Her first day of a new job. Leaning on the counter in the kitchen, Kate ate Lena's cold leek and feta pie. She had decided to forgo figuring out how to make coffee. Kate hurriedly wiped her mouth and headed to brush her teeth. Dressed in slacks and a buttoned blouse, she glanced at herself in the hallway mirror. "That'll have to do," she said aloud, before starting out the door with a bag of therapy supplies in the travel bag hoisted on her shoulder.

Once outside, Kate paused beside the glass door of the apartment building. The morning air was warm, and the scene bustled with activity. As she approached Queen Olga Street, she was met with a stream of people. Men carried briefcases, gray-clad street sweepers busied themselves with their carts and brooms, and children in blue-and-white uniforms were pulled along by hurrying mothers. She joined them with apprehension, hoping to find her way to ELEPAAP without getting lost.

Kate followed the flow of pedestrians, stopping with them at busy intersections and slowing to cross smaller streets. She was awed by the few graceful two- and three-story villas that had survived from an earlier era. Multitudes of posters were plastered on any available space, from political announcements and commercial advertisements to notices of musical events. Kate stopped when a communist red sickle and hammer caught her eye, out in the open. She'd never seen anything like this at home. She repositioned her bag and continued walking.

Most buildings were modern concrete structures with stores on ground floors and apartments above. Kate had seen things like this in the movies, but these storefronts had names and signs she couldn't translate. With purposeful steps, she tried hard not to be overwhelmed by the strangeness of it all.

The noise of traffic accompanied her past sleeping restaurants and past storekeepers raising up metal security grilles. Kate stepped over a thin stream of sudsy water from a drainpipe and glanced up to a balcony, spying a woman with a bucket and wet broom. Everyone seemed busy with morning tasks or in a hurry to get somewhere.

On most of the long blocks, a kiosk sat in the middle of the sidewalk. Newspapers and magazines were clipped with plastic clothespins to rows of twine. Candy, packs of cigarettes, and trinkets were on display. A man seated inside the kiosk gave change to someone who had completed a call on a gray telephone on the counter. This seemed to be the Greek version of a pay phone.

Finally, Kate crossed over onto Christovasilis Street and approached the center. Excitement and trepidation jockeyed inside her. With background sounds of voices, she climbed the marble staircase and went right to Kuria Argero's office, as Lena had instructed. Wishing Lena were by her side, she soldiered on and knocked on the doorframe of the office.

"*Kalimera, Kuria Argero.*"

"*Ah, Kalimera, Thespinis Katerina,*" Kuria Argero said, calling her "Miss Katerina." "*Theleis café?*" offering her coffee by gesturing to her own half-full cup on her desk.

"Ohi, efharisto," Kate declined with, "No, thank you."

Kuria Argero glanced at the phone on her desk ringing repeatedly, shrugged her shoulders, and gestured for her to wait a moment. Kate studied the face of this woman seated at her desk whose strong features and short, dark hair made her appear more handsome than beautiful.

Kuria Argero switched to English. "Welcome to ELEPAAP, Katerina. Let us get started. The children have not arrived." Kate followed Kuria Argero down the stairway to what would be her therapy room. Together they moved furniture in place. Kate chose to have her desk near the window. They put a small table and children's chairs in the center of the room and the other adult chair near her desk. In the corner was a specially designed chair she knew was for children who could not sit independently. The padded seat and circular tray were obviously homemade. This special seating and children's table and chairs provided a familiar anchor for Kate, reminding her of the rehab center where she'd last worked. The vast, fading linoleum floor, however, highlighted the emptiness of the rest of the room.

"Would you like to start later today? We have Kuria Bouras coming in with her son." She checked her watch. "She is not coming for another hour. I am afraid he is . . . " Kuria Argero seemed at a loss for the correct word. "Two years old. Not smart. Small head. You understand. He drinks from a bottle. Only mashed food." Kate suspected Lena had already spoken with Kuria Argero about the plan for starting therapy first with feeding clients.

"I'll be happy to see him. *Ti ora?*" The phrase asking, "What time?" was one of the first Kate had learned from the LP *Learning Modern Greek in Record Time.* She briefly thought of the distance she had traveled from cracking the code of Greek words, slumped in her beanbag chair in Colorado, to standing here at ELEPAAP.

"Ten o'clock. *Theka.*" Kuria Argero repeated the number in Greek. "Welcome, Katerina. *Kali arhee.* Good beginning." Kuria Argero smiled warmly before rushing back upstairs.

An empty bookcase was ideal for the books, games, and a collection of wind-up toys she'd brought with her. She'd have to search for other ways to give color and life to the mostly vacant space. Kate set out the specialized cups and spoons for the first session. Before long, it was almost ten o'clock.

Zipping up the lime-green polyester smock she'd bought in a medical supply store in Lubbock, Kate headed upstairs, determined with each footstep on the winding marble stairway to build her confidence. She could tackle this job of being a speech therapist in a foreign place. She would have to.

A dark-haired mother waited on the bench beside Kuria Argero, her child propped in her lap. He appeared to be microcephalic, with his head small in proportion to his body. Kate smiled her best smile.

"Kalimera." She tried to keep her voice steady.

"Kuria Boura . . . Thespinis Katerina," Kuria Argero said proudly. Kate's tutor had taught that when addressing someone, the last "s" in a name was not used. Kuria Argero explained Kate would help with her son's feeding difficulty.

"Hairo polee," Kate hoped her words sounded authentic enough.

"And this is Aleko," Kuria Argero introduced the child. Kate knew the boy's small head likely indicated low intelligence. Some type of medallion was pinned to his shirt, and a bib around his neck was wet from drooling. His eyes searched her with curiosity as he sucked on his fingers.

"*Yeia sou, Aleko.*" Kate stooped to say "hello" and touched his arm. He continued sucking on his fingers.

Kuria Bouras stood, repositioned Aleko over her shoulder, and accompanied Kate down the stairway. Once in the room, Kate motioned for her to have a seat.

Kate smiled and made a gesture of drinking. Kuria Bouras pulled a baby bottle from her purse, lay her son in her lap, and began feeding him. Kate nodded, using a few Greek words *etsi, etho,* and *kala,* for "like this," "here," and "good," as she adjusted the mother's arms so the boy would be sitting upright. This would help him swallow properly and establish the basis for a better position for eating.

With this unexpected change of posture, however, the boy's expression slowly changed from pleasure to pout and finally into a full scream. Kuria Bouras quickly put her son on her shoulder, rocked him, and whispered into his ear. Before Kate could suggest something different, Kuria Bouras hurriedly thanked her and fled out the door. Unsure what to say if she had followed her out, Kate sank down into her chair.

"Too fast, Kate. You went too fast. How stupid!" She squeezed out the words, blaming herself. This was not the way she had imagined her first session.

As she studied herself in the mirror, a distraught face stared back at her. There were still traces of the coed who had been named one of the Baylor Beauties her junior year in college, slim figure, hazel eyes, and ready smile, except her smile quivered as she fought to keep back the tears that threatened to stream mascara down her cheeks. Kate grabbed a tissue and daubed below her eyelids. She swallowed hard and went toward the stairs, wondering if Kuria Argero had learned about the disastrous session.

The rest of her morning was less eventful as she observed children in their physical therapy sessions, matching faces with names on her schedule. She ended her day with Soto sitting in front of the mirror trying, as she had instructed him, to keep his hands firmly on the sides of his chair and repeating a series of vowels, "*ah, ee, o, ou.*" If he could stabilize his arms and keep himself straight, he would have a better chance of controlling his body when he talked.

"Tiny steps," she pantomimed. Kate wanted to retrain the way he used his breath in combination with sounds, starting with vowels as the smallest building blocks. It could be a basis for keeping his muscles from freezing when he tried to say something. Soto seemed to understand this new strategy for his body to stay calm when talking. He made it through a few series of vowels, but then stopped and repeated the same phrase, pointing a wavy finger in her direction. He laughed heartily.

"Sorry, Soto. *Then katalaveino.*" She shook her head, telling him she didn't understand.

A familiar voice came from the doorway and greeted her. "Yeia sou, Katina." Yiannis had come to pick up his son. "Soto is telling you his new joke."

Kate was relieved their conversation had reverted to English. "That's what I thought, but I couldn't understand."

"In Greek, we call a speech therapist, *logo therapeftria* or 'word therapist,' since *logo* is 'word,' you see." Yiannis explained, and Kate nodded. "The similar word *alogo* means 'horse,' so he is calling you instead his 'horse therapist.' It is his own personal joke for you." Hearing his dad's explanation, Soto burst forth with a laugh that ranged across several pitches, due to poor control of his vocal cords.

Kate joined him in laughter and reached over and gave Soto a hug. "Please tell him I am happy to be both his 'word' and his 'horse' therapist."

"Come with us to the farm for lunch?" He gestured to his car parked outside. "No more 'out with Americans' but 'in with Americans' today?"

"I'm not sure what you mean."

"The phrase 'out with Americans' is used at protests." His smile was wide.

"Oh. I see." Yiannis's jest had the opposite effect than intended, reminding Kate of her experience at the movie theater. His engaging smile, however, quickly helped diffuse her worries. "Efharisto, but another time. I don't know how to say, 'rain check' in Greek, but I'll figure it out."

Yiannis gave her a mock salute and left, Soto shuffling under his father's arm.

Slipping back into her chair, Kate began writing notes from the day.

"Knock knock." The voice came from a petite, young woman at the door, someone Kate had seen only from a distance. She appeared to be of similar age to Kate. "I am Georyia, the teacher." The woman sported a half-crooked smile that conveyed both warmth and a little bit of amusement, like she was ready to tell a joke. "Georyia like 'Georgia' in English." Her dark-brown hair was short, curls on top and sides, her nose slightly prominent. She walked with an erect posture at an unhurried pace.

"Hello, Georyia." Kate motioned for her to sit down.

"How is it going for you?"

Kate was relieved to hear Georyia's English was fluent. Many on the staff had limited English skills. Georyia pronounced the "h" in her words with the form of the Greek *x*, a throaty exhalation causing the word "how" to sound like "xow."

"Okay, I guess. Other than making my first child cry and have his mother run out."

Georyia clicked her tongue and shook her head back and forth. "Greek mothers. Sometimes they can be difficult. And it is always hard to begin. I am also new here." Georyia explained she had just finished her studies in special education and moved to Thessaloniki. "We will be new classmates in this place." She raised her eyebrows, signaling anticipation. "Please come to my home someday after school for lunch?"

"Oh, Georyia, that would be wonderful. Efharisto." Kate gladly accepted.

"I will be most happy to have you." Georyia rose to leave.

"One minute. I have a question. The jewelry some of the children are wearing?" Throughout her morning, Kate had noticed something like a small blue eye or on others a medallion pinned to sweaters or shirts.

"Oh, yes. You may see modern things like our cars and fashions, but part of Greece still lives in older times. Babies in Greece are given this pin to scare away the Evil Eye, or a medal of the *Panayia,* the 'Holy Mother,' to keep the children safe from sinful spirits. Many people believe our disabled children have been cursed." The smile on Georyia's face was gone. "It was not so long ago these children were hidden away." She shook her head again. "Our poor children. I guess the magic protection did not work." Kate sensed the cynicism behind this comment.

"Efharisto." Kate thanked her.

"*Parakalo, Kaitie,*" Georgia responded with, "You're welcome," but pronounced her name with a short "a," sounding almost like "cat-ee." It joined Katina and Katerina in the list of monikers she was acquiring.

Buoyed by the conversation, Kate watched Georyia disappear through the door. Maybe—just maybe— she would find both a new friend and a home here at ELEPAAP.

fourteen 🌿

*W*orkday by workday. Afternoon by afternoon. Evening by evening. It was mid-October, and Kate's new life was gradually becoming easier. Daily walks to ELEPAAP were no longer a worry but rather a chance to learn more about her new home.

In high school, Kate had been taught Greece was the birthplace of Democracy, and she was experiencing it firsthand. The first elections since the collapse of the dictatorship were coming later in the month. All along Queen Olga Street, Kate studied the gallery of vibrant political posters plastered on walls, fences, or any other available space. Each political party's logo was emblazoned in its specified colors, not unlike the color-coded advertisements for sorority and fraternity club events in her college days, her most readily available reference point.

Kate knew red was the color of the communists. In conversations after work, Georyia explained about other political parties. "Blue is the New Democracy party—the Center Right. The green and a symbol of the rising sun is a new Socialist Party called PA-SOK." She then looked directly at Kate.

"Kaitie, you cannot imagine what it is like to have our freedom—after seven years of the junta." Kate knew it was impossible for her to understand fully what Georyia was telling her, yet she had the sense democracy was reemerging from the ashes. And she was here to witness it.

The previous conversation with Lena about America's role in the dictatorship had continued to be a concern. Kate was also picking up other clues about her country's involvement. Colleagues at ELEPAAP were comfortable enough to joke with her.

"Katerina, have your bosses at the CIA paid you this week?" Such comments, always made in a good-natured way, still caused a hitch in her chest. She would force a smile and attempt to joke in return. But she continued to be haunted by the possibility that America had played a role in the coup replacing a democratically elected leader and put the military in power.

There were two other characteristics of the Greek populace: an ever-present tendency for conversation and a penchant for reading newspapers. It was rare to see Greeks without newspapers tucked under their arms or papers spread out on desks or counters of the stores she walked past.

Weekends were spent on the farm, with Kate returning to Thessaloniki Sunday evenings by bus. The Stylianou farm had become a second home. Kate had her familiar perch in the kitchen, watching Lena make her own filo, the tissue-thin sheets of dough for pies—cheese, leek, or sweet squash. Out the back door and down the wooden steps, another world awaited with Yiannis's orchards and the richness of animal life.

In addition to her task of sweeping the kitchen floor, Kate often took food scraps to the very large pig in his pen at the edge of the property. As she tossed leftovers of lunch in his direction from her plastic pail, Kate said aloud what she couldn't tell anyone else. "I miss home so much. Talking to my family whenever I wanted. My friends. And even hamburgers." The list of her own rendition of the homesick blues changed with each delivery, but the sentiment remained constant. Sometimes after giving the pig his final scraps, she'd sit on the overturned pail, study the mountains in the distance, and let loose with slow tears. The release was cathartic, another word Kate learned had origins in the Greek word, *katharizo* or "to clean."

As time passed, Kate had also become more at ease with Yiannis and his playfulness. He was like an older brother—one with a wicked sense of humor lurking behind an often-serious expression. Kate remembered first meeting Yiannis and her shock at seeing the scars on his face.

Lena had explained to her one evening in the kitchen. "Yiannis was on his way back from a technical fair in Germany to purchase machines for the shoe factory. There was a terrible car accident in Yugoslavia." She lifted the thin, wooden dowel used for rolling the filo. Lena's usually warm smile faded. "It was a shock when they called me. I was home alone with the boys, who were very young." She reached for flour to dust away the stickiness of the dough. "After two days in the hospital, he came home. Slowly, the scars disappeared for me." Lena's momentary recollection of anguish gone, she continued to roll out another layer of filo and lift it into the large rectangular pan, drenching it with olive oil before beginning the process again with the next sheet.

"Oh, Lena," Kate shook her head. "I can't imagine how scary that was." For Kate, those scars were now also becoming almost invisible.

One Sunday afternoon, Kate found Yiannis sitting on the balcony that faced the highway, the outline of a monastery in the distance. "Katina—I have found it for you." He peered over his newspaper, motioning with his eyes to come sit in the chair next to his. "Here," pointing to a movie advertisement.

"Fellini?" She could now easily read Greek names in capital letters.

"We start with Fellini. You know him? The Italian?"

It was another of those moments Kate realized the limitations of her world knowledge. She followed reviews of foreign films in *Time* magazine but had seen only a few and never one by Fellini. "I've read about him."

"What a good fortune for you to come to Greece to become educated. Not a moment to lose!" He cackled. "*Eight and One-Half.* This one I like very much. Fortunately for you, all such films banned by the junta are coming back—very fast." The extent of the censorship in Greece was still hard for Kate to comprehend.

"You must go to the Fargani. It is a small theater in my old neighborhood. Nearby is the Kamara—the Arch. You have seen it?"

"No, I don't think so. Oh—maybe in that book." Kate had found *Old Salonika* in Yiannis's library in the apartment and studied page after page of old photographs of the city.

Yiannis explained the Arch was a remnant of Roman occupation, now a centerpiece of a busy street in Thessaloniki, surrounded by shops, restaurants, and tall apartment buildings. "Do you know that the Kamara was built in the fourth century—how many centuries before your America was born?" His expression was one of mock superiority, as he blew on his fingernails and shined them on his shirt.

He picked up a cigarette, waving it unlit in his fingers. "Thessaloniki was once a very important crossroad between the East and the West. It was the home of Greek, Turkish, and Jewish people—all living together in harmony."

She hated to admit that one year ago she barely could have

found Greece on a map. Kate pushed back in her chair as she struggled to take in all this information. Yiannis sparked his lighter and brought his cigarette to the flame.

"Greece was under Ottoman rule—you know Ottoman, the Turkish empire? From the mid-1400s. The Greek War of Independence did not begin until 1821. And it took one hundred years more for Thessaloniki to once again become part of Greece." He shook his head, as if he couldn't believe how many years northern Greece was ruled by the Turks. He fell silent, taking a deep drag of smoke.

Gazing into the distance, Kate tried to piece together this mountain of history he was sharing. She interrupted the silence. "The Fargani? I'd like to give it a try. Maybe you can write the bus number down for me?" She was gradually more emboldened to go new places in the city.

"Yes, yes." He wrote a number on the newspaper border and tore it off. "You take the bus for the street Egnatia and get off at the stop for Kamara. You will see a store on the corner that sells floor coverings. Turn right. You will think you are in—what is it—alley? But straight ahead is the cinema Fargani." Kate took the paper, tucked it in her jeans pocket, and thanked him. Another new frontier of learning beckoned on the horizon.

fifteen 🌿

The next week after work and lunch on the balcony, Kate summoned her courage and boarded the bus that would take her into a new part of the city. The Fargani was located down a small alleyway in an ancient building that must have been Turkish, she guessed, from the rounded turret on top.

Yiannis had said only a few Ottoman buildings remained in Thessaloniki after the departure of the Turkish people in the 1920s. Kate had been astounded to learn about a massive, compulsory population exchange between Orthodox Greeks living in Turkey and Muslim Turks in Greece.

"There was a genocide in Turkey of the Greek Orthodox by the Turks. Between 1914 and 1922. Very terrible times. After that, Greeks living in Turkey were expelled and the same for Turks living in Greece."

This trip to Greece for a speech therapy job was opening up the world for her.

Approaching an older man seated behind a small window at the theater entrance, Kate indicated by gesture she wished to buy one ticket. Inside, she made her way through a darkened lobby to an even darker theater. The seats were thinly padded and screeched when opened.

The movie began. Large ornate numbers "8 and ½" announced

the film "di Federico Fellini." Kate had read about surrealism but had never seen anything like this before. She struggled to comprehend the strange movie unspooling before her eyes, made even more inaccessible by Italian dialogue with Greek subtitles. A man stuck in traffic in Rome escaped from his car and elevated into the sky. A Romani woman pirouetted on the beach. Long-dead family members dressed in white danced upon dunes. Her confusion gradually gave way to another sensation—an eager willingness to follow Fellini's tale. Kate half-smiled at the exotic world spreading out before her. Eventually, the screen went dark. It was over.

Slightly disoriented from the movie, Kate made her way back to Queen Olga Street. In Yiannis's library in her apartment, she munched on cheese and bread while examining a book in English she'd found about European filmmakers. She searched to find an explanation for what she had just seen.

From then on, Kate's new routine was to spend at least one afternoon a week seeing films Yiannis recommended. She had always liked puzzles, and watching movies in a language she didn't know, with Greek subtitles that disappeared before she could attempt to read them, was a new form of entertainment. Kate was free to use her imagination to figure out the plot, creating in her mind whatever she wanted. After Fellini, other Italian and then French New Wave movies cascaded into her life.

A few weeks later, Kate waited in what was becoming her usual afternoon seat midrow in the almost empty Fargani. *Potemkin*, a Russian silent film made in the 1920s by the director Sergei Eisenstein, came onto the screen. Kate watched the horrifying scene of Cossack soldiers, loyal to the Czar, as they marched in precision down flights of stone steps and fired into an unarmed crowd. A mother, her injured son in her arms, appealed to the troops, but was shot. An older woman was hit by a bullet in the face. A baby carriage bumped down the length of the stairs, abandoned after the infant's mother had been killed. Kate was riveted. On the crowded sidewalk back to her apartment, she replayed the scenes in her mind. Despite the strange beauty of the slow-motion, black-and-white images, the horror of innocents being gunned down stayed with her. An unsettled reaction grew.

Growing up in Texas, Kate knew the Russians only as evil, and communism as the enemy of all good American values. She was now seeing another side of the story and a reason Russians rebelled against the Czar and started a revolution.

Back in Yiannis's library that evening, Kate found a memoir in English by the film's director Eisenstein. She read about the meticulous filming of the Odessa Steps scene with the soldiers marching and the runaway baby carriage. Into the night, page by page of this book, she had the sense of sneaking into someone's backyard where she wasn't supposed to go. What would her grandmother think if she knew Kate was reading a book by a communist? An American flag decal had ridden next to an "America: Love It or Leave It!" bumper sticker on her silver Buick. Her grandmother had always admonished her grandchildren not to "do anything you've got no business doing." *Is this something I've "got no business doing"?*

Kate's solo movie dates filled her afternoons, giving her companionship with towering figures on the screen. Her time spent with Fellini, Bergman, and French New Wave directors also fostered new questions about personal relationships. Extramarital affairs on the screen rekindled her suspicion that Jim had a girlfriend when they were married. Kate had always viewed marriage as sacred, but now she began to wonder. *Maybe the Europeans have it right—maybe affairs are part of human nature and not a sin, like I was taught in church?* Life was feeling much more complicated than she'd thought possible.

One day walking back from work, the marquee at a movie theater one block from her apartment advertised an American film. Kate translated the names Barbra Streisand and Robert Redford. She stopped. She had seen *The Way We Were* in Waco when still happily married to Jim, before she had her heart shattered.

Kate checked the time and hurried home for a quick lunch. Later, sitting with a handful of Greeks waiting for the movie to start, she thought back to the long tables of gifts on display in the living room of her parents' home in June 1970 before her wedding to Jim. Those four years seemed a lifetime ago. She was all set to marry the boy of her dreams, a handsome law student who would carry her along to imitate the lives of her parents by having children and raising them to marry and have their own children, the never-ending line of happy stories like a series of mirrors reflecting continuously upon themselves.

Now, Kate was in an almost empty movie theater in Greece with the oversized faces of Barbra and Robert ending their own marriage, Greek subtitles running across the bottom of the screen. Despite her evolution over the past two years since the divorce, she couldn't escape occasional moments of heart-stabbing sadness. *Couldn't I have fought harder to stay married and settled down in a normal life?* Just as quickly, Kate countered that argument. *And see Jim bored with me and avoiding my face when we made love?* Still, the illusion of being happily coupled with Jim beckoned like a beacon in the fog at times like these.

She remained in her seat, soaking up the last strains of music during the credits. Slowly, Kate made her way back to her apartment, sifting through her own memories of the failure of her marriage.

Later that evening, Kate sat on the balcony and watched the shimmering lights from cruise ships slipping out of the harbor. A shudder ran through her body. *Am I letting go of the fantasy life I've had since I was a little girl? Am I making room for something new?*

Kate had no idea what would replace her childhood dreams or what she would find next in her life. But now, in her mind, she saw the image of her beautiful wedding dress drifting far out into the distance. Flying. Dancing. Twirling. Falling. And disappearing into the dark waves of the Bay of Salonika.

sixteen ✿

October warmth filtered in through the open balcony door in Kate's kitchen. Although it was nearing the end of the month, the weather remained mostly sunny and mild. She munched on a breakfast of boiled egg and cheese slices, taking sips of Nescafe made with Carnation milk. The *International Herald Tribune* was spread open on the small kitchen table. This paper, and the weekly European edition of *Time* magazine, helped Kate keep up with news from the United States and around the world since her arrival in Greece several weeks before.

Hearing noises from outside, she stopped reading. Often Kate had wondered about her neighbor. There were never signs of life across the metal railing of the balcony next door. The mop, bucket, and clothespin bag she'd seen every day for the past few weeks had stayed in their places.

Kate peeked out the door and glimpsed someone vigorously shaking a dustmop. Venturing out, she greeted a middle-aged woman with jet black hair. "Kalimera."

The woman jumped with surprise, then greeted her with a broad smile, revealing a slight gap between her front teeth. "Kalimera," the neighbor answered, quickly running a hand over her hair as if to make sure her coiffure was in place.

"Eimai ee Katerina." Kate introduced herself and stuck her

hand across the railing separating the two balconies. *"Eimai etho,"* using a phrase that said, "I'm here." After saying it, Kate realized that was a silly thing to say—of course she was here—but that was all she could think of.

The woman wore a flowered housecoat, reminiscent of the kind Kate's maternal grandmother wore when doing chores. She wiped her hand before offering it to Kate and greeted her with, "Hairo polee." Recognizing Kate was a foreigner, she asked, "English? French?"

"English, please. I'm from America." Although she could never be sure how the news that she was an American would be received, something about this woman's friendliness made Kate move past any hesitation.

"Hello, Katerina. I am Margarita—like the flower. The daisy. Rita for short. I traveled with friends to Italy and have returned. Everything is a mess."

"Welcome back, Rita." Kate was relieved they could speak in English.

Rita brushed back a wayward strand of hair that had fallen across her forehead. "Are you a friend of the Stylianou family?"

"Yes. They're letting me stay in their apartment. I'm working at ELEPAAP—a speech therapist for Soto and the other children."

"Tch, tch, tch." She clicked her tongue. "Poor Soto." She shook her head slowly and sighed, a sad expression momentarily taking over her face. After a few seconds, she brightened. "They are a very nice family."

"Yes. They've been wonderful to me."

"Your family in America is Greek?" Rita asked.

"No. I answered an ad for ELEPAAP in a journal. I'm slowly

learning Greek and helping mothers with feeding their children more properly." Rita winced, an expression Kate had often noticed from passersby on the sidewalk outside ELEPAAP.

As they continued to talk, Kate studied Rita's face, which was attractive in an unusual way. Its characteristics were slightly different from most Greeks, with her wide face and sharp nose, dark-brown eyes, and a deeper color of olive skin. "I live with my two brothers—Demetris is older, and Antonis is younger. Of course, I do all of the work in the house," Rita gestured to a basket of wet clothing waiting to be hung out. "We have a small factory where I work in the office also. Do you know what is a *trikuklo*?"

Kate nodded, as she had seen the three-wheeled delivery vehicles that crowded the streets of Thessaloniki, and Lena had explained the word meant "three circle."

"Some of those are from our factory. Our father started the business many years ago."

Hearing the pride in Rita's voice, Kate said, "Polee kala." She had the urge to say something positive, but "very good" was what she remembered. They smiled at each other in the ensuing quiet.

"Do you know today, October 26, is a very special day in Thessaloniki?"

"Yes—St. Demetrios Day. We have a holiday from work." Lena had invited Kate to the farm, but she'd decided to do household chores and study her Greek textbook.

"Bravo. He is the patron saint of our city. There are many name-day celebrations for all who are called Demetris, like my brother." Rita paused. "Would you join ours?"

Greek people observed name days rather than birthdays, since many Greeks were named after saints. They celebrated the holy day of their namesake instead. She hesitated. "I don't know. I promised myself to spend the time studying Greek."

"The party is tonight. You will have the opportunity to practice what you learn in the day. You will come?"

Not knowing how to refuse the invitation, Kate nodded her head. "Efharisto."

"Our entrance is downstairs next door. Your building is 84-B, and we are 84-A. Push the button for Kozakis. After eight o'clock." She laughed and added, "We Greeks do not have early gatherings."

They said their goodbyes and Kate went back to her breakfast. *What have I gotten myself into?*

Two hours later, she closed *Conversational Greek,* stretched, and decided to go for a walk. Greek flags hanging from balconies flapped in the breeze, a festive atmosphere in the bright sunshine. On the seaside promenade, couples strolled, children ran ahead of their parents, and older men in twos and threes, heads bent and hands behind their backs, flipped worry beads. She was amazed at the speed with which they circled these short strands of beads rhythmically through their fingers.

A sudden sense of aloneness sunk any bright mood she might have had to match the glorious sunshiny day. Everyone seemed to have somewhere special to go. Kate sighed, a feeling of isolation overpowering her. At least this evening, she was invited to a party.

seventeen

inishing the final page of the most recent *Time* magazine, Kate glanced at her watch and was surprised at the time. She hurried to the spare bedroom where she kept her clothes in the armoire and flipped through the choices. There was only one. The teal pantsuit she'd worn on the plane and on the first day she visited the center. It was decidedly less fashionable than what Kate saw on the streets of Thessaloniki. Here, women dressed in an upscale way, with midi skirts and boots and cowl-neck sweaters. Mannequins in dress shop windows displayed sleek outfits complemented by elegant shoes and bags. She would ask Georyia to go shopping after the next payday, but tonight this would have to do.

Kate checked her makeup in the mirror as the elevator descended. She headed outside and went to the door directly on the right. After announcing herself over the intercom, the buzzer sounded, and the door opened. The lobby of Rita's building was much the same as Kate's, with a shiny, marble-tiled floor, and an elevator. She pushed the button for the fifth floor.

Down a narrow hallway, an open door waited for her. Rita had transformed into an elegant hostess, sparkling jewelry accenting her close-fitting fuchsia dress. Kissing her on each cheek, Rita welcomed her into a living room decorated with an Oriental rug, tapestry-covered chairs, and a leather couch.

"Welcome to our home." She smiled. The room was empty. Kate was the first guest.

"Americans. You are always on time." The baritone voice from around the corner was soon connected to a man in sports jacket and turtleneck sweater, bearing a surprising resemblance to the American singer Dean Martin. Graying hair and dark eyes, he showed a hint of Rita's features. A strong scent of cologne accompanied him.

"Katerina, this is my brother Demetris."

"Oh—what is it I say for a name day?" Kate knew there must a special greeting.

"*Chronia polla.* Many years. You must learn this. It is very much part of Greek life." Demetris smiled broadly. Kate hoped she could remember the phrase, especially since the word for "years" was *chronia,* the basis for English words like "chronology."

Rita gestured to a chair. "Please sit. The others will come soon. Our younger brother, Antonis, is celebrating tonight with friends. You will meet him another time." Rita disappeared through the doorway.

Demetris sat across from her, adjusting his jacket as he sat. "I am sorry that my English is not good. My sister—she studied more in school."

Rita reappeared carrying a tray with a tiny crystal bowl sitting atop a crocheted doily. It was filled with *gluko,* the fruit preserves she had been served at her first visit with Lena's mother. A glass of water and a small silver spoon were also on the tray. Rita and Demetris watched Kate as she struggled to eat two spoonfuls. It was quite sweet.

"Kala," Kate said and then wished health to them, "Steen ygeia sas," before drinking the water. At least she remembered that much.

Kate sat back in the chair. The glass case of a hutch was filled with china and delicate objects. The room was decorated in a different style from the homes of Lena and her mother. It was fancier and had a pastel color scheme rather than a casual style and earth tones. This was reminiscent of the living room of one of her grandmother's friends, where Kate and her girl cousins went for Saturday afternoon tea parties. She remembered her childhood sense of awe at ceramic figurines of ballerinas, crystal bowls, and a sparkling chandelier similar to the one hanging in Rita's living room. Something fluttered within. For a moment, Kate had a deep wish for her family to be sitting in the empty chairs across from her now.

Just then the buzzer sounded. As a string of guests began coming through the doorway, Rita kissed each visitor on both cheeks and thanked them for the gifts in their hands—boxes of pastries, flowers, and candies. Kate realized she had brought nothing. She had grown up in a less formal way of calling on friends, where one would usually just show up at somebody's house. Here, there were definite rituals of hospitality and visiting. The Old-World customs of Greece. Kate was trying to fit in, but she wasn't doing a very good job.

The evening continued with Kate remaining in her chair and regretting she didn't have something fancy to wear. No one else wore a pantsuit but wore cocktail dresses and high heels. Fortunately, the conversations were primarily in English. She talked mostly with the women, answering questions about life in America or hearing about someone's family in Chicago or Boston. Rita served homemade cheese pies and small oblong meatballs in a spicy tomato sauce.

"This is a recipe my mother brought from Smyrna—now it is

Izmir in Turkey." Rita spooned the meatballs onto a plate for Kate. "*Soutzoukakia,* they are called."

One of Rita's friends explained, "Many of our families came from Turkey with the exchange of populations in 1922." Kate, nodded, having heard stories about the Greeks who had lived centuries in Turkey before being uprooted and coming to settle here in the early part of the century.

"*Ouzo?*" Demetris approached and offered. She knew about this Greek drink but had not yet tried it.

"I guess so." She raised her shoulders. He nodded to his sister, who came back with a tray that had a small glass and a bowl of ice cubes. Demetris opened a miniature bottle with blue lettering on the label, poured clear liquid into the glass in Kate's hand, then plopped in three ice cubes. The ouzo immediately transformed into a milky white liquid.

"It will go down better," Rita said.

Surprisingly, Kate liked the strong licorice taste. She took another sip and smiled at Demetris. "Efharisto." He grinned back and rejoined his friends congregated in another part of the room. Their drink of choice was Johnnie Walker scotch. Kate recognized the red-and-gold label. The conversation from the men's side of the room grew louder and more animated with time. Kate's insecurities lessened with each icy sip of ouzo.

During a lull, Kate watched Rita move about, envious at the graceful way she maneuvered among her guests. Her head buzzed slightly from the ouzo, and her thoughts roamed. The scene sparked memories of a visit last summer to the home of her Greek tutor in Denver. Kate's parents had driven up from Texas and accompanied her.

Although the hospitality that afternoon was not as extensive as this evening, there were similarities. After coffee and pastries, they had been served watermelon to eat with forks and knives, instead of picking up thin slices to eat, as was the habit in Kate's family.

As they ate, her father had whispered, "We are looking at centuries of civilization here." He raised his eyebrows and nodded his head in appreciation.

The recollection wove back even further in Kate's mind to her childhood. One of her favorite excursions had been to the watermelon patch on her grandmother's farm. The grandchildren would pile out of the large gray Buick and chase across rows of West Texas dirt to a watermelon patch. They watched in anticipation while their grandmother detached a melon from a vine, raised it high above her head, and dropped it onto the ground. Small hands gouged the sweet insides, and they gobbled watermelon while juice dribbled down their chins and forearms.

The outings always ended with a seed-spitting contest. The idea of eating watermelon with a knife and fork was something unheard of, something more distant than the far away horizon beyond the cotton rows of those afternoons. Now, Kate leaned back in her chair as the memories of the past melted into the scene in this Greek living room, far away in time and geography.

The evening ended with pastries, liqueur-filled chocolates, and honey-drizzled baklava. *"Efharisto, Rita. Eitan oraio."* Kate thanked Rita and told her, "It was beautiful." She made sure her walk to the elevator was as steady as it could be, after the many glasses of ouzo.

Kate fumbled with the key in the lock to 84-B and swayed her way across the lobby. She punched the number for the fifth floor. The elevator lurched, and she grabbed the railing to keep her balance, bringing her up close to the mirror. All at once, an immense sadness overcame her. She shook her head and blurted aloud, "What was wrong with me? Why didn't Jim love me?" Tears wetted her cheeks. There it was again. Jim. The ouzo had shaken loose old feelings.

The elevator stopped at her floor. Kate went inside her apartment and switched on the light. She headed into the kitchen for a glass of water, an aspirin, and two slices of bread—her routine to fend off hangovers that she'd learned in Colorado.

Again, she thought of Jim, sighed, then chided herself. "That's gone, Kate. It's all in the past," she announced to the empty room. Kate scrutinized the small kitchen. This place, this apartment so foreign just one month ago, was beginning to feel like home.

Kate remembered her words to Rita when her day had started. "Eimai etho. I am here." She steadied herself and repeated them, this time with a new meaning. "You are here, Kate. Yes, you are here."

eighteen

The following Friday evening, Kate squeezed her way past fellow passengers on the bus heading into downtown Thessaloniki. Georyia had taken her on this route once before, teaching her how to buy a ticket, where to stand, and how to negotiate an exit. But this was the first time she tried it on her own. Kate's body shifted with each bump and turn of the road, as her hands gripped the metal bar of a nearby seat for balance. The bus was full, and what if she couldn't find her stop or make it to the door in time to get off?

Keeping her eyes focused out the windows on the sights that passed by, Kate was aware of strangers' bodies in the close quarters. She avoided eye contact but took in the smells of cologne, cigarette smoke, and body odor. A blur of faces and colors crammed beyond her peripheral vision. Outside, pedestrians on the packed sidewalk moved in waves, and neon signs and lights shined in store windows. The evening marketplace was coming to life.

She scanned the buildings they passed, keeping watch for the unique architecture of the popular Aristotelous Square. Curving arches fronted the buildings, giving an almost fairy-tale feeling, a story from a faraway land. The landmark would be the signal for her stop.

Finally, Kate spotted the square and joined the throng of people rushing down the steps and onto the sidewalk of busy Tsimiski Street. Hemmed in by the crowd, she followed the flow for several paces before breaking off to one side to get her bearings. On the right was a large outdoor space that stretched down to the waterfront. Shops and restaurants lined either side of the semicircle alongside the open square.

Her destination was the sea walk, the continuation of the concrete promenade along the city's edge beside the Bay of Salonika. It ran the length of the city, and the segment near her apartment had become one of her favorite places.

The sun was setting over the water just as she reached it. Lights from coffee and pastry shops twinkled on. The city stretched high up into the surrounding hillsides like an amphitheater, with thousands of glimmerings in the dusk. This was another of those moments of disbelief at where life had brought her. After making a full rotation to take in the view, she joined the activity on the sea walk.

A black-clad grandmother herded a rambunctious toddler. Women strolled arm in arm engaged in animated conversations. Old men, hands behind their backs, clicked worry beads in neverending circles running through their fingers. A young man in an army uniform, head shaved, embraced a girlfriend as they sat on a red bench overlooking the water. Kate passed scene after scene of people fully rooted in their lives.

In the gathering darkness of evening, she moved among them invisibly and as noiselessly as the large freighters making their way from the docks and heading out to the Aegean. *Xenos.* The Greek word for "foreigner" was the same as for "stranger." Kate was both. Loneliness surrounded her like a thick scarf wound around her neck.

As Kate headed back toward the bright lights of the city, the freshness of the evening air and the pace of her steps sparked a renewed energy. *Stop being a chicken. You can handle Tsimiski Street.* Her gait quickened with the decision. Kate walked past the shops and restaurants that bordered the outdoor park, where small children rode tricycles and groups carried on lively conversations. She wouldn't get lost if she went straight back up to Tsimiski where she'd gotten off the bus.

At the crowded corner, Kate passed a cart loaded with *koulouria,* the sesame bread rings that seemed to be a national staple. Their aroma beckoned, like the ethereal finger from cartoons she had watched as a child. A cardboard sign indicating fifty lepta, or half a drachma, was propped next to a box already filled with coins and paper bills. This honor system in a huge city on the busiest street corner in Thessaloniki astonished Kate. Before heading back to her apartment, she would see if she had exact coins to buy an evening snack. She didn't trust herself to try to make change, since she didn't yet know the Greek currency too well.

Swept along with the stream of shoppers, Kate noticed a distinctive window display. Books with English, German, and French titles were propped in the window of Molhos Bookshop. A foreign bookstore. She couldn't resist.

The faint, musty smell of old books greeted her as she entered. Foreign language magazines covered the table across from an ancient cash register. A woman in a blue cotton smock was perched on a stool, watching customers and handling transactions. Kate smiled, the woman nodded, but the expression on her face did not change.

The main floor offered tourist guides, Greek books, and stationery items. Venturing up well-worn wooden treads of a curving staircase to the second floor, she found rows of foreign books. Quickly locating the English language section, Kate trailed her finger along the spines of the volumes. Since her arrival, her days had been consumed by the Greek language, with its rapid-fire sounds and hieroglyphic-like curving letters. *I can't believe it! English all around me!* She was ecstatic. These were words that didn't have to go through a transformation in her brain to be understood. This was her language. Her domain.

Gradually, though, Kate's excitement morphed into melancholy. She didn't realize how dreadfully she had missed something so simple as a collection of books, all in English. The books' prices penciled inside were an unwelcome surprise. Too expensive. "No way," she said under her breath. Maybe the magazines downstairs would be in her budget.

At the bottom of the winding staircase, Kate approached the magazine table and was stopped as she recognized the cover of *Ms.* magazine. She was transported to the orange couch in her apartment in Colorado Springs, studying the pages of *Ms.* from start to finish. Still recovering from her broken marriage, Kate's journey toward healing had been helped along by the feminist movement. This magazine had become one of her guideposts.

Heart racing, Kate grabbed the magazine and hurried to the cash register. *"Parakalo, poso?"* asking, "Please, how much?" The woman stared at her, then released a small smile and wrote numbers on a scrap of paper. She could afford it. Happiness flooded inside her. After being helped to count out the right combination of paper money and coins, Kate grinned at the clerk. She struggled to put together the words to ask about the possibility of getting future copies.

At that moment, the woman relaxed. Her eyes brightened, and she reached to shake hands. *"Eimai Demetra. Ela se mena allee fora."* She was Demetra and invited Kate to come to her next time.

"Katerina." She introduced herself, smiled again, and wished Demetra a good evening. A bell above the door tinkled as she left the bookstore and returned to the busy sidewalk.

With steps now more confident, she rejoined the crowd. This evening Kate had made one small bit of progress in broadening her circle of familiarity. She hoped that Molhos and Demetra would become anchors, as she wandered the streets of this city with hundreds of thousands of people, trying not to get lost.

Kate stood at the edge of the sidewalk and checked her change purse, pulling out a fifty lepta coin and headed for the koulouria cart. She could already taste the sweet bread ring with sesame seeds on top.

nineteen 🌿

"Come for lunch today?" Georyia invited Kate, as they met outside Kuria Argero's office Monday morning.

"Efharisto, Georyia. That would be wonderful." She was eager for the chance to expand their conversation beyond their usual few minutes of chatting in Kate's office and their brief bus trip to the city center.

Just after two o'clock at the end of the workday, they left ELEPAAP and walked toward Queen Olga Street. Georyia carried herself in a calm, deliberate manner. Her steps on the sidewalk were unhurried, her interactions relaxed when buying a fresh loaf of bread, and her pace leisurely leading up the stairs and down the hallway to her apartment, located a few blocks from their workplace. It was a contrast to Kate's own usual tempo.

Georyia disappeared into the kitchen. In the small living room, a couch and two chairs encircled a dark-wood coffee table. The style was casual, decorated in earth colors, with various curios and trinkets arranged about. She saw a miniature bronze replica of the Parthenon, a doll dressed like a traditional Greek guard with pleated skirt and funny rolled-toe shoes, and a tiny windmill reminding her of a 1960s Hayley Mills movie that might have been set in Greece.

Kate expected they would eat soon, so she was surprised to see Georyia saunter in, sit at the opposite end of the couch, and light a cigarette. Kate watched her take a slow drag and blow the smoke out of the corner of her mouth. In Colorado, Kate and her friends shunned cigarettes in favor of the marijuana joints they rolled on album covers. In Greece, cigarette smoking was everywhere. Almost a national pastime.

Although their conversation was lively and entertaining, it was nearly three o'clock and Kate's stomach rumbled. Lunch was the main meal of the day, usually followed by a siesta, which allowed Greeks to stay up late in the evenings. At home, Americans typically sped through their days and tucked themselves into bed early. In contrast, nighttime for Greeks seemed to be the equivalent of another day.

At last, Georyia extinguished her cigarette and motioned Kate into the kitchen. It was slightly smaller than the one in Kate's apartment. Georyia poured olive oil in a pan over a low gas flame, releasing a delicious aroma. After cracking and slipping two eggs into the pan, she scrambled them with a fork. The next step was to chop a fresh tomato and edge it along with small pieces of feta cheese into the egg mixture. The dish was completed with a sprinkle of oregano.

Back in the living room, they balanced the plates on their knees. *"Polee oraia."* Kate complimented, "very nice" after her first forkful. "And this bread is yummy." The golden loaf of bread which Georyia had sliced sat in a basket on the table. "It's a good thing I do a lot of walking, or I couldn't fit into my clothes." She was finding Greek cuisine to her liking.

Offering more bread to Kate, Georyia asked, "You notice we have bread at each meal?"

Kate nodded.

Georyia put her fork on her plate and settled back on the couch. "Do you know that during the Second World War, Greece was occupied by Germany and Italy?"

"I know Greece recently celebrated Ohi Day, but I understood that was saying 'no' to Mussolini when he invaded."

"Yes, well Mussolini had to ask his friends, the Germans, to help. It was called the *Katohi* or 'Occupation', a very dark period in our history. The Nazis exported most of our food products back to Germany and left the Greeks with little. There was a severe famine, and everywhere was hunger and starvation. Bodies of the dead were left on the streets and loaded onto carts. Terrible stories."

Kate was quiet.

Georyia continued. "There was no bread during the Occupation. So we now keep bread on the table to remember. At demonstrations we shout, *psomi, paitheia, eleftheria*. Bread, education, freedom. Bread is first, you see."

Offered the basket again, Kate reluctantly obliged. Her appetite had been diminished by the conversation. Still, she ran a chunk of bread around her plate to soak up the last drips of olive oil and bits of feta.

Georyia's voice was soft but straightforward. "After the Second World War, we had a Civil War here. I do not suppose you know?"

"No." Kate shook her head.

"It is a long story, and now that the junta is gone, I do not have to whisper to tell you." Georyia's expression was somber. Kate braced herself. Was this burgeoning friendship going to be hijacked by politics? Until now their conversations had been about the children at ELEPAAP and the many questions they each had about the other's life experiences.

Georyia finished her food, then placed her plate on the table. "In the Second World War, when Greece was occupied, the collaborationist government's army had many Greek fascists and Nazi sympathizers. But an army of resistance fought them, mostly in the mountains. They also tried to keep food from being stolen by the Germans." She stopped to light a cigarette. "After the war ended, there was a battle for power between the government's army and the resistance, who were, by then, mainly communists. Your county and Great Britain were on the government side."

"But I learned in school about the Marshall Plan that aided Europe. Didn't that help Greece?" Kate hoped America would be viewed as the good guys in Georyia's version of the story.

"Yes, but the rightist government used some of the aid to defeat the resistance. After three years of fighting, the government won, with many killed on both sides. Thousands of communists were put in prison or left Greece." Georyia stopped. "I am searching for a word in English. It is when someone takes the place of someone else."

"Substitute? Proxy?" Kate said.

"Proxy. That is it. They say the Greek Civil War was the first proxy fight in the Cold War between the East and the West, a defense for NATO against the Soviet Union. It is one of the reasons your CIA supported the junta." Georyia slowly took another deep draw on her cigarette.

Kate hesitated. "Do you hate America?" She waited for the answer with apprehension.

"Ohi, ohi, Kaitie." Georyia rushed her words. "Greece has the blessing and the curse of geography. We are a small country, and we will always be on the chessboard of the big powers." She stubbed her cigarette.

Kate's voice was subdued. "There is so much that I didn't know about your country before I came here." Kate wiped her mouth with a napkin and put her plate on the table next to Georyia's. "Do you know the book *Alice in Wonderland*?"

Georyia smiled gently. "Of course. Let me guess. You are feeling like Alice falling down the . . ." She tried to remember the English words.

"Rabbit hole. That's exactly how I feel. Especially when it comes to politics and my country's role in the world." Kate struggled to smile but couldn't.

"Kaitie, meen stenohoriesai." Georyia urged her "not to worry." "Like children who come into the classroom for the first time, there is much they do not know." She leaned forward in her seat. "You start with your own understanding. You take what you are learning here—you will find your way." Georyia placed a hand on Kate's knee. "Do not rush, *koristi mou.*" Her use of the term "my girl" was sweet and genuine.

"Efharisto, Georyia." Kate rose to leave. "For everything. Food and conversation. And the bread." Georyia laughed and patted her on the shoulder.

It was after five o'clock when Kate started back to her apartment. As she moved along the sidewalk starting to fill with people, her head whirled with all Georyia had told her.

Suddenly, in her mind she was a young girl, sitting in the dark at the Palace Movie Theater in her hometown. She heard strains of music accompanying newsreels presented before the show started. Licking her way around a cinnamon cube lollipop, she watched scenes of American troops being welcomed on foreign shores, a voice booming the heroic exploits of soldiers and crowds cheering for them. That was how she had grown up. Those images were vivid in her mind. The faces of her father and uncle in their military uniforms had watched from framed photographs as grandchildren chased each other in her grandmother's hallway.

Although more recent scenes of American soldiers in Vietnam had been added, Kate still believed in the praiseworthiness of the American military, despite seeing the documentary about Vietnam on her second night in Greece. A boy from her hometown, a West Point graduate killed in that war, was a local hero. But Kate was learning American soldiers were seen very differently by people in other parts of the world. Especially here.

Lost in those thoughts, she found herself at the corner of Queen Olga and Markos Botsaris streets, standing between a queen and a Greek hero in the liberation war from the Ottoman Empire.

Starting out two months before, Kate had no idea her Greek adventure would put a new spin on almost everything she thought she knew. But now it was happening.

twenty 🌿

"Katerina, please bring your passport with you tomorrow," Kuria Argero had said on Wednesday afternoon, as she rushed to the waiting van with a child in tow.

"*En daxi.*" Kate had responded with "okay," assuming it was a formality for some kind of paperwork. The next morning, however, she was surprised by what greeted her amid the constant busyness of Kuria Argero's office. Kate fished out her passport from her purse to hand it over.

"Kalimera, Katerina." Kuria Argero gestured for Kate to keep her passport and flashed a broad smile. "Today you will go to the *Allothapi.*"

Kate was puzzled. "I don't know what that is."

"Ah, sygnomee," she apologized. "The Bureau for Foreign Workers. For foreigners working in Greece."

Kate tried to keep her voice steady. "I have to go there?"

"Yes. We are a little late to tell the government you are here." Kuria Argero was nonchalant. "But no worries—it's Greece!" She laughed. "You will take the Stathmo bus—the route for the train station on other side of the city—but you do not go all the way to the end. There are twelve stops before you get off. Here. I wrote them for you." Kuria Argero pushed her glasses on top of her head, handing Kate the list. She then gave Kate what appeared to be an application and a letter on the center's stationery. "And these you give to the bureau."

"But, I—" Kate wanted to explain she'd never been to that part of the city or taken that bus line.

Kuria Argero interrupted as she reached for the ringing telephone. "I am certain you will not have a problem." She smiled again before conversing on the phone cradled on her shoulder.

Holding on more tightly than usual to the railing as she headed down the winding marble stairway, Kate desperately wished she could turn to the right into her therapy room rather than go out onto the street. *Just another new challenge, Kate. You can do this.* She urged herself on as she left the building and headed toward Queen Olga Street. A new bus line. Dealing with Greek bureaucracy. Alone. Worry stirred in her stomach.

Kate gripped the exact change for the ticket in her fist as she waited to see a bus with Stathmo written on a dashboard placard. Finally, it came. She pulled herself up the steps, purchased the thin paper slip of a bus ticket, and took a seat. At this time of the morning, there were fewer passengers than at rush hour, so she could sit down. She noticed the mostly empty metal seats and the series of leather straps hanging from a bar attached to the ceiling. Stray bits of pink paper tickets littered the floor.

Fraying the edges of the directions from Kuria Argero, Kate listened intently to the driver up ahead as he announced each stop. Doors whooshed open and closed every time, making it easier to tick them off. She folded the paper down, name by name, after each one. As more passengers came on board, Kate kept her eyes either on the list or outside the windows, blocking out any curious stares.

She had become accustomed to being recognized as a foreigner. Once more she chided herself for bringing her shiny Colorado ski jacket to Greece, rather than trading it for something that would have attracted less attention. Greeks wore coats of wool or other heavy materials in colors of grays, browns, and blacks. Kate knew she stuck out even more as a foreigner with her bright yellow.

Gradually, Kate's concerns about the bureau were overtaken by her interest in the scenes sliding past the windows of the bus. The route traveled along the Via Egnatia, which she'd learned was built during the Roman occupation of Thessaloniki in the second century. Kate had spent hours studying the city's history in a book from Yiannis's library. Photographs from those pages now came alive in the sculptured vignettes that comprised the Arch of Galerius, an imposing monument constructed by a Roman emperor to depict his victory over the Persians. Kate almost gasped at the sight of the Rotonda with its minaret that reached to the sky. It was exotic and like something from a fairy tale.

Along the broad street of shops and tall buildings, a Byzantine church from the Middle Ages sat across from ruins of an ancient Greek forum. *All those centuries squeezed in together right here. Three months ago, you were in your bedroom in Texas. Just look where you are now!* She smiled as she settled back in her seat, continuing to keep track of the names on her list. History was on parade outside the windows.

The bus made frequent stops, with brakes squealing, passengers stepping down onto crowded sidewalks, and others pushing their way in. Recognizing her stop was the next one, Kate slipped her purse strap over her shoulder, stood up, and grabbed the leather loops as she made her way to the door. Again, she heard the metallic whine of the brakes. Doors slapped open, and she went down the three steps onto the street.

Kate was startled at the surroundings. This part of the city was different from the more prosperous sections downtown and along Queen Olga Street, with their gleaming shopfronts of European fashions, fancy restaurants, and coffee shops. In this part of Thessaloniki, the restaurants were stacked closely together, with luncheon offerings displayed in rows of steaming metal pans inside each one. Clothing stores announced prices in marker on cardboard rather than printed on sleek plastic placards.

Fortunately, the entrance to the Allothapi was obvious with groups of foreigners littering the steps, some with checked scarves around their necks and some with much darker skin than she was accustomed to seeing. Kate pulled open a heavy glass door and climbed the stairs to a large hallway. A chorus of clacking keys and dinging bells of typewriters spilled out into the lobby, instantly reminding her of visits to her grandfather's office at the bank when she was a little girl. She was transported to a place stalled in the 1950s. The ceilings were high, and fixtures overhead provided a modicum of light.

Kate joined a group reading the directory of offices. She laughed to herself at the name in English of the Director of the Bureau of Foreign Workers—Captain Hercules Markakis. Captain Hercules sounded like a Saturday morning cartoon character. Kate joined a line that crept slowly toward an office at the end of the hallway. Three employees were seated behind a desk with stacks of papers in front of them. No one seemed to be in a hurry. A boy delivered coffee to the employees, holding the top handle of a mobile serving tray with small cups balancing on a platter underneath.

She waited as the man behind the desk exchanged a handful of coins for his coffee and took a leisurely sip. "Passport." He seemed indifferent. After perusing it and her accompanying documents, he fastened several large colorful stamps to the letter from ELEPAAP with a straight pin, closed her passport, and directed her to a nearby office.

Kate read the nameplate on the half-opened door indicating it was the office of Captain Hercules. A man sat behind an oversized desk with piles of papers. Smoke from a cigarette balanced on an ashtray curled upward in a ribbon. His head was bent in concentration. The name was not as comical as it had seemed earlier. Even seated, he was a large man with a sturdy build. He wore a tight-fitting business suit, and his dark hair was carefully combed in place. The scent of men's cologne enveloped him.

Burrowed in her yellow parka, she stood beside the chair in front of his desk, pressing her thumbnail behind the nails on her left hand. Unease crept in. What would she do if there was a problem with her papers? She would be at the mercy of this person in an office in a building in an unfamiliar part of the city.

Kate studied the wall with a series of black-and-white photographs of men in military dress. The scene triggered the memory of an old movie, *Seven Days in May*, the story of an attempt by army officers in the United States to take control of the government in Washington with a coup. Perhaps the movie plot was not too far from what had happened here in Greece? Kate had heard stories from her friends about prison and torture during the dictatorship. She shook her head, trying to swat away her suspicions about this man, seated a short distance away, and what role he might have played.

Captain Hercules raised his head and changed the bored ex-

117

pression on his face to a wide grin. He studied her for a moment. "Please, Miss . . ." He glanced at the papers she had handed him, "Miss Adams. Please sit." He gestured to the chair. His too-eager smile and lingering gaze quickly put her on guard. He studied her application, then pinned her with his eyes. "So now I know who to call if my children need an American babysitter some evening."

Kate wasn't sure if this was meant as a joke. The tension in her body rose. Smiling politely, she kept herself on the edge of her seat with an erect posture.

Captain Hercules tapped a silver pen as he read the pages, then scrawled a signature. "Miss Adams, we hope you have a successful time in our country and bring help to our children." He stopped. "These poor disabled children. May God be with them. And with you." Kate was surprised by a momentary kindness in his eyes, which quickly, however, disappeared. He stood, moved toward her, and offered his hand, which stayed a few moments longer than comfortable to Kate.

She murmured a quick "efharisto," pulled her hand away, and left.

Relieved to be finished with Captain Hercules, Kate rushed into the hallway and ran headlong into a young man. "Excuse me," they said simultaneously, then both laughed. He was about her age and had a round face, blond hair, and deep-set eyes. He gestured, smiled, and said, "After you" in heavily accented English as they continued toward the staircase leading to the street.

As they left the building, Kate hesitated. "Pardon me. Do you know which bus goes along Egnatia to Queen Olga Street?" She hadn't thought to ask Kuria Argero the name of the bus to take back to ELEPAAP.

"No problem. I can go to the city center on the bus to Egnatia. We will wait together. I am Branko," he said, putting his hand out in her direction. She took it, having learned the custom in this part of the world of shaking hands, even with someone in her age group.

"Hello Branko. I'm Kate." She heard herself roll the "r" in his name easily, rather than the usual American pronunciation of the letter.

As they waited for the bus, Branko asked, "American?"

"Yes. From Texas. You?" Kate asked

"Yugoslavian. Belgrade." His voice had a hint of pride. She wouldn't be able to find his country or his city on a map.

Just as they began to chat about their reasons for being in Greece, Branko said, "Here. This one." He pointed to a bus rounding the corner. Once on the bus, they stood next to each other, movement occasionally pushing them together. Noise from the road kept conversation to a minimum.

The bus approached the city center. "My stop is next," Branko said, glimpsing in her direction.

"Goodbye, Branko. Nice to have met you." Kate smiled, then started to turn away.

Branko quickly said, "Would you like to have a coffee on Saturday night?"

Kate paused. "Sure, that would be nice." She knew she needed to check this out with either Georyia or Lena. It wouldn't exactly be a blind date, but she knew nothing about this man smiling nervously in front of her. Kate decided to be in charge of their connecting and asked, "Can you give me a phone number, and I'll call you?"

"Here. This is my office." He reached in his wallet for a business card and shook her hand again, another formality for saying good-bye in this part of the world.

Kate watched as Branko faded into the sidewalk crowd. "My first date in Greece. With a Yugoslavian," she whispered to herself. The bus jerked into motion, taking Kate back alongside the battles carved on the Arch of Galerius and toward whatever waited next on her horizon.

twenty-one

By the time Kate returned to ELEPAAP, the school day was ending. She threaded her way through the stream of children and staff on the sidewalk. Climbing the marble staircase, she had an immense sense of relief being on the other end of the task, which had confronted her a few hours earlier. Kuria Argero was again on the phone, holding the receiver a distance from her ear as an animated voice spilled out. Kate mouthed words indicating she'd completed the task and received a nod and a smile. She backed out the door, listening to Kuria Argero as she attempted to interrupt the torrent of words coming from the phone.

Heading down the hallway to Georyia's classroom, Kate was grateful to find her friend seated at her desk, straightening a stack of notebooks. "You'll never guess what happened on my adventure this morning," Kate said. She explained about meeting Branko and the possibility of a date. "I really don't know anything about him, and I'm a little nervous to meet him somewhere by myself."

Georyia listened and nodded her head in agreement. "Would you like that he come first to my apartment? I will play the role of village . . . what is the word . . . something about matches?"

"Matchmaker?" Kate was horrified at the thought. "But Georyia this is only coffee," she protested. Quickly, Kate caught the mischievous smile on her friend's face and realized she was joking.

"You give him my address. I will write it for you. Eight o'clock this Saturday?" She stood up to leave. "I hope that will give you enough time to become pretty for your new romance," she said, striking a pose of primping and running her hands over her hair. They both laughed and headed out the door.

Back in her apartment, Kate ran her finger around the name on the business card as she listened to the series of telephone rings. "Branko Stepanavich" a voice answered. Kate introduced herself.

"Ah, yes. Good afternoon, Kate. I am happy that you call me."

She offered the invitation to meet first at the home of her friend, gave him the necessary information, then hung up quickly.

Heading directly for the balcony, Kate contemplated what had occurred. She was pleased at the prospect of a date. From her vantage point, she watched the scenes below. School children raced along in their blue-and-white uniforms, and men with briefcases hurried home for their midday meal.

The memory of another first date floated into her mind—in Wyoming, soon after moving there following her break up with Jim. A fellow teacher had arranged a blind date. She'd met Wayne at the restaurant in the Holiday Inn in Casper. He was cute enough, polite, and not overbearing. Most notably, he was her first date after so many years with Jim.

A cocktail waitress showed them to a table and impatiently fidgeted with her notepad while waiting to take their order. Kate was unexpectedly overwhelmed with emotions. She'd never been in a situation like this before. She had never even ordered a drink. She had no idea what to say or do. Wayne ordered a gin and tonic, so Kate copied him. The drink was strong—too strong—and she barely tolerated it. The evening ended soon, with Kate in tears, offering apologies for not being ready to date just yet.

Fortunately, that was two years and several boyfriends ago. Still, some of those early uncertainties resurfaced again now. She had until Friday afternoon to call Branko at his office and cancel, if she needed to. Kate sighed and left the balcony to find something in her fridge for lunch.

Finally, Saturday evening arrived. Kate zipped the yellow ski jacket over her teal pantsuit as the elevator groaned to the lobby of her apartment building. At the bakery around the corner, she watched the salesperson package the three pastries she had selected. Kate knew by now that you did not go to a Greek home for a visit with empty hands but rather with sweets or flowers. Aware of the crowd pushing behind her, Kate hurried to open her purse and find the correct paper bills. The clerk motioned for the money in Kate's hand and counted out the right amount.

"Efharisto." Kate was met with a quick nod of the head, indicating "You're welcome."

She was learning the vast lexicon of Greek gestural communication. "Yes" and "no" gestures were the opposite of those used in America. "Yes" was a slight nod to the side, chin leading. "No" was a vertical lifting of the head, often accompanied by closed eyes and sometimes a tongue click. Kate cradled the box of pastries and left the crowded warmth of the bakery for Georyia's apartment.

Soon Kate, Georyia, and Branko sat in the small living room of Georyia's apartment, drinking coffee and two of them smoking cigarettes.

Branko puffed a stream of smoke into the air. His blond hair was cut short, his smile hesitant, and he was resolute in keeping on his black leather jacket. Jiggling his lighter in his fingers between sips of coffee, he seemed content to answer questions rather than to ask any of his own.

"So, Branko," Georyia began after blowing smoke off to one side, "what is your work here?"

"I am a *ch*emist."

"A *ch*emist?" Georyia responded with interest.

Kate was amused they both used a soft "ch" rather than a hard "c" for "chemist." Even despite everything she was learning about politics, Kate held firm to the notion of the superiority of her American way of life. Contrary to what she might be hearing from Georyia, Lena, or Yiannis, in her mind America was still better than any place else. She worked hard to keep out anything conflicting with that viewpoint, removing it as quickly as her grandmother would yank weeds out of her garden.

With the help of Georyia's interviewing skills, Kate learned Branko had arrived in Thessaloniki in August. He liked to hunt pheasant and quail in the countryside on weekends and liked American pop music. The room fell silent when Georyia went to the kitchen for the pastries. Georyia brought the confections in on a tray, and the three of them traded nods of satisfaction as they ate them.

"Steen ygeia sas." They toasted to health with the glasses of water that always accompanied sweets.

Conversation stalled. Branko said to Kate, "I believe it is time to go, yes?"

"Sure. Thanks, Georyia, for the coffee," Kate said as she stood and slipped her jacket on. Branko shook Georyia's hand then placed his hand on Kate's back as they moved to the door. She quickly moved away from his touch, having no desire to lean into it.

Outside in the brisk evening air, Branko hailed a cab. Kate sat a distance apart from him as they wove through traffic, each glancing out the windows of the taxi and saying little. He was attractive enough, but Kate was finding little compelling about him.

Arriving at Aristotelous Square, they walked beside the arched walkways of the buildings outlined by strings of lights. Tables in front of each coffee or confectionery shop sat out in the chilly evening air.

"How about this one?" Branko suggested as they approached a spot where they could watch the activity on the outdoor park at the square and look out onto the bay. It was the same area she'd strolled past on Friday evenings, where she'd often had a sense of longing, seeing couples sitting together. Now, Kate and Branko became one of the couples. Being a café patron rather than a spectator, however, didn't feel as satisfying as she'd thought it would. Seated at a small metal table, Branko ordered for himself.

"One coffee and one Coca Cola," then waited for Kate.

I guess that's what they do in Yugoslavia. She ordered coffee. No Coke. "So Branko, how long do you think you'll be in Greece?"

He answered, then proceeded to explain Balkan geography and his career plans to her. She tried to remain interested in the conversation, but Branko was boring. Kate missed the liveliness and laughter of her Greek friends. Where was the communication without words, the animated gestures and facial expressions?

Kate was relieved when the evening was over, and they finally stood at the entrance to 84-B. "I would be pleased for you to call my office again. Or you can give me the number at your work?"

Rather than disclosing she had a phone in her apartment, Kate responded, "My work doesn't allow personal calls, but I have your number. Thank you for the evening." Kate deflected a hug with her outstretched hand for a farewell. Riding up the elevator and gazing in the mirror, she fluffed her hair and then watched herself make a decided gesture of "no" side to side, American style. There would not be a second foray into the Balkans for her.

Later as she slipped under the covers, Kate stared up at the bottom of the bunk bed above. She'd purposefully chosen this bedroom in order to have a balcony outside. Tonight, the smallness of the space was comforting.

In the darkness, Kate's thoughts traveled to the fresh memory of sitting outdoors in the café tonight, seeing beyond Branko out to the waves dancing in the bay and at the fishing boats tied to the dock. They rocked and bobbed in the reflection of the city lights. They moved but remained anchored. And that fit with what Kate was doing, finding a new steadiness in the midst of changes. She was going to be fine in this life expanding day by day. Night by night.

twenty-two

Sunlight and the sounds of farm animals drifted through the open living room windows on a bright Sunday morning the next weekend. Yiannis, sitting in his armchair, called to Kate. The previous week he'd asked, "What is the size of shoe you wear?" Now, he stood and presented a shoebox sporting a design of chain links, the trademark logo of *Alysitha*, the Stylianou factory.

Yiannis's brown eyes reached out beyond his dark-rimmed glasses. "*Mademoiselle, pour vous,*" indicating the box was for her. He then sang a French children's song, each verse faster than the preceding one, ending with a prolonged trilled "r" sound. He clicked his heels and bowed at the waist.

Kate opened the box, quickly donned new white sneakers, then stood in front of him, showing them off, taking turns with each foot. "And to christen them," she said with a flourish of her hand toward her feet, "do you think I can take a hike back there?" Kate had seen the mountain behind the farm. In Wyoming and Colorado, she had developed a love of walking in nature.

"*Vevaios,*" he told her. "Certainly." He gave her directions.

Ten minutes later, in a heavy sweater and her new white sneakers, Kate walked the gravel driveway heading past the orchards and through the green metal gate. Turning left, she was careful to stay in the weeds along the highway and away from the cars and trucks that roared by. At the fence marking the end of the Stylianou property, she traveled away from the asphalt and onto a dirt road in the direction of small hills and a larger mountain. Yiannis had told her Thessaloniki was on the other side of this mountain.

The late November sun warmed her shoulders as she strode past Yiannis's olive trees on her left and tall brown grasses on her right. A jab of familiar homesickness lodged in her chest like a taut balloon, now that she was alone and away from the Stylianou family. She thought about other hikes in the company of friends she'd left behind. *Do you realize where you are, Kate? Don't think about where you aren't,* she chided herself.

Several more minutes and she was at a high enough elevation to see the farm, which now resembled a child's structure made of blocks. The noise of cars and buses honking their melodic multitone signals below was barely audible. Up ahead, a collection of metal sheets, boards, and sticks were bound together in a curving shelter for animals. A gleam of light flashed in the distance. Kate heard their noise before they appeared.

Cresting the hill, a scattering of goats bleated and jangled their deep timbered bells as they scrambled over uneven surfaces. The figure of a shepherd appeared ahead, coat tossed on one shoulder, long staff in his right hand as he held something to his ear with his left. Passing in front of her several hundred yards away, he didn't pay her any attention. He listened to a small transistor radio. *This is so cool.* Homesickness was shoved out of the way.

Kate shaded her watch from the bright sunlight to check the time. The Stylianou family would be eating later, since it was Sunday. She had time to go farther, so she continued up the rocky path. Unexpectedly, down below to the right, other figures clambered over the rocks. They were not goats. The voices of half a dozen boys carried up to her in English. American English.

Unlike the shepherd, they noticed her watching them from a good distance away. "Hey look," she heard the boy in the lead yell. "She probably thinks we're going to rape her." Kate was shocked by the words. The boys appeared to be twelve or thirteen years old and had no way of knowing she could understand what they said. Still, they seemed too young to be malicious. She had been told there were American families living in Thessaloniki, working for US business interests. Perhaps they were a roving band of offspring out for a Sunday hike. Kate shook her head as she watched them disappear over a knoll. *Those little brats.* Their bravado was offensive. They had intruded into her beautiful hike.

Ready to begin her descent, Kate shook her head again, thinking about their brazen attitude. Unfortunately, this was the second time within one week she had come upon arrogance of her fellow Americans. The previous Wednesday, she and Georyia were having dinner at an Italian restaurant, a few bus stops away from her apartment. Kate dug her fork into the pasta with tomato sauce and lots of freshly grated Parmesan, twirling the strands in a large spoon just as her father had taught. Over her shoulder, she heard a conversation readily accessible to her. In her mother tongue. This was the first time she'd heard American English since arriving in Greece. Two men in leather jackets, with expensive briefcases and short haircuts, yelled out "American" to her. They had put paper drachmas on the table and were heading for the door.

Kate was surprised by her excitement at the prospect of meeting other Americans in Thessaloniki. She had excused herself, wiping her mouth with her napkin. A small flip of elation tingled as she approached them. Kate detected a curiosity in their eyes. She smiled broadly. "Excuse me. The States?" she asked eagerly.

"Yes, ma'am. You?" The taller one answered for them both. The three stood near the doorway and exchanged introductions. They both appeared similar in age to her. The taller one was the more handsome of the two, but there was something about way he pushed his chin forward when talking that hinted of condescension. His friend scanned the scene with disinterest. Both men were working for an international oil company with an office in Thessaloniki.

"But we're hoping it's just temporary," the second one spoke up. "We can't wait to get out of here and move onto the Middle East. That's where the real action's at."

"And what're you doing here?" the taller one asked. When she told them about her job, they regarded her skeptically. "Really? In Greek? Whew. Hats off to you, little lady." The term "little lady" hit her like a baseball bat.

Although annoyed, Kate wasn't ready to give up the chance of new companions. She tried again. "I really like Thessaloniki. The people. The hospitality. The beauty of this place. I'm excited to be here!"

They rolled their eyes at each other. They obviously didn't agree.

"I'll tell you what I want," the taller one said. "I'm gonna get me some of those Greeks to take me up in the mountains near Yugoslavia and do some hunting. That's about all these Greeks'd be good for, if you ask me." He smiled smugly.

As quickly as she could, Kate wished them well and hurried back to her table and sat down.

"What happened?" Georyia asked.

Kate shrugged her shoulders. "I thought maybe I'd find some-one from home to hang out with." She shook her head. It was more than disappointment. She toyed with her food, then pushed the plate away. Kate was aware of her own tug-of-war. One part of her longed for something familiar, something from home after these many weeks of constantly working so hard to adapt to a new place. The other part was offended by the demeaning way they talked about Greeks, about the people who had opened their homes and their hearts to her. The phrase "ugly American" pushed into her mind.

"Kaitie, are you okay?" Concern had taken over Georyia's face.

"Don't worry. It was just weird talking to people from home." Kate didn't want to share with her friend what the men had said, so she was quiet most of the walk back to her apartment.

Now, Kate stood on a rocky ledge surveying the Greek countryside. It was after two o'clock. From the winding road, the Stylianou's villa with the red-tiled roof was visible, a tiny, frosted cake. She shook her head again, thinking about both experiences with Americans, as well as the night at the cinema with the Vietnam documentary.

As the weeks had continued, Kate was beginning to feel embarrassed. Her country had done some awful things, especially here in Greece. She still loved her country. She didn't know how to reconcile the tension.

Maybe it's just bad timing—these two things happening so close together, she worked to convince herself. Kate scanned the expansive landscape. A circle of tall cypresses surrounded the red stone buildings of a monastery far off on the horizon. Mount Olympus stood grandly in the distance. The beautiful city of Thessaloniki hid on the other side of the mountain. Her eyes landed on her new sneakers, now dusty and scuffed.

She sighed and headed back down to her new family waiting for her.

twenty-three 🌿

It was an early December evening when Kate set out for Molhos Bookshop. The weather had a decidedly wintry feel. She had been surprised this Mediterranean country fell into obvious seasonal changes with lower temperatures, wind, and rain. Kate had assumed it would be sunny and warm all the time. Even though her yellow ski jacket often drew unwanted attention, at least it provided protection from the elements.

The bookstore had become one of her favorite places in the city, and she made weekly trips there for a European edition of *Time*, possibly a *Ms.* magazine, and to skim the English language books. And just this past week she had learned the bookstore's history.

Lena had been driving Kate to the farm for the weekend. "I see you have found our city's treasure," Lena said, glancing at the bag on Kate's lap with the bookstore logo.

"Yes. I've been there many times. It's always wonderful."

"Someone from the Molhos family was my classmate at Anatolia, our English-speaking high school." Lena was silent for a few moments. "I do not think you have learned the story of the Molhos family." Her eyes stayed on the road. "Our city has a tragic story for that family and others—the story of the Salonika Jews."

"I hadn't thought about Jews being in Greece." She'd had no

reason to think of Greece as anything but comprised of Greeks. Her lack of world knowledge kept showing up as woefully inadequate.

Lena glanced in the rearview mirror. "Yes. There are a small number of other ethnic groups in Greece—Armenians, Albanians, Bulgarians, and a few Turks. But during the Second World War, a horrible event occurred. In Thessaloniki, the Jews owned many businesses. They had their synagogues, own social organizations and newspapers, and everyone got along. Until the German occupation. The Germans and Fascists treated the Jews very badly and finally made Jewish families leave their homes and move into ghettos."

Lena was silent for a few moments. "Later, they loaded the Jews onto trains. Fifty thousand of them, Katina. The trains took them to concentration camps, and many were killed immediately on arrival. After the war, only a few survived to return to Thessaloniki. A small number reclaimed their stores. One of them was Molhos." Lena glanced over at Kate. "And that is the story of your bookstore."

Kate was stunned. She knew about the Holocaust, but never had such close proximity to its reality. Another story of history had now come alive for Kate. A horrific one. They drove along in silence the rest of the way to the farm.

The conversation with Lena caused a decidedly different mood to the December evening's visit to Molhos. In the past, she had noticed an older gentleman hunched over a desk at the far end of the room on the second floor. The top of his head was balding, white hair fringed around his ears. Kate had observed the thick lens of his oversized glasses. Now, she perceived him differently. Was he a member of the Molhos family? She glanced at him, then turned her head away quickly, only imagining what history he might have endured.

Leaving the warmth of the bookstore, Kate headed out for a few more errands. There was a palpable buzz in the air. Small multicolor rectangles of paper were showered from passing cars and swirled in the air. Kate grabbed one. *Abasilikee Demokratia* or "Democracy without a King." The referendum. She had heard about it from conversations at work. This was the vote to either keep the King of Greece as the figurehead of the country or to end the monarchy.

Kate was surprised to see security police surrounding one of the storefronts she passed. Signs in the window indicated this was the political headquarters for the monarchists. Police guarding the sparsely populated office glared straight ahead, expressionless. Her eyes traveled to the tops of the surrounding buildings. Men in black overcoats and walkie-talkies were stationed there, scanning the crowd. They held machine guns. Kate wasn't sure why there was so much security around the area, but a chill traveled through her body. *This isn't a movie, Kate. This is real life.* Hurriedly, she cut short her shopping expedition and headed home.

Back at 84-B, she stopped by to see Mama Mary, as she had begun calling Lena's mother, hoping to learn more about what was happening. Aunt Sophia was also visiting. After being welcomed warmly, Kate joined them in front of a small black-and-white television.

"It is the King—Constantine." Aunt Sophia, who always spoke English with her, explained. "He makes his final appeal to the Greek people. From London where he is in exile. Do you know of the election?"

"Yes. I heard about it at work." Kate watched the man read from papers in his hands. Surprisingly, his round face and features didn't appear very Greek to Kate.

"Tora theleis na yurizeis se mas?" Mama Mary wore a sour expression and shook her head back and forth as she spoke to the television, asking if the king now wanted to return. She followed by wondering where he had been when the dictators had taken over the country. Kate watched Mama Mary make a gesture of throwing the palm of her hand toward the television. A *moutza,* she had learned, meant something like "go to hell."

Kate listened to King Constantine as he spoke haltingly. "Why is his Greek that poor?" she asked Aunt Sophia.

"The family are not really Greek. They are from the House of Glucksberg. Long ago, they were given the throne of Greece, and now we have to pay very much money to them because they are our royal family."

Mama Mary made the sign of the cross over her chest. *"O Theos mazi mas,"* asking God to be with them. Older Greeks still asked for help from God, even though the church had been complicit with the colonels during the dictatorship.

Kate knew the current Greek democracy was still in its infancy. Perhaps there was the threat of another coup? Maybe that's why she had seen so much security in Aristotelous Square. *What on earth would I do if the government was overthrown again?* Kate worried. Glancing at the two women seated nearby, she instantly knew she would be okay. Her Greek family would protect her. Shortly, she bid Mama Mary and Aunt Sophia goodnight and walked the stairs one flight up to her apartment.

After midnight, Kate was awakened by loud noises from the street below. Grabbing a robe, she rushed onto the balcony. Car horns honked continuously. People riding atop cars majestically waved huge Greek flags.

A banner read, *Abasilikee Demokratia*. The people had won. Marchers, arms linked together, stretched out across the expanse of the broad avenue. Some carried candles.

"Apopse yiortazei o laos!" Tonight the people celebrated. Their words echoed in rhythmic waves, followed by a full-throated singing of the national anthem.

On the opposite side of Queen Olga Street, other pajama-clad people on balconies waved their own flags. These Greeks, who had been stuffed inside their homes for seven years of dictatorship, could now stand outside in the open with their political views. Kate rejoiced with them. Despite the cold and the late hour, she continued to watch until the last stragglers of the group passed.

twenty-four

"Please come for coffee some afternoon," Kate's upstairs neighbor Fotini invited, as the elevator ascended. They had initially met in the lobby of their building, and Fotini's husky laugh and ebullient personality always filled the elevator every time they were in the small space together. She and her husband, Takis, lived in an apartment on the sixth floor, just above Kate.

Fotini's green eyes and brownish-blond hair were striking. Kate was learning Greeks came in a variety of appearances. They didn't all have dark eyes and hair. She found this new neighbor compelling and hoped to get to know her better.

"I'd like that very much. Just let me know when."

"Tomorrow? Takis will be at his office, and we can—I think it is 'chat'—without a man." Fotini laughed heartily.

The next afternoon Kate walked up one flight of stairs and knocked on the door. Mindful of the Greek tradition of never coming to a visit empty-handed, Kate carried a small box of her favorite almond cookies from the bakery around the corner.

"Thank you, Kaitie. Please, this will not be necessary the next time. Come in," Fotini welcomed.

Kate was interested to see how Fotini's place differed from her own. They seemed to share the same floor plan except the space of her bedroom below was, instead, a sitting room and study in Fotini's apartment. Books lined shelves floor to ceiling. A television on a stand nearby was draped with a colorfully embroidered fabric, the kind many Greek women worked on as sewing projects, often with beautiful metallic threads.

The two sat on a green tartan couch and shared the cookies and an afternoon coffee, a htepeti café or "beaten" coffee. This warm, foamy drink was becoming Kate's favorite. Instant coffee and a small amount of boiling water were poured in a cup, whipped into a froth with a spoon, then supplemented with canned Carnation milk.

As she sipped her coffee, Kate was momentarily stunned seeing a nearby basket of newspapers. The mastheads bore the sickle and hammer logo of the Communist Party. Kate knew that each political party published its own newspaper, and one's political leanings were apparent by whichever newspaper they bought. Fotini watched her reaction.

"Kaitie, you are surprised to see our newspapers?" Fotini's expression was one of amusement.

"Well—yes." It was impossible for Kate to hide her uneasiness.

"Maybe we are the first communists you are meeting in Greece? At least the first you are aware of." Fotini then let out her trademark husky laugh. "Do not be frightened. There are many of us in Greece, and we are really very nice people."

Kate smiled tentatively. She took another sip, not knowing what to say. "In America, communism is something that is—do you know the word 'taboo'? At least that's how it was where I grew up."

"Yes, I know the word. And I know that in America we are not very popular," Fotini said. "But in the last election there was a communist—Gus Hall—on the ballot for your president."

Kate shook her head. "I have no idea who you're talking about."

"Gus Hall is the leader of the Communist Party in your country. He was on the ballot for president in the last election with Nixon." Fotini was matter-of-fact. "Before Nixon left on the helicopter and Ford moved in," she added with a joking tone.

"How do you know all of this?" Kate was both curious and embarrassed to be lacking in what apparently was basic information to Fotini.

"Newspapers. Television. What happens in America touches the rest of the world, impacting our lives each day."

"It's so strange that I have to come halfway around the world to learn so much about my own country."

The conversation shifted, as Fotini wanted to know more about Kate's job, how she was finding things in Greece, and if she had a social life. They laughed together after Kate shared the story of her date with Branko. Fotini then explained her own job in the architectural department at the university and how she'd met Takis. She had a talent for entertaining stories, and the afternoon passed quickly and pleasantly.

Walking back down the stairs to her apartment, Kate wasn't sure what to think about Fotini or communism. Similarly, as when she read the Soviet filmmaker Eisenstein's book, Kate was curious about communism. But she remained apprehensive.

On subsequent visits to the apartment one floor above, Kate continued to discover a different America than the one of her upbringing. She learned more about the American Communist Party. Somewhere in the archives of her mind were black-and-white newsreels of Joseph McCarthy and the phrase, "Are you now or have you ever been a member of the Communist Party?" But she really didn't know much about that chapter of American history.

One afternoon over coffee, Kate picked up a thin book with a black-and-white photograph on the cover of a young Black man with an Afro. "George Jackson?" The name was unfamiliar.

Fotini translated the title from Greek as *Blood in My Eye* and explained it was a memoir by Jackson, a Black Panther killed in prison. Kate remembered a related incident a few years before in a California courtroom, involving the activist Angela Davis, with the bountiful hairstyle, where a judge was kidnapped and killed.

The next week Kate found the book in English at Molhos and bought it. Sitting on the couch in Yiannis's library with a tensor lamp leaning over her shoulder, she was disturbed to read Jackson's description of growing up Black in America. It was a road that had led him to the idea of revolution. In America. Kate knew there were race riots in big cities, but she didn't know anything about a revolution.

Even worse, she rarely had thought about the life of the Black people where she grew up. Kate knew they lived in their own section of town and were mostly poor. She'd driven with her mother to drop off their maid, Totsy, at her house, if it could have been called a house. It was a shack. Had her mind been so filled with dresses and boyfriends and football games that she had paid no attention to the reality of what life was like elsewhere in her town? The Soviet films Yiannis recommended had begun her introduction to communism, and now her awareness of injustice was being expanded in visits with Fotini and by George Jackson's book.

One afternoon as they finished their coffee, Fotini ran a hand through her hair, as if contemplating a next move. She smiled. "So, are you ready for a new adventure?"

Kate grinned back and cocked her head in the Greek manner

for yes. It was a movement that had invaded her own vocabulary of gestures.

"On Saturday is a demonstration about Cyprus." Greece and Turkey had been fighting over Cyprus. Although the battles had ceased between the two countries, hostilities on the island of Cyprus continued. "Of course, the US keeps us to play at war with Turkey, so it is time to shout a little. Come and join?" Kate was staying in Thessaloniki for the weekend instead of going to the farm. She was ready for something new and accepted the invitation.

twenty-five 🌿

When Saturday came, Kate's ski jacket was perfect for the chill as she waited with Fotini at the bus stop, but she knew the bright yellow made her stand out. She had promised herself to buy a new coat. It was time to stop putting off that task.

The ride to Aristotelous Square was different from her usual expeditions of browsing at Molhos or wandering alone in the city. Kate tethered herself, holding onto the leather strap in the moving bus, but inside she was not steady. It was her first demonstration of any kind. She had avoided the few small anti-Vietnam protests on her conservative college campus.

As they neared the downtown area, her excitement sparred with apprehension. Stepping down from the bus, Kate was caught in a crush of people heading in the same direction on the sidewalk.

"This way." Fotini grabbed Kate's hand and pulled her through the crowd until they reached a group, some of whom held signs with red lettering and hammer and sickle logos. Her breath caught. *What have I gotten myself into?*

Fotini introduced her to the group. They greeted Kate with smiles and seemed genuine in welcoming her. Some of Fotini's women friends wore stylish coats and had modern hairstyles, while others were more plainly dressed and appeared of modest means. Fotini's husband, Takis, gathered with other men, and he greeted her with an enthusiastic wave.

Heartened by the warm sun and the crisp December air, Kate gradually released any worries about where she was and who she was with. She smiled, being on the threshold of a new adventure to share in letters with friends back home. Aristotelous Square was filled to bursting, people gathered together as far as her eyes could see.

Then, like a train gathering speed, the noise began. Bullhorns led thunderous chants in Greek of, "Out Forever from NATO" and "Murderer Kissinger." The words stung. Kate knew a special venom was reserved for US Secretary of State Henry Kissinger, but it was jolting to hear him called a "murderer" in full-throated jeers. A chant of "Americans Out" could have been the stuff of a secret joke that she, an American, was here *in* their midst. But today, it wasn't funny. Her body tensed. *How could I have been so naive as not to expect this?*

From a podium far away, a series of speakers shouted speeches into a microphone. The crowd noise was too great for Fotini to translate. They then began moving. Belatedly, Kate realized they were marching the few short blocks from the square to the American Consulate, which sat in a prime location facing the Bay of Salonika. She was pressed in the throng of bodies, but Fotini held her sleeve as they inched along with the group. Regret and fear swirled inside her.

Voices bounced off the buildings they passed. Up ahead, the four-story consulate was fortified with a thick wall around its perimeter, rolls of barbed wire on top. At the main entrance, heavily armed US soldiers stood beneath a large American flag fluttering in the winter breeze.

Seeing the flag caught Kate midstep. For the past several weeks she had been captivated by the heady excitement of her friends' freedom from the dictatorship. Her political education had been moving ahead. Until this moment. It struck Kate in a new and shocking way that she was, right now, going against her country and all she had been taught.

A memory leaped to her mind. She was in her high school English classroom, practicing a presentation for the National Honor Society program. The society's sponsor, Mrs. Ogletree, sat at the back of the empty room, her thin legs folded to one side, eyes fixed on Kate through navy-rimmed glasses, gray hair pulled back in a tight knot.

"Do it once more please. And this time slow your words. Make them sing out!" Mrs. Ogletree encouraged.

Kate began again. "I am an American, and I speak for democracy."

The script, written by an Ohio high school girl, painted a montage of various kinds of American students, markedly different from Kate's classmates, mostly White and Protestant, who would be listening to the speeches in the auditorium the next day. Kate particularly remembered the reference to a Jewish student studying his Torah.

"Hear, oh hear, O Israel, the Lord our God the Lord is one." The piece was a recognition of America's greatness as a melting pot for all religions, extolling the ideals of American democracy.

It still seemed true to Kate. Yet for the people of Greece, she knew those words would be meaningless, perhaps laughable.

Shuffling along with the group, Kate's thoughts continued. She had always been mostly a good girl, never bucking authority, questioning very little. Was that now shifting? This moment of the clash between the two nations, as well as the conflict within herself, gripped Kate with fright. A deep chasm had opened up inside and she was falling, falling, falling.

One street away from the consulate, a car was parked off to the side. A man, wearing a dark overcoat, bent through the window and pulled out a walkie-talkie. He straightened to scan the crowd. There was something familiar about him. Then she remembered her visit to the Bureau for Foreign Workers. Captain Hercules. She had heard stories about the Greek security police and their tentacles reaching throughout the Greek population. Captain Hercules was obviously more than a bureaucrat.

Kate and her fellow marchers were getting closer and closer to him. Her bright yellow ski parka was the one she'd worn in his office. Even though the crowd was large, she couldn't hide or blend in. She would have to pass in front of him, a few feet away. As Kate walked by, she could see from the corner of her eye that he looked in her direction. She tried hiding her face, but it didn't matter. He would see her yellow jacket.

As the crowd gradually moved forward, Kate dared not look back. She was in the company of communists, his enemy. And now he knew it. Kate was also in the company of her new divided self. Where was she headed? And what would happen when she got there?

twenty-six ✿

Two days after the demonstration on Saturday afternoon, Kate sat in her room at ELEPAAP, which she had brightened with an alphabet poster from Georyia and curtains from Lena. The joyful colors did not calm her worries.

Over the weekend, she'd repeatedly questioned attending the demonstration with Fotini. Something fragile had been taken from within and smashed to the ground at the barricade of the American Consulate. How was she going to piece the shards together again? Each time she flashed on the sudden appearance of Captain Hercules, Kate berated herself. Would there be ramifications from the Bureau for Foreign Workers? Had it been a horrible mistake to go?

Kate glanced out the window, listening for sounds signaling the van's arrival and the distraction it would bring. She hoped her day with the children and staff would create a respite from the intensity of Saturday's experience that still lingered.

She smiled at the first name on the list for today: Demetris Repanithis. He was the boy she'd seen on her first visit to ELEPAAP, as he and his mother were getting off the van. The one who had gone straight to her heart. He was always carried around the center by his mother and was probably six or seven years old. His smile was bright, despite the severe cerebral palsy that twisted his arms and legs.

Demetris's mother, like several others, had apparently been hesitant to enroll her child in speech therapy. Fortunately, Kate's Greek was improving, alongside a confidence in her therapy techniques. From smiles and comments, she knew she was gaining a favorable reputation. But there was still a cohort of parents suspicious of Kate and her skills. She hadn't forgotten her very first session when Kuria Bouras rushed out of the room, cradling her crying son.

Arranging two adult chairs and bringing the specially made padded seat from the corner, Kate waited for the van. She reviewed the list and made additional notes for the other children she would be seeing. Then she heard doors slamming outside and the buzz of voices. The children had arrived. Kate listened for the sound of footsteps outside her open door.

"Thespinis Katerina?" The woman's voice was soft.

Kind eyes and a timid smile lined the face of Kuria Repanithis. Demetris was wrapped in her arms. Her brownish-red hair was in a style that required minimal care, and she was dressed in black, the sign of mourning for a relative.

"Kalimera. Yeia sou, Demetri." Kate wished them a good morning and said hello to the boy. She had mastered the art of greeting, infusing it with her Texas friendliness in an effort to make new clients feel comfortable.

"Katheiste, parakalo." Kate gestured to a chair, asking Kuria Repanithis to please sit.

Demetris's eyes were a pale color of blue, and his skin was light and smooth, almost like porcelain. Her greeting had created waves of excited movement throughout his body. His squirming on her lap was something Kuria Repanithis seemed to be well-practiced at containing. Cerebral palsied children often had difficulty controlling not only their bodies but also their emotions, resulting in overflowing extraneous movements.

"Then sou eipa tharthoume steen kali kuria?" His mother's tone was reassuring and musical. Kate had heard similar words other times from mothers, telling their child they were coming to see a "nice lady."

"Uhnn," Demetris voiced a sound Kate recognized as an affirmation of what had been said, accompanied by a purposeful blink of his eyes. This was a good sign. Demetris was using one of the few things he could control—his eyes—to communicate.

Kate watched Demetris's eyes dart about, following the conversation and responding with appropriate facial expressions. She had been trained to observe clues of a child's comprehension of language, and Demetris seemed to understand what his mother was saying. Kate hoped Demetris did not have intellectual limitations, as did some children with cerebral palsy.

"Kuria Repanithi, ti thelete?" Kate was accustomed to using the plural form of "What do you want?" This was a switch from the singular and used to show respect for a person one didn't know well. Kate was asking what priorities Kuria Repanithis had for her son.

Demetris's mother responded slowly and with gestures to make sure Kate understood. *"Then troyee kanoniko fayeto, kai ton eho xapla."* He ate puréed foods and she fed him lying back in her arms.

She continued, quietly. *"Then milaei. Thelo na milesei. Alla then xero."* Kuria Repanithis confirmed he couldn't talk. She wanted him to be able to speak. Her voice trailed off after confessing she didn't know if that would ever be possible.

As his mother talked, Kate reached out to stroke Demetris's hand, seeing if he would tolerate her touch and judging how pliable his muscles would be if she tried moving them in new positions. Demetris watched her intently with his large, beautiful eyes, taking in everything going on around him. Satisfied with the inroads she was making, Kate decided to go to the next step.

"Demetraki," Kate switched to the diminutive form, an affectionate way of talking to children. *"Thelis na gnorizis teev karekla mou?"* She asked if he wanted to meet her special chair. *"Eho paihnithia."* And she had toys. Kuria Repanithis smiled at her son's excitement with this last statement.

Demetris blinked affirmatively. Kate removed the tray from the specially made chair and slowly Kuria Repanithis manipulated his legs around its center post, holding him in place until Kate could push the rounded semicircle tray in front of him. Since the chair provided support with its curved back, Demetris could sit independently instead of in his mother's arms. The expression on his face changed abruptly to fear and concern. Tears welled in his eyes. Instantly, his mother used her lyrical voice to reassure him he was fine and special toys were coming. Kate watched with admiration the talent of this mother and her skill in assisting her son.

Behind her back, Kate hid two wind-up toys, one in each hand. She then revealed them, positioning the toys far apart in opposite directions. Asking him which he preferred, Demetris quickly turned his head toward the right hand which held a mouse on a bicycle. With this simple test, Kate determined that he could use his eyes to communicate to others. By presenting a choice of two objects held in different directions, caregivers could let Demetris show a preference. Did he want a drink, or did he want a cookie? Did he want a book or a toy? Kate would share this approach with teachers and therapists upstairs. He could begin to rely on adults other than his mother for understanding his needs. Demetris could become more independent.

Next, Kate wound the wind-up toy he had chosen. Demetris chortled with glee, watching the mouse pedal around on his tray. It stopped. He looked at her. Kate then used a shortened version of *ki allo* for "more," by asking him, *"Allo?"* Demetris blinked. This wasn't good enough for Kate. She wanted him to respond vocally. With two syllables. Could he imitate what she was saying? Could he use two sounds rather than the single sound she heard him say? She overemphasized the two parts of the word. "Al-lo?"

"Ah-uh," came the response.

Kate wound the mouse, watching Demetris's reaction, while glancing at his mother to see if she understood what had just happened. Her eyes were moist, and her smile was wide.

"Bravo, Demetraki! Akouses ti eipes?" Kate cheered him and asked if he heard what he said. He blinked and grinned a smile even brighter than before. Kate explained he could use this word to tell others if he wanted more of something. *"Boreis na miliseis!"* telling him, "You can talk!" Her heart was twirling flips with delight for him.

Kate encouraged Kuria Repanithis to have Demetris use this version of the word to ask for "more" often and in as many situations as possible at home. She would see them again later in the week for another session.

Kuria Repanithis's eyes locked with Kate's after she had scooped Demetris into her arms before going out the door. "Efharisto, Thespinis Katerina." Her voice faltered.

After they had gone, Kate sank down into her chair. She twisted the tiny lever of the wind-up toy and watched the mouse move his legs furiously on the pedals of the bicycle. Kate smiled at the creature. Maybe, just maybe, she had done something good on this day.

But before she could bask fully in this happiness, Kate recalled the image of Captain Hercules scanning the crowd at the demonstration. *Have I put all this in jeopardy? Will there be consequences?* She wondered what her responsibility was as an American, and her responsibility as a human being.

Kate put the wind-up toys in their box and pushed the padded chair back to the corner. "Allo?" she whispered to herself, echoing the word she'd taught Demetris. She straightened, gazing out the window. She hoped this would be the beginning for Demetris to learn communication with words. Kate also hoped for herself a discovery of how to navigate this new version of her own world.

twenty-seven

A haze of smoke filled the air. Greek folk music from the stereo could barely be heard over the din of conversation. Kate sat with Georyia the next Saturday evening in a living room filled with people. They were at the apartment of Georyia's friend Eleni, a heavyset nurse with a ready smile, who was quizzing Kate about life in America. Greeks seemed to have an insatiable appetite to hear what things were like in the United States.

"Boyfriend in America, Kaitie?" Eleni blew cigarette smoke over her shoulder.

"Only *ono* boyfriend?" Kate said with a laugh, hoping Eleni knew she was joking. She then raised her head and clicked her tongue, Greek-style, to say "no." No boyfriend. Kate didn't know when, if ever, she would share the story of her failed marriage to Jim. Divorce was rare in Greece, and Kate still considered hers as an embarrassing failure, a secret not to be divulged. Nor could she imagine describing her life in Colorado where smoking marijuana and sexual freedom were commonplace. Getting high and having casual sex didn't fit into Greek society.

Eleni laughed and shook head from side to side. "Ready for a good Greek, then?"

"Vevaios!" Kate flashed a smile. She sipped her retsina, a resin-flavored white wine she was learning to tolerate. At first, the smell had reminded her of the Pine Sol underneath the sink in her mother's kitchen, but she could now swallow tiny sips without difficulty.

The intercom buzzer sounded. Another guest was joining the group. Kate briefly paused her conversation with Georyia and Eleni as someone opened the door. Eleni grabbed Kate's attention back to the conversation offering her a cigarette. *"Tsigaro?"*

"Ohi, efharisto," thanking her. "I'm not that much of a Greek yet."

"Siga, siga." Eleni laughed telling her, "slowly, slowly," hinting that it was only a matter of time.

A figure passed by. Kate was shocked to glimpse one of the most handsome faces she'd ever seen. It reminded her of the marble bust of a young man from fifth century BC on display at the Archaeologic Museum, which she and her neighbor Rita had visited the week before. But this person with perfectly sculpted eyes, nose, and mouth was very much alive. The young man with a head of dark curls was making his rounds to greet everyone.

He approached them. Georyia spoke to him in English. "Thanasi—this is Kaitie, our American. We work together at the school for disabled children. Kaitie, this is Thanasis."

Kate stood to greet the dark brown eyes and the sweet smile framed by a mustache and beard. A wave of excitement ran the length of her body.

"Hello, American." Thanasis shook her hand. There was an openness to his countenance, like a warm invitation. His hand was soft and strong at the same time.

"Hairo polee," Kate responded, reluctantly releasing the grasp of his hand.

"Milas Ellinika?" He asked if she spoke Greek.

"I'm learning." She switched back into English, not wanting to risk stumbling over the Greek words that sometimes failed her when she was excited.

"Welcome, Kaitie. Thank you for bringing good things to Greece." His smile was charming. Thanasis paused before moving onto another group of friends.

Kate sat back down and took a few more sips of retsina, trying to keep her eyes away from this new attraction in the room and hoping not to seem too obvious. *He's gorgeous.* She munched on a tyropita and took another sip of retsina, feeling a buzz inside her body not resulting from alcohol but from something more intoxicating.

Across the room, Thanasis was deep in discussion with Eleni's brother, Nikos, listening intently while Nikos gestured with forceful motions to emphasize his words. A few times Kate thought he glanced her way, causing her breath to quicken. Presently, Thanasis and Nikos both donned their jackets and moved toward the door. Kate's eyes followed the slim figure of Thanasis. He stopped, turned directly toward her, then cocked his head to one side in a farewell gesture. He locked eyes with her. Then he was gone.

Like a balloon slowly deflating, any interest Kate had in conversations with other people gradually disappeared. The evening crawled to an end. Strolling on the sidewalk back to Kate's apartment, she asked Georyia, "Who was that handsome guy Thanasis?"

"Ah—kalo paithi." Georyia called him a "good kid," the latter word referring to "'child,' *pedi* being the Greek root in words such as "pediatrics." Figuring out these connections of Greek to English was helping Kate expand her vocabulary. Georyia switched to English. "He studies at an engineering trade school here. He is from Eleni's village and lives with Nikos."

"Polee oraios anthropos," Kate said, letting Georyia know she had found him to be a "very beautiful human." She wasn't sure of the words for "ridiculously handsome." Kate added, *"Ohi san ton Branko."* They both giggled with, "Not like Branko."

"Ellinas then einai?" Georyia used a phrase to indicate "after all, he is a Greek, isn't he?" Kate appreciated the underlying humor of mock pride. Georyia often sprinkled in a bit of ironic joking whenever possible.

Kate hesitated. "Maybe he has a girlfriend?"

Georyia raised her shoulders and lifted her hands indicating she didn't know. They continued down the street, Kate's mind wandering.

After three months in Greece, she was beginning to get her bearings. Kate had struggled to learn the language and carry out a daily routine. She had worked hard to adapt the principles of speech therapy from English to Greek, creating new strategies every day.

Perhaps now it was time for a different challenge. Meeting Thanasis had pricked something inside her, a sensation she hadn't had since her time in Colorado. Thoughts ran happily through her mind as Kate and Georyia walked. The prospect of meeting Thanasis again, or some similarly handsome young Greek man, gave a buoyancy to her step. She smiled broadly into the chilly evening air.

twenty-eight

*D*ays in December passed too quickly. It was becoming impossible for Kate to avoid thoughts of the upcoming Christmas holiday and the gloominess that accompanied them. This year would be her first time away from her family for Christmas, their most anticipated holiday of the year.

One Sunday at the farm, Kate chatted with Yiannis on the balcony over a late-afternoon coffee. "You know that Christmas is coming next week." He stopped to flick his cigarette into the ashtray between them.

Kate forced a smile. "Christmas without my family."

As youngsters, she and her brothers and cousins had created their own Christmas Eve pageants at their grandmother's house. Kate loved the music, the decorating, pecan fudge, divinity, and other special Christmas treats.

Yiannis's voice brought her back to the balcony. "We plan for you to be with us. In Greece, we observe two days of Christmas. On the second day, we will celebrate a special tradition of the villages." He smiled at her impishly. "I hope you have not become too attached to the *gourouni*."

Kate wondered what the "pig" had to do with this conversation. "Actually I have. Why do you ask?"

Since one of Kate's tasks after weekend meals at the farm was to take him scraps of food, she had grown fond of the animal. The gourouni had become her confidant. She talked to him as he snorted and munched his way through the vegetable peels, leftovers, and fish carcasses. Kate shared thoughts with him no one else would hear and always experienced relief after their one-sided conversations. Emptying her plastic bucket was like letting go of something pent up inside.

Yiannis continued. "In the villages on the second day of Christmas—a pig is killed."

Kate's breathing stopped.

"Since it is our first Christmas on the farm, we will invite family and friends for a feast. My cousin, the one who drives a taxi in Thessaloniki, learned to do the slaughter growing up in my father's village." Yiannis stubbed his cigarette. "You will be privileged to see the National Geographic version of Greek holidays up close!" Kate knew Yiannis delighted in bringing in American cultural references whenever he could.

She spoke haltingly. "I'm not so sure I can handle that."

"Ah, Katina. I thought you were a tough Texan. *Kappa Kappa Texas*?" After learning she had gone to the Cyprus demonstration with Fotini, Yiannis enjoyed teasing her, pretending she was the head of her own Texas Communist Party. The issue of her allegiance to America continued to rest uneasily.

Kate attempted a smile and finished her coffee in one long sip. She swallowed again to remove remnants of bitter silt-like grounds that remained in her mouth. What she couldn't get rid of was impending dread.

Back in the room where she stayed on weekend visits, Kate gathered her things before catching the bus back to Thessaloniki.

As she stuffed a sweater into her travel bag, she thought, *Killing a pig as part of a Christmas tradition? It's barbaric!*

Kate was thrust back into her early days in Greece and the sense of being somewhere foreign. Why did Yiannis have to recreate this village ritual? And how could she possibly witness it? These thoughts tumbled through her mind as she waited on the asphalt for the bus to arrive.

When Christmas morning finally came, Kate joined Lena in the kitchen. Sitting in her usual ladderback chair, she cut a piece of bread and spread it with honey from Yiannis's bees. Lena deftly moved a skinny dowel over small mounds of dough, broadening them into thin circles for layers of filo.

"Katina, I think it may be different in your country, but in Greece our most important celebration is not Christmas, but Easter." Sprinkling flour on the plastic tablecloth she continued, "Greeks believe that the *anastasi* of Christ—I cannot remember the word—is more important than His birth."

"Resurrection?" Kate offered.

This theological perspective was something she had never considered, despite years of Bible study in the Baptist church. Christmas had always been the centerpiece of their family and church lives. *Easter more important than Christmas?* Kate disagreed but wasn't sure why. She toyed with stray bits of flour, trying to stay focused on their conversation. Her mind wandered, imagining what her family would be doing each hour of Christmas Day. Lena rotated the oven dial for the *kolokithopita*, the sweet squash pie, to bake.

Later that evening with the boys in bed, Kate joined Lena and Yiannis as they listened to a recording in English of *Amahl and the Night Visitors*. Kate sank into the cushion, relieved Christmas was finally over. Earlier, Lena had gifted her with a phone call to her family for a conversation that threatened to break open the dam of emotions. Fortunately, she kept her tears at bay.

With a wisp of sadness, Kate recalled another Christmas evening a few years before when her dad had played a recording of this very opera, the story of the Magi told from the point of view of a young disabled boy. Down the hallway Soto slept in his bed. He was perhaps around the age of Amahl, but Soto struggled to speak, rather than having the sweet soprano boy's voice that sang out from Yiannis's stereo set. Lena's head was bent down as she concentrated on sewing a button on a shirt. Yiannis's eyes were closed as he listened, a cigarette resting in his fingers.

Despite her melancholy, Kate had a momentary sense of peace. Until she remembered what awaited tomorrow. The pig would be slaughtered. Even the beautiful music couldn't quell her uneasiness.

twenty-nine ✎

From the kitchen window, Kate heard the slamming of car doors and excited voices down below. For once, the stacks of plates and glasses littering the kitchen were a welcome sight. Washing the dishes would be a good excuse to delay joining the group. Kate listened to the rising and falling tones of Greek voices, like flags flapping in the wind.

Just then another noise came, this one from inside the house. It was Soto shuffling his way into the kitchen. With one hand on a chair for balance, he shoved a foot with an untied shoe toward her. Kate doubled the last bit of lace on his second shoe and tugged it. Soto again secured his balance and drew an imaginary line across his throat with a shaky finger, mimicking an executioner's stroke. His mouth pulled to one side, he paused before articulating slowly the three syllables of her name. "Ka-ti-na." He teased with a hint of devilment.

Kate wasn't able to hide her dread of what was about to happen to the pig. Soto must have noticed, as he gently moved his wavering fist under her chin, a gesture for her to "buck up." It was sweet and caring. A moment later, Soto was gone. She could hear his half-octave of laughter echo as he carefully made his way down the stairway outside the kitchen.

Back at the sink, her trepidation deepened. Shortly, she heard

Lena's familiar footsteps coming up the wooden stairs. "Katina. Enough time in the kitchen." She had come to refill her red metal tray with sweet squash pie and more small ouzo glasses. "We want to impress our friends that we have imported immigrant labor from America but not to think that we have a slave," she said. Seeing Kate's face, she stopped. "Katina—I hope that—"

"Lena! Katina! Grigora!" Yiannis was yelling from downstairs for them to "hurry." Kate stiffened. How could she escape what was about to happen? She wished her feet could become stuck and keep her on the kitchen tiles.

"Ela Katina." Lena urged her to "'come," gently grabbing her hand and leading her down the stairway.

Soto and Aris joined a crowd of men and boys next to a pile of evergreen branches. Women, small children, and older people watched from a short distance away, gathered around a table underneath a vine-covered gazebo. Kate easily recognized Yiannis's cousin by the large knife in his hand, its blade glinting in the sunlight. Black hair was plastered to his head like a synthetic sculpture. A cigarette rode his bottom lip.

Yiannis herded the pig from his pen toward the gathering. Time slowed as Kate watched his attempt to escape. The taxi driver raised a mallet, hitting the pig squarely on top of his skull to stun the animal before slitting its throat. His snout swerved to the ground, legs beginning to crumble. Kate turned away, closing her eyes and pressing her lips together. When she looked again, the pig rested on a nest of evergreen branches. Steam arose from blood puddling on the ground. Shock overwhelmed her. She was nauseous.

Kate stepped apart from the crowd. Immobile. Presently,

Yiannis made his way over to her. A black fisherman's hat sat jauntily atop his head. His sunglasses reflected the morning sun. He stopped. A curious smile spread across his face before he spoke. "Vietnam, Katina. Vietnam."

Kate was stunned. Both at the words and that Yiannis had thrown them at her. Keeping his gaze fixed, he smiled and raised his eyebrows. Yiannis made a small bow, then left to rejoin the men. She was transfixed on the grass where she stood. With unbelieving eyes, she watched him walk away.

The men tied a rope to the pig's feet and hefted the lifeless body onto a hook. Children chased each other around. Women's high-pitched voices and laughter drifted from the seating area. Kate hurried back upstairs to the kitchen, almost tripping on the top stair. She slammed the wooden door and sank into a chair. Kate shoved her head backward, hoping to keep tears from spilling down her face. Her heart beat wildly.

"Yiati, Yianni?" Kate repeated aloud her question of "Why?" It had been an unexpected crushing blow. *He saw how shocked I was at the pig being killed. And he compared it to what America is doing in Vietnam.* That much she understood. Kate knew his words were aimed not at her but at her country. She was a stand-in target for America's atrocities in Vietnam and also for what had happened during the dictatorship here in Greece. But this understanding didn't lessen the way his words cut deeply to her core.

Kate stood and stared out the window. The pig was hanging feet-first as men crowded around to dismantle her confidant. Wiping tears with the back of her hand, she took a deep breath and went to the sink. Kate willed herself to open the faucet, grab the thin sponge, and soap the small ouzo glasses. The kitchen started to fill, as Lena and other womenfolk focused on preparing the afternoon meal.

Lena approached and placed a gentle arm around her shoulder. "Are you all right?"

"En daxi, Lena." She could at least pretend to be okay. Their brief interaction ended as Lena was beset with a multitude of questions and requests.

Into the afternoon the boys played soccer on the brittle December grass while the adults enjoyed their Christmas feast. Kate filled her plate with potatoes, squash pie, and salad, avoiding any meat, and went through the motions of socializing with those seated around her. Yiannis was in another part of the yard, engaged with male friends and members of his family. Their paths didn't cross during the rest of the festivities.

It had been arranged for Kate to ride back to the city that evening with Lena's parents. Everyone gathered in the driveway. When it came time to say goodbye to Yiannis, Kate hovered by the car. She was hesitant. He came toward her, reached out his arms, and gave her a warm hug before pulling back to fix her with his eyes. "You know we love you. Sometimes I cannot help myself with my politics. But you are part of our family, and nothing can change that. You understand?"

His eyes, the smile, the genuine affection radiating toward her told all she needed to know. She nodded her head and then spoke, her voice now strong. "I've told you I come from a family of cowboys, right?" She raised her hand with a gesture mimicking a gun. "Watch out for Kappa Kappa Texas." Her hand then transformed into fingers of a salute from her forehead. Their eyes locked.

At this moment, Kate's friendship with both Lena and Yiannis was as solid as the flagstones beneath her feet. Throughout the short but incredibly long three months she had been in Greece, they had been her support and were now her family. They had helped her transform from the hesitant person Lena picked up at the airport into someone who was learning to live independently in Thessaloniki with its hundreds of thousands of people, in the midst of a boiling pot of political uncertainty.

And they had given her the gift of becoming Katina.

thirty ✿

*J*anuary arrived in full force. Thessaloniki didn't have the snows of Wyoming and Colorado, but some days brought icy winds that sliced like a knife when Kate ventured out on the sea walk. Surprisingly, life in Greece was becoming routine. Kate was at home on the sidewalks walking to and from work. Her ease with the language was growing, and therapy strategies with children were becoming clearer. She had even begun to take on private clients in late-afternoon hours. Saturday evenings not spent on the Stylianou farm were an occasion to go with Georyia to a taverna, an evening restaurant, or to visit friends.

It was one such evening that her life took a decidedly different path. Shivering outside Eleni's apartment building, Georyia spoke into the intercom as they waited to be buzzed into the lobby. They climbed the stairs to the apartment on the second floor and found the door ajar, leaking voices and music from inside. Kate recognized him among the dozen people milling around. Something flipped inside her chest. It had been a month since meeting the handsome Thanasis, who tonight wore a black corduroy jacket over a multicolored sweater and a white shirt. The whiteness of the collar set off his dark hair and the curls that framed his face.

Thanasis stopped midsentence, smiled at Kate, and raised his glass in her direction. Kate returned the smile. In the small bedroom off to the side, Kate took off the stylish gray wool coat Georyia had helped her buy in the agora—the marketplace—this past week. She was glad to have a substitute for her yellow ski parka. It gave her a new confidence. Carefully, she folded her coat and placed it on the pile of other coats. Kate retucked her new apricot-colored blouse into her tweed, A-line skirt. After two years of mostly jeans and flannel shirts in Wyoming and Colorado, she was coming back to the world of fashion that had marked her high school and college days. "Welcome back, Kate," she had told herself in the mirror before leaving her apartment. Now, she tried to push down the butterflies flying wildly inside her, before heading toward the noise of the crowd in the other room.

Kate willed herself to approach Thanasis and stood directly in front of him. He spoke to her in English. "And how are you finding Greece, Miss America?" Kate was taken aback by his sense of informality and playfulness. She was also relieved he spoke English beyond the basic greetings.

Momentarily at a loss for a response, she nodded in the direction of the tiny kitchen. "I would say I'm impressed by Greek hospitality, except I don't have a drink."

Thanasis smiled and bowed. "*Amesos.* Immediately." He reappeared with retsina for her, and they clicked glasses, wishing each other good health. "Steen ygeia mas." Their eyes met briefly. With that, the butterflies of apprehension changed into sparkling fireworks.

Kate followed Thanasis as he found space for them to sit together on a couch. Throughout the evening, she was pleasantly surprised by the way Thanasis stayed nearby and acted as her interpreter during conversations. It reminded her of how Lena's son,

Aris, explained the rules of soccer with a slow pace and simple terms. Thanasis used this same patient process as he included her in conversation, except their topic was solely about politics, the lifeblood of this country.

Kate had been learning the spectrum of political parties in post-dictatorship Greece, from the far right to the far left. She also realized party affiliation was often a means of identity for people, especially university students.

She took a sip of retsina. The jolt of alcohol made clearer the reality she sat on a couch in Greece, learning about the variations of socialism and communism. What would her family and hometown friends think?

"Eimaste Evrokommounistes," Thanasis told her. Reverting back to English, he explained he and his friends identified with Euro-communists, believing wealth should be shared. No one could be too wealthy, and no one could be too poor. She had been taught such ideas—socialism or, even worse, communism—were evil. Kate thought back to the book she'd read by the Black activist George Jackson and to the economic disparity that existed in her hometown. *Are all these political ideas more complicated than I thought?*

"Eurocommunists are not the same as the other Communist Party?" Kate questioned him, thinking of Fotini who belonged to a Soviet-leaning Greek Communist Party.

"Ohi." Thanasis accompanied his "no" with a tongue click. "We do not think the Moscow regime would ever work in Greece. Too many rules." He laughed.

Remembering how Greeks didn't like to form lines even waiting for a bus, Kate understood what he was saying. Sitting close by, his knee occasionally brushed up against hers, making it harder for her to concentrate fully on their conversation. She was pleased to learn Thanasis was a serious person, but she was even more thrilled with the added bonus of his physical contact.

Noticing Georyia by the door with her coat in hand, Kate stood to leave. Thanasis brushed her shoulder as he rose beside her. "Would you like to come to a lecture tomorrow morning? Kyrkos is here from Athens. A professor—very smart."

"Will they check my passport at the door?" Kate asked, only partially joking at the prospect of being in a gathering of communists. She couldn't believe she was seriously considering the invitation. But neither could she imagine giving up the chance to see Thanasis again.

"Do not worry. We will keep you in disguise as one of us." Thanasis accompanied his teasing with a warm grin.

Kate smiled back with a Greek affirmative head nod and gave him her address. They settled their rendezvous time, and Thanasis touched her arm as they parted.

The imprint left by the touch of his hand remained with Kate long after she slipped her arm through the sleeve of her new gray coat and followed Georyia out into the winter night.

thirty-one 🌿

The next morning, Kate checked her appearance in the hall mirror. At the last minute, she exchanged her new midi-length gray coat for her yellow ski parka. The longer coat was too formal for the jeans and sneakers she wore. The yellow jacket would have to do. Working to calm her excitement, she smirked at herself in the mirror. "This sure is gonna be a different kind of Sunday morning."

Kate had logged hours in the pews of Baptist churches in her lifetime. Going to a communist lecture on this day was a universe away from growing up sitting with a Bible in her lap and searching for scriptures the pastor quoted. Even though her church days had thinned out over the past two years, her youthful Sunday memories were never too far away.

Today she was excited, most of all, to be with Thanasis. Kate scanned the scene and waited outside the door of 84-B. The first glimpse of Thanasis in the daylight didn't disappoint. He was just as handsome as she'd remembered, if not more so. In a sudden rush of insecurity, she hoped her own appearance was satisfactory.

They didn't know each other well enough for the usual greeting of kisses on each cheek, so both wished each other a "kalimera." Their eyes stayed connected for a brief moment.

"So, am I Greek enough for the inspectors?" Kate asked. He was perplexed. She rushed to explain, "You know. The people at the door checking for American spies." Kate was only half-joking.

Thanasis grinned back. "You do not look like a spy."

Just as Kate savored the lighthearted banter, a dark thought surfaced. Captain Hercules and the demonstration. *And I had to wear this stupid jacket?* But it was too late to change. Glancing again at this attractive man walking beside her, those worries soon evaporated.

They headed across the gravel parking lot to Queen Olga Street, less busy on this Sunday morning than the usual racetrack. A small blue-and-white taxi pulled over, and Thanasis gave the driver their destination, following with a "parakalo." She liked his politeness with the taxi driver, rather than what could have been a perfunctory command to someone to do his bidding.

On the way, they shared casual conversation, comparing her growing up in a small town with his in a village. During the few moments of silence, Kate viewed scenes on the sidewalk, pleasantly empty on a Sunday morning. Waiters in white shirts and black pants set small metal tables and chairs outside of coffee bars. Greeks loved sitting outdoors, even in chilly weather. After several minutes and several neighborhoods, the cab stopped, and the driver cranked the handle of the meter to show the fare due. Thanasis paid, and they scooted out of the seat.

The neighborhood was familiar. "The Fargani!" she exclaimed, as they rounded the corner, seeing their destination was the movie theater where she often watched foreign films. "I've come here lots of times to see movies," she told him, her smile wide and her voice ringing.

"Koultouryiaris eisai?" Kate knew this was a compliment. Thanasis was asking if she was "cultured," a word she had learned meant someone who engaged in interesting activities. Thanasis's

expression made it seem like she'd won his approval. This thought, the familiar setting, and their shoulders touching intermittently helped calm worries about what lay ahead.

As they neared the theater, Kate smiled at the notion of heading to a Greek communist lecture in an old Turkish building, worlds away from Sunday School classes at the First Baptist Church. Those classes wouldn't start for several hours. Perhaps the lesson would be from Letters to the Thessalonians. She had only recently learned this New Testament book by the Apostle Paul was written to the people of Thessaloniki. As a child, Kate had paid scant attention to the maps on the walls of her Sunday School class. Teachers would point out the geography of the Holy Land and the Ancient World to fidgety children, sitting on wooden chairs in a circle. And now Kate was actually in the company of those people called Thessalonians.

"Ela apo etho." Thanasis told her to "come this way," making a space for her amid the crush of people trying to fit into the single doorway at the Fargani. She was grateful he spoke Greek to her in this crowd, hoping her true identity was hidden, despite the coat. Kate had a strong sense this was enemy space for an American. She grabbed onto Thanasis's sleeve, trying to steady the nerves that began to unspool inside.

Most of the people pressing against her were young men and women, similar to Thanasis in age. Many wore bell-bottom jeans, sweaters, and black wool pea coats. Most males had beards and shoulder-length hair, and the females had either short or long hairstyles and little, if any, makeup. Cigarette smoke and a hint of body odor commingled in the crowd.

Once inside the theater, she was struck by how odd it was to enter with the lights fully on. Usually, she would find her way in the dark and wait for a moment of illumination from the screen to find a seat. This morning the theater was crowded to capacity. Kate and Thanasis found seats in a back row. Three chairs on the stage were occupied by a bearded young man, an older woman beside him, and a distinguished, middle-aged man in slacks, black turtleneck sweater, and jacket.

"That is Kyrkos," Thanasis whispered to her. "He is a professor of uhm . . . politic—"

"Political science?" Kate asked.

"I think, yes. Political science. He studied in Paris and was in exile during the junta. He is—" Thanasis stopped, as the young man came to the podium.

The lectures that followed for the next hour were incomprehensible. The speakers spoke rapidly, and she soon gave up trying to understand anything she heard. It was similar to her experience with the foreign films she'd seen here. She understood neither the language nor the Greek subtitles, freeing her to create her own dialogue and storyline.

Kate watched the speakers, their gestures, and the audience reaction, especially when the words *Ameriki* or *Amerikani* were used. The crowd's jeers reminded her of that other movie theater, seeing *In the Year of the Pig,* when she'd first come to Greece. The fear she'd experienced that night now was back. America. Vietnam. Those words. Those warring countries. And what Yiannis had said to her at the pig slaughter.

Anti-war protesters at home expressed the same anger that was being hurled now toward the United States. Even after the murder of the students at Kent State, Kate hadn't gone to demonstrations.

173

It had been horrible, she knew. But the event had happened in May, just a month away from her June wedding. There had been so many other things to think about—invitations, engagement parties, and her wedding portrait. Kate had been insulated inside her own world.

And now she was an American in a sea of communists listening to a lecture she couldn't understand and subjected to an onslaught of hatred directed at her country. Just then Thanasis's shoulder pressed against hers. "Do not worry." There was a sweet sincerity in his eyes. "We will discuss later." She nodded, grateful he understood her discomfort.

Kate glanced at Thanasis again, whom she didn't really know. She realized her tendency to believe the best in people, either from an innocence or lack of sound judgment or both. Thanasis seemed very nice, but she wondered if she had too quickly entrusted herself to this handsome man whose arm rested next to hers.

Was this same naivete somehow similar to the naivete of her earlier life with frilly bridesmaids' dresses and flower arrangements while soldiers died in Vietnam? Incredulously, Kate was in a room full of strangers, listening to the rising and falling tones of Greek words coming through the loudspeaker system.

Eventually, Kate settled back into the thin padding of the seat, her mind continuing to wander. Her own journey, even to this point, had not moved in the straight line she had expected from her life. The twists and turns were gifts, however, providing unimagined experiences.

Kate was startled back to the present by applause as the audience gave a standing ovation. She rose beside Thanasis, clapping with feigned enthusiasm.

Walking out of the theater, Kate was again self-conscious of her yellow jacket, her appearance, and her citizenship. Thanasis's arm on her back guided her through the crowd to an unoccupied area.

His next words came as a surprise. "Kaitie, I am sorry," he said. "I must attend a study group because it is the week of examinations. I will take you home now." Kate froze. *Was this his quick exit from her life?*

Thanasis placed a hand gently on her shoulder. "I would like very much to have a dinner with you on Saturday. Will you forgive a delay of our discussion?"

There was an earnestness to his expression. Her body relaxed. "That would be wonderful, Thanasi." The warmth of the sun had broken the chill of the winter day. "I know my way back home from here," she said.

Thanasis bent slightly, placing a kiss on each cheek. She watched as the crowd enveloped him. Kate headed toward the sea.

thirty-two ✢

"Have you visited the Kastra?" Thanasis raised his voice over the din of streaming traffic rushing down Queen Olga Street in the brisk Saturday evening air. He was referring to the castle, the ancient fortress walls at the top of the city. In previous trips to Aristotelous Square, Kate had squinted to see them as she surveyed the city stretching up the hillsides like an amphitheater.

"No, but I'd like to very much," Kate shouted back.

Thanasis scanned the traffic for an empty taxi, an almost impossible task this evening. As they waited, shoulders touching, Kate squirmed inside with delight standing next to him. It had been quite some time since she knew this kind of happiness. His repeated attempts of raising his arm to flag a taxi finally paid off, and they hopped inside one.

The taxi climbed gradually upward, leaving behind concrete multistoried apartment houses stacked next to each other block after block as they entered an older part of the city. Here the dwellings were two or three levels of the more traditional type of architecture she had seen visiting mountain villages with the Stylianou family. Many of the houses were made of stone with wooden-shuttered windows. The streets were smaller, almost like something from a storybook.

"Wow. This is so different from any part of Thessaloniki I've been in," Kate said. "It's like a world away from where we were just ten minutes ago." She was filled with a matchless sense of good fortune, with the scenes outside the taxi window and Thanasis's leg resting next to hers.

"This is called *ano poli.* 'Above the city' I think it translates," Thanasis explained.

"Ano poli," she repeated.

Thanasis said, "And somewhere here is the birthplace of Ataturk."

"Who?"

"Ataturk—the father of modern Turkey. One of the only Turks the Greeks admire. He brought modern democracy to Turkey. He lived here before the population exchange."

Kate had become aware of the compulsory expulsion of Greeks and Turks early in the century. Many of her friends talked about the treacherous journeys of their parents coming to Greece from Turkey as small children.

"Oh!" Kate gasped, seeing remnants of the ancient fortification. "These must be the famous walls that protected the city from invaders. Yiannis showed me drawings of the old city and said the walls once ran completely around Thessaloniki." What remained now were stretches of stone barriers of varying heights. *So much history.* Kate had seen ancient ruins down below, but something about seeing these relics high atop the city was even more thrilling. Thessaloniki's connection to centuries of its past was now coming to life.

Thanasis tapped her shoulder to take in the view from the rear window. Below them, a dazzling array of lights spilled on the hillsides leading down to the center of Thessaloniki and the Bay of

Salonika. She saw illuminated cruise ships tethered offshore, seeming like toys from this elevation.

The walls became more prominent as the taxi curved toward the top or *acropolis*, literally "high city," as she had learned. But instead of an ancient past, an active neighborhood appeared. Bright lights revealed people strolling in groups of twos and threes, on a *volta* or "walk," one of the traditional pastimes of Greeks everywhere. Folks spilled out of restaurants and small variety stores. The ever-present kiosks did an active trade of cigarettes and newspapers. They passed a park with its red benches and trees whose trunks were painted white. Thanasis signaled the driver to pull over. Kate reached for her purse. "Please, let me pay for this—" only to be met with another form of nonverbal communication, his head shifted to one side and an expression telling her not to be ridiculous.

Like something from a magical scene, they walked under strings of white lightbulbs that crisscrossed overhead outside a taverna, where Thanasis guided her, his hand resting on her back. Small tables and chairs were unoccupied in the chilly evening air. Once inside, a comforting warmth and the aroma of meat and frying potatoes met them. Sounds of boisterous voices and strains of recorded music of a bouzouki, an instrument resembling a mandolin, rose up into the clouds of cigarette smoke.

They found a table at the back of the crowded floor. Tonight felt different from other outings with friends. Perhaps it was the avant-garde appearance of many of the patrons. Men in sports jackets and turtlenecks, women with intricate earrings and colorful scarves. Everyone smoking. Perhaps it was because she was with Thanasis. He gestured to a waiter, and promptly, two small glasses and a small copper pitcher appeared on their table. "Their own retsina." Thanasis smiled as he poured their glasses full.

The waiter, a young man with white shirt open at the collar and black slacks, pulled a pad from his pocket, continually scanning the room for signals from other customers. Thanasis ordered plates of the cucumber and yogurt dish tzatziki, smoked eggplant appetizer, feta cheese, fried potatoes, and souvlaki, marinated beef on skewers.

"Steen ygeia mas." This was their second time toasting to health, the universal Greek ritual. They kept their eyes on each other a few seconds. Then, Kate reached toward the ever-present basket of fresh bread on the table, and Thanasis lit a cigarette. She took pleasure in watching him draw smoke in and release it into the air, tamping the ashes into the square metallic ashtray on the table.

"So now will you let me into the secret club of Mr. Kyrkos and the *Kou-Kou-Es*?" Kate asked, showing she had learned the shorthand of initials for the *Kommounistiko Komma Esoterikou* or "Communist Party Interior." This European-affiliated party was in contrast to *Kou-Kou-Ex*, the Moscow-allied one.

With a slowed pace and simplified words Thanasis explained Kyrkos's vision of a Greece whose government provided all its citizens with the essentials to live a healthy life, with rights for the working class guaranteed. Kyrkos advocated for a framework of representative government. As they ate and drank, Kate listened as Thanasis wove a story of the twentieth century, beginning with liberation from the Ottoman Empire through two world wars, the German occupation, the Greek Civil War, and the most recent military dictatorship.

By the end of the meal, Kate's head was full of Greek political history, seeing for the first time how many of the pieces fit together. Until now, the fragments had been separate. This small country had struggled for freedom from outside forces, often as a pawn in a larger political game. *So, this is why the Greeks resent the United States so much.*

After a few pitchers of retsina, Kate was lightheaded, but from more than the alcohol. She was in prolonged, intimate contact with this handsome, engaging man whose knees pressed into hers below the wooden table and whose arms touched hers above it.

Newly awakened feelings of desire had been kindled. They were in a restaurant on a hill surrounded by ancient castle walls, twinkling stars in the sky above, and city lights of Thessaloniki below. She had no wish to stop herself from hurtling forward to whatever was next.

thirty-three 🌿

*A*t the door to 84-B Kate didn't hesitate, knowing she was about to step over a line. "Would you like to come up?" At this moment, she knew she was being reckless. She didn't care. Thanasis responded with a broad smile and affirmative tilt of his head. In the ride home in the taxi, their kisses had been soft. Sweet. Restrained. As the elevator climbed to the fifth floor, something else entered. Passion. Urgency.

Barely had the door to her apartment closed than Kate and Thanasis were in each other's arms. In high school, Kate had discovered she enjoyed passion, necking in a parked car at the edge of a cotton field. It was how teenagers in the Bible Belt dealt with natural urges, also known as sin in their community.

After the devastating end to her marriage with Jim, she stayed away from intimacy for almost a year. But its return came with a new intensity amid the loosened sexual restrictions of the '70s and the gift of marijuana in the Rocky Mountain highs of Colorado.

Kate wasn't sure how things were in Greece regarding sexual proprieties, but her pleasure in sex was something she'd brought with her. Now, she abandoned any reluctance and pulled Thanasis into the double bed in the bedroom off the hallway.

They fit together surprisingly well, and their lovemaking was both easy and satisfying. Afterward, Kate nuzzled into the softness of his neck, just below his beard. Eventually, he sat up and kissed the top of her head. "I will go now. I do not want to be a surprise for your neighbors." His voice had a mischievous tone.

"You don't think it's a good idea to make them jealous of their resident American?" Kate asked, propping on her side. She fastened the sheet under her arms and watched Thanasis gather his clothes. *Damn. He was handsome.* In the dimness of the bedside lamp, Kate could make out broad shoulders that narrowed at the waist. She glanced briefly at the lower half of his physique before pulling herself to a sitting position.

"Do you want coffee tomorrow?" he asked as he buckled his belt.

"Yes, but no. I'm going to see my friends tomorrow at their farm. Monday night?" she asked.

Thanasis signaled agreement with a nod of his head. *"Yeero stees octo?"* asking if "around eight" would work. Kate had learned for most Greeks, there was no such thing as an exact time designation. Around was the closest it got.

Thanasis approached the bed, and they both leaned in for a kiss. Kate watched him leave, then listened for footsteps on the marble floor and the click of the front door closing.

Those sounds and the groaning elevator gears that signaled his exit would become part of a new routine. She and Thanasis met a few evenings during the week and spent Saturday nights together, except for the ones she was at the farm. They were becoming a couple.

thirty-four ✿

One evening, Kate and Thanasis strolled along a row of braziers that dotted the sea walk beside the Bay of Salonika. They were greeted with the aroma of roasting chestnuts from the cookstoves whose flames slit into the night sky, like campfires along the city's edge. Thanasis stopped in front of one, exchanging drachmas for a paper bag. The old man behind the flame smiled, giving a hint of missing teeth, his eyes narrowed to screen out the smoke. They found an empty bench near the water. The bag of cooked chestnuts warmed Kate's hands, the smell of carbon and nut rising to her face.

"This is how it is done." Thanasis reached in and grabbed a chestnut, tossing it back and forth between his hands before peeling away the charred outer covering and extracting a creamy paste. She opened her mouth, feeling his fingers underneath her chin as he guided the warm chestnut meat inside her mouth. For a brief moment, she closed her eyes and tasted, surrounded by snatches of Greek words, taxi horns bleating in the distance, and the splash of waves against the sea wall.

"*Kaitie mou.* I will take you to my mother's village one day." Kate loved how he used the possessive pronoun for "my." He stopped to open a chestnut of his own. "My mother's village is the name of these—*kastana.* And I am sure because you are a teacher of words you can guess why the village is called Kastanas—I think it is 'chestnuts'?" She nodded. "When we visit, you can pretend to be a Greek, and when I come to America, I can pretend to be an American cowboy." Something about his words triggered a momentary disquiet, but Kate chose to ignore the feeling and instead shifted the conversation elsewhere.

"I can't believe you Greeks have such a fascination with the cowboy part of American culture. When I told the driver of the school's van that I was from Texas, do you know what he said?"

Thanasis clicked his tongue and lifted his head, indicating he did not.

"He made his finger and thumb into a gun and said, 'America. Dallas. Kennedy. Bang bang.'"

Thanasis responded matter-of-factly. "You Americans are famous because of cowboys and your movies and your President Kennedy. But in the world today, you will not find many places where you are popular. When your soldiers leave Vietnam, you will make more friends again." Here once again was the criticism of America. Although it had become easier for her to understand that view, something still prickled. Kate hadn't realized that now she was overseas, she would be a representative of all that was American.

Passing the bag of chestnuts to Thanasis, they sat in silence. In the night sky, she couldn't see the outline of Mount Olympus, but she knew it was there. From her balcony, Kate had become accustomed to imagining the face of God in the mountain's profile and seeing how it changed throughout the varied lighting of Aegean days. The myths of Olympus and the romance with this man had become part of her life.

Thanasis was right next to her, their legs touching and his

arm around her, sensations that had become sweetly familiar in a very short span of time. But it was his comment about coming to America that was unsettling. How could she have Thanasis—a communist—sitting around her family's dinner table? She shook away the thought and reached for another chestnut in the bag.

Kate was aware she avoided thoughts of what would happen when it came time for her to leave in June. She couldn't worry about that now. It was as though she was wearing a pair of heavily scratched sunglasses, seeing light and shadows ahead of her but nothing in detail. Kate was enjoying herself too much to take them off. She had fallen in love.

thirty-five 🌿

Everyone in Thessaloniki seemed to be repeating the same words. *"Erhetai O Theodorakis!"* "Theodorakis is coming!" The name of the composer Mikis Theodorakis was a vague ghost twinkling in Kate's memory. She recalled hearing the soundtrack from the movie, *Zorba the Greek,* in her father's art studio over their garage, where he painted as a hobby on weekends. On the album cover, a man's arms were outstretched, one foot raised off the earth, dancing. The plinking strings of some unusual-sounding instrument were interspersed with dialogue from the movie.

Kate had listened to the record as she watched her father run his paintbrush across the canvas on his easel. Heavy scents of oil paints and turpentine permeated the room. She loved spending time tucked away with her father, talking, and listening to music, and watching him paint. Propped on the floor against a couch, she heard the actor Anthony Quinn's Zorba teaching a young Englishman about life, thundering at him, "So what good are all of your books if they tell you nothing about death?" Back then, Zorba had existed in a faraway part of the world, thousands of miles from where she sat with her father, as tumbleweeds danced across the streets of West Texas in stinging sandstorms.

Now, on her daily walk to work, posters were plastered everywhere of Theodorakis with arms outstretched as a musical conductor, a fury of hair rising from his head. This very Theodorakis was coming to life. Soon he would be in Thessaloniki.

Sitting in her room at school one day, Georyia explained in her measured, patient voice. "As a youth during the Resistance, Theodorakis was tortured in a prison camp on the island of Makronisos. Later, he was elected to Parliament. In the dictatorship, he was jailed and beaten, then sent into exile. He toured the world to build support for a peaceful overthrow of the junta and now has come home."

Georyia's gaze was beyond the window and garden outside. "It was a crime to listen to his music, so we played his records quietly with our doors locked." She faced Kate. "The Beatles we could not listen to. Anything the colonels thought dangerous was not allowed. There was a list of prohibited songs and books and movies."

Kate imagined her friends gathered around a radio with the volume low, listening to music or news from the BBC, fearful of noise leaking out into the hallway. They never knew if a neighbor might become an informant. She let this information wash over her. She didn't know what to say, so she listened.

"And now he comes to Thessaloniki for the first time since his return to Greece. It is a great joy for us!" Sometimes Georyia's explanations had the feeling of books she read to the children in her classroom. This one seemed the happy ending to what had been a frightening story.

On a deeper level, Kate was slowly understanding the horror this country had suffered. She finally broke the silence. "Do you think we can go see him?"

"Maybe Thanasis can get tickets for our *parea*," Georyia proposed.

Kate was now familiar with the Greek custom of a "circle of friends" going places together as a group. "I'll check with him." Kate's voice was quiet, made somber by the thought of what had happened to this man whose music had once filled her father's studio.

On the evening of the concert, Kate, Thanasis, Georyia, and their group of friends walked to the large indoor arena that was the *Palais des Sports* on the grounds of the Thessaloniki International Fair. The crowd was huge and slowly squeezed into entrances and into the amphitheater seats surrounding the stage.

Pandemonium erupted when Theodorakis appeared onstage, dressed in black, hair blazing. A group of singers and an orchestra of bouzoukis, guitars, drums, percussion, and a clarinet followed him. The entertainers took their places in chairs lined up on the stage while Theodorakis bowed to the ocean swell of the prolonged applause. The crowd was on its feet, clapping and yelling, some waving red flags.

When everyone finally sat, Thanasis explained, "In Greece, we give our most applause for the composer." Here was another difference between American and Greek culture, giving praise to the composer rather than the performer. Also, Kate realized she'd never been in one place with this many people, except maybe a college football game. Her heart raced with excitement.

The music started. Giant thunderstorms of emotion that had been contained for years were set free. The audience sang along with every word of the rousing songs and mouthed the words during the quiet ballads. Although she had heard lots of Greek music, there was something about this live concert that highlighted the distinctively eastern quality of the music's minor key tones. With each song, Thanasis tried translating.

"This is about prisoners in their cells communicating to each other by tapping a code."

The upbeat melody hardly fit with the picture of prisoners in jail. And for another song, "Greeks will not be slaves again to dictators." Surveying the crowd, she had no doubt of the will toward freedom of everyone here.

After two hours of music and a brief exit from the stage, Theodorakis reappeared and spoke to the hushed crowd of thousands. Kate could understand a few phrases, and Thanasis helped her with the rest. "Now we go to the sweet past," Thanasis explained.

Theodorakis lifted his arms and ushered in the songs that had made him famous and beloved in earlier years. They were songs that everyone in the country seemed to know. Kate could even sing along with some parts, as she had heard them sung many times by her friends.

The plinking sounds of the bouzouki, the minor key, the words that were beginning to roll off her own tongue, all combined to envelop and embrace her in a way that, at this moment, were not foreign. Thanasis's arm draped around her shoulder. The man onstage, his hands alternately waltzing or chopping with staccato motions, was directing not only music but a movement. And Kate was beginning to feel like she was part of it.

thirty-six ✤

The next Monday morning in the hallway outside Kate's therapy room, Kuria Zeta, one of the children's assistants, drew deeply on her cigarette, blue eyes scanning to see if anyone might be watching her sneak a smoke. *"Ah Katerina. Kourastika."* Kate smiled back sympathetically to the fifty-something year old woman in her light-blue work smock who confessed, "I am exhausted." Kuria Zeta often took her breaks here, giving them a chance to chat.

"Katerina, then boreis na voithisis ton Giorgo?" Kuria Zeta asked Kate if she could help Giorgos, one of the children at ELEPAAP. Kate had seen how Kuria Zeta assisted him, an older boy with cerebral palsy, in his attempts at communications, recess, and helping him to the toilet.

Kate thought Giorgos was probably around thirteen. When not in his wheelchair, he scooted himself around with his arms, as his legs were curled underneath him and mostly useless. He had some use of his hands to get what he needed, though the movements were wavelike and his fingers imprecise in their grasp. He couldn't talk, but he communicated through facial expressions and a series of gestures he'd developed on his own, using them with others, especially his best friend, Lakis.

This other boy was bright-eyed and about half Giorgos's size.

And he was deaf. The two were inseparable companions at school, somehow knowing what the other wanted, getting along beautifully in their own private world of understanding.

Giorgos's hair was shaved; his brown eyes were large and expressive. He came to school each day in the van and was a vibrant part of the community of disabled children. As she watched him being lifted in the van to leave, Kate had often wondered what his life was like at home.

Kate paused before responding. She didn't know but would ask Kuria Argero.

Kuria Zeta stubbed her cigarette in the coffee cup she used for an ashtray. *"Ee mama tou."* Her voice changed to a mocking tone saying "his mother" as she mimicked someone primping her hair. Kuria Zeta resented that Giorgos's mother seemed to be minimally involved in her son's life and was interested only in dressing up and going out. At least that was Kuria Zeta's opinion. *"Kaeimenos . . . ."* Her voice broke. This word for "poor thing" was frequently used in referring to the children of ELEPAAP.

Two days later, Giorgos smiled broadly as he sat in his wheelchair in Kate's room. Kuria Zeta was by his side, encouraging him with his first session. Kate asked Giorgos a series of questions she had designed to determine a basic level of a child's understanding of language. She had translated this test from assessments used in her prior jobs. Georyia collaborated to make sure the words and sentences were appropriate for Greek children.

Kate had observed Giorgos respond to conversations around him appropriately and laugh at jokes in the right way. She needed, however, to make sure that whatever she was asking him to do would be something that he actually understood. She didn't want her students to be parrots who only imitated words but rather to communicate in a meaningful way.

In between questions, Giorgos raised a curling finger on his right hand and waveringly placed it above his upper lip, like a mustache. Then he brought his left hand up, pretending it to be on a steering wheel.

"Nai agori mou. O Babas tha parei kainourio aftokinito." Kuria Zeta translated for Kate. "Yes, my boy, your father will get a new car," nodding her head at Kate to indicate this was one of Giorgos's frequent communications.

"Bravo!" Kate nodded to him with approval. Giorgos smiled, pleased that she understood his message.

Giorgos resumed his sitting position, both arms anchored on his crossed knees, like a "proper gentleman."

Satisfied with Giorgos's comprehension, Kate proceeded. She adjusted his chair so he could see himself in the mirror. *"Giorgo, boreis na anoikses to stoma sou—kai na to cleisis?"*

Could he imitate her opening and closing his mouth, the most basic movement to make sounds and possibly learn to say a word? He tried. He tried. The more he tried, the effort caused his lips to stick together. Just then, his lips formed a pout, and tears spilled down his cheeks.

"Agori mou gleeko. Meen stenahoriese." Kuria Zeta pulled him toward her, saying, "My sweet boy. Don't worry." Kate patted him on the back and waited for his sobs to subside. She shook her head in disappointment. He was not a candidate for learning to talk.

"Giorgo." Kate wanted to distract him. Her wind-up toys never failed. Hearing the tiny noise of the gears, Giorgos alerted. That gave her time to grab a piece of thick posterboard. With light pencil strokes she divided the surface into four sections. In each quadrant, she drew a picture that represented something he might need to communicate beyond his current system.

Giorgos would wave his hand in a fist when he wanted to go to the bathroom. He brought his hand to his mouth when he wanted to eat. He used a thumb to his mouth when he wanted a drink. *What else does he need to say?* Kate drew stick figures of children for his friends, a soccer ball, the playground, and a book. Giorgos closely watched while Kuria Zeta narrated the drawings.

Asking him to identify what she had drawn, Giorgos successfully pointed to each one, smiling broadly every time. She explained, with help from Kuria Zeta, that this would be his "talking board." He could use it at school to point to what he wanted. And he could take it home. His finger flew up to position above his lip. Yes, he could show it to his father.

Giorgos and Kuria Zeta left with the posterboard under his arm. She could hear his squeals of delight. Kate sat back in her chair, pleased that this picture communication board might be the first step of helping Giorgos unlock more of what he wanted to say. This would be only the beginning, with more complicated messages to be incorporated gradually.

At the end of the day when the children had left, Kate wandered upstairs. Glancing in Georyia's classroom, she noticed something white in the corner of the room. It was the communication board face down on the floor. It had not made it home even the first day.

Kate's spirits fell. *Why didn't I go upstairs and teach him how to use it?* She picked up the board. Georyia appeared in the doorway.

"I see the board didn't make it home."

Georyia shrugged her shoulders. "Unfortunately, there was lots of *fasaria*. It was one more thing that we did not do." When Kate had learned this Greek word, she thought it sounded exactly like what it meant. "Commotion."

"Georyia—ego ftao." Kate conceded it was her own fault, using *ego*, the Greek word for "I." Switching to English she confessed, "I didn't teach him or you what to do with it."

"Siga, siga." The phrase "slowly, slowly" applied to many things in her life. "We will make it work, Kaitie." She gathered papers from her desk and put them in a satchel. "Let us go have lunch and discuss."

Kate nodded her head to the side in the Greek way of expressing affirmation. She had learned sometimes words weren't necessary. But communication was. That's what Giorgos deserved. And that's what she and Georyia could make sure he would have.

thirty-seven 🌿

"**I** can't believe all this traffic!" Kate watched the steady stream of headlights. She shouted to Thanasis and Georyia as the three of them waited to cross Queen Olga Street and catch a taxi to the outskirts of Thessaloniki. It was nine o'clock on Saturday evening, yet the crowded sidewalks and unending lines of cars made it seem like the entire city was awake, not bringing the day to a close.

Nightlife with Thanasis, Georyia, and their various friends had come crowding into Kate's life, somewhat limiting her time at the farm. On most weekends, their evenings started late and would usually end around two o'clock. *Glendi,* or "entertaining with friends," seemed like a national pastime. Tonight would be her first time at a bouzouki dinner club with food, drink, and dancing. They were meeting friends at *Poseithonas,* a beachfront restaurant named appropriately enough "Poseidon," the Greek god of the sea.

The dining room was sprawling, with every table full of people feasting, exchanging stories, and laughing. A wall of windows faced the beach. *This must be heaven when the weather is warm!* In one corner, amplifiers were set up and musical instruments rested on chairs.

Dinner started with the usual appetizers, but then waiters swept in with plates of exotic dishes of stewed octopus, fried calamari, and seared mussels. Apprehensive at first to try these unfamiliar dishes, Kate searched for the smallest bites to sample. Her next forkfuls were larger and more frequent. She found the bounty of Poseidon to her liking.

With the meal finished, Thanasis addressed Kate. "You will look good on a cigarette," he said. She had smoked only marijuana in Wyoming and Colorado, shunning cigarettes even in college when some of her sorority sisters had tried them. Kate's small retsina glass had filled several times, allowing her to venture over a new edge. She took a cigarette from Thanasis and put it between her lips. His lighter approached.

Kate took a cautious puff, not wanting to take in too much smoke. Small breath by small breath, she got the hang of it and liked taking this kind of smoke into her body. She watched the paper as it burned, disappearing into fumes, joining the clouds of haze that hovered near the ceiling above.

As the evening progressed, the white paper tablecloth became littered with empty plates, half-full glasses, and ashtrays crammed with cigarette butts. Electric bouzouki music reverberated throughout the large room. Fellow diners drifted to the dance floor, hands joined, and fingers snapping in time to the music. Captivated, Kate watched the graceful movements of groups of people dancing hand in hand with one another. The music pulled her back to the *Zorba the Greek* soundtrack from her father's art studio.

Thanasis drew her closer with his arm circled around her shoulder. *"Ela na horepsoume."*

Kate raised her head and clicked her tongue at his invitation to dance. "No," she answered Greek style. She would be too embarrassed. Across the table, Georyia moved her head in the direction of the dance floor. Eyeing first her friend, then her lover, Kate smiled. Of course. She would join them.

Standing unsteadily between the two of them, Kate held onto their hands and slowly followed their steps, crisscrossing her feet, then changing directions and repeating the same pattern. The music was slow enough that she could keep up with their movements. Gradually, she relaxed. Something ran the length of her body with a gentle swaying. *I'm dancing!*

They stayed on the dance floor for a few more songs before returning to the table. *"Bravo! Boreis na horepsis Kalamatiano."* Georyia congratulated her on learning to dance whatever the name of the dance was.

Kate wasn't interested in a Greek lesson now. She was carried away by the event. Thanasis filled her glass with retsina and lit another cigarette for her.

As the evening wore on, the music became less lively and slower, almost mournful. And the dancing changed.

"This is *Zeibekiko*," Thanasis explained.

Kate didn't understand why it was called this, but rather than ask for an explanation she sat and watched. A series of solo dancers stretched arms out to either side and swayed to the music, like soaring eagles spreading their wings.

Georyia leaned over the table. "This dance was only for men before. Now women are allowed." Her voice was full of approval and pride.

Each solitary dancer was surrounded by friends, crouched on bended knees, clapping in time to the music and offering encouragement.

Extinguishing her cigarette, Georyia leaned over again, a serious expression on her face. "In this dance you show the story of your soul." Before Kate could protest, Georyia pulled her arm. "Now you must try."

With retsina tamping down any resistance, Kate let herself be drawn to the dance floor. Thanasis and Georyia took their positions in front of her. Smoke drifted across Thanasis's face from the cigarette clamped in his mouth. Kate began. Strains of the minor keys of Greek music commanded the snapping of her fingers as her arms reached outward. Kate improvised, moving and spinning her body, exploring and finding a new space in her soul that had not existed before.

thirty-eight

The calendar brought March. Kate and Thanasis sat on the balcony in the morning brightness, their chairs close together, legs touching, and feet propped on the railing. Thanasis handed her a cigarette and leaned over to light it. Monday was a holiday, and they were taking advantage of an extra day together with a lazy start.

Thanasis sat back and lit his own cigarette. "I have a surprise for you. We are going somewhere special." Sun dappled the water on the bay in the distance and caught the edge of the metal ashtray on the small table. "A new Greek celebration for you—*Kathari Theftera*."

"I know what that is. 'Clean Monday' or something like that." It was a day off from ELEPAAP, but Kate was uncertain of the reason for the holiday.

"Tomorrow begins the time before Easter when many people do not eat meat," he said. Kate knew Catholics in America observed Lent, but she didn't know much about the practice or even the religion. In her small West Texas town, most Catholics were Mexican Americans, a community set apart by culture and economics.

Thanasis continued. "The women wash their pots and put them outside in the sun to dry away anything to do with meat. To make them clean before fasting." Thanasis tapped the ashes from his cigarette. "In all of Greece the custom will happen. But instead of washing, we are going with friends to the seaside."

"The seaside!" Kate's voice rose with excitement. "Which friends?"

"Stelios and Makis. And others. Also, a special person from Athens."

"From Athens? Who?"

"It is a secret," Thanasis teased, putting his finger to his lips.

"Sometimes I like secrets," Kate played along. "Should I wear my new dress?" She had bought a French-inspired sack dress. Wearing it with her new stylish black boots made her feel like one of the fashionable Salonika women on the streets of the city.

"Vevaios!" Thanasis responded.

Kate stubbed her cigarette and kissed the top of his head before disappearing inside.

Within the hour, they were in the back seat of a taxi. "So now will you tell me about this famous person from Athens?" Kate snuggled beside him, watching the tall buildings being replaced by single-family residences as they headed out of the city.

"You will meet Giorgos Farsakithis. He is famous in Greece because he is an artist, but also because he was tortured in prison during the junta. His crime was to be a communist."

Kate stilled. Prospects for the sunshiny outing had now changed. "How do you know him? Why is he here?"

"He is here to visit friends. The jails released political prisoners when the junta fell in July. This is his first time to come north to Thessaloniki."

Kate winced, flashing on stories of the torture of political prisoners she'd heard about. Thanasis had not answered her question about how he knew Farsakithis.

Her enthusiasm gone, Kate asked, "What will he think of me?"

Her heart raced. She had been accepted by Thanasis's group of friends and no longer worried about her status as an American when they went out. Now, however, she would be with a group of strangers, which included someone who had been a political prisoner.

"*Koukla*—please do not worry." He reached for her hand and cradled it. "They are friends." When Thanasis had first called her *koukla,* meaning "doll," she was taken aback. At one time, it would have been demeaning, especially considering her feminist views. But the way Thanasis said the word was sweet and tender. Now, Kate was neither reassured nor comforted. She shifted her attention to the scenes sliding by outside the window.

At once, Kate was back in the movie theater watching *In the Year of the Pig* on her second night in Greece, hearing the jeers and shouts at the screen with any mention of her country. Despite all of Kate's positive experiences in Greece, her fears of being called out as an American still lurked below the surface. *What's going to happen? Surely this man will automatically hate me after all that's happened to him*. Kate sat in anxious silence.

The taxi slowed and exited the main road. A sign marked the entrance to a village: Nea Michaniona. Many villages throughout Greece were called *Nea* or "new," renamed to commemorate towns in Asia Minor abandoned in the population exchange between Greece and Turkey.

As Kate caught glimpses of sparkling water in the spaces between a series of beachfront restaurants, she clasped and reclasped her hands.

"*Etho, sas parakalo.*" Thanasis signaled to the taxi driver, "Here, please." A group of a dozen people stood outside, shaded from the bright sunlight by the restaurant's awning. She recognized Stelios and Makis, Thanasis's friends.

Stepping out of the taxi, she heard laughter and watched as those gathered took turns clapping the back of a figure in a dark coat. A wave of fear washed over her. He must be the famous artist. Kate wished she could disappear.

Thanasis guided her to the circle of people, his hand gently on her back. The figure at the center of attention pivoted. His full head of graying hair was combed in a style reminiscent of Elvis's pompadour. Dark eyes danced and reached out to her, along with a smile surrounded by lines of wrinkles.

"Enchante, mademoiselle!" Speaking French, Farsakithis said he was pleased to meet her. He offered a slight bow, keeping his arms to his side rather than offering a hand to shake.

"Hairo polee," Kate said, working to keep her smile from wavering.

Introductions continued around the group. Stelios, one of Thanasis's closest friends, greeted her with the customary kiss on both cheeks, his lips lingering longer than she would have liked. He was taller than Thanasis, broad-shouldered, with stubble that made him always seem a few days past a shave. She didn't like him. Something about him was sleazy, but Kate hadn't yet worked up the courage to share this with Thanasis.

Makis was short with a rounded physique, clean-shaven face, and dark eyes that sparkled with sincere welcoming each time she'd met him. The others in the group were mostly older and dressed in neat but modest clothing. They reminded her of some of the Moscow Communist friends of Fotini's she had met at the anti-American demonstration. This group differed from the younger group of

Eurocommunists that Thanasis was aligned with. *Why is he with these people?*

Kate was momentarily struck by how easily she avoided paying attention to any inconsistencies from Thanasis. Did she really know him that well? Kate was in love with him, and she relied on him more and more to navigate her social and political life, just as she had done with Lena in her first days in Greece. And wasn't that her pattern? Defaulting to others—her parents and then Jim—to make decisions? After the divorce, Kate had struggled hard to gain her autonomy. She hoped she wasn't falling back into old habits.

Making their way toward a line of small tables pushed together to accommodate the group, Thanasis made sure to sit next to her. Conversation and laughter became more boisterous as the retsina flowed. Farsakithis reached for the small glass near his plate. Kate's stomach dropped. Misshapen hands grasped the tumbler. On each hand, a thumb and a few digits acted together, much like a claw.

Thanasis whispered into her ear, "During prison they made him pay for his communism by damaging his hands."

Kate put her head down to keep from staring. This was the first time she had seen the work of the junta up close. She was shocked. Nausea threatened. As Kate lifted her head, Farsakithis sent her a sympathetic smile. She tried to be inconspicuous as she watched him tear off a piece of bread from the loaf and dip it into the yogurt and cucumber tzatziki.

How can he paint with hands like that? She thought of her father who painted in his studio above their garage. His hands held a paintbrush with precision as he deftly repositioned his fingers to get whatever effect he intended.

This artist with broken hands showed her kindness despite

what her country had been complicit in doing to him. How could America, even indirectly, have sanctioned such crimes? Kate grabbed her own retsina and took a few large gulps.

A plate of golden fried calamari was placed squarely in front of him, and Farsakithis exhorted the group up and down the table. Kate was able to understand his Greek. "Eat, eat, friends. The Americans may come back again tomorrow!"

Thanasis glanced her way, joining the others to see if she had understood what he said. The retsina had given Kate newfound courage. Cocking her head to one side and then lifting her own glass, she rejoined in Greek, "We're already back!" Laughter exploded and arms reached in her direction to clink her glass in a toast, saluting her humor.

A young girl with a basket of carnations approached the table, one of the parade of vendors with goods to sell to restaurant patrons. Flowers, cigarettes, lottery tickets, and photographs were routinely offered to diners. Thanasis motioned the girl over, pulled a wad of bills from his pocket, and shouted, *"Kokkino!"* demanding red carnations for everyone at the table. Red, of course, was the color of communism.

Small plates continued to arrive and were passed up and down the table. Eggplant salad, fried squash with garlic sauce, fresh sardines, loaves of bread, and retsina, retsina, retsina. Farsakithis regaled his friends with tales from prison, a naturally large presence at any table. Kate's proficiency with Greek was improving enough for her to follow some of what he said, and Thanasis supplemented.

The scent of the red carnation pinned to her dress transported Kate back home to the bouquet she had gathered at the cemetery after her grandfather's funeral. It had been easier to conceal tears of sadness at the loss of his kindly presence by hiding behind a handful of carnations in the back seat of the large gray Buick on the way home.

The glow of memories of large family dinners and afternoons running and playing in her grandmother's backyard flooded in. Family bonds had been strong enough to sustain her when her marriage had broken apart, softening Jim's rejection and the failure of her marriage.

Her family. What would they think of her having lunch surrounded by members of the Greek Communist Party? They were patriotic Americans. An American flag stood at attention on her grandmother's front porch. How could any of them begin to understand these new views she was developing about her country?

The late afternoon slowly became evening, and lights from small boats danced on the waves in the distance. The lively cadence of Theodorakis songs played from a stereo. Kate followed the group to the beach to dance. Pushing away thoughts of her loved ones, she fell under the spell of this exotic music and the whoosh of waves lapping the shore.

As she danced, an attractive woman with erect posture glided in her direction, dark hair festooned with her red carnation. She had been seated at the far end of the table during lunch. They hadn't spoken, but she had sent warm smiles in Kate's direction. The woman's arms waved gracefully overhead as her fingers snapped in time to the music. She surprised Kate by leaning in and kissing her lightly on both cheeks before delivering her message in English. "Welcome! You are now one of us." The woman eyed her with intensity, waiting for a response.

Stunned, Kate forced a smile and stumbled away from her, not knowing what to say. She stretched her arms out in an attempt to resume dancing. *One of them? How did I give the impression I've chosen sides—against my own country?* Frantically, she scanned the crowd to find Thanasis. She wanted to leave. He had moved away from the group, the arm of a man around his shoulder, making animated gestures with his other hand.

Kate found her way back to the table. She fingered the feather petals of the red carnation Thanasis had pinned to her dress, recalling the way his thumb played on her skin as he anchored it to her bra strap. Kate lit a cigarette, drew deeply on it, and watched the glow of the paper being consumed by fire.

Worry played inside as she tore a paper napkin into strips, trying to make them equal. Kate liked these people, but yet there was something troubling about being in their presence. Despite the banter, she sensed a seriousness different from Thanasis's other friends. Kate knew at the end of the evening, she could leave behind the person they thought she was and once again, simply be an American speech therapist working with cerebral palsied children.

Taking the strips and tearing them into smaller squares, she pushed them back and forth on the tablecloth. Something had happened today. Returning to the person she was before meeting Farsakithis was no longer possible. Kate reached for the bottle of retsina on the table and drained it into her glass.

thirty-nine 🌿

Kate's head was still clouded with too much retsina as she walked to work the next day. Scenes from the night before in Nea Michaniona crowded in. On the taxi ride back to Thessaloniki, both she and Thanasis had been unusually quiet. Resting her head on his shoulder, she was comforted by his embrace but unwilling to have a conversation about Farsakithis, the dark-haired woman's comment to her, or Thanasis's connection to this group. She sensed this group was more hardline in their politics, and she wondered what he was doing with them. Thanasis was lost somewhere else, staring out the window.

"Thespinis Katerina. Eiste etoimee yia mas?" The quiet voice from Kuria Repanithis came from the hallway, asking if she was ready for them.

"Elate." She asked them to "come" and arranged Demetris's special seat between chairs for the two of them. As Kate asked how things were going, Demetris beamed at her, smiling broadly.

Kate listened as Demetris repeated an approximation of *allo* that she had taught him to request "more."

"Bravo, Demetraki!" She praised him.

Kate, Demetris, and his mother joined in a moment of laughter, pleased with what he had accomplished. Kate noticed his tongue could move slightly to the roof of his mouth, a position for the consonant "n." Maybe he could use this movement combined with opening his mouth to make a vowel sound for the word *nai* meaning "yes." Although he already indicated this with his eyes, Kate hoped he could say the simple word. After a few tries, he succeeded.

Before they ended, Kate proposed something else. The word "no" was two syllables in Greek. Ohi. He wouldn't be able to say the aspirated "h," but he could try for "o" and "i." Glancing at her watch, she knew there wasn't enough time for further practice.

"Mathima yia spiti," she told them. "Lesson for home."

Standing at the door, Kate prolonged the syllables *"a—dee—o"* for "goodbye."

Unprompted, Demetris struggled but imitated the three syllables *"a—ee—o."*

Now, Kate beamed a smile at Demetris and bid farewell to his mother, both adults with moist eyes shining. She dropped into her chair and brushed back her tears, not only of happiness for Demetris's progress but also pent-up emotions from the confusion of the previous day. Noise from the hallway marked the end of any further thoughts of Nea Michanonia.

Kuria Zeta pushed Giorgos and his wheelchair into the room, his communication board under his arm. His head bobbed with excitement, his finger wriggled under his nose, and his hand pushed the board toward Kate. She guessed he was indicating his father liked the board.

Kate asked Giorgos if he would like her to make one for home. A series of nods followed. Kuria Zeta and Kate spent the next half hour proposing a list of items to Giorgos who would nod to the side for "yes" or lift his head up for "no." She would create the board and have Kuria Zeta write a note to his father requesting he call her for instructions. As Kuria Zeta disengaged the wheelchair brake to take him back upstairs, Giorgos made a kissing movement to Kate with his lips. She worked to hold back her tears. *What's wrong with me?* She was not usually this emotional about her work.

As she prepared for her last appointment of the day with Soto, Kuria Argero knocked on her door to say Soto had to leave early for a doctor's appointment. Although she loved her sessions with him, Kate was relieved for an early end to her day. She had tried to disregard her headache from too much retsina the night before, but now she could relax and give in to lingering remnants of a hangover.

She imagined Soto sitting in the chair she had set out for him, hands gripped to either side of the seat, practicing slow breathing. Kate put away the flannel board and its felt pieces—a face and red cutouts to represent lips showing positions for vowels *ah, ee, o, ou* they used for practice before adding consonants for simple syllables. Together they were building a way of easy talking.

Accomplishing this in the quiet of her room was one thing, but would he ever be able to use these strategies when he was out in the world? Soto's excitement to talk caused his arms to retreat to abnormal positions, and his lips to pull to one side of his face. Could he change enough to be able to speak more clearly? Kate wasn't certain. *And wasn't that what brought me to Greece after all? To help the son of the Mrs. Stylianou from the letter?*

Kate put away the therapy materials, grateful to have fully inhabited her professional identity. Two private sessions awaited later this afternoon. And then, as usual, her evening would be spent with Thanasis. She slumped into her chair, thoughts again of Thanasis and last night. *Why am I hesitant to ask him about his connection to those people? Is there a reason to question his honesty?* Kate twirled a strand of hair, let it go, then twisted it again.

She thought back to last October when she had waded on the beach in Metamorphosis with Lena. Kate was fascinated by the sea since she'd never spent time near it before. That day she had seen how her footprints in the sand would soon be washed away by the actions of waves, as though nothing had ever happened.

Did questioning Thanasis risk a turbulence that would preclude a return to what had, until now, been the intimate relationship she'd so yearned for? *Do I dare? But do I dare not to?*

forty ✿

The taxi screamed up Martiou, the street officially named Twenty-Fifth of March commemorating Greek Independence Day of 1821. For Kate, Martiou was the large avenue that intersected Queen Olga Street. She crossed it twice daily, on her way to and from work. A few blocks down to the right was the Bay of Salonika, and its promenade. This was her first time heading in the other direction. Kate glanced at Thanasis as they went farther into a part of the city unknown to her. "Suez. That's a funny name for a nightclub. Why do you think it's called that?"

Thanasis sent her a curious smile, then shrugged. "Maybe a grandfather of someone worked on the Suez Canal? I know it is popular, but I do not know the history." He resumed staring out the window on his side.

"Fotini called it the 'heart of the beast' when I told her where we were going." Fotini had said it was a favorite gathering spot for political activists. Thanasis nodded to let her know he had heard the comment but offered no further explanation. She held his hand tightly and squeezed it. She needed to reassure herself of the realness of their connection, especially at times like this when Thanasis seemed to be slightly out of reach.

Kate was confused. Like a juggler spinning multiple plates, she tried balancing several concerns. *What's really going on with his political connections? Why does he seem so distant lately? Am I losing my independence?* Being in love again was exhilarating, but what price was she having to pay for it?

Before leaving for the restaurant, Kate had made herself ask Thanasis about his connection to the group at the restaurant with Farsakithis. He said they were good people, and he had friends from different political parties. She shouldn't worry about Anthi, who had tried to welcome Kate to the Communist Party. *"Ee retsina ftaei."* He blamed it on too much retsina.

She pushed herself to believe what Thanasis told her. But it was not just her imagination that Thanasis was occasionally lost in thought these past few weeks. The wonderful moments still abounded—laughter, a deepening friendship, and physical gratification—but he was preoccupied, drifting away. Something was changing.

Brakes screeched, and the taxi driver punched the meter on the dashboard. Thanasis reached in the pocket of his black corduroy jacket and peeled off some drachma bills. Kate followed him out of the taxi. Nothing resembled a restaurant. On both sides of the street, doors were open, and lights were on inside small stores selling appliances, carpeting, and furniture. The agora stayed open later on Saturday nights, especially for villagers coming into the city for shopping.

This part of Martiou had none of the tall apartment buildings, flower shops, or movie theaters prominent in Kate's area. Thessaloniki was a city of varied neighborhoods, and this one was decidedly less cosmopolitan, reminding her where she had registered as a foreigner worker and met Branko. Standing in the semi-light, she smiled, thinking of herself before Thanasis had come into her life. Despite the new worries, she loved their time together.

"Ela, Koukla." Thanasis urged her to come and guided her on the sidewalk. He opened a door indistinguishable from others along the street. Inside, rows of long tables spread out in a cavernous open space. Smoke rose to the rafters like low-hanging clouds.

The recording of a popular song she had heard at the Theodorakis concert blared from a speaker. Its refrain celebrated martyrs of the struggle. "When they perish, life pulls uphill." Something about the Greek lyrics stirred her heart. She remembered the concert and the red flags in the audience waving in time to this song, an anthem in the Greek resistance against the dictatorship. Increasingly, she understood the scars left by those terrible years.

Kate scanned the room. The music and a sense of gaiety pervaded. The feeling of belonging she'd experienced at the concert came again. She breathed a sigh of relief. With Thanasis by her side, Kate relaxed into her place in this new world.

A figure beckoned from the far side of the room. To Kate's annoyance, it was Stelios, gesturing to empty places at one of the long tables. Plates were already lined up on white butcher paper.

"Yeia sas paithia." Stelios greeted them with the customary words, calling them "children" and embraced first Thanasis, then Kate. "Hello to you, Miss, and how are you this magnificent evening?" Stelios took pride in his English and used it almost exclusively with her.

Kate greeted Thalia, one of Stelios's several girlfriends she had met. Even with Thalia at his elbow, Stelios let his hand wander to the small of Kate's back and remain there as she greeted the rest of the group. Conveniently for Stelios, Thanasis's back was to them. Kate quickly stepped away in the direction of Makis and his girlfriend, Anna. She had to talk to Thanasis about Stelios soon.

"Hello again, Kaitie," Anna kissed her on both cheeks and slipped an arm into Kate's, helping her to step over the picnic table-like wooden plank for seating and plop down beside her. "So how is it going?" Anna began in English.

Kate vacillated between a desire to speak Greek to feel part of the group, and wanting to have a more meaningful conversation, which could only happen in English. She chose English.

"I'm doing okay, I think. Some days it feels like the six months I've been here are a twinkling of an eye and some days it seems like I've been here forever." Anna indicated confusion, apparently trying to understand the idiom. "A 'twinkling of an eye' is when something happens fast, while your eyelids are blinking."

Anna smiled and repeated the phrase, most likely tucking it away for future use.

Kate worked to catch Thanasis's attention and motion him in her direction. He left the others and headed toward her.

"En daxi?" Thanasis was checking if she was okay and made sure their eyes connected before sliding his body next to her side as he sat. Kate smiled and nodded.

"We eat the usual," Makis said. Kate had come to expect beef or lamb souvlaki sprinkled with oregano, tomato and cucumber salad with tangy olives, tzatziki and eggplant salads, feta slices, and french fries. And retsina. Of course, retsina. She was also learning that although the never-ending discussions at Greek restaurants were of as many opinions as the snakes on Medusa's head, the table fare was usually pretty much the same on most menus.

"Miss Katerina." Stelios waved his cigarette expansively as he addressed her formally. "One year ago this place was a *mystiko*—a 'secret.' We could not have this music, we ate our souvlaki, and pretended to speak of the weather. And now here we are. On the . . . I do not know the word. Help me. Brig of a new . . . ?"

"Brink?" Kate said.

"Yes. Brrrink." He rolled the "r" for effect. "Brrrink of a new revolution!"

Fortunately, someone farther down the table grabbed the group's attention with a joke. Kate sought out Thanasis to get a translation for what she hadn't understood. However, he wasn't laughing with the group. He was focused on someone entering the room.

"I will be back." Thanasis kissed Kate's cheek and left the table.

At that moment Anna and Thalia asked Kate about American movies. Kate had been surprised at the popularity of American cinema in Greece in the face of such strong anti-American sentiment.

Thanasis and Stelios spoke with a middle-aged man. The man kept his leather jacket on as they stood near the doorway, heads hunched in conversation. Anna and Thalia pressed her on details of famous American cities, and Kate confessed that she'd actually never been to New York City or Chicago. Her eyes stayed on Thanasis across the room until he eventually came back to the table.

"Who's that guy?" Kate asked.

"A friend," Thanasis replied casually, as he poured retsina for both of them from the small, copper pitcher.

"Why doesn't he come sit with us?" Kate asked. She had a vague, uneasy sense he was keeping something from her.

"He has many people to see." Thanasis put an arm around her and brought her closer to him. Reluctantly, she dismissed her concern.

The evening of eating, drinking, and conversation dragged on. The ashtrays overflowed. Thanasis excused himself again. Kate toyed with the cold french fries in front of her. She refilled her glass and tapped a cigarette from the pack she'd recently started carrying in her purse.

Although she had bought a lighter, Kate often preferred the small box of matches from the sidewalk kiosk. She was pleased with her newfound expertise of effortlessly striking a match and lighting the cigarette poised between her lips. Especially after a few glasses of retsina, the thought of "good girl gone bad" made her smile. She scrutinized the room, spotting Thanasis in conversation with Stelios and the unknown man, who had reemerged. The smile left her face.

Thalia and Anna had moved into a conversation about some intrigue at the university where they both worked. The swift chatter of their Greek was too difficult to follow. She focused instead on the servers who were cleaning up. Waiters at the Suez wore blue jeans and T-shirts rather than the usual white shirts and black trousers at other restaurants. They balanced plates on both arms and scooped up the small retsina glasses in groups with their fingers.

Thanasis waved at her and nodded his head toward the door. *"Telika!"* she muttered to herself in Greek. "Finally."

Brisk, smoke-free air greeted them on the sidewalk. Thanasis hailed a taxi. Settled in their seats, Thanasis whispered in her ear, "Sorry, Koukla. I had not seen my friend for a very long time."

"Thanasi. I'm not sure what's happening. You seem to be—I don't know. It's like you disappear sometimes." There. She'd said it out loud.

"I am sorry, my love." He pulled her closer. "I do not want you to worry about the *leptomeria*—'details' I think—of the concerns of my friends." He found her eyes.

The sweetness and sincerity of his smile were hard to resist. Kate considered pressing the issue further, but she wanted to believe him. She had always worked to avoid conflict in her life, and, not for the first time, she chose the easier path.

"Okay. I'll trust you, Thanasi." Something passed between them. She was surrendering. This time, he squeezed her hand. Kate cleared her mind. The spinning plates were landing safely back into the juggler's hands.

Thanasis and Kate settled back into the silence sitting between them. On the radio, an announcer ran through the results of the day's soccer matches in a fast-moving river of vowels and consonants. A small, cardboard double-headed eagle, emblem of Thessaloniki's hometown soccer team PAOK, bounced from the rearview mirror where it hung, dancing in the air as they headed home.

forty-one 🌿

Morning light invaded the room. Thanasis kissed Kate's bare shoulder. She nestled into the softness of his neck wishing they could stay like this for hours. Instead, he slid away. She watched as he got out of bed and dressed.

Kate was surprised to hear the slow turning of the telephone dial from the hallway. Thanasis spoke in a low voice. She couldn't make out the words, but she could hear his tone. It was rough. It was angry. The receiver clicked on its cradle.

As Kate followed his sounds to the kitchen, an unsettled feeling breached her contentment. A striking match lit the gas burner and a spoon scraped inside the small, one-handled briki used for making coffee. Before long, he appeared at the doorway with two white demitasse cups. Thanasis half-smiled and nodded in the direction of the balcony.

Determined to ignore her concern, Kate stretched her legs toward the end of the mattress. She squeezed her eyes shut and deliberately chose instead to recall Thanasis's hands moving up and down her back when she had straddled him a few minutes before. One more stretch before she donned jeans and a shirt lying nearby.

On the balcony, Thanasis sparked the lighter for a cigarette for Kate, cupping his hand to protect the flame from the breeze. He lit his own and settled back in his chair. Kate let her cigarette smolder and instead arranged her chair to watch him against the backdrop of early-morning Sunday traffic. Blue-and-white taxis raced down Queen Olga Street, their multitone horns sounding warnings to anyone foolish enough to be in the way.

Kate moved the rim of the small cup back and forth across her bottom lip before taking a sip. Smoke curled up past his head as Thanasis exhaled a long stream. He was distant again. Stretching her leg, she ran bare toes along the curving calf under his jeans. Thanasis pulled the strands of his beard, a familiar gesture when he was contemplating something. Kate withdrew her foot.

"Hey, are you okay?"

Thanasis was startled, as though she were reeling him back from far away. *"Kala eimai."* He assured her he was fine. He sipped his coffee.

Kate persisted. "I heard you talking to someone. What was that about?"

"Nothing important. Stelios wants me to do a favor."

The name hit with a thud. Stelios. Kate drew up energy, like filling a bucket of water from the ocean and fighting the current to bring it to the surface.

"Thanasi, I've got to tell you something. I don't feel comfortable around Stelios."

She watched the profile of his face. He didn't flinch. No visible movement. Kate fought an impulse to rush in and negate what she had just said, in case the news was unwelcome. Instead, she focused on the people getting off at the Salamina bus stop.

Thanasis shifted his head to one side, acknowledging what she had said. He took another sip. Placing the cup back on the table, he said, "What is the problem with Stelios?"

Kate stared back at eyes that did not dance as they usually did when they found her. His face wore a mask. A chill ran through her body. She took in a breath. "He takes liberties with me." Thanasis's expression changed to reflect confusion, most likely with her words. She tried again. "He keeps his hands on me too long. The way he kisses me hello is different. I know he's your friend, but he doesn't act like he has any loyalty to you."

Thanasis bit his bottom lip and nodded his head. "I am sorry." His eyes were fixed beyond the balcony. "I know he is not always polite. That is who he is—he is hungry. No, that is not right word. What is the word for *orexi*?" He faced her again.

"Appetite." Kate knew the word well, as Greeks always wished each other "good appetite" before meals.

"Yes. His appetite is always large. Since we were small. Stelios had big ideas and a big thought about himself." He reached for Kate's legs and pulled them onto his lap, rubbing her shins. "I promise to talk to him." A tender smile returned to his face.

The tension in her body receded. Still, she wondered about the favor for Stelios. Later. For now, she would pace her questions, even though she knew she was falling back into bad habits. Kate had never wanted to make Jim mad by asking too many questions at one time. His anger wasn't a spark of flame, but more like embers glowing and ready to ignite if she said the wrong thing. Thanasis's displeasure was different. He might show annoyance, but it was always momentary.

Kate changed the subject. "What shall we do on this beautiful day?" It was the name-day celebration for King Constantine and Saint Helen. Constantine was the Emperor of the Byzantine Empire in the fourth century. Legend had it that his mother Helen discovered relics from Jesus's crucifixion. Helen and Constantine were among the most revered saints in Orthodox Christianity.

"I have somewhere I need to be."

Kate's body stiffened, and she quickly switched her legs back to the balcony railing.

"Stelios, right? A favor for him?"

The pleasant expression drained again from Thanasis's face. Kate wished this wasn't happening. She didn't like it when things got off balance or messy.

Thanasis lit a second cigarette before explaining. "There is a special celebration in the village of Langathas, a short distance from here. For Constantine and Helen. Every year a group of people walk on burning coals to show their faith in God."

"What does this have to do with Stelios?"

"Not Stelios. His favor is a different matter." Thanasis's focus was again on the Bay of Salonika. "It is important only to me." He drew on his cigarette, then balanced it on the ashtray.

Minutes passed before Thanasis brought his gentle, familiar gaze back to her. "Villagers carried this ritual with them from Eastern Thraki—you know the area? When they were refugees and came to Greece." Kate nodded. Many of her friends had family who had been forced from Turkey in the 1920s. The compulsory population exchange between Greece and Turkey was a centerpiece of the history of northern Greece.

He bent toward her, continuing his slow and deliberate explanation, just as when they'd first met, and he would describe the intricacies of Greek politics. "Long ago, a church of the Saints Constantine and Helen was burning, and villagers heard voices of the saints from inside the church asking for rescue. Some went in to get icons and did not get burned. This is to memory . . . to . . ."

"Commemorate."

"Yes. That. To give honor to the saints." Kate was surprised by the extent religion intertwined with everyday life in Greece. Even the blatantly nonreligious ones like Thanasis still had orthodoxy as their framework. "They are called the *Anastenarithes*, which in English means . . . I am not sure."

Kate went inside to consult her dictionary. "It means 'to sigh,'" she explained when she sat back down. "That's a strange word for a religious group."

"I believe it is because they do not yell from pain from the fire, but only make a quiet noise. I had relatives in Langathas. I did not tell you, I do not think. A cousin of my grandfather. He married someone from Langathas. The Anastenarithes took him in, and he also walked on fire."

"He didn't get hurt?"

Thanasis raised his head and clicked his tongue. "Believers walk on the coals and have no problem. It is a sign of their faith in God. They believe you come out a new person on the other side of the circle."

Kate flashed back to standing in a pool of water above the altar at the Baptist church where she was raised. Her baptism ceremony. She was eleven years old, skinny, shivering, and afraid. Someone helped her change into a white robe and squeezed her hair into a bathing cap. The rubber strap under her chin pinched. Reverend Arbuckle assisted her into the dim light of the baptistery and onto a stool. He spoke to the Sunday night congregation in the darkness below them.

"The angels in heaven are rejoicing that Katie is coming into the fellowship of Jesus."

His voice had echoed off the white tiled walls around them. Covering her mouth and nose with one hand, he used the other to pull her backward into the water. She only heard parts of the words he spoke, although she knew them from watching many baptisms with the congregation.

"Into the liquid grave she goes with her blessed Master, to rise and walk again in a new life."

Kate had coughed and spluttered as he brought her up from the water. Her legs were shaky as she had headed up the stairs back to the dressing room. Trembling, she wondered if Jesus was already beside her or inside her or wherever he was supposed to be. For a few weeks, she tried to feel like a new person, listening to the sermon rather than opening the Nancy Drew book she'd checked out from the church library. But it didn't last long. She tried to be nicer to her younger brother, but that didn't last long, either. Kate wasn't exactly sure what to believe.

Those questions had hovered over her into adult life as she veered away from baptisms and Bible stories and from always being at church on Sunday mornings. Now, as she sipped the last of the bitter coffee, Kate knew this trip to Greece had made her a new person in a different way. In this setting with the noise of Greek traffic and the blue of the Aegean, Thanasis was telling her about a religious ceremony with fire rather than water.

"Why go to Langathas today?"

"I need to see the Fire Walking. I need to go back to my early life."

"Can I come with you?" Kate tried to keep from sounding like she was begging.

He didn't answer.

She tried again. "You don't really believe in all that stuff, do you?"

He was slow to respond. "It is not a question of believing. It is about memories. The cousin of my grandfather is long dead, and the relatives moved away. I am thinking today of when I visited as a small boy. I must go back to something old." He moved his chair to face her. "You do not know me."

This seriousness fit with a complexity she was beginning to see in him. Over the past four months, Kate had come to know Thanasis as loving and dependable. But there was something in this moment that matched the uneasiness she had recently sensed. Was he moving away from her? And what about the people he kept secret from her—at the restaurant with Farsakithis and last night at Suez?

"I have boxes in my life." His voice was earnest.

"Boxes?"

"Different parts. There is an English word. Departments?"

"Compartments?"

"Yes. Compartments. Sometimes they stay together in a line. Sometimes they get knocked over and not in the line."

Kate knew he was trying to use his English to tell her something important. "I think we all have different parts of ourselves—"

Thanasis interrupted. "My parents learned of my American girlfriend." He began counting on his fingers. "They are not happy. My parents do not believe in my way of politics. Again, not happy. My friends ask me to do things that I do not want to do. Number three, not happy."

"What kind of things?"

"They are not important for you to know."

A door had shut and left her standing outside. "Thanasi—

you're pushing me away. Is that what you want to be doing?" She paused before admitting the painful part. "Maybe this whole thing of us being together isn't such a good idea." She surprised herself. His family was pressuring him about her. What were his friends wanting him to do? And politics—the politics were always there. Their time together had made life in Greece a wonderful carnival ride. Perhaps the ride neared its end.

Thanasis was like a young boy lost in a crowd. The noise of honking taxis and screeching brakes filled the space.

He spoke quietly. "I feel obliged to go to Langathas today. To find a way to make the boxes . . . go back in a better line. I do not know if . . ." He pulled the strands of his beard as the sunlight crept onto the balcony. He stubbed his cigarette and finished his coffee. Thanasis stood and lifted her up, bringing her into a tight embrace. "The clock for us is still going around. It has not stopped." He kissed her deeply, leaving a taste of coffee and smoke. He whispered in her ear, "Do you want to come with me? To Langathas?"

Kate pulled back and found the eyes that, at times, overtook her. "Yes. Very much."

"I will come for you at three o'clock. I will borrow a car from a friend." Thanasis signaled his leaving with a kiss on the top of her head, his sweet signature of affection.

Kate listened to his footsteps disappearing down the hallway followed by the closing of the door. She glanced at the table. Thanasis had forgotten his cigarettes and lighter. She helped herself.

forty-two 🌿

*M*usic from the radio drifted out of the car windows as Kate
and Thanasis left the city. It was the first time she had ridden
with him in anything other than a taxi or a bus. "So, tell me again
about this car?" Kate asked, wondering how it had materialized.

"From a friend. Someone you do not know." Thanasis switched
the dial to a different radio station. Kate was taken aback by his
minimal response. Remnants of concern from their morning conversation returned. Her chest tightened.

"It just seems funny for us to be in a car together," Kate said,
searching for a way back to connection.

His hands rested easily on the steering wheel. "On the farm of
my grandfather, I drove the tractor from very young." He had read
her mind about his driving skills.

Kate laughed at the thought of him as a small, curly-headed
boy careening through fields. "You on a tractor? I like that picture."

Thanasis smiled. Kate pushed back into her seat, but still unable to shake her wary feelings.

Continuing on the road for half an hour, conversation came
sporadically. The plinking bouzouki music from the radio was a
soundtrack for scenes of lofty Italian cypresses surrounding small
Byzantine churches. Blood-red poppies dotted the fields. *Maybe this
wasn't such a great idea. I should have gone to Lena's instead for her*

name day celebration. But just as quickly as that thought formed, Kate knew Thanasis would still have filled her head no matter where she was. She was connected to this man in an almost obsessive way. The possibility she had already abandoned her independence twirled in her mind as she toyed with the knob of the window crank. Kate shook her head with disappointment in herself.

They exited the main roadway and joined a stream of other cars. Single, stone houses with red ceramic tiled roofs appeared. "Langathas?" Kate asked.

"Langadas!" Thanasis jokingly changed to an anglicized pronunciation and reached over to goose her knee, one of his playful gestures. He was back again—his old self. Kate dismissed her worries and reached out to stroke the soft part of his neck beneath his curls. Thanasis followed the traffic and parked in a field. After shutting off the engine, he bent toward her for a kiss. It was soft and long, ending with a caress on her cheek.

Kate watched Thanasis get out of the car and gather their jackets from the back seat. She admired his lithe body, the way his movements flowed from one to the next, his handsome profile. The past days had been a roller coaster, but she willingly signed up to continue the ride.

Dust from the field coated her shoes as they followed the crowd to the far side of the village. Vendors sold bread rings topped with sesame seeds, as well as souvlaki and chestnuts from the grill. Music from transistor radios and the enticing smell from braziers created a festive atmosphere.

"Isn't this supposed to be a religious ceremony?" Kate asked Thanasis.

"We Greeks are never far from our stomachs." He slipped his

hand in hers and squeezed it. As they moved into the crowd, she glanced at him, hoping he could find whatever had brought him here.

A faint smell of smoke in the air reminded her of homecoming bonfires before high school football games. Despite the recent uncertainties, his hand gave her strength as it pulled her into another new experience. With him by her side, Kate didn't care she was probably the only non-Greek in Langathas that day.

Ahead, a group of people milled about in a yard while others lined up to enter a small house. Kate and Thanasis took their places with the crowd and waited. He puffed on a cigarette, and she studied those in line. Mixed in with villagers in their Sunday best were city people, women with stylish outfits and prominently displayed gold crosses around their necks. They were markedly different in appearance from Thanasis's friends.

Finally, it was their turn. Bending slightly to fit through the tiny doorframe, Kate immediately sensed an electricity. The crowded room had low ceilings, and rugs covered the uneven surface of a packed dirt floor. Sweet-smelling smoke drifted from an incense burner. Red scarves intertwined with an assortment of icons on a mantel over an empty fireplace. Onlookers ringed an open space for some kind of ritual already underway. A group of half a dozen men and women danced from one end of the room to the other, back and forth and back and forth. Some held icons, the sacred paintings she knew to be Constantine and Helen, while another carried an oversized Bible.

In one corner, three older men sat on stools, singing and accompanying themselves with a drum and small stringed instruments played with a bow. The snatches of words she caught from the songs told stories of kidnappings, wolves, and a young Constantine going to war. Minor key tones and nasal voices melded together.

A few of the dancers twirled red scarves to the beat of music that snaked around the room. "Red scarves?" Kate whispered to Thanasis. "Does that mean they're communists?" In Kate's mind, the color had become associated with that political party.

Thanasis clicked his tongue *tch* and raised his head, the familiar gesture indicating negation. "They are the opposite of communists. That red is for the blood of Christ."

Kate remembered *Kokkino Pempti* or "Red Thursday," the day during Holy Week of Easter to dye eggs red and to hang red tablecloths or rugs from balconies to honor the blood and sacrifice of Christ. The transition from the previous night at Suez to this was jolting, but she was captivated by the scene.

The dancers were like typical Greeks she would see on the street, middle-aged with plain clothing. The facial expressions, however, made them unusual. Making eye contact with no one, the dancers stared ahead while gliding past one another, as if in a trance. One woman caught her attention. She twirled her red scarf with intensity, snapping it in time to the music.

The musical background and the motion of the dancers captured Kate. It was as if she were being transported into a magic fable. Something released inside her. She swayed from side to side. The warmth of the room, the incense, and the mesmerizing cadence took her further away from consciousness. Kate was aware only of being deeply lost in colors and fractured images.

Abruptly, someone bumped her. The spell had broken, and she was jostled out of her reverie. Thanasis's eyes were fixed on the door. Kate watched as a man in a leather jacket left the room. Although she only saw his back, there was something familiar about the figure. Thanasis's focus was held by something.

"Who is that?" she whispered.

"We must go." His voice was jagged.

Once outside the house, Kate reached for his hand. "What was that about? Are you okay?"

From Thanasis's eyes came the familiar connection, but there was also something else. A glimmer of uncertainty. "Please. Do not worry." His gaze stayed with her for a moment, like he weighed something in his mind. Before she could form another question, he pulled her forward. "Come. We do not want to miss it."

A sliver of fear pricked her chest. She grabbed his hand tightly as they followed others to a field. A sizable crowd had already gathered in a semicircle around a smoldering bonfire. Two men began to break up the burning wood with long poles and rake it into a large circle of glowing red-and-orange embers. The group quieted.

Steady drumbeats, like a message from an oversized heart, sounded from the direction of the small house. Day had melted into dusk. Embers from the fire glowed intensely. Kate's curiosity overtook her uncertainty.

Letting go of Thanasis's hand, she moved in front of him to get a better view. A procession of the men and women dancers from the house appeared out of the darkness. They carried white candles, shadows of flames playing across their faces. Barefooted, they approached with determined steps, wearing the same trance on their faces as when they had danced. Those accompanying them carried the icons and the large Bible.

The Fire Walkers strode through an opening in the crowd and

approached the outer edge of the circle. The drum abruptly changed to a rapid, feverish beat. Handing off the candles to their escorts, they skipped and danced over the glowing coals, kicking up sparks from the embers with their bare feet.

Riveted, she watched their movements as they ran over hot cinders. Once across the diameter of the circle, they ground their feet in the dirt and raced back again to their starting place. One part of Kate searched for any tricks used of stepping so lightly on the coals to avoid getting burned. Another part was transfixed, almost believing a miracle was happening. Kate again found the woman who had twirled her scarf. She wore an expression of fearlessness.

After three complete trips, the drum stopped, ending in one loud, sudden bang. The group's leader shouted a phrase Kate didn't understand. She sought a translation from Thanasis.

He was not there.

Instead, she was face to face with an elderly Greek woman, clad in black, making the sign of the cross repeatedly upon her chest. The old woman gazed beyond Kate with milky eyes, moving her head rhythmically and chanting. Startled, Kate stepped back and scanned the crowd for Thanasis. She didn't see him.

Standing on her tiptoes, she searched for his familiar figure. "Where is he?" She choked the words out in a whisper, barely able to breathe from a rising fear. The spectators were leaving. The Fire Walkers, standing in a group, were enveloped by a swarm of people.

An old man walked by with buckets of water in each hand, giving her an inquisitive glare. He began dousing the fire. Clouds of dust and ash billowed in the air. Kate coughed and walked away from the smoldering circle, away from where she had last seen Thanasis.

The car. It took a few turns before she found the place she thought they had parked. The car was not there, but then, she hadn't paid attention to its appearance. Still, no empty cars waited. Kate retraced her steps to try the opposite direction. She hoped to find Thanasis leaning against a car, smoking a cigarette, ready with a simple explanation. But she didn't. As the minutes passed, Kate worked to keep her fear from becoming panic.

Evening chill slipped into her open jacket as she stumbled in the direction of noise and lights, toward what she thought was the center of town. Most villages had bus stations in a central location. Kate was hesitant to ask for directions from any passersby, so she moved forward, searching for the bus station logo. *What could have happened? This is not like him at all.* But the words haunted her as soon as they formed in her mind. It was the second time today the subject of her knowing or not knowing Thanasis had come up.

Fear swam inside like a school of disoriented fish. She dropped to a nearby bench, wrapping her arms around herself and rocking back and forth. Kate was alone. She was more alone than when she'd first stepped off the plane eight months before. *Stop it. Get hold of yourself.*

Moments passed. Eventually, she calmed.

Kate started moving again. She would get a bus for Thessaloniki, then take a taxi home from the bus depot. Maybe he would be waiting at her apartment when she got there, with an apology for a huge misunderstanding. *But what if something bad has happened to him?* Kate shivered but kept walking on the uneven sidewalk.

The center of Langathas was bordered by the usual array of small stores. Streetlights brightened the night. It was still early for Greeks. Since it was Sunday, villagers in their best clothes strolled arm and arm, back and forth on their ritual voltas. Foreigners were an unfamiliar sight in villages, and she wasn't sure if anti-American sentiment existed here. Without the protection of Thanasis or her friends, she once again lurched back into the vulnerability of her early days in Greece when she feared being berated because she was an American.

She spotted the bus terminal up ahead and made her way into the stark lights of the station. A scattering of people waited on benches around the mostly empty room.

"Thessaloniki?" she asked the ticket agent.

"*Stees ennea,*" he answered, eyeing her curiously. Kate understood the next bus was at 9:00 p.m., so she fumbled with the correct combination of paper drachmas for the ticket. The bus wouldn't leave for another hour. At the snack bar counter, an indifferent attendant handed her the Nescafe and tyropita she ordered. Shedding her jacket, she settled into a small chair next to a wobbly table.

Kate took a sip of coffee and tried remembering the morning conversation with Thanasis for any clue to explain why she was now sitting here alone. She recalled the night before at the Suez, his preoccupation on the balcony, his secretiveness about the car, and his expression in the house of the Fire Walkers. It was all a jumble. Kate dug her thumb behind each nail on her left hand, the process becoming faster and more intense the longer she sat. A loudspeaker interrupted her thoughts with the announcement of the bus to Thessaloniki. She hurriedly finished her coffee, leaving the tyropita untouched.

The bus drew away from the lights of the village center and drove past the empty arena that had earlier been filled with the crowd and bonfire. Kate tried keeping her head toward the window and the dark countryside. On previous outings, buses had seemed quaint. Tonight, the half-empty bus was different. The eyes of the bus driver found her in his rearview mirror. A black-clad grandmother with her plastic bags of dandelion greens squinted at her from the corner of her eye. Even an icon of the Virgin Mary, decorating the front of the bus and illumined with a small light, was of no comfort. Kate toyed with her necklace, her mind still working on the puzzle of Thanasis and his disappearance. *Should I be mad? Worried? What do I feel?* She studied her reflection in the window. "Afraid," she whispered to it.

The hope of finding Thanasis waiting in her apartment faded into the shadows of the deserted lobby. She rode the elevator to the fifth floor and hurriedly switched on all the lights in the apartment. Everything seemed in place.

Walking out on the balcony, Kate spied Thanasis's lighter and cigarettes, remnants from their morning together. The sight of the empty chairs stopped her. Something was terribly wrong. Kate outlined the shape of the cigarette pack with her finger, then ran it across the smooth plastic of the lighter. She grabbed them and left the balcony. There was a soft thud as they hit the bottom of the trash can.

Kate switched off the lights and went to bed in the darkness.

forty-three

Walking to work the next morning, Kate was numb. Street noises were too loud. People pushed past. Even the posters on the walls proclaiming, "Victory to the People" seemed a hollow promise. The city's charm and her sense of adventure had evaporated.

The van hadn't yet arrived at ELEPAAP, so she hurried inside and sought out Georyia upstairs in her classroom. Luckily, she was there. Recognizing something was amiss, Georyia reached out with *"Vre, koritsi mou,"* affectionately calling her "my girl." Instead of risking any emotions in this more public setting, Kate motioned for her to come downstairs to her therapy room.

They sat in the small children's chairs at the far end of the speech therapy room, next to the window that faced the front garden.

"What happened?" Georyia always knew when it was time to change to English.

"I have no idea. Yesterday we went to Langathas."

"The Fire Walking?"

"Yes." Kate nodded. "Thanasis left me there. He . . ." Her voice stopped and the tears began. "He told me some story about needing to go back there where he had good boyhood memories. I convinced him to let me go along. But then he disappeared." She took a deep breath. "I was so scared. And I was mad. I had to take a bus back home by myself." Kate wiped her cheeks with the backs of her hands. "I don't know what to think. Why would he do that? I haven't heard a word from him, and I'm worried that something bad has happened." She shook her head back and forth, finally not knowing what else to say.

Georyia seldom rushed her words. Kate waited. Georyia's voice was calm. "Those students. You must understand that the students are in a difficult situation now. During the junta, we were kept inside a cage. We could see out and listen, but there was nothing we could do. Now we are out of the cage and are free. Some are searching to find what to do next." Georyia quieted. "People died for these freedoms. Like at the *Polytechnio*—"

"I know. We saw the documentary last week." Kate and Thanasis had seen a film about an uprising at a university in Athens during the dictatorship. Sitting in the darkened theater with lights shifting across her face, she'd watched with horror the images clandestinely shot by a Dutch journalist. Thanasis sat motionless beside her.

Students in Athens had barricaded themselves in the Polytechnic University, calling for the overthrow of the junta. Kate understood most of the Greek words accompanying the footage, messages from a pirated radio station inside a classroom. Over the airwaves, they begged for support for their uprising against the colonels and their foreign supporters the United States and NATO, even urging the soldiers to join them. It was devastating to hear the young, desperate voices name her country as their enemy.

The grainy film showed an eerie scene illumined by spotlights in the early morning hours. A lone tank crept slowly toward the central gate. Students stood behind iron fences and perched atop concrete pillars. They waved a large Greek flag and sang the national anthem. Almost in slow motion, the armored vehicle broke through the steel gate. Figures hurtled downward from the impact, some crushed by the grinding treads of the tank. Shocked, Kate witnessed the deaths of these young people. It could have been Thanasis or any of his friends. Kate had squeezed her eyes shut and bent her head. After the movie ended, silence, rather than conversation, had accompanied them back to her apartment.

Georyia's words were edged with bitterness. "Forty of them died. Students and also protesters outside the walls. The tank and the soldiers' machine guns showed no mercy." Her face and its expression were pulled down by gravity and by experiences Kate never had to endure in her sheltered life in America. "For you it was a film. For us it was life."

Kate's eyes traced the patterns of the linoleum floor of the therapy room. Squares and lines ran over the buckled and uneven surface. She shook her head and whispered, "Awful. I could see that it was so horrible." It didn't seem like Georyia was accusing, but rather she was confirming something Kate now knew to be true. Unfathomable killings, tortures, and cruelty had happened in this country.

"I do not know details, but some student groups are planning what to do next. Revenge, I think, is the word."

"You believe Thanasis is in a group like that?"

Georyia shrugged her shoulders.

"I don't understand. But do you at least think he's okay? That nothing's happened to him?" Kate wished desperately for assurance.

"I cannot be certain. I believe you will hear from him. There will be some explanation. He is a good person." Georyia again shifted her focus to the garden. "There are many . . . parts to this life you have come to in Greece. It is not a simple story like we read to the children."

Suddenly, they heard excited voices on the walkway. The van had arrived. The conversation would have to be continued later.

"Come for lunch?" Georyia asked.

"I can't. I have private lessons."

"Come by later if you want." Georyia stood.

"Efharisto, Georyia." Kate whispered, then began setting out supplies for her students on the schedule.

forty-four

T he days crawled by. It had been three days since the Fire Walking ceremony and three days she had not heard from Thanasis. Her emotions constantly crashed into each other—anger, sadness, disbelief. During the day, Kate went through the motions of work at ELEPAAP and private lessons in the afternoons. In the evenings, she sat on the balcony hoping to hear from Thanasis. She struggled to keep her fear away, fear that swelled with each passing night of quiet. *What's happened to my lover, my best friend?*

Wednesday evening after picking at the food on her plate, she forced herself to venture into the spare bedroom with the double bed, the one she had shared with Thanasis on Saturday night, the room she had avoided.

Just as she grabbed an empty glass on the bedside table, the sudden ringing of the telephone in the hallway startled her. The tumbler fell from her hands and struck the metal leg of the table. Stepping over broken shards, she ran for the phone.

"Koukla?" It was Thanasis. His voice sounded raspy and distant.

Kate held her breath. Then her words spilled out. "Thanasi. Where are you? I've been sick with worry. Why did you leave—" Relief and anger battled against each other.

"Kaitie, I am very sorry. Believe me. I am sorry. I want the— the . . . opportunity to tell it all to you. But I cannot say more now. You will meet me Friday night?"

"You can't just expect me to—"

"Come to the old part of the city. Ten o'clock? The Hotel Oneiro. *Oneiro.* Like 'Dream.' Please?"

"But Thanasi—"

Again, he crowded her out. "Please, Kaitie?" His pleading words pressed.

"I don't know. I don't—"

There was a finality in his voice. "I must go. I wait for you Friday."

And he was gone before she could give an answer. Only the steady buzz on the phone line remained. Kate replaced the phone on its cradle and somehow found herself on the balcony. The chair usually occupied by Thanasis was empty, colored by flashes of light from the circling Ferris wheel in Luna Park. Hearing Thanasis's voice again had amplified his absence, opening a deep cavern in her chest. Small fires of anger still burned, but a rush of relief spread inside her that he was safe or presumably safe.

Kate wavered. Stuck in both emptiness and chaos. Finally, she spoke to herself aloud. "I've got to see this through." She considered talking to Georyia or Lena and Yiannis, but she shook her head. *No. This is your story—yours and Thanasis's. Nobody else knows what has happened between you—they can't help. It's yours to deal with, Kate. You can and you will.* Coming to that conclusion brought a momentary stirring of strength, which was just as quickly replaced by uncertainty.

Kate thought back to early September, eight months before. Her decision to come to Greece alone, in a time of turmoil in this country, was either an act of bravery or foolhardiness. But she had pushed forward and come. Now, she was again faced with decision that echoed a similar risk. Thanasis was no longer the person she had thought he was. *But who is he? My lover? Someone not to be trusted?* Perhaps both.

The lights of Luna Park began to dim. Bumper cars raced and collided in one last round before the park shut down. A few minutes passed. Her decision was set. She would play this out. She must. Kate watched the riders climb out of their tiny vehicles and head toward the street as darkness smothered the scene.

forty-five ✧

On Friday evening, the taxi careened along the curving road beside the ramparts of the Kastra, topped by battlements from the Byzantine era. In the semidarkness, the ancient walls were like an imaginary backdrop, adding to the surreal nature of the evening and the past few days. The Kastra was where Kate had come on her first date with Thanasis. As the taxi climbed higher and higher, the city below became a distant sprinkling of lights. Bouzouki music whined from the radio.

They entered the village, driving past the taverna where Kate and Thanasis had dined in the winter. Tonight, the tables were set outside underneath crisscrossed strings of lights and teemed with diners. How Kate wished she and Thanasis were among them, nestled together, clinking retsina glasses, sharing a meal and the magic that had been their lives these past few months. She steeled herself against those tender memories, at the same time hoping to recapture the life they'd once shared.

The noise of the busy square faded as the taxi left the village behind and moved into the darkness of less populated streets. The glass of retsina before leaving the apartment had helped Kate when she first got into the taxi, but now, twenty minutes later, her courage was failing. She could tell the taxi driver she'd changed her mind.

"Etho?" The taxi driver signaled they had arrived. Kate shoved away her doubts and reached into her bag. As soon as she passed him the paper drachmas and climbed out, he sped away before Kate could ask him to wait. His red taillights disappeared around the corner.

The hotel was on the outskirts of the village. The area was completely dark and quiet, save the pounding beats and flashing lights of an outdoor discotheque farther down the street.

The Hotel Oneiro was an older, three-story building with missing shutters. A naked light bulb lit the entrance, revealing a sign with the name Oneiro painted in blue letters surrounded by a cloud to illustrate a dream. She hesitated. *What on earth have I gotten myself into?*

Shifting the purse on her shoulder, Kate's resolve wavered like a wobbly tower made of cards. She wanted to believe Thanasis would be able to explain everything, and they could go back to their life together before all of this happened. Hoping her optimism was justified, she grabbed the strap of her purse even more tightly, took a deep breath, and ventured forward.

Kate tried the heavy wooden door, but it would not budge. She stepped back and pushed again. Frustration momentarily overcame her fear, and she kicked hard against the bottom part of the door, causing it to release and fly open. The door banged loudly against the wall. A harsh voice from somewhere on the first floor bellowed obscenities. Then she heard another voice.

"Koukla?"

A pair of bare feet appeared on a wooden stairway. Then the jeans. The small waist. The partially unbuttoned shirt. The broad shoulders. The dark beard. The beautifully sculpted face framed by curls. And the kindness of his eyes that she recognized even in the shadows. Her heartbeat quickened as she watched him approach. He lifted his arms in her direction, an invitation for an embrace. Kate backed away. As he came toward her, she pushed him away. Her voice wrenched from her throat. "What the hell is going on, for God's sake?"

He motioned for quiet holding up one hand, his fingers gently touching her lips with the other. Kate yielded as the warmth of his arm gently reached around her back. He guided her up the small wooden stairway to the second floor, and she remembered how it was to be in tandem with him, walking along the promenade next to the sea or in city crowds. A scant hint of relief with that familiarity battled her sense of apprehension. They moved farther into the darkness of the hotel. Rooms they passed showed no sign of activity. Light came from an open doorway at the end of the hall.

Kate hesitated at the entrance. Once inside she was surprised to find a spacious living room, well-furnished with a large black leather couch, chairs, and a glass table. A small kitchenette was off to one side. The couch sat in the middle of the room, and beside it was a serpentine wrought iron lamp with a fringed lightshade. Brightly colored pillows of reds and yellows were arranged on the sofa, and a decorative blanket was thrown over the back. On the table a bottle of retsina and two glasses waited.

Thanasis shut the door behind her. Ignoring his gentle nudge on her back, Kate hovered near the door. He walked past her to the couch, settling himself and motioning her to join him. Kate continued standing. "What is this all about?"

"Please, Kaitie. Please sit." He gestured again, his familiar smile imploring her. "Koukla. I am very sorry."

Kate relented, slowly approaching him, and perched herself on the edge of the couch at the other end. "Sorry? That's it?" She glared at him. As she waited for a response, Kate sensed a slight quivering of her lips she was unable to control.

His voice was subdued. "I did not want to leave you at Langathas. Please know that. My friend followed me to the ceremony to remind me of my obligation."

"What obligation?" Kate shook her head back and forth.

"No details. I cannot. But I want to say that sometimes we have to make ourselves do a small bad thing for a greater good."

"Is this about politics?" She spit the last word out like it was a piece of bitter fruit. The tiny hint of affection a few moments earlier disappeared.

"Politics? You Americans—"

"'You Americans?' Since when did I become just an American? Where are we? What is this place?" Kate's voice filled with anger.

"So, you do not feel comfortable being called an American?" A slight edge of bitterness invaded his tone. "Is that not what you are?"

He was correct. Despite her recent experiences, which had made her want to run away from that fact, she could not. Kate wasn't sure how to answer. She sat in silence, anxiety and confusion circling inside. She searched his face for a clue, something familiar. His tender eyes were at odds with his mouth, now set in a grim frown.

He nodded toward the table. "Please—have something to drink with me. Greek hospitality." Thanasis deftly uncorked the retsina and filled the two small glasses, handing one to her.

Without taking a sip, Kate placed the glass back on the table. The situation didn't feel safe for a drink.

"You are right. I am obliged to tell you where we are. You know my brother, Kostas, who lives in Montreal? This is one of his places.

He likes to stay here when he comes back to Greece. He has visitors here other than his wife, if you understand what I am saying." Thanasis moved slightly closer. He lit a cigarette. She shook her head to refuse his offer of one to her.

"You saw the Fire Walkers in Langathas. Like them, sometimes we have to go places that we would not go in our daily lives unless there is . . . say . . . a larger purpose? I apologize for the . . . inconvenience that I may have caused you."

"Inconvenience?" She heard her voice rising. "Thanasi, do you know what you did? How frightened I was? You left me stranded, with no warning, in a small village in a country that is beginning to feel stranger to me by the hour."

"Strange? Of course. It was just a question of when the tourism would fade." He parked his cigarette in the ashtray, putting both hands on his thighs and facing her.

"Tourism?" Her voice trembled. "What are you talking about?" She found his eyes. "Thanasi, I was hoping that you would—that you could explain all of this craziness to me, but I see I was wrong."

She grabbed her bag and headed for the door. It was then she felt the firm grip on her arm. "Let go." Her voice was steel. "Let me go right now!"

Instead of releasing her, he guided Kate back toward the couch, positioning himself between her and the direction of the door. His grip was too strong to break. "That is not possible. You see, I . . . we need your help." It was as though she was suspended in mid-air. *Is this really happening?*

"Stop! You're hurting my arm. What's wrong with you?"

Releasing his grasp, Thanasis gently rubbed her arm, reminding her of moments of tenderness before this horrible evening.

Kate closed her eyes. She still had one last hope there could be an explanation to this whole thing and she could go back to being lost inside his kisses and getting even more lost making love with him.

Kate wanted to give him a chance to explain, as she struggled to understand what had happened to the lover who had captured her heart. She wanted to feel safe with him again. Tears gathered in her eyes.

Reluctantly, she sat back down on the couch. Thanasis scooted closer, his leg touching hers. The sensation of his body beside her, even now, only added to her terrible confusion. They sat together in silence. He then moved a short distance away to pick up his unfinished cigarette, taking a long drag. Smoke hung in the air.

"Koukla, you must understand I did not start out with the idea of hurting you." He stubbed his cigarette in the ashtray. "I did not know how much I would love you." His voice faded with those last words. His fingers twisted the cigarette, long beyond the point of extinguishing.

"Love me? If you love me, why are you doing this to me?"

Thanasis reached and stroked her cheek gently with his thumb. He opened his mouth to speak, then closed it. Finally, he said, "I did not know my friends would ask me to get help from you. And that I could not say no to them."

"Say no to them for what? When did this happen?" Her voice shook. "Were you using me from the start?"

"No, my Kaitie. Long after we met, I was approached about the importance of my American girlfriend." He hesitated before again raising his eyes to find hers. "I will not tell you anything except that we need an American passport. We need your passport."

His words chilled her. A sudden current of fear replaced the soft feelings his touch had resurrected.

"I tried to find another way but could not." His gaze lingered for a few seconds.

It was now clear, illuminated just the way fireworks light up the nighttime sky. This was no longer a romantic adventure novel. This was real. This was dangerous.

Kate was startled by the jangle of a telephone ringing. Moving to the kitchenette, Thanasis reached for a phone on the counter and pulled the handset back to the couch. He was now at the far end, away from her. The cord swayed in the air with his actions.

"Ela." Thanasis made contact with someone on the other end of the line. She heard a rapid string of words from a male voice and watched Thanasis nod his head, momentarily distracted. Her thoughts raced. *Who's on the other end? Is someone else coming? Will they take me back to my apartment and make me hand over my passport?* Frantically, she looked around the room. The door was the only way out. Kate didn't remember him locking it when they came in. She desperately hoped she was right. Then her eye caught his cigarette lighter on the table.

From the other end of the couch, Kate reached for his cigarettes and the lighter. Thanasis noticed, assuming she was getting ready to smoke. He nodded his head before resuming the call. The voice at the other end of the line grew louder. Thanasis tried to interject but was cut off. There seemed to be some disagreement about what to do next. He turned his back fully to her, gesturing with his free hand to make a point.

This was her chance. Kate brought the cigarette to her mouth, pretending to light it. He half-glanced in her direction and shifted away once more. Carefully drawing the lighter alongside her body and beside her shoulder, she reached toward the fringe of the lampshade. For a fleeting moment, it was as though her hand belonged to someone else. Although in an awkward position, she was able to catch a spark on the first try. The flame jumped to the hanging tassels, igniting them instantly. Kate bolted upright and rushed around her end of the couch.

"Kaitie!" Thanasis yelled, seeing the fire. He grabbed in her direction, but she was out of reach. In the process, his arm knocked the lamp over into the pile of pillows. He screamed, then tried to smother the flames with the blanket. She bounded for the door and grabbed the doorknob. It released. Flying down the hall, she ran away from his cries.

Kate stumbled down the stairs, her feet slipping on the treads as she struggled to keep her balance. She shoved open the outside door, escaping into the night air and ran the few blocks toward the discotheque and the line of taxis waiting out front. Only when her hand closed around the metal door handle of the taxi did she glance back at the hotel. The street was empty.

Kate slid into the back seat, breath still coming in gasps. "Parakalo—grigora!" Kate urged the driver to please hurry, then blurted out her apartment address. The taxi driver punched the meter and glowing numbers appeared. Squeezing her eyes shut as they drove off, Kate kept herself from looking back. The taxi sped toward the scattered lights of Thessaloniki down below.

forty-six 🌿

The driver let her off on busy Queen Olga Street and rushed off for more fares. Kate hurried to the entrance of 84-B, unlocked it, and pulled shut the lobby's heavy glass door. The elevator was waiting, but the mirror inside dealt an unwelcome shock. Lines from tears trailed black mascara down her cheeks. It was her eyes, however, that made her catch her breath. Blank. Empty. She placed her back to the mirror and pressed the number five.

The motor engaged, the sound like the groan of an ancient animal distracted from slumber and reluctantly pushing upward away from the earth. In the small, enclosed space, another reminder of the terror of the evening made itself a passenger on the elevator. It was the smoke, the smell of it in her clothes, faint but distinctly there.

She exited the elevator with her key in hand. Even as Kate pressed it into the lock on her front door, her shoulders sank as she allowed herself to begin to relax. She was home, or at least she was in her home in Greece. Going from room to room, Kate switched on lights and checked the locks of the three balcony doors. Momentarily assured of her safety, she rushed to her bedroom, jerked open the desk drawer, and grabbed her passport, lying where she had last left it. She exhaled an audible sigh of relief.

Sitting on the bottom bunk bed, she opened the small booklet.

Her sunshine-bright smile came from her picture. It seemed like years ago rather than just nine months when she sat on the round stool, posing in the photographer's studio across from the courthouse in her hometown.

Fear gripped her throat. *What could they have wanted this for?* Studying the front of her passport, the words The United States of America jumped out. She thought of the most obvious symbols of her country in Greece—the consulate in Thessaloniki and the Embassy in Athens. *Are his friends trying to get into one of those buildings?*

Kate's finger rubbed across the imprint on the front as her eyes wandered around the room, searching for a hiding spot. Beside the bed was a bookcase with sliding doors on the bottom, where Aris and Soto had left a stash of their comic books. Squatting next to it, she slid open one side and took out the collection. Kate thumbed through until she found it. *Yes—this one.*

On the cover of the comic book a smiling cowboy with a large white hat lounged on the back of his horse. It was Lucky Luke, the popular European comic book hero created by a Belgian cartoonist. Kate had been surprised at the huge popularity of cowboys in this part of the world. Connecting with her own Wild West heritage gave her a momentary jolt of confidence. Kate slipped her passport between the pages, placed it in the middle of the stack, and slid the doors shut.

In the bathroom, she washed the smeared makeup from her face, not bothering to brush her teeth. Kate walked back to her bedroom with the lifeless tread of a zombie. She kicked off her shoes and stripped away her dress. Switching off her bedside light and closing her eyes, Kate strained to push away thoughts of

Thanasis and this country. She needed to clear her mind. There was a process she'd devised right after Jim had left. It was the only way she had been able to stop her uncontrolled sobbing when she realized their marriage was over.

Even though her body shook underneath the sheets, Kate made herself go back in her mind to the Palace Theater, the movie house in her hometown. First, she visualized a hand holding a white cloth and wiping the top of the display counter in the snack bar off the lobby. Small circles started at the left end of the case and continued polishing the glass. Gradually, each box of treats on the shelf down below came into view: Slo Pokes, Cherry Mashes, Charms lollipops, Big Hunks, and Black Licorice Nibs with palm trees and a camel on the box. To the right at the end of the case, the rhythmical rain of popcorn flew out and blanketed layer after layer of soft white slopes inside the glass box.

Her feet followed pale green linoleum squares that met the lobby carpet with its pattern of oversized green leaves on a maroon background. A set of heavy swinging doors led into the first layer of darkness. On the right, she passed a water fountain with a wad of pink gum resting on the drain.

Rather than going left to the ladies restroom and its graffiti walls of thick red lipstick names and messages, she headed into the darkened theater. Bouncing images on the screen played to rows of empty seats. Murals on both side walls displayed scenes of West Texas history. On one side, Coronado and his Spanish conquistadors peered over yucca plants, surveying the barren landscape. On the other side, cowboys sat on horseback, ready to lasso a calf just out of reach, with a real rope affixed to the wall. Kate found a seat near the back. Her eyes watched conjured scenes from her favorite movies on the screen. But rather than drifting off to sleep as had been her habit, Kate saw the handsome face and the sad eyes. Thanasis. In her mind the screen behind his head filled with flames, and she again heard the wail of his scream.

Kate's eyes opened and were met by the darkness of the top bunk overhead. Her breath came in short bursts. She tried to place herself again at the snack bar off the lobby and imagine the pungent smell of buttered popcorn. She reached out to feel the cool edge of the glass case and then walk toward the heavy swinging doors. This time, however, as she reentered the darkness of the theater, she found herself in the hallway at the Hotel Oneiro. Kate wrapped her arms around herself and rocked from one side to another.

When sleep did come, it was restless. In one dream fragment, the handsome cowboy actor Audie Murphy rode his horse across an expanse of land toward a castle with battlements. Blue-and-white Greek flags flapped against the sky.

forty-seven 🌿

Kate jerked awake to sunlight peeking through the shutters from the balcony. The fitful night was finally over. Images of the previous evening with Thanasis burst into her mind. The steely grip of his hand on her arm. The sound of his cries as he battled the fire she had caused. Kate buried her face in her pillow, stifling sobs of despair. Waves of emotion gradually slowed before finally subsiding.

Sitting upright, she surveyed the room. Except for her dress puddled on the floor, everything appeared the same as the past several months, when she would first unlatch the glass doors and then pull a cord to raise a slatted window shade to welcome the new day. But things weren't the same. Inside the cabinet and buried within the stacks of comic books was her passport, safely protected in the land of Lucky Luke. What had once been her ticket to adventure now made her a target. After a few moments, she forced herself to follow the routine of opening up her room and stepping out onto the balcony.

Figures moved along the promenade beside the bay. From her earliest days in Thessaloniki, walking beside the water had been a salve to her soul when she was homesick, never failing to bring a sense of peace. *Do I dare leave my apartment and give myself the gift of a walk today? There'll be lots of people there. I'll be safe.* The thought instantly changed when she noticed the purples and blues of a bruise forming on her arm where Thanasis had grabbed her. *I can't go out. What if some of* them *are waiting for me outside the apartment?* It was still impossible to think Thanasis would allow any actual harm to come to her. But, then again, the impossible had already happened.

Kate sat again on the bed, leaning forward and putting her head in her hands, caught between the security of staying in her apartment against her need to be on the sea walk. Tiny clicks from the alarm clock on her dresser filled the silence. Then, gathering strength from deep inside herself, Kate stood. "You're not keeping me in, Thanasi. No way," she said aloud, faintly heartened by the resolve she heard in her own voice. She hurriedly dressed.

There were no signs of activity in the hallway as she spied out the door. Pressing the down arrow button, she heard the elevator rumble to the fifth floor. When it arrived, she glanced through the small window to make sure no one was there. Again, Kate avoided herself in the mirror as she descended, unwilling to confront her hollowness inside.

The lobby was empty. Cautiously, she slipped out the door of 84-B and glanced in both directions before choosing a small byway to the left rather than busy Queen Olga Street. The neighboring fish taverna, Mimi, on the corner, was closed after a busy Friday night of dining and bouzouki music. She stepped around a stream as a boy poured water from a bucket to sweep the sidewalk clean. The neighborhood vegetable vendor's back was to her as he busily arranged rows of peppers and tomatoes in his storefront. Nothing on this familiar street was out of the ordinary.

Reaching the gray expanse of the sea walk, Kate reflexively

scanned the passersby for the familiar figure of Thanasis, as she had done the many times she'd met him for a rendezvous. *How can he have changed?* Pain jabbed at her heart. Kate heaved a deep sigh and began walking.

Usually she would go right, toward the outline of buildings in the distance. Today she went in the other direction, away from the busyness of the city coming to life. She needed to focus on the solitude of the horizon, onto the openness of the bay. The sun rode the waves. In the distance, a hulking cargo freighter crept toward the open waters.

Kate tried to bring some order to her thoughts, but they were like pieces from different jigsaw puzzles dumped on the floor together. She needed to tell someone what had happened and get help. Lena and Yiannis had taken Lena's parents to their seaside home in the village of Metamorphosis. Georyia was in her hometown for the weekend. Kate's hands clenched and unclenched with her steps. The authorities were not to be trusted. She had heard enough stories about the Greek police to know that any chance to pounce on leftists would be an excuse for an extreme response. The hands of Giorgos Farsakithis gripping his glass of retsina with crippled fingers flashed into her mind.

However frightened she was by what Thanasis had done to her, she still couldn't risk what might befall him if she went to the authorities. Kate continued walking. The memory of Farsakithis circled back into her mind, tweaking something. She could go to her upstairs neighbors, Fotini and Takis. They knew the leftist political community quite well. She had faith in them.

Her rhythmical steps on the concrete had been a comfort in her first days of being alone in Thessaloniki. *"Solvitur ambulando,"* the

Latin phrase she had learned in her college classics course meaning, "It is solved by walking." This walk had provided what she hoped would lead to a solution.

Kate breathed a deep sigh of relief. For the first time in countless hours, a sense of balance returned. She was hungry, not remembering the last time she'd eaten. Since Fotini and Takis might not be up yet, Kate would grab a quick bite of breakfast in her kitchen before finding her friends. Relieved, she exhaled again, heading back to 84-B.

forty-eight

K ate approached her apartment building with caution, scanning
the scene before she unlocked the door to the lobby. Again,
she avoided the elevator mirror and kept her eyes on her sneakers as
she neared the fifth floor. Sliding the key into the lock, she was
grateful to be back safely.

Just as she shut the door to her apartment, her skin prickled. A
smell of smoke came from inside the apartment. Cigarette smoke.
Before her awareness could form a question, two strong hands
grabbed her shoulders. Kate gasped. A head came into her peripheral vision and a mouth whispered in her right ear, "Good morning,
Miss."

Stelios. His head was lodged over her shoulder. She tried to
squirm away but could not. Fear stabbed the middle of her chest.

"Stelio, please." Kate worked to keep her voice calm.

"Please, what?" There was a teasing sarcasm in his words.

"Let me go."

"Immediately." Instead, he moved her away from the door,
keeping his hands on her shoulders. His face was close, and she
smelled the tobacco on his breath.

Stelios pushed her through the doors of the library and onto the
sofa. He placed a chair for himself squarely in front of the only exit.
Her heart raced. "What are you doing here? Where's Thanasis?"

Never long without a cigarette between his slender fingers, Stelios took a fresh one from the pack and flicked his lighter. There was a quick burst of light before he maneuvered his cigarette toward the flame. His eyes were cast down, momentarily leaving her free from his stare. He surveyed the bookshelves that ran from floor to ceiling with an expression somewhere between appreciation and a smirk.

"I see you have found a very comfortable nest here in Greece." His eyes traveled around the room, again taking in Yiannis's extensive library. He then viewed her through a veil of smoke. "You asked where he is, but you did not ask after the health of your friend that you tried to roast like an Easter lamb. Is it not polite first to ask about his condition?"

Prompted by a twinge of guilt, she asked, "How is he?"

"He was injured—but he is not out of the game."

Kate remembered Thanasis's cries as she ran out of the room. "How badly?"

"His arm needed attention. Painful, but nothing to keep him in the hospital."

A small measure of relief ran through her body, but she was hesitant to ask anything else. The shock of being grabbed and pushed into the room had kept away the question of how Stelios had gotten into her apartment. He moved something back and forth in his hand. Stelios's habit of flipping and twirling worry beads.

This object, however, was too shiny for worry beads. It was Thanasis's silver key chain with a small blue amulet of an eye, meant to ward off evil. Among the keys was one to her apartment, which she'd given to him a few weeks ago. *How could he?* Like a blistering slap to the face, the word "betrayal" forced its way into her mind. Thanasis knew Kate despised his friend. *He gave the key to Stelios.*

"Magic!" Stelios bounced the key chain in his palm and smiled. He must have read her mind. Now as he stretched his long legs out in front of him and crossed his arms, he cocked his head. "Well, Miss, I wonder how your President Ford will be of help to you now."

Kate shifted her position on the couch. She remained silent, not wanting to show her fear. Instead, she focused on the fingernails on her left hand, working hard to keep her hand steady. Moments passed.

Plink! Stelios skipped the keychain across the hardwood floor to get her attention. She transferred her gaze to her right hand. Detachment was the only way she could think to counter his power over her at that moment. Kate thought about her passport buried in a stack of comic books in the next room. Maybe he'd already searched the apartment and found nothing? *That's got to be the reason he's here—to finish the job Thanasis started.* She worked to contain a rising panic.

Stelios glanced at his watch. "We have many things to discuss. But let us keep our hospitality." He stood and retrieved the keychain. Stretching his arms over his head, Stelios nodded toward the kitchen. "Coffee?"

The kitchen can't be a more dangerous place than being stuck in the library, Kate reasoned. She pushed up from the couch and quickly scooted past him. Stelios stood beside the library doors, blocking the hallway and denying access to the front entrance of her apartment.

Heading into the kitchen, she hurried to the single door leading to the small balcony off the kitchen, with its access to the quadrangle of other apartments.

"No, no, no. Not that way." Had she moved faster, she could have rushed out and perhaps yelled for Rita or a bystander—some housewife airing bedsheets—who would hear her signal of distress. But Stelios would most likely have grabbed her. The thought of his hands on her body made her recoil in fear and disgust. He directed her toward the chair between the refrigerator and the kitchen table, hemming her within a perimeter easy to guard. Since the early morning heat was beginning to permeate the apartment, he cracked ajar the balcony door for air to circulate.

Stelios opened the cupboard and found two demitasse cups and the canister of coffee. With movements echoing those of Thanasis, he measured fine brown powder into the small one-handled coffeepot, added water, lit the gas ring, and began stirring and waiting for the coffee to boil almost to the top. He poured the bubbling hot coffee into one of the cups. Stelios repeated the process a second time and brought both cups to the table. Another canister on the counter caught his eye. It was coconut macaroons her mother had sent for her birthday. Stelios helped himself. She watched him smile in approval and nod his head as he crunched into the sweetness.

If I had a gun right now. Kate shocked herself with this thought, but she was desperate. She was a prisoner in her own apartment, trapped in a country where the letters on signs were curved and twisted. Where a person who was a tender lover one evening could become an enemy the next.

Kate readied herself to force the issue. "What do you want?"

Ignoring the question, he pushed back from the table and shook a cigarette out of the package in her direction. Kate took it, figuring she could buy more time. She moved her head away as quickly as she could after Stelios neared with his lighter. Playing the end of the cigarette back and forth on her lip, Kate steadied herself as her thoughts raced. She waited for what he would say next.

Brrring. Brrring. The ringing of the gray telephone in the hallway next to the kitchen made her jump with surprise, just as when she'd first moved into the apartment. She was dropped back in time, into those first days and nights in Greece with their scrambled emotions.

Brrring. Brrring. Stelios clicked his tongue against the roof of his mouth as he lifted his chin up in the quintessential Greek expression of "no." The ringing persisted, then finally stopped. Stelios dropped his cigarette into the mud left at the bottom of his coffee cup.

"Miss America. Coming to poor little Greece to give us help," Stelios whispered with his head down as he tapped the lighter onto the table. "And did not your CIA come to the aid of poor little Greece, to keep us on the side of America and in the fold like good sheep? Did not your CIA help the colonels to keep their feet stepped on our necks?" His voice grew louder. "Did not your CIA make possible the killing of the students at the Polytechnio? Do we not have a right to make America pay for the death and tearing down of our country?" Stelios's voice was now a shout.

Kate shook from his outburst. Her fingers trembled as she guided her cigarette back to the ashtray. *But that wasn't my fault!* she thought but was too afraid to say aloud. The Polytechnio had been Georyia's first guess.

The images had haunted Kate. The grainy footage now played in her mind again. The tank ramming through the gate of the university while students stood on top of the walls and waved Greek flags. The murder of the students. The vivid description of torture from those imprisoned. Kate now understood even more clearly the fury at America, but she could never justify paying back violence with more violence, as Stelios suggested. It would be wrong, very wrong.

Kate shifted in her chair. This kitchen had, over the months, become her reading room during breakfast, and the place where she attempted some of Lena's recipes, like her favorite green beans with tomatoes. Now the room transformed into something ominous. Stelios had invaded her private space and she was his hostage. *If it's my passport he wants, why not make me give it to him now?*

A new fear inserted itself. She remembered his hand riding her back, his lips staying too long on her cheeks, all in the presence of Thanasis. Now it was just the two of them. Alone. He had long muscular arms under his shirtsleeves. *Can I defend myself?* His eyes pinned her. Her breath caught. She was afraid. She steadied her fingers to grind the cigarette into the ashtray.

Kate glanced down the hallway. "I need to go to the toilet."

Stelios got up, making room for her to pass, then followed her. His presence was a menacing shadow. Outside the door, he signaled for her to wait. Keeping her in his line of vision, Stelios knelt in front of the bathroom door and broke the wooden match he'd taken from the kitchen, sticking it in the key cylinder of the lock. He was making sure she couldn't lock herself in. "Please. You may take your time."

As she closed the door, she heard Stelios dialing the phone in the hall and speaking to someone. Curious, Kate cracked open a space to peer through. Stelios's arm gestured wildly in the air as his voice became louder. His anger unnerved her, reinforcing the notion she had to do something. Kate took in a deep breath and let it push out through her lips. After hurriedly using the toilet, she washed her hands, watching the soapy water swirl around the white basin and disappear into the drain. She reached for the towel.

The seriousness of her expression in the mirror elicited the image of her grandmother. The look on Kate's face was one she'd seen many times from that beloved woman, like when it was time to catch a chicken in her backyard and wring its neck for a chicken and dumplings dinner. A cowgirl raised in the wilds of the Texas plains, her grandmother strode everywhere with fierce pride and always did what had to be done, no matter how hard.

"What would you do, Gran?" she whispered. Something shifted. Kate had come from tough stock, and she would, at this moment, call on that toughness. Her eyes now stared back with a new determination. She would fight Stelios, and she knew exactly how.

Folding the towel and placing it on the silver rack, Kate fluffed her hair with her fingers. She practiced what she hoped would be a seductive expression. She was chilled by the thought of what she must do next, but she could think of no other way. Her protective older brother had taught her how to defend herself if the occasion arose. And it had. Kate was ready.

Stelios stood in the hallway staring at the phone, stroking the straggly remnants of beard on his chin, a confused expression on his face.

Kate approached him slowly. "Problem?" she asked with a gentle voice.

He didn't respond but rather glanced at the phone again with confusion. Kate forced herself to keep moving toward him, pasting a smile on her face. Her hand reached out to his shoulder. He showed surprise. Kate began to rub small circles, working her way down his arm.

"Stelio—I know that for some time you have wanted me." She tried to read how he was responding to her advances. He didn't move away. Kate anchored her body directly in front of him and moved closer, nuzzling her head on his chest, under his chin. She made sure her back was in the direction of the kitchen, necessary to make her plan work. He relaxed and molded himself into her. It was all she could do not to be repulsed by the feel of his body and the acrid tang of his armpits. Kate steadied her balance. With one swift motion she pulled her knee up and aimed it directly at his groin, making contact.

Stelios bent over in pain.

Not losing a moment, Kate ran into the kitchen and made her way outside. She vaulted over the railing to Rita's balcony, kicking over a pot of red geraniums in the process. Furiously, she pounded on the glass door, "Rita—Rita!" Peering through the gauzy kitchen curtain into the kitchen, there was no shadow of a figure responding to her knocking.

Kate kept watch on her own kitchen door while continuing to pound her fist, fearful that at any moment Stelios would appear and drag her back inside. She scanned the quadrangle of apartments, but there was little movement, only the retreating back of a woman on an opposite balcony who had finished hanging her laundry. The scene was eerily quiet, quiet enough for her to hear the sound of her own front door slamming shut.

Was that Stelios? Did he just leave? Kate waited, trying to piece together what had just happened. *The phone call—what was it about? Am I safe or will he come back?* Several minutes passed without hearing any noise from inside. Slowly, she stepped over the railing, back into her kitchen and into the hallway. There was no sound. There was no movement.

The chair in the library sat alone in the middle of the room. Had Stelios really gone? After checking both bedrooms and making sure he was nowhere in the apartment, she wedged a chair under the front doorknob. Kate rushed to the bookcase in her room. Reaching into the stack of comics, she let her breath release in one great sigh. Her passport was still there. *Why did Stelios leave?* She fought back the urge to curl up on the floor and sob. Instead, she ran out of the room.

Heart racing, Kate opened the door to the hallway. Everything was quiet. She bounded up the open stairwell to Fotini's apartment. The descending maze of stairs to the bottom floor met her with silent emptiness. She rang Fotini's doorbell. Its buzzer echoed inside. Footsteps did not. *Of course. Saturday with beautiful weather. They've probably gone out of the city.* Lena and Yiannis wouldn't be back until tomorrow. Georyia was away. Kate was on her own.

Gripping the handrail, she went back down the stairs. The key slipped out of her shaking fingers. Just as she bent to retrieve it, Kate had a frightening thought. The key. Stelios still had her key.

forty-nine 🌿

O nce back inside her apartment, Kate again wedged the chair against the front door and headed to the kitchen. Propelled by frenetic energy, she dumped remains from the coffee cups and ashtrays in the trash and worked to scrub away any trace of Stelios's visit. She righted Rita's geraniums, swept up the spilled dirt, then headed to the library to move Stelios's chair back to its rightful place.

As the momentum drained from her body, Kate went to her usual seat on the balcony.

Thanasis's chair was empty. She imagined him stretched out with a morning coffee, cigarette smoke drifting from the ashtray, carefully explaining his vision for Greece and for the world. Kate had loved getting lost with him in his dreams. *He's gone, Kate. That other Thanasis is gone.* She sat. Lost. Watching the scenes below.

Since it was Saturday, fewer people populated the sidewalks, moving, like the traffic, at a more leisurely pace. Housewives carried their market purchases soon to be transformed into a delicious lunch before a lazy afternoon siesta. Lives following the security of a routine. Lives that had not been completely overturned, as hers had. Kate picked up her key up from the table and turned it over and over, bringing herself back to the problem at hand.

The shape of the key reminded her of the locksmith's shop she passed daily on her way to work. Kate grabbed her purse and left. Except for aromas of cooking that wafted up the stairwell, there were no other signs of life in the building. The elevator descended. Guardedly, she looked out to make sure no one was around. Kate pushed open the heavy glass of the front entrance. Again, she scanned in both directions and headed down Queen Olga Street with rapid footsteps.

"Be open. Be open," she whispered.

A bell tinkled as she walked through the door of the locksmith shop. "Parakalo." Kate started, then went on to explain she wanted to change the lock on her door. The elderly man with snow-white hair wrote a figure on a piece of paper.

Her hands trembled. He shook his head from side to side, a compassionate smile spreading across his face. *"Meen stenahoriese paithi mou,"* telling her not to worry and calling her his child, a frequently used term of affection, adding that it was only a lock.

Kate wrote the address, paid him, and arranged for the new lock to be installed that afternoon. She started back to the apartment with quick strides, sneaking peeks around every few steps. People and buildings began to blur. The enormity of all that had happened the night before and this morning caused her heart to pound. Kate didn't know whether she could make it back to her apartment. She moved out of the stream of pedestrians toward the side of a building, propping herself against a wall and stood still. Moments passed. Then, visualizing her grandmother's bustling pace, Kate worked to recreate those same movements and willed herself forward.

Once more she went through the agonizing process of coming back to 84-B and to her apartment, reliving the fear of Stelios's surprise greeting in the front hallway. As she walked past the telephone, Kate wished she knew how to contact Lena and Yiannis in Metamorphosis, but she'd never thought to ask for the number. When they returned from their weekend, Kate would call and tell them the whole story. She was certain they would understand the need to change the lock.

Kate stretched out on her bed and drifted off to sleep, only to be shocked awake by the door buzzer from downstairs. Dizzy and disoriented, she located the intercom panel. Her breathing was in rapid, shallow bursts, but she calmed enough to ask for identification. Satisfied with the explanation by the tenor voice of a young male who gave the name of the key shop, Kate buzzed him in and waited for him at the peephole of her apartment door. She recognized the light-blue vest often worn by workmen and opened the door.

The polite young man did his work quickly, checking twice to make sure the fit was perfect. After he left, Kate went to the kitchen and patched together a meal of bread, cheese, and cold green beans she'd made earlier in the week.

Evening finally came. One more time Kate wedged a chair against the front door as an added precaution. It was unnecessary, she knew, but it would help her sleep more easily. As Kate settled in her usual place on the balcony, a space that had become her sanctuary, tears made the slow trip down her cheeks. So much in her apartment and in the last several months of her life was imbued with Thanasis. Again and again, she tried understanding what had happened to him. *How could he have transformed from a loving presence into something this unrecognizable? He gave his key to Stelios. He left me vulnerable with that monster.* There was so much she couldn't fathom.

Watching the playful reveling at Luna Park, Kate speculated on the coming days. There were only a few weeks left before ELEPAAP closed for the summer. She could count on Lena, Yiannis, and Georyia for steady support. Kate would find a way to stay in Greece until then. To tough it out. Leaving the children and her friends before the end of the year was not an option. Something she would not do. Even after all of this.

fifty ✿

The next Saturday afternoon, Kate watched Lena move about the kitchen, struck anew by the natural beauty of her friend—olive complexion, dark hair tied back, eyes deep with a calm and certain wisdom. Lena divided a mound of dough into eight small balls and set them in a row. Sprinkling flour onto the patterned oilcloth on the table, she reached for a long, thin dowel. The process of rolling out filo dough had begun.

On the stove, slices of leeks wilted in olive oil. Kate remembered one of her first days in the kitchen when Lena had pulled a large tin from underneath the cabinet and announced, "Our own—from last season's crop of olives." She had poured thick golden olive oil through a funnel into a smaller bottle with a spout for easier handling during cooking.

Later that day, Lena had opened a door downstairs in the storeroom to show Kate large jugs of oil and vats of olives soaking in brine, alongside bags of almonds and pistachios, all products of their farm. And now she watched Lena add another splash of oil to the pan. The constant presence of olive oil in daily life had now become routine for Kate.

"Katina, Katina." Lena shook her head, her voice tinged with sadness. This was a departure from her usual stoic approach to life, both for herself and others. Kate assumed Lena's attitude was the result of raising a disabled child in a country where such children were often hidden away. But today that stance was softened. Lena stopped rolling the dowel and watched Kate reach for a paper napkin to dab her eyes. Her hopes of recounting the story to Lena without tears had failed.

"*Then xero. Then xero.*" Kate had used the phrase "I don't know" too many times over the past few days.

The previous Sunday evening when she knew they were home from Metamorphosis, Kate called Lena and Yiannis to tell them about Thanasis and Stelios and changing the lock. On Monday, Lena made a special trip to ELEPAAP to check on her. Georyia had been updated over lunch at the end of the school day.

The remainder of the week passed without incident, as Kate stayed close to home except for work and private lessons. Walking in crowds and coming back to her building were times of high alert, followed by anxiety each time she entered the apartment. Evenings were spent alone, with meals on the balcony and her emotions awash with worries and disappointments. Mostly Kate kept asking, *Why? Why? Why?*

Now she struggled to find a smile from somewhere inside. Kate had been nicknamed "Sunshine" by a high school boyfriend because of her cheery disposition. It seemed like lifetimes ago.

Lena straightened and pursed her lips before leaning over the table to continue expanding the first mound of dough. The ball became thinner and thinner with each stroke of the dowel, growing wide on the table. Lena carefully lifted the almost translucent layer of dough and draped it inside a large pan, slathering it with oil. The fragrance from the leeks and heat from the oven enveloped Kate in a comfort and a security that had been lost to her this past week. As she watched Lena's familiar cooking rituals, Kate relaxed into the chair.

Lena spoke as she worked. "I did not see this happening. I know that students are getting more and more troubled. But I did not believe Thanasis would go to this extreme. If that is what happened."

Several weeks before, Kate had brought Thanasis to meet Lena, Yiannis, and the boys. On the backyard lawn, she'd watched the tenderness with which Thanasis played soccer with Soto. His kicks to Soto as goalie were perfectly timed for the boy to scoop up the ball to save a goal. Perhaps Lena was remembering the visit as well.

"*Kalo paithi.*" Lena frowned, acknowledging that Thanasis seemed a "good kid," the quintessential phrase no matter what a person's age.

Since Kate's arrival in September, Lena had played the role of both friend and parent. Although only a few years her senior, Lena had steered Kate with authority through all her early decisions. And now she was trying to help again.

"We do not want you to leave us." She moved to the second ball of dough and briskly rolled the dowel in different directions, making another circle spread on the table. "I hope there is a way we can make you feel comfortable again."

Kate bit down on her thumbnail before responding. "The apartment feels safer since I got the lock changed, and I mostly take the bus back and forth from work and my private lessons. I don't go into the city or on the sea walk." Her new routines had brought a measure of security, but she had no joy in her life. "I don't know, Lena. Maybe if I go back home and spend the summer with my family, I'll be able to figure it out."

Lena kept her concentration on the filo while asking, "And Thanasis?"

"The phone rings at night, and I think it's probably him." Each evening sitting on the balcony, she listened to the echoes of ring after ring from the hallway. "I don't answer it. I know it's not my parents since I already called them to say I was coming back home for the summer."

Her mother had answered with barking dachshunds in the background. It had almost broken the dam of pent-up emotions. Kate would wait until she got home to tell them as much of the story as she would decide to share. "I thought Thanasis might try to come to my apartment, but luckily, he hasn't. He may be ashamed. He may be still recovering from the fire. I have no idea where he is." She shifted in her chair.

Kate sipped water from the glass she held. "Oh Lena, I'm mad and hurt and . . . to be honest, I'm scared." She turned the glass around and around. "Especially after what happened in Athens with the guy from the embassy and the 17th of November group." Her voice wavered.

A week ago, an American had been assassinated on his way to work at the American Embassy and the group, which named themselves after the date of the Polytechnio incident, claimed responsibility. "I really can't imagine Thanasis would have any connection to those people." She paused, her thoughts hurtling about.

"But why my passport?" Kate continued. "Maybe for something like that here in Thessaloniki? To try to get into the consulate?" Her stomach churned as she recalled the newspaper photo of a body covered in a sheet on a road outside of Athens. Kate's *Time* magazine reported the story as an ordinary bureaucrat killed by leftist extremists, but the Greek newspapers identified him as the CIA Station Chief. Kate fought the idea that Thanasis would be involved with people who did that. *Could he really have gone that far?*

Lena again nodded her head side to side, clicking her tongue as she moved to the stove. She stirred the leek mixture, lowering her face to smell the simmering fragrance. She straightened. *"Pou pame tora?"* using the familiar Greek phrase expressing bewilderment of "Where do we go from here?" Lifting a dishtowel covering a bowl, Lena drained water from slices of feta cheese.

"Lena, have you ever been really stupid about love?" Lena's quizzical stare made Kate rephrase her question. "Had feelings that didn't make sense?" Kate stopped, hesitant to admit either to Lena or herself the feelings she still had for Thanasis.

"After all this, I can't really hate him. I don't want to believe bad things about him—that he was part of something so . . . so horrible. He was just different from anyone I've ever known. Isn't it so unbelievably ridiculous of me to still feel this way?" Kate shook her head at her own foolishness.

Lena spread another layer of filo in the pan before answering. "The heart. It is a curious part of ourselves. Especially for someone like you, I think." She considered Kate. "You have a very tender heart, Katina. It makes you love very much, but it also leaves you without protection sometimes. You came here. You loved us. We loved you. You loved Thanasis. And you were hurt." She stirred the leeks back and forth in the pan. "It is all coming from that thing that keeps beating until we close our eyes for the final time." Lena shut off the burner.

Kate gathered remnants of flour on the table with her fingers, creating a line and then making a wavy path through it. The memory of the waves at the beach in Metamorphosis returned.

October. It was the first time she had seen the Aegean close, when she had gone with the Stylianou family for a weekend outing. It was what they called *mikro kalokairi* or "little summer," when the weather warmed, possibly for the final time in autumn. She had rolled her pants legs up so she could follow Lena as they waded on the sand and into the shallows of the sea. The falling sun colored the sky in shades Kate had never thought possible. The sea washed warm on her feet as they walked on the softness of beach sand, and Kate was happy, something she hadn't been in such a long time.

Now, sitting on the kitchen chair, Kate knew her capacity for emotions had grown, stretched exponentially from joy to fear and now immense sadness. She watched Lena move across the tile floor of the kitchen. Peacocks honked from outside the window, a sound that had become as ordinary as the taste of feta Lena was crumbling into the leeks.

"Ah, Katina." She shook her head as she coaxed the last bits of feta from her fingers, wiping them against the edge of the bowl. "Now, can I ask our labor imported from America to please go to the garden and cut some dill?" Lena ran water over her fingers, wiped her hands on her apron, then lifted it to mockingly shoo her out of the kitchen.

Kate's footsteps echoed on the wooden stairway outside the kitchen. At the bottom of the stairs, she brushed the tops of basil growing in a pot, bringing her fingers to her nose to breathe in the scent. Basil in colorful pots or painted tins was everywhere in Greece, and Kate could never pass by without reaching to rub the leaves and smell the fragrance. Kate would miss the basil, her friends, and this country.

All week her decision of whether to leave Greece for good had teetered back and forth like the scale at the corner sweet shop weighing her favorite almond cookies. She needed to cut Thanasis out of her heart completely and leaving seemed the best way to make that happen. She didn't want to stay in Greece if it meant living in a prison she had to create to feel safe. Kate was becoming more certain of this with the passage of time. Perhaps tonight she would tell the Stylianou family she would not be coming back after the summer. At this moment, the scale had moved past its balance point and finally landed on one side.

In the distance, the mountains stood guard on the horizon. Mount Olympus, where the mythological Greek gods fought, deceived, and slayed one another was barely visible. Coming into this ancient land with its layers of history and civilizations, its exotic sights and tastes and smells had been like walking into a book, a book nearing an end. Kate let out a wistful sigh and walked toward the garden.

fifty-one

Georyia placed their cups of afternoon coffee on the small table in her living room. It had been exactly one month after the frightening visit from Stelios and one day after ELEPAAP closed for the summer. Already the tears were starting for both Kate and Georyia.

"Vre koritsi mou," Georyia addressed her girl. "Do not think you have finished with Greece." Her eyes conveyed a sadness her stoic smile attempted to hide.

Kate heard the words. She just wasn't sure they were true. *Will I ever come back?* Blinking away tears, Kate reached into her bag and pulled out the Christmas tin from the cookies her grandmother had sent in December. Inside Kate had wrapped earrings and a necklace Georyia often admired. "For you, my friend. It doesn't even begin to compare with everything you've given me." Kate smiled. "And there's no rule you can't come to America and see me sometime. *Ekthromi! Ekthromi!*" Kate mimicked the chanting of school children asking for an "outing." Her shout faded and the corners of her mouth trembled as she tried to maintain her smile.

Georyia replaced the earrings she was wearing with the dangling silver ovals and draped the beaded strands around her neck. She then snapped her fingers rhythmically and moved her head about, mimicking the *rebetiko* singer Sotiria Bellou, who sang "outcast" music from earlier in the century.

When first introducing the lyrics to Kate, Georyia—always the teacher—had explained the singer's words. She sang that although she was a good woman and open-hearted, she played men like she was rolling the dice. Georyia shared how Greeks often spoke of fate as a "roll of the dice." The clatter of dice on backgammon boards in coffeehouses throughout Greece was pervasive. Kate had not played Thanasis, but had he played her? Kate's trip to Greece had been a chance to test her fate. Sipping retsina with Georyia, laughing, singing, and dancing together, were times she hoped would always be sealed in her memory.

"Thank you very much, my friend." Georyia's voice faltered.

At the end-of-year party at ELEPAAP the day before, Kate had bid farewell to the staff and children. They thought she was heading back home just for the summer. Only Kate and Lena knew she was leaving for good. She shared the news with Georyia in private after the school assembly.

Gathered with children, parents, and staff in the large space on the second floor, Kate had scanned the room. Demetris sat in his special chair with his classmates rather than in his mother's lap. His mouth moved, attempting to join in with a few words of songs whenever he could. Giorgos was smiling, his arm fixed over the shoulder of his best friend, Lakis. The communication boards had become more complex, and he used them at times, but Giorgos's own invented gestures were still his easiest way to interact.

Soto, tender-hearted Soto, tried to join in the singing, but the emotions of the final day of school overtook him. One fist was stuck in front of his chest, the other arm straight down at his side, his head pulled to the left and his lips also tugged in that direction. Soto had made significant progress in Kate's room. He could articulate longer sentences more clearly in front of the mirror. Would he ever be able to replicate this clearer speech outside of a therapy room? She had her doubts.

Working hard to keep her own emotions in check, Kate stood at the back of the room and watched Georyia direct the children in one song about a beautiful butterfly and another about a clever fox. The diminutive and adored teacher presented awards to the children. Each one received a special commendation for their progress or simply their efforts. Kate had so loved this group of children and adults and this shabby old building. She hoped she had made some difference in a few lives.

Now, in this last visit to Georyia's apartment, she let her suppressed emotions flow freely. Together they reminisced over their times together, laughing through their coffee and a few rounds of cigarettes. Georyia's lips curved to the right as she blew cigarette smoke off to the side. Her eyes widened as she mischievously asked, "Do you remember when we went shopping for the gray coat and your package got stuck in the door of the bus and you kept shouting, '*Ta rouha mou*'?"

Kate brightened. "I thought I was saying 'My clothes'—and you told me I was really saying 'I have my period.' I couldn't figure out why everyone on the bus was smiling at me." Their giggling was cathartic, from the Greek *katharsis* or "to cleanse." There was a magnitude of sorrow within Kate that needed to be washed away.

Finally, the topic of Thanasis came up. "Kaitie, I feel . . . how do I say it?"

Kate watched as Georyia struggled to find the right word.

"Regret that you met Thanasis because of my group of friends."

"Ohi, ohi," Kate told her. "It was really one of the best parts of my being here. Until it became the worst." She laughed, but it was a laugh edged in bitterness. "Georyia, you only started the adventure going forward. I fell in love with Thanasis and then he became someone I didn't know. And it ended." Her voice betrayed the emotion of a pain still fresh.

She ground her cigarette into the ceramic ashtray on the small table between them. "I wonder if I'll ever know what really happened." She paused, a tangible heaviness inside. "But that's not your fault. Not at all."

Georyia shook her head in bewilderment and blew another cloud of smoke off to the side. They sat in silence for a few moments until it was time to leave. The two women stood. Kate bent to hug her friend, this small woman who had taught her to shop and to dance, who had made her laugh and led her into the circle of friends that had changed her life.

They held each other in a long embrace without any more words. Once Kate stepped out into the hall, she turned one last time to see her friend framed in the doorway. Georyia's fingertips were on her lips then into the air as she sent a kiss in Kate's direction. Kate returned the gesture and pushed open the heavy glass door and stepped onto the sidewalk, leaving Georyia for the final time.

fifty-two 🌿

The elevator gears announced the arrival of the Stylianou family before they knocked at her apartment door. Lena had said they would stop by on their way to a vacation in the mountains. As Kate would be leaving the next day, this visit was her last chance to see them. Keeping her tears in check, she opened the door and greeted them.

"Mesa ee Amerikana! Mesa ee Amerikana!" they shouted in unison. "The American inside!" The Stylianou family marched into the front entry hall, hands raised in fists, in the style of demonstrators. Even Soto's arm snaked and wove above his head. Their words were a play on the phrase often used at protests urging Americans to get out of Greece. They were, instead, exhorting her to stay.

She hugged each one of them, remembering her first meeting. Lena, with her gracious smile and stunning beauty, running to the airport shuttle bus in her skirt with colors of the American flag. Yiannis, initially a gruff and frightening presence, who had become her cultural godfather. Soto, whose first words to her had been in English with his practiced, "hello," followed by octaves of laughter. Aris, handsome and kind, who slowed and simplified his Greek words to teach her everything she needed to know about the sport of soccer.

They stood together in the hallway. Lena began to sing the

words from a popular song, *"Tha xanartheis"* saying, "You will return." Kate hoped she would, but she also knew soon Greece would be far away.

"Katina, pou pas? Piso ston Kurio Ford? Toulahiston tha kaneis to Kappa Kappa Texas ekei?" Yiannis asked if she could really go back to President Ford, and that the least she could do was form her own chapter of the Texas Communist Party.

"Vevaios!" she assured him, then buried her face in the collar of his shirt.

He patted her back as she straightened and moved out of his embrace. "It is not too late to leave your suitcase here and come to the mountains. Special village ouzo and even maybe a pig roast?" He resurrected the memory of Christmas and the pig slaughter at the farm.

Kate's laugh was muffled from her tears. *"Allee fora,"* she promised him with the words for "next time."

As usual, Soto's emotions hijacked his head and mouth to one side, making it hard for him to say anything. Even the usually talkative Aris hunched his shoulders and said only a word or two of goodbye.

"Se agapame Katina." Lena was the last to leave, telling her, "We love you." She then thanked Kate for everything she had done for them.

"Ohi, Lena. Ego efharisto." It was she who must thank them. They hugged one another firmly, each reluctant to let go. Though not yet a year in the making, their friendship had been deep and steadfast.

The door closed and Kate slid to the marble floor, with silent tears and the baffling question of why she had to leave.

fifty-three

The following day on the balcony, Kate scanned the scene from Queen Olga Street to the bay for a final time. Checking her watch, she ground her cigarette in the ashtray. Her plane was scheduled to depart in four hours. She would need that much time to find a taxi, get to the airport, and wade through customs for her international flight.

After a fanatical morning of cleaning and straightening, Kate had restored the apartment back to its original state when she'd first walked through the door only ten months ago. Before it became her home. With her suitcase packed and her passport safe in her bag, it was time to leave.

The cigarette and ashes in the small silver ashtray on the balcony table were now the only evidence left that she'd ever been here. Kate picked it up and headed back inside. In the hallway, she paused. Her life—her very essence—had been rearranged in these rooms. *What pieces of myself am I leaving that can't be packed in a suitcase?*

In the kitchen, Kate dumped the contents of the ashtray into a plastic bag to throw away in the lobby downstairs. Soon the silver disk was rinsed, dried, and back in its place. Her eyes landed on the chair occupied by Stelios on that horrible morning. The memory hung like a haunting spectral presence, sending a shiver through her body.

She made one final trip back into the library. Following the routine of the many times she had walked in there, Kate pulled the cord to close the outside shutters, then lifted the handle of the glass door to secure it. The room was dark, like everything in it had disappeared.

Kate was startled by the loud shriek of the telephone. She barely missed tripping over her suitcase waiting in the hallway. All week long she had avoided answering the phone, which rang each evening, afraid of the possibility it could be Thanasis. Now, she lifted the receiver and waited.

"Koukla?" He sounded hoarse. "I did not know if you were gone."

She gripped the receiver. Her voice stuck in her throat.

"Kaitie?"

Any words were lost to her.

He continued. "Stelios explained what happened. I wanted to tell you myself that I will never forgive what we tried to do and—"

"Stop."

"No, Koukla, I am sorry, but I cannot. I must tell you that I never had a plan to hurt you. The bad things I said to you at the hotel? That was someone else talking. Stelios was wrong to frighten you. It went very far in the wrong direction and—"

"Thanasi, what happened to you? Why did you do what you did? How could you?" The words ran out of her mouth, tripping over each other while tears streamed down her face.

"That is why I called. I must have the chance to see you." He pleaded.

"It's too late for that. I'm leaving today. I'm leaving Greece and you. I can't forgive you for what you did. Not ever." Like a storm that had been building, the clouds finally burst. There was a feeling of liberated space in her chest instead of the squeezing that had taken residence there.

"Koukla." She could tell by the wavering tone of his voice he was crying. For a brief moment, she wondered if she had ever seen him cry. But she couldn't let him in. It was over.

Kate pulled the phone off the table, edging down against the wall until she was seated on the floor facing the library. She saw the chair where Stelios had sat and tormented her. "You knew how I felt about Stelios. You gave him my key, and he was here. I was so scared, and then he just left. I've been living in hell all this time not knowing what was going on." She stopped to take a breath.

Thanasis jumped in. "My Kaitie. Please do not leave without seeing me one more time." His voice had become a whisper.

Kate wrapped the gray phone cord around her finger until the tip grew numb. Frozen, she held the receiver, unable to speak or move. There was silence until the sound of Thanasis, again repeating "Kaitie," vibrated in her ear. She unraveled the cord.

Without saying a word, she placed the phone back on its cradle and ended the call.

fifty-four ✿

The taxi driver tossed the bruised yellow suitcase onto the sidewalk in front of the airport, slammed the trunk, and sped away. Kate stood alone on the hot pavement. Her overstuffed travel bag and purse weighed heavily on her shoulders. A vast emptiness brooded inside.

On the drive she had watched the familiar landmarks of Thessaloniki speed past the window of the taxi, while she replayed the conversation with Thanasis. She was depleted, but at least she had said what needed to be said. Kate had stood up for herself, a task that had always been difficult throughout her life. But the memory of his pleading voice was trapped in her head.

Outside the airport, the palm trees and carpet of grass baked under a hot June sun. No one noticed Kate on the sidewalk except a skinny man with widening circles of perspiration on the underarms of his khaki uniform.

"Miss—luggage?"

Kate nodded and followed the wobbly handcart into the airport, past men sprawled on the lawn, smoking and sharing stories. Their voices and laughter filled the space between them. Greeks, she had learned, had a penchant for socializing with one another. She caught snatches of conversation in passing.

Once inside the cavernous terminal, Kate was immersed in crowds of Greeks loosely clustered in lines for the Olympic Airways flights to Athens. She went instead to the area for international flights. A few tourists, some directly from the beaches and smelling of cocoa butter, waited ahead of her in the line. Automatically, Kate swiveled her head, on guard for obvious Americans. She'd become practiced at keeping her distance from the sometimes-brassy loudness of that distinct group. The air of superiority that often surrounded them had become offensive.

Sighing deeply, she realized how completely she had separated herself from her Americanism over the past months. Now she was swaying on a rickety suspension bridge between two groups on opposite sides of a chasm. *Where do I even belong anymore?*

"Next please." The voice of the Olympic agent, addressing the person three spaces ahead, jerked Kate away from her daydream and back to her place in line. Just as she was pivoting away from the crowds, something stopped her.

At the far end of the terminal, the doors opened. In the crowd, Kate noticed a movement that was familiar and well-worn in her mind. Many times she'd met him on a crowded sidewalk, recognizing him after sifting through the images of the crush of strangers, when the pieces had slid together and he had suddenly appeared. Thanasis. He was coming toward her.

Quickly, Kate spun away. But, as had always been the case, there was, once again, the unmistakably fierce pull of his presence. He was reentering her life. Kate kept her eyes forward.

"Koukla?" She heard the way the consonants and vowels tumbled over each other in one fluent push. Kate briefly caught the sweetness of his hesitant smile and the kindness in his eyes. She followed the lines of his muscular shoulders to see his left arm wrapped in bandages, a macabre souvenir from their last time together. Kate tried to will the tears to stay in the safe confines of her eyes. But they wouldn't. She lowered her head and placed her hand over her mouth to muffle her sobs.

"Koukla, ti ekana?" Kate heard his wavering voice asking what he had done to her. She straightened, swallowed her tears, and gradually regained her composure. She faced him. The rage she had poured out on the phone call had dissipated her anger.

The beautiful depth of his eyes peered into her. His question was simple. "What is the time of your flight?"

She considered the clock above the ticket counter and calculated. "I will give you twenty minutes." Remnants of fury resurfaced. "Is that enough time for you to explain yourself to me? Enough time to tell me what all of this has been—what happened to you—before I get on the plane and leave this place forever?" Her voice trembled.

Thanasis nodded toward the small coffee bar in the corner. Just like old times, their bodies were a single mind moving together in space. With his good hand, he dragged along her large, yellow suitcase.

While Thanasis went for coffee, Kate settled at a table away from the banter and noise of the travelers. She placed her shaking hands on the small circle of the Formica table, waiting for the three-card-Monte game that would be spread in front of her. *Will I even know if he's telling the truth or not?*

Setting their demitasse cups on the table, Thanasis retreated for a plate of pastries before joining her. He took a sip of his coffee and ran his tongue along the top of his mustache. The familiar movements stirred memories and a begrudging affection.

Thanasis began to speak. "There is something I did not trust to tell you." He took a breath. "I did not think you would understand so that you could help."

Kate kept her eyes down as she picked at the cream pastry on the plate. *Was this a big mistake? Letting him back in even for this brief moment?* Being with Thanasis was natural and foreign at the same time.

"My friends." He stopped. "When the colonels took power, they did horrible things. We could do nothing." Thanasis rubbed his fingers back and forth over his mouth. "I tried to tell you once but—" He seemed unable to continue.

Kate paused, then quickly finished her coffee. The final sip was liquid, followed by a muddy blend of finely ground beans. Thanasis watched her place the cup on the saucer. She did not swirl the grounds and invert the demitasse, as she had numerous times in the past. It was the custom of village women, after coffee, to "read the cup." Someone practiced in this art of fortune-telling would turn the cup over and study the patterns left by the grounds. The contours of the brown swirls would be interpreted to forecast the future—a trip, money, romance.

Thanasis pressed his lips together, then said quietly, "I see you are not willing to have your future told by the lines of coffee."

"By the lines or by the lies?" Kate met his eyes and pushed her chair away from the table. Her patience had reached an end.

"Wait." He gently grabbed her hand just as she stood to reach for her suitcase. Swayed by the warmth of his hand and the urgency in his eyes, she relented and sat back down.

"Before you came into my life, I was part of something. During the junta. You do not know what it was like to sit and watch them killing us. The Polytechnio."

Again, Kate remembered the scene of students at the university on top of the walls, waving flags, before the tank came crashing through the gate.

He continued. "They were students. Like us." Thanasis kept his eyes on the table, his face drawn. "They were murdered." He stopped again. "You remember the stories?" He glanced at her. "The beatings and electric shock treatments. The street in Athens people avoided because you could hear the cries of torture coming from the jail?"

She knew this was not fiction. However, she asked, "What does that have to do with you—and what you did to me?" She emphasized the last words, pounding them out, leaving the final one to hang in the air like an indictment.

Thanasis winced. Kate had hit him deeply. "Was this part of a plan all along? Did you use me?" Her voice faltered.

"Ohi, Koukla!" His eyes implored her to believe him. He reached out to take her hand again, but she pulled away from him. Kate was trying very hard not to cry.

Thanasis seemed to gather himself for another try. "You did not meet Leftheris. We made certain of that."

"The one at the Suez?" Kate remembered seeing an older man, someone who did not join their group at the restaurant.

Thanasis nodded. "His nephew was one of the students killed at the Polytechnio. He desires to strike back."

"The 17th of November Group? You're connected to them?" Kate gasped. Fear plunged in her chest like a runaway elevator.

"Not like that. They are a much larger group in Athens. We do not do anything directly, but Leftheris wants to give support if they ask. That is why we wanted your passport. To get into the consulate here, if necessary."

Kate's heart tumbled. These people were supporting the group that had murdered an American. Even if he was CIA and had done horrible things, it was a step too far. Although she had only recently entered the political situation here, Thanasis and his friends had lived it many years. Desperately, she worked to balance in her mind the junta's crimes as justification for the killing in Athens.

Thanasis shifted his arm in its sling, a wounded bird. His voice was low and worn out from his effort to explain. "Before Stelios could get your passport, we learned of the killing in Athens. At your apartment, Stelios called Leftheris and was told to leave. We knew the police watched us, and we could not risk anything." He paused. "Stelios is gone. He is in Crete. He did not pass his examinations and will work for his uncle in an electrical shop in Chania. He is no longer a problem for you—or for me."

Kate stared at the untouched pastry. She could not rid her mind of memories of Stelios in her apartment. His bullying. His threats. His smell when she forced herself to embrace him. Her fear. Her fighting back to save herself. Thanasis said he was gone. She was relieved but wasn't sure if that was enough.

Her heart raced with fear that Thanasis was connected to this man Leftheris who was supporting the terrorist group. She struggled to reconcile the remembered sweetness of her lover with the hard reality of political murder. Rather than look at him, she scanned the airport lobby. Most everyone seemed to be in a lighthearted mood. Getting ready for trips, ready for new adventures. Her own bright shiny adventure had morphed into a nightmare. She willed her eyes back to Thanasis.

"The night at the hotel, you changed into someone I couldn't recognize. Then you gave the key to Stelios. He held me prisoner in my own apartment. Am I supposed to forget all of that?"

"I know that you cannot forgive me for what I did."

Moments of silence passed. Thanasis watched her. The question was queued up in her mind. She surprised herself by wishing for the answer she knew she wanted. "And now are you done with these people? Is it over for you?"

Thanasis was slow to answer. "I believe so. I hope that the blood from the assassination in Athens was enough." He took a deep breath. "I do not think there can be enough American blood to equal what we went through. But I do not want it to go further." The sincerity of his eyes was replaced by a weariness, an expression of defeat.

She rose. "I've got to go." The intention of her words, though, did not translate to movement, as she stood in place. He reached out to her with his good hand. His grip was not firm. It was not demanding or overpowering. It was more like a plea.

"How much time do we have?" he asked.

She knew he was not talking about today's flight. Kate remembered when they had gotten ready for their vacation together in early May. They were heading to Thasos, an island off the coast of northern Greece. She had opened her apartment door to find him with a small rucksack over his shoulder, T-shirt stretched across his chest, and blue jeans small at the waist and belled at the bottom. His devilish smile. Dark brown curls. A sweet kiss on his lips for her.

When he'd seen the items scattered on her bed, he mockingly shook a finger at her. "You must remember to never take an alarm clock or an umbrella on a vacation." There was a part of him like Zorba—living life to its fullest and throwing off societal constraints whenever possible. How she loved that thrilling ride with him.

Their days on the island were lunches of fresh bread, feta cheese, olives, and wine. Their afternoons were spent hiking over dunes to find a private beach for making love, where waves crashed, and sand pelted them. In the evenings, they strolled along the waterfront past a row of tavernas, with their strings of lights reflecting on the water and fishing boats rocking on gentle waves.

And in these past months, Kate had learned another idea of what home could mean to her. He had become, in a way, her new home. There was a sense of belonging to another person. It was what she'd hoped for with Jim. She had yearned to know someone deeply and to understand the disparate corners of their being. Despite the barriers of language and culture, Kate had found a deep connection with Thanasis. But everything had changed at the Fire Walking ceremony.

Thanasis, with his bandaged arm, struggled to stand to be closer to her.

Ding-dong. Kate's reverie was broken by the bell calling for attention to flight announcements. In the past, the sound reminded Kate of a giant doorbell with a surprise behind a door, waiting to be revealed. However, there was nothing humorous about the signal today. Its signal now meant it was time to leave Greece . . . to leave a life she had carved out for herself with wonderful friends and work that had only begun. She would be leaving the man who now put his arm around her shoulders, offering another chance to find a way back toward each other. Panic flooded inside of her. *Should I rush to catch my flight? Should I stay? Could I stay?*

When she had packed her now battered yellow suitcase atop her pink flowered bedspread in her childhood home, she had no idea what awaited her in Greece nor of the changes to come. Now she was independent, adventurous, and had lost at least some of her naivete.

An image of her grandmother appeared, standing in the doorway of her bedroom when she'd come to say goodbye. Gray hair swept up into a French twist, bustling with purpose wherever she went. Her grandmother had always warned not to ignore second chances.

"A second chance is like a bird landing on a branch, just there for a minute before flying way off into yonder and gone forever."

Her thoughts circled and circled. Here was the opportunity to continue the path she had started when she flew out of Texas and into a broader world. That impulse of daring rumbled inside her now, overriding any concerns for her safety.

Thanasis's words urged. "If you do not stay, this is a book you did not finish."

Kate leaned into him, savoring his warmth. She straightened up and reached into her bag for her ticket. Scanning the airport for the exchange desk, Kate slipped out of her chair. Her departure might come in a day, a week, a month. But today would not be her day for leaving.

Thanasis smiled and grabbed her suitcase. Kate hesitated. He was taking control of her bag and, in some way, of her world again. There was still a small space for a different voice to move through her body and rise to the surface and say "no."

Today, that voice was being ignored.

fifty-five ✦

On the taxi ride back from the airport, Kate sat close to Thanasis. She welcomed the familiar touch of his arm around her shoulder and his leg next to hers, but doubts about her decision still roiled. Traveling closer into the city, Kate watched scenes pass by that she'd bid farewell, just a few hours before. *I can leave anytime. I can leave anytime,* she repeated to herself, hoping she had not made a mistake.

They passed her former apartment on Queen Olga Street and headed to the flat Thanasis shared with his roommate, Nikos, who was gone for the summer. In her mind Kate tried to bring some order to this sudden change of plans. She was jumping back into a life she had decided to leave behind.

Arriving at Thanasis's building, they hauled her luggage across a small lobby. Political fliers and paper ads for neighborhood restaurants were scattered across the floor. Kate had been here a few times, but today everything seemed different—cramped and un-kempt. Thanasis hoisted her suitcase onto the only chair in his bed-room. Constant noise from the busy street outside filtered through the slats of shutters.

Alone at last, they embraced for the first time in weeks. Eyes closed, Kate was amazed by how natural it felt. She was home. Before they moved toward the next stage of intimacy, Thanasis removed his shirt, then carefully unwound the gauze from his left forearm to reveal his scar. It was almost star-like with lighter striations branching toward his elbow. She watched him refresh the bandage.

Kate faced away. The wall she had built around her heart was beginning to crumble. She sensed his approach from behind. Thanasis carefully wrapped his arms to encompass her. She turned and molded herself into him as they both shook with sobbing waves of emotion. No words. Only a coming together of bodies.

The next morning, Kate awoke early and waited for his eyes to open. She followed the cracks in the ceiling as she sensed the touch of his warm body beside hers. Kate heard the dusky voice in her ear.

"Etho eiste?" using formal grammar as he asked, "You are here?" Kate moved on top of him and nestled in. At this moment, she was assured that her decision to stay with him was right.

Things, however, were not the same this time around. The Greek philosopher Heraclitus had said one couldn't step into the same river twice because the river was constantly changing. Unquestionably, their time together was changed.

Now, Kate's life was exclusively with Thanasis. Lena and Yiannis were at their summer home in Metamorphosis, and Georyia vacationed on Santorini with her sister. She was alone with Thanasis, without the distractions of work or friendships. Together, they drifted through days and evenings. And the river kept flowing past.

How long would she stay in Greece? She wasn't sure, as she'd told her parents when she telephoned. Until the end of the summer or would she return to her job at ELEPAAP in September? It was uncertain. Just as when she'd first met Thanasis, Kate figuratively put on heavily scratched sunglasses. They allowed her to see only lights and shadows rather than to focus clearly on what might be ahead.

Gatherings at the apartment with Thanasis's group of friends lasted past midnight. Kate had met some of them before, like Makis, one of his best friends. Others, she had not. Staying on the edge of conversations, Kate remained slightly apprehensive. She listened and watched, always seated next to Thanasis and anticipating something, although she wasn't sure what. Smoke clouded above their heads, empty retsina bottles crowded under the small table. As with most Greek conversations, politics was the main topic.

With the previous November's election, the first since the junta ended, a conservative government had stabilized in place. A variety of new political parties vied for constituents. Their own Eurocommunist Party was strategizing ways to compete with other groups.

On one such evening, Kate poured herself another half glass of retsina and listened. She now understood the idealism at the core of what Thanasis believed and could differentiate it from the extremism that had caused his earlier actions. *Didn't his group advocate taking care of the less fortunate? Like at the Baptist church where I was raised?*

When talk moved to the upcoming parliamentary elections, Kate ferried empty bottles to the kitchen. As glass clanged in the trash bin, her emotions shifted. She was disoriented, as though stranded on a seesaw tipping backward, finding herself alone in a closet-sized kitchen with the roar of Greek conversation as background. *How can I so easily go from being at home with Thanasis one moment to feeling alienated the next?*

A male voice from the doorway interrupted her thoughts. "Kaitie?" She jumped. Makis was at the kitchen door. Instantly on guard, she remembered being alone with Stelios. But Makis was the "good one" of Thanasis's boyhood friends. Short of stature and slightly overweight, Makis radiated kindness. His usually merry eyes, however, now showed concern. "Sorry. I frightened you?"

Seeing the earnestness of his expression, Kate relaxed a bit. "Yes," she admitted. "But that's okay. I was lost in my thoughts."

He hesitated. "I am obliged to apologize to you for the horrible event with Stelios." Makis studied his sneakers and shuffled his feet. "I hope you understand we did not agree with what he did. He brought shame on his friends, especially Thanasis." His eyes searched hers. "You understand?"

Kate ran her hand across the counter, fingering the bumps and cracks. "To be honest, I'm still trying to sort it all out. The whole thing was terrifying. Being left at the Fire Walking ceremony, and then the hotel, and Stelios at my apartment." As Kate listed the betrayals, she wondered, *Was I too quick to trust Thanasis?*

The silence between Kate and Makis contrasted with the noise from the adjoining room.

Makis spoke again. "Stelios is gone. He was a bad person. We tried to hide our eyes from the worst parts of him. That was a mistake. I am sorry."

Flooded with memories of Stelios in her apartment, Kate shook her head slowly. "It was really awful."

"Kaitie, please know that despite bad feelings for your government, we hold you and the people in your country high in our hearts. I have my aunt and cousins in Chicago." He paused. "The dictatorship was a very hard time for Greece. We still try to find our next steps." Just then laughter broke out in the living room. "Come, let us not miss out on something good," he urged her with his infectious smile, one which seemed like a hug.

Back in the living room, Kate perched on Thanasis's lap and worked hard to catch the fast train of words that ran past and crashed into each other. Her eyes were closing.

"Koukla, go to bed." Thanasis ran his finger down her cheek. She knew he would wake her when he came to bed, and they would fall into each other once more.

She bid the group a goodnight. The men and women smiled back with genuine warmth. But there was still an awareness that she was a foreigner, *xena,* and would always be one.

fifty-six 🌿

Kate waded deeper and deeper into the river of her new life. Two more weeks passed. It was getting harder to withstand the rushing current of late evening meetings and piles of cigarette butts and raised voices of Thanasis and his friends. Despite the sweetness of their days together, Kate worried whether Thanasis would be able to resist the dangerous politics that had driven him to an extreme in the past.

Although she tried to avoid it, the scar on Thanasis's arm was a reminder that she had to stay alert. Kate knew she needed to ask questions and get reassurance. *But do I need to do it right now?* It was summer in Greece. She was living the life she'd seen in travel brochures. Sun and sea and beaches. For a bit longer, Kate willed herself to ignore her concerns, acutely aware of her risky decision.

Together as a group, Thanasis and his friends met at the same seaside village on weekends, taking a break from city life. They frolicked in the sea and spent evenings at tavernas. Kate and Thanasis stayed in an apartment owned by his uncle. The one-bedroom space in a new complex was small but with a balcony where they could watch the blue Aegean catch the evening sunset.

Kate found it increasingly difficult, however, to disregard unsettling signs. *What am I doing? Am I being foolish to rush back into a life with him?* Worry twirled in her head, alongside yet another concern. This one came from the outside. Thanasis grasped her elbow more tightly when they passed someone sitting on a bench, hidden behind a newspaper. That same man, in sunglasses with slick, combed-back hair, always seemed to be around, appearing on the corner or standing near the news kiosk. *Who is he?*

One afternoon after shopping at the small market down the street, Kate placed their straw basket on the kitchen counter. She handed Thanasis the chunk of feta cheese wrapped in white paper and dripping inside a plastic bag. Buying time by inhaling the sweet fragrance from an oval loaf of fresh bread, Kate closed her eyes and steadied herself. Then she asked, "Thanasi, is someone spying on us?"

Thanasis kept his back to her as he moved a knife through the hunk of feta cheese to make thinner slices and de-salt in water. Kate had heard of "shadow" men from the Greek security who followed suspected leftists or "terrorists," as they were called in the Western press. Thanasis ran water into a bowl with the feta slices before putting a plate on top to protect against any insects coming in through an open window.

He faced her. "I am obliged to say you are correct." She read a hint of concern in his eyes. "The security police did not disappear with the junta. They are around and suspicious of leftists everywhere. But we do nothing wrong." He moved close and wrapped her in his arms. "Please do not worry. We do nothing wrong," he repeated in her ear. Kate wanted to believe him. She relaxed into him, working hard to dismiss fears of being swept up into some new political intrigue.

But there was still another concern. *Am I ceding myself again to a man?* It was a familiar feeling.

Alone at the beach that afternoon, Kate watched seagulls swoop overhead and felt the gusts of wind blowing past. The strong breeze reminded her of the wind on the hill outside her apartment in Wyoming. In her early days in Casper, two years ago, she would sit there and stare at the outlines of mountains in the distance, comforting herself after her marriage had abruptly ended.

She remembered the surprise phone call one November evening after she had moved to Wyoming. It was Jim. His confident, steady voice had wavered.

"I've been thinking." He paused. "How 'bout we reconsider the divorce? Maybe I rushed into this thing too fast." Jim had initiated the divorce in Texas, but Kate hadn't received the final court papers.

Sitting on the green shag carpet in her bedroom, Kate slipped her finger inside the coils of the phone cord and listened until he stopped talking. She'd had suspicions about a girlfriend, someone at law school. It was time to confront him. Jim stumbled over his words, ultimately confessing. Kate quickly ended the conversation. Despite moments of melancholy and missing him, she knew that conversation had been the beginning of her independence. It led to the confidence which eventually brought her here to Greece.

Now, Kate scooped up fine beach sand, letting it move slowly between her fingers. *After working so hard to stand on my own, am I letting it all slip away? Am I losing myself again to a man I adore?* Thoughts, like confused acrobats searching for their landings, tumbled through her mind. In this new relationship with Thanasis, it was once again not just the two of them. But instead of a girlfriend, the other woman was his politics. Thanasis's idealism was part of what she loved about him. It was also why she doubted he could ever be a permanent part of her life.

Kate dug deeper into the sand with both hands. *What happens if I stay with him?* After all her feminist reading and striking out on her own to Wyoming, Colorado, and now Greece, would she get swept away by another man? Kate stood up and walked into the sea, the choppy waves kicked up by the wind. She swam against the swells, proving to herself she could fight them. Then she reversed course and let herself be ferried back to shore.

fifty-seven

The next day, Kate and Thanasis walked through the seaside village of whitewashed houses, passing painted olive oil tins of flowering geraniums and roses. She had suggested they go for a late lunch, just the two of them. The small restaurant near the beach sat under a tin awning, squash vines winding in and around wrought iron supports. The green tendrils on the overhead beams created chandeliers for the chickens pecking at dropped pieces of food on the cement floor. A young boy brought a basket of bread, and Thanasis signaled for retsina. Taking her first sip, Kate wished she could let the meal proceed lazily into the late afternoon. But she could not.

"I need to talk to you." There was an absence of surprise from his face. "I thought this stuff with politics was over—didn't you promise me that?"

Thanasis toyed with his glass, making a new wet circle on the white butcher paper covering the table. He kept his eyes down. "Koukla, I promised you would be safe. And I try to stay away from anything . . . dangerous." He shifted in his chair to face her directly. "To stay away from politics is to lose part of myself. I cannot make it go away from my life. Just as I could not let you go away from me." He reached for her hand and traced lines on each of her fingers. His expression was pained.

Despite these words she'd imagined he would say, something inside was starting to break. "I don't know, Thanasi. I just try to go along one day into the next, so happy to be here with you. But it's a struggle not to think . . . not to worry."

"I know. I wish it was not this way." He sighed and shook his head.

Kate took another sip of retsina. The blue Aegean sparkled in the distance. "I'm going to Metamorphosis tomorrow to see Lena and Yiannis. I need to get away for a few days."

Thanasis nodded his head to one side, indicating he understood. He took her hand, kissing it tenderly, just as the boy arrived to take their order.

She downed the retsina and gestured for a refill, wanting to get lost in a cloud of delusion. To live only in the touch of Thanasis's lips and the familiar taste of fresh fish drenched in olive oil and lemon.

The next day she dressed, packed her small travel bag for the trip, and they headed together for the bus stop on the highway. "We'll meet in the city next week?" she asked.

Thanasis nodded, kissing her long and hard before Kate climbed the steps of the bus for Metamorphosis. She watched through the window as he became smaller and smaller, until he disappeared.

fifty-eight 🌿

The landscape of Halkidiki rolled by outside the bus window. Kate scanned scenes of red-tiled houses in nearby villages, wild azalea bushes in pinks and whites, and sunlight glinting off occasional glimpses at the blue of the Aegean.

Kate recalled the day she had opened a volume from the encyclopedia set in her parents' den to study the geography of northern Greece. Halkidiki, the large peninsula on the northwestern side of the Aegean, was compared to a hand with three fingers jutting into the sea. A photograph of a bust of the philosopher Aristotle indicated this area was his birthplace. *Kate—you had no idea what was coming your way.*

Today she traveled from the first finger of Halkidiki to the second. The third, Mount Athos, was closed to the public. It had been occupied as an Orthodox spiritual center since the tenth century. Kate remembered when she'd learned about the area during her first days in Greece in the Stylianou home.

"Those are from Mount Athos." Kate had jumped at the sound of Yiannis's voice. Standing in the living room, she was examining a set of starkly beautiful black-and-white photographs. An older monk stood barefoot on a dock gazing out to the sea; a younger monk slipped a small book into the folds of his robe; an ancient monastery perched high on a promontory.

"Mount Athos is the third protrusion of the Halkidiki

peninsula," he'd told her, holding out three fingers from his hand to illustrate. "This is the closest you will come to seeing inside Ayion Oros or the Holy Mountain, as it is also called. Only males are allowed—no women or children."

"These photographs are beautiful. Where did you get them?" Kate asked.

"They are my own. It is something I do as a hobby. Of course, I had more time for it before the children and the farm."

"I had no idea of your talent." Kate was astonished. Yiannis didn't respond but rather scanned the wall with a wistful expression on his face.

Their conversation had been in September, and now it was early August. Kate was heading to Metamorphosis for a respite from Thanasis and a long-delayed talk with Lena and Yiannis. She hadn't seen them since their farewell in her apartment, the day before her originally planned departure date.

When Kate had called to say she'd made a last-minute decision to stay in Greece, Lena sounded concerned. Kate assured her she was safe. She would come to Metamorphosis and explain everything. She also hoped she could leave her big suitcase at the farm rather than keep it at Thanasis's small apartment.

Now as the bus wove through streets of villages to pick up additional passengers, Kate replayed her decision to stay in Greece. *Has it really been worth it? Does this glorious summer with Thanasis outweigh what I may have gotten myself into?*

One thing was certain. Lena and Yiannis had become her family. They would be a sounding board for whatever decision was bubbling underneath. On the beach in the distance, waves rolled in slowly and rhythmically, following the imperative of the tide.

fifty-nine

"Katina—one more chair, please," Aunt Sophia said as she nudged open the screen door. She held a tray with bowls of cucumber and yogurt tzatziki and a smoky eggplant dip, a plate of feta cheese, and a salad of tomatoes, onions, peppers, olives, and parsley.

Kate rearranged the chairs around the table on the veranda of the Stylianou summer home. Lena emerged, carrying a platter of roasted lamb and golden potatoes, festooned with sprigs of fresh oregano. As usual, a loaf of bread was in the center of the table. Afternoon lunch with the extended family was ready to begin.

Trees surrounded the two-story white stucco house, protecting them from the early afternoon sun. The home was not fancy, but it provided the family with all they needed for their months' long summer vacation. Yiannis helped Soto to his usual place next to Lena, and Aris snagged a spot beside Kate. She affectionately rubbed the top of his head, smiling at Lena's parents and aunt as they took their seats.

"*Kalos eerthis, Katina,*" Yiannis welcomed her back to them as he raised a small glass of retsina in her direction.

"*Kalos sas vreeka.*" Kate responded with the usual. "Good to find you." It was indeed good to be in the company of these loving people. She was comforted being here and away from the increasing tension with Thanasis. Kate savored the softness of the potatoes with hints of olive oil and oregano. She was surprised by an unexpected relief in detaching from Thanasis, an awareness of her sense of self by being apart from him.

The group exchanged news and highlights of the summer thus far in Metamorphosis. Kate sketched out her time in the seaside village with Thanasis and his friends. Only Lena and Yiannis knew of the frightening events with Thanasis and Stelios, so she glossed over the topic of her reversal of plans with Lena's parents and aunt. She spoke of not wanting to miss the glories of a Greek summer.

The boys went off to play, and Lena's parents and aunt excused themselves to rest.

"So, Katina, it is time for your story." Yiannis lit a cigarette and pushed back in his chair. Unlike when she was with Thanasis, Kate never smoked with Yiannis. It was a habit Lena frowned upon, always begging her husband to give up cigarettes.

Kate took a deep breath. She toyed with breadcrumbs on the tablecloth and told them what had happened. She ended by saying, "I knew that he was hurt in the fire at the hotel, but seeing his arm wrapped in bandages really hit me hard. He convinced me to hear him out. So I did."

Yiannis jumped in. "Your passport? Did he explain?"

"Yes." Kate bit her lip. "The nephew of one of Thanasis's friends in Thessaloniki was killed at the Polytechnio—"

"Does this involve the 17th of November?" Yiannis asked, his pitch rising. Although the violence of the vigilante group, named for the day of the university killings, had not spread beyond Athens, its reputation was known throughout Greece.

"Not directly," Kate said. "Thanasis and his friends were never a formal group, but the uncle asked for their help if the organization wanted to do something in Thessaloniki. My passport might have made getting into the American Consulate possible." Even though her voice was calm, Kate's heart jumped as she again remembered the newspaper picture of a body covered with a sheet lying beside the highway. "The killing really frightened Thanasis. He says he's opposed to violence. I want to believe him."

The reassurance she hoped to find in their expressions was not there.

Kate continued. "I decided to take a gamble and give him another chance. But not to be as trusting as before." She shook her head. "I don't know. I'm starting to worry. I know he can't stay away from politics. Lately I thought someone was watching us, so I asked him. He admitted it was someone from the Greek security force." Kate took a sip of retsina, working to calm herself.

Yiannis leaned forward on his elbows. "Katina, this is not a game. Your passport gives the protection of your government, but that may not be enough to keep you out of trouble."

"I know. But there's another problem." Sadness pulled the muscles of her face into a deep frown. "I love him, and I really don't want to leave him." She picked up her fork and moved it around her plate. "But I'm afraid to stay."

Yiannis took a long drag from his cigarette and blew out smoke slowly. "We lived through many terrible times in the dictatorship. And as a country we are not as far removed from danger as we wish. What happens in Greece is not make-believe or movies. It is real."

"But Thanasis wouldn't do anything to put me at risk. I really believe that." Kate's voice was pleading, hoping to convince Yiannis. And perhaps herself.

Yiannis reached out, gently touching Kate's hand. "Be careful, Katina. Be careful."

Lena gathered the plates and began scraping remnants from each onto the large platter. "Katina, I have told you before that you have a heart that is . . . Yianni what is *evaistitee?*"

"Sensitive," he answered.

"Yes, very sensitive. You have had many shocks in your time with Thanasis, and I can see that, despite everything, you have not stopped loving him." She stacked the plates. "That must be very difficult." Lena faced Kate directly and emphasized her words. "You are strong. You left your home and came here and became part of our lives. And now you consider having him in your life. I have faith you will find your way."

"Efharisto, Lena." Kate's voice broke as she thanked her. "But I really don't know that I deserve that kind of faith." Attempting a smile, she followed Lena inside, carrying a load of dishes. She longed to fall into their familiar kitchen routine and into the security of simple acts. And also, to draw from Lena's calm strength.

Kate gazed at her friend's face framed in partial shadows from sunlight creeping through the single window above the sink. Lena hummed while soaping and rinsing dishes before handing them over for Kate to dry. She suspected these shared times were dwindling. Although her conversation with Yiannis and Lena was riddled with doubt, deep inside Kate knew her final decision was nearing.

Her mind wandered to a discussion she'd had with Georyia about the word "nostalgia" and its Greek roots *notos* meaning "return" and *algos* meaning "pain." The suffering caused by a yearning to return. Kate sensed a hint of this pain, even though she had not yet left. Most likely these times would soon only exist in memory.

sixty ✬

H orns blared and brakes squealed as Kate waited on the crowded sidewalk of Egnatia Street, the broad boulevard in an area of Thessaloniki not far from the bus depot. She was waiting to meet Thanasis. He was late.

During her time in Metamorphosis, Kate and Thanasis had been out of contact, except when he'd phoned to schedule their rendezvous. The call was brief, and she detected a heaviness in his voice. He asked her to meet him at 5:00 p.m. at the Kapani market, a mismatched collection of many single shops joined under one large roof. It had been in existence since the early days of the Ottoman Empire in the fifteenth century.

Kate had been to the Kapani once before, when she was beginning to explore Thessaloniki. One evening she'd wandered the narrow aisles amid pyramids of glistening olives, hanging goat and lamb carcasses, and bounty from the sea packed in ice but still with the unmistakable aroma of fish. A myriad of items were for sale—long-handled coffee brikis, fabrics, suitcases, icons and other religious items. The shops were crowded together in a maze of never-ending stalls. Merchants hawked their wares in a cacophony of pitches. Today, it seemed that years had passed, rather than months, since that first visit to the Kapani.

Apprehension clawed within as she waited outside, hemmed in

by traffic on one side and crowds of shoppers on the other. Kate pretended to search her bag for a lighter, cigarette balanced between her fingers. She kept her head down, a strategy to avoid the occasional car that slowed, with male voices reaching out to her through open windows. Their shouts were in German, French, English, or whatever nationality she appeared to be to them.

Kate jumped as an arm reached around her shoulder. The touch, the push, and instantly she was matching Thanasis's familiar stride down the sidewalk. Kate dropped the unlit cigarette into her bag and relaxed into his arm, joining him a few steps before they stopped for a kiss. She savored the comforting warmth of his lips and moved her face to nuzzle into his neck, as she always did.

His handsome face made her heart leap, and Kate instantly reconnected with the best of what it was like to be with him. Affection washed completely over her. All week long in Metamorphosis, Kate had played a ping-pong game back and forth with her decision to leave. But here he was, knocking her off balance with a burst of affection. They kissed again, this time with more intensity.

Gradually, she disentangled and stood back to regain her footing. Then, just as quickly as the rush of happiness at being together again had overwhelmed her, a boomerang of concern whizzed past. She stopped. "Thanasi, why did you ask me to meet you here? What's going on?"

He kissed her once more, shouldering her travel bag and nudging her to keep going alongside him. "Please, walk with me."

With his arm around her, their legs moved together and lulled her into something familiar, something she craved. Kate relented, squelching her frustration that he had avoided her questions. Midstride he reached down and brushed another kiss on her cheek.

They headed away from busy Egnatia and onto narrow streets on an incline, taking them up into an older part of Thessaloniki. Early evening shoppers, heading toward the city center, dodged past them. Lights were coming on in the coffee shops they passed. Men crowded around small tables with their demitasse cups of mud-brown coffee, smoke curling from their cigarettes. Dice clattered on backgammon boards.

Thanasis's grasp of her elbow was gentle. His thigh, in tandem with hers, was the axis that kept her moving forward. Moving, moving, moving. Thoughts flashed in her mind, like scenes one saw from a fast-traveling train. *Where is he taking me? What happened this past week?*

Kate's tolerance reached its limit. She stopped again, breaking away from him. "Where are we going? Talk to me." Her tone was firm.

"I am sorry for the hurry." Thanasis stroked her cheek with his finger. "We will see friends of mine. I wanted you to meet them before, but it was not the right time."

"I don't get it." Alarm bells of danger clanged in her mind.

"Koukla, come for a coffee with my friends. We will leave after that. I promise."

Kate hesitated. His eyes pleaded with her. Wary, she nodded her head to the side, signaling assent. Although instinctively she knew she shouldn't, Kate was trusting him again. But it was no longer a blind trust. This time she was on guard and ready to do whatever she needed to keep herself safe.

They were now in the midst of smaller apartment buildings, structures without the shining glass doors and marble-tiled lobbies of her old neighborhood on Queen Olga Street. Thanasis slowed his pace as they reached the front of a nondescript multistoried building. He pulled open a heavy glass door, cracked in a few places. They went inside. Kate worked to quell her mounting uneasiness.

The lobby was poorly lit by a single light bulb dangling overhead. Cooking smells of onions and garlic in olive oil slipped into the stairwell as they climbed. They turned corner after corner on the stairs. At last, Thanasis led Kate down a hall and knocked softly. He identified himself, and the door opened into a small living room neatly arranged with a couch, coffee table, and a few chairs. Stacks of books and newspapers were piled on a desk in the corner.

The man at the door was slightly familiar.

"Kaitie, this is Leftheris." The middle-aged man stuck his hand in her direction and greeted her warmly in Greek. Recognizing the name, Kate stopped cold. Thanasis continued, "I told you about him."

So, this was Leftheris. The one whose nephew was killed at the Polytechnio. Her heart plummeted. *What's going on? Is he the one pulling the strings? The one who wants my passport?* Kate knew she was in dangerous territory. She faltered, moving inside reluctantly only with the urging of Thanasis's hand on her back.

Another person joined them from a small kitchen off to one side. A woman she recognized. Kate remembered her from the dinner with the artist Farsakthis, recalling her erect posture, perfectly coiffed dark curly hair, and finely chiseled features. "We meet again, Kaitie. I am Anthi." This was the woman who had made Kate feel uncomfortable by welcoming her to the communist movement that night while dancing on the beach. Anthi wiped her hands on the dishtowel she carried and put both hands out to Kate. Her grasp was firm and her focus intense. Anthi asked if they'd had their afternoon coffee yet.

Thanasis answered, and Anthi disappeared into the kitchen to move to this next round of Greek hospitality. Kate's breath caught in her throat. Quickly, she began to map out an exit plan. She could excuse herself now and head for the door.

Thanasis must have sensed her apprehension, as he urged her to please sit. It was only for coffee. His smile attempted to reassure her. Kate was momentarily paralyzed. Reluctantly, she followed Thanasis to the couch and slid to sit close beside him. He set her bag on the floor.

Anthi brought in coffee and a small plate of cookies on a tray. Kate worked to keep her hands steady as she reached for her cup. The opening conversation was awkward, as though this was just the first round for something else that was to follow.

It was Anthi who took the lead. "We want to apologize to you for the problem with Stelios at your apartment and the discomfort that he caused you. Unfortunately, sometimes he becomes a little overzealous." Kate now remembered Thanasis telling her Anthi had an administrative position at the university, which explained her command of English.

Kate stared at her squarely. "I hardly think overzealous even begins to describe what he did to me," neither smiling nor offering any other comment. She made herself take another sip of coffee.

Anthi nodded and pressed her lips into a smile before continuing. "Thanasis has been very . . . let us say forceful . . . in asking us not to involve you in any plans that we have."

Thanasis sat motionless beside her.

"With difficulty, we persuaded him to bring you to our home to speak with you ourselves."

Kate's breathing quickened. The murders at the Polytechnio.

The 17th of November group with its revenge assassination and bombings in Athens. *Are they planning something in Thessaloniki? Is that why they need me and my passport?*

She glowered at Thanasis. He spoke quietly, his words addressed solely to her. "Kaitie, you are not obliged to do anything you do not wish to do." He placed a hand on her knee.

Anthi narrowed her eyes, seeming to consider how to continue. "As you know, your government caused great harm to our country. We would like to, I think Americans say, 'move on' from it. But for many of us that is not possible." She tilted her heard toward Leftheris. "We know you understand the pain of Leftheris and his loss. We know from Thanasis that your heart is good."

Kate placed the cup on its saucer, unable to take another drink. Her heart pounded a staccato drumbeat.

Leftheris spoke. "We ask you to consider how you could help us. Please do not give an answer now, but perhaps you will find a way to repair some of the damage done by your government. You are in a . . ."

"Unique," said Anthi.

"Yes. Unique position to contribute."

He wore a pained expression. Kate's momentary pang of sympathy, however, was not enough to win her over. Leftheris pushed back into his chair, placing both hands on his thighs, and staring at the floor.

Disbelief joined the whirl of fear and anger rising up inside. Thanasis had brought her here and put her in this position. After all the promises he made that he was done with these people.

"It is only a conversation." Thanasis began attempting to justify his actions.

Kate found his eyes and shook her head forcefully side to side before speaking, her words trembling with emotion. "I don't know what you're asking me to do. I don't want to know what you're asking me to do. No! No! No!" Her voice was a shout. Kate rose from the couch.

"Kaitie, please wait."

She heard Anthi's words but ignored them. Kate grabbed her travel bag, rushed to the door, and yanked it open. She needed to get away from all of this as fast as she could.

Kate ran down the hallway and headlong onto the curving flights of stairs, skipping her hand along the railing to keep her balance with the heavy bag on her shoulder. Thanasis's footsteps sounded behind her, but she managed to cross the lobby and run out the front door before he could catch up to her.

A hand touched her shoulder lightly. He had overtaken her. Kate whirled around. "How could you? How could you do that to me? You said you were finished with anything dangerous. It's over. No more." She spit the words out of her mouth like bullets.

"My Kaitie." He moved toward her, his hands resting gently on her shoulders. She shook away from him.

His voice pleaded. "I am very sorry. Leftheris and Anthi only wanted the chance to talk with you . . ." His words trailed off.

Kate's voice shook. "Why did you do this, Thanasi? Are you crazy?" The words tumbled out of her mouth. "After everything we've been through? You know that I won't—I will never have anything to do with Leftheris and Anthi. No matter how small or no matter how much they—or you—beg me. I will never be part of any kind of plans. Never. Do you understand?"

"Yes, I do. But . . ." He shook his head.

Kate read the pain in his eyes. In her time with Thanasis, she had come to understand his deep loyalty to his friends. His allegiance to them and his political idealism were at the core of who he was. Moments passed. Her breathing slowed. Her anger quieted. Her face dropped into sadness.

Thanasis tried again. "I understand my mistake. Please. Please do not end it like this."

Kate looked into his eyes, realizing what she already knew. His passion for what he believed in and his love for her would always be in a battle. It was clear she would never win that war, no matter how much either of them hoped it could be otherwise.

A group of older children raced past them on the sidewalk, their carefree shouts and shrieks filling the space around them. Kate watched them disappear around the corner, their gaiety in sharp contrast to the scene between the two of them. *How did we get here?* By the expression on his face, she knew he shared the same question.

Tenderly, Thanasis pulled her into an embrace. It was with reluctance she relented. Kate struggled to find some way to fight against her depth of feelings for him. She could not. What she had so fiercely hoped for in a relationship was to love and be loved, to be seen, to be treasured by someone. And she had found that in her private moments with Thanasis. The depth of her struggle to hold onto that bond with him was palpable. She folded into his arms.

"*Synhorese me.*" He was asking for her to forgive him. They rocked together back and forth. He whispered in her ear. "Give us one more small time together. I promise to keep my politics away from you for as long as you are here. I promise."

Kate wanted to step away from him. She wanted to be finished with all of this confusion and hurt. Instead, she was irresistibly pulled back into his orbit.

Thanasis moved slightly away. They locked eyes, and he began to sing a song by Kostas Hatzis, a Greek of Romani origin they had seen perform at a small bar in the city a few months before. On stage with his guitar and dressed all in black, his meltingly beautiful voice sailed over the room filled with devoted fans sitting in rapt attention.

Thanasis's voice reached out to her. It was one of her favorite songs, the title translated as "From the Airplane." A lover seeks to bring comfort to his beloved who has been embittered by life. They will fly high up in the sky and see the world below like a painting, houses like matchboxes, and people like strolling ants. Everything will appear trivial, and she will be able to forget her pain. Thanasis's voice quivered with the last word.

Like a moth flying directly toward a light bulb on the porch in the summertime, Kate found herself once again driven toward this man. She fell fully into his embrace. *One last time,* she told herself, as the fabric of his shirt brushed her cheek, and she inhaled his familiar, smoky scent. She would let herself live in this magic just a little longer.

sixty-one 🌿

The light of morning slipped through the shutters and created patterns of wavy lines on the bedroom floor of Thanasis's apartment. From outside, a jumble of noises from cars and buses crept in as well. It was still early, but Kate's mind was fully awake. More sleep was not a possibility. Slipping out of the tangle of Thanasis's arms without waking him, she paused. Her eyes couldn't help but see the contrast of the stark whiteness of his scar against the golden summer color of his arm. The remnants of what she had done to him. The reminder of what he had done to her.

At the apartment after the fiasco with Leftheris and Anthi, Kate's anger at Thanasis had spilled out again. "We don't see each other for a week, and this is the welcome I get?" Her voice was strong, almost shrill.

He had asked for her forgiveness multiple times, admitting his mistake. What more could he say? What could he do to make it up to her? She had slammed herself on the couch in the small living room and fumed. Still, she smiled when he had appeared in the doorway with a half loaf of bread balanced atop a plate of olives and feta cheese, a bottle of retsina with two glasses, and a dishtowel draped over his arm like a waiter. A grin curved one side of his mouth, and his eyes sparkled mischievously.

Throughout the evening they skirmished repeatedly over what

had happened. The first bottle disappeared and a second one took its place. Their words grew in volume and intensity, with Thanasis trying to justify the need for retribution against the forces that had ravaged his country. Kate argued adamantly that more violence would neither solve Greece's current problems nor bring back those who had died. Yet, by the end of the evening they found their way back into each other's arms and to the magnetism that bound them together beyond beliefs and beyond words. Two empty bottles, the remnants of feta cheese, crumbs of bread, and a few olives remained in the living room. Kate and Thanasis headed to the bedroom, any boundaries between them dissolved by the heat of their passion.

Now, despite a slight dizziness from too much wine the night before, Kate quickly dressed in her blue jean shorts, T-shirt, and sneakers. She left a sleeping Thanasis and headed to the sea walk, her morning routine since moving in with him. These few miles of concrete bordering the Bay of Salonika were her retreat for solace and reflection, just as they had been since her earliest days in Thessaloniki.

Kate successfully crossed the busy boulevard to reach the promenade, then stretched her legs into the long stride that had become her modus operandi for walking and thinking. To her right, the city awakened. To her left, waves rocked small fishing boats tethered to the dock. The sun sparkled and winked. Up ahead she could make out the large cylindrical shape of the White Tower, the symbol of the city—the city that had become hers. Now a museum, the tower was built by the Ottomans in the fifteenth century and had been the scene of a notorious prison and mass executions.

Step by step she worked on solutions to the problem that played hide and seek in her mind. *When to leave? How to leave?* It was no longer whether to leave. Her days with Thanasis were coming to an end, as she feared the possible danger of being with him and his friends. And then there was something else. Despite her deep love for Thanasis, she was being pulled back to her homeland. *How have I been changed by everything that's happened? Who have I become? What will my life as an independent woman in America be like now?* She was curious.

As she observed the scenes right and left, Kate noticed a dark and steady presence several steps away. *Someone is following me!* Glancing back, there was a pinprick sensation of a familiarity in the sturdy build and neatly combed hair of the man behind her. She hastened her pace and kept her gaze straight ahead. The figure was gaining ground. It was him. Captain Hercules, ostensibly from the Bureau of Foreign Workers. Since spotting him the day of the demonstration many months before, however, she was certain he was part of the security police. Kate hadn't seen him since then, but she had not forgotten who he was and what he stood for.

"Miss Katerina." The voice hooked her. She stopped.

"Kalimera," she offered, lodging her trembling hands in the back pockets of her shorts.

Despite the warmth of the day, he wore a black overcoat.

"Kalimera," he answered and motioned to a nearby bench. "Please. May I have a word with you?"

"Certainly." Because of her upbringing, she had always respected authority. And Captain Hercules was definitely an authority.

"Miss Katerina," he continued with formality, "I am speaking with you now as a personal conversation and not in my official capacity. This is 'off the record,' I think it is called."

Kate sat at the far end of the bench, her heart racing. She had no idea what to expect. She wasn't sure what personal meant. *Is he going to ask me out on a date?* She remembered her discomfort at his office, and how creepy it felt at the time. She feared, however, this was something more serious. Kate thought of Thanasis and Leftheris. Her stomach knotted.

"Yes, sir." There it was again. Her early training kicking in. The voice of her grandmother was in her head. "You always use 'ma'am' or 'sir' to be polite."

Captain Hercules fixed his eyes on Mount Olympus. His hair was graying at the temples, something she hadn't noticed in the office. Though his face was cleanly shaven, the line of a beard was attempting to break through, as was a glimmer of perspiration. Lips that were thin stayed, at this moment, in a neutral position. His eyes were like black marbles. "You understand that in this country we are fighting very hard to keep the security—the public order."

Kate nodded. At least now she knew he was not asking her out.

"And, as you know, there are certain elements wanting to create *haos,*" using the Greek pronunciation of the word for "chaos."

"Let me be very clear with you. I know that for whatever reason—maybe for *love,*" he emphasized the word caustically, "you have associated with people who are not, we can say, in your best interest."

It was true. She was on the radar of the security force. Her fingers kneaded the outer seams of her shorts in small circles. "But Captain Hercules, I have many friends here in Greece. I'm not limited to just one group of acquaintances." She struggled to make some kind of defense.

"Do not pretend. We know about your communist boyfriend and his group."

Kate didn't know what to say. She couldn't deny her close association with Thanasis or his cohorts. She and Thanasis must have been seen going to visit Leftheris and Anthi the day before.

"I have come to say you must be careful if you do not want to end up in a very bad situation."

His words chilled her. "What do you mean? What kind of situation?"

Captain Hercules responded by turning his head to one side and nodding, in a typical Greek gesture indicating something negative.

Kate struggled to continue. "And why are you telling me this? I'm sure there are many people that come through your office each day."

"That, Miss Katerina, I am not sure myself. I think I was . . . touched . . . is that the word? You came to Greece to work with our children. To try to help them and to teach them to speak. *Ta kaeimena paithia mas.*" He stopped after he said, "our poor children." His eyes softened. Kate had the sudden recollection of that day in his office, and how he had spoken about the disabled, momentarily letting down some kind of guard.

He continued. "We all have our Achilles Heel—yes, we Greeks have a myth for everything. And one of mine is these children. I had the occasion to see them going into your center in their mothers' arms. The faces of the mothers when they think no one watches. It is a heartbreak." He studied his hands. Kate vaguely remembered one morning at ELEPAAP when someone in a dark overcoat surveyed the building from the bakery across the street.

He shifted his focus back to the bay. His voice was quiet. "Growing up in our village there was such a child. He was hidden away, but I often saw him through a window. All of my life the picture of him alone in the dark while we played outside in the sun—it does not leave me." They sat in silence as a trio of elderly men passed by, their hands behind their backs juggling strands of worry beads.

Kate finally found words. "Are you telling me I need to end my friendships?"

Captain Hercules rose to leave. "My protection of you has limits. And it is moving quickly beyond those limits. Very quickly. Also, you must tell no one about this talk." He stood to walk away.

"Captain Hercules," she called. He stopped. She stuck out her hand to him. "Thank you, sir." Kate's response was not a polite reflex. This time it came from deeper inside her. She was convinced somewhere within him there was a place of goodness, a place that made him reach out to help her. He shook her hand and left.

Kate sidled back onto the bench, stunned. She watched the black overcoat until it vanished into the distance. Her thoughts whirled frantically, like one of the West Texas sandstorms from her childhood. *What does he mean by "a very bad situation"?* And he had emphasized the word "quickly." She stood and resumed her walk, her pace accelerating. Kate had now been given the answer to the question of *when* to leave. She still didn't know *how.*

sixty-two 🌿

Kate kept up her brisk steps along the sea walk, trying to fight a rising panic. A man in a short-sleeved blue shirt bumped into her.

"Sygnomee, Thespinis," he apologized and continued a few steps.

She froze. *Was he one of them?* Kate watched as he greeted a friend and walked into one of the many coffee shops that dotted the promenade. Relief. She resumed her speed, shaken from what she had just learned. Kate recalled scenes from the seaside village of the man behind the newspaper, the man on the corner, the man lingering too long at the sidewalk newsstand while she and Thanasis bought cigarettes. *The security police have been watching us.*

The knowledge she was being surveilled was as unsettling as the rest of her conversation with Captain Hercules had been. She jumped at the sound of a flock of pigeons flapping as they rose from a breakfast of breadcrumbs on the cement. Reluctantly, Kate reversed direction back to Thanasis's apartment. The question of *how* to leave her lover was still a tangled knot.

"You must tell no one about this talk." Captain Hercules's words played in her head. She needed to warn Thanasis. *How can I do that?*

Fluffy white clouds moved overhead, letting the sunshine through intermittently and dance on the waves of the bay. Up ahead the magnificent bronze statue of Alexander the Great, rising into the sky, appeared. The city of Thessaloniki claimed him as their own. Sitting astride his horse with sword in hand, the ancient hero was perpetually racing into battle. She found a bench near the towering statue, with Mount Olympus on the other side of the Bay of Salonika as a backdrop behind him.

Kate closed her eyes and waited for the pounding inside her chest to slow. The image of Captain Hercules, his face glistening from the heat of the day, reappeared. "That was so scary," she whispered to herself. She shook her head slowly back and forth. *Is all of this really happening to me?*

Sunlight pressed against her eyelids. Greece. Politics. Love. Danger. None of these existed in her life one year ago. They had inserted themselves and forged new places in her heart, mind, and soul. This lovely place on a map had become home to her. Kate opened her eyes and sighed. "But Greece is not my home," she whispered. The realization she must leave everything here was like a heavy stone being dropped into the well of her being.

She and Thanasis had already made plans to go away for the weekend. *Do I dare to do even that?* Kate needed time—she wanted time—just one last weekend with Thanasis to explain their time together had finally come to an end. Her lips trembled.

A mother holding the hand of an unstable toddler passed by in front of her. The child's finger pointed up to Alexander the Great, as his mother repeated, "Alogo, alogo" the word for "horse." How easily he copied it, unlike so many of the children at ELEPAAP. *What about them?* In the past few weeks, Kate hadn't thought much about what would happen if she failed to come back in the fall, even though that had been her original plan. *Who will help my children? How can I leave them?* She rhythmically bit her thumbnail. Around and back. Around and back. An idea came to mind. *I'll recruit someone when I get back home—a Greek American speech therapist to come to ELEPAAP.* Kate would make sure not to abandon the children.

She leaned back onto the wooden slats of the bench. Just as she had outgrown the fairy tales associated with her glittery white wedding gown, Kate would leave behind the romance of the revolutionary movement she had come to know in Greece. She half-smiled, remembering the excitement of the Theodorakis concert, red flags waving, the crowd united in song, the arms of the black-clad figure with his blazing head of hair. The struggle for a more just society was real. That much of Thanasis's dreams seemed true to her.

Wherever she would live in America, Kate could search out like-minded people who also believed in a more equitable society. People who wouldn't disregard the way America used small countries like pieces on a chessboard by supporting military dictatorships. She refused to bury what she had learned in Greece.

The phrase "heavy heart" had always sounded cliché. No longer. She could barely stand the immensity of weight within. The lessons she learned in Greece had been difficult ones. Seemingly good countries could do bad things; seemingly good people, like Thanasis, could do bad things; seemingly bad people, like Captain Hercules, could have good motives.

Kate watched the young boy and his mother continue along the sea walk as he struggled to keep his balance. Like him, she learned to stay steady in the face of new challenges, always working to remain upright as she kept moving forward.

Sadness accompanied a question. *What would my life be like if I hadn't boarded the Olympic flight last September?* She would never know. She only knew what a large debt of gratitude she owed to her decision. Kate took in a deep breath and slowly let it out.

"Home," her voice whispered the word. She knew it was time to go home. Her body, though, resisted standing up to head back to Thanasis's apartment. She knew that action would be her first step of leaving. Of saying goodbye. *Will this be the final time I'll walk beside the dancing waves of the Bay of Salonika? Will this be my last time to feel a part of this city I love so much?*

Kate shaded her eyes from the sunlight to find Alexander's face. He stared straight ahead. He would always be focused on the horizon, always ready for the next battle. She had no choice but to move forward to what awaited.

sixty-three

"Efharisto." Kate thanked Thanasis for the coffee he placed in her hands as she sat on the balcony at the beach house. The dread that had stalked her since their arrival the night before finally grabbed her shoulders and stopped her. She had no choice but to launch the conversation that would begin the end of their time together.

Thanasis kissed the top of her head. His knee pressed against hers as he settled into his chair. Kate ran her lips back and forth on the rim of the cup, pressing it more and more firmly. She knew she had to tell him about her conversation with Captain Hercules. To warn him. To lay the foundation for her leaving.

Earlier this morning lying beside him, Kate understood today would be their last day together. It would be her final time ever to wake up and feel the warmth of his head, his neck, his arms and legs, and the comfort of his skin. Kate had never been connected in such intimacy with anyone. Others hadn't known how to hold her in just the right way, to move together in lovemaking that led to simultaneous satisfaction.

Her time with Thanasis was moments strung together on a necklace she had worn with pleasure over the last few weeks, just as she wore his hands around her body when they were in bed. Alongside him was where she wanted to be, despite the danger and despite the knowledge it would have an end. Today would be that end.

With her head still on the pillow, Kate had agonized about whether or not to tell him she was leaving. She played it out in her mind and let the tape go forward. He would bargain for a few more days. She would have to stand firm and not allow his words and his touch to persuade her to stay. There was nothing to gain by telling him directly. She could avoid the pain of that scene. And she would.

Hours later after a swim in the sea and lunch at their favorite restaurant on the beach, Kate watched Thanasis on the balcony as he eyed the horizon. She took a sip of her Nescafe, then another before putting her cup down. "Thanasi, I've got to tell you something." She reached out and caressed the softness of his neck beneath his curls before continuing. "I'm getting more and more afraid about getting caught in the middle of something."

"Yes. I know that." His words were slowed.

Biting her lip, she stopped before forging ahead with the difficult part. "Yesterday morning on my walk, I was followed by that captain from the security police—the one I met when I registered for work. The same one at the demonstration."

Thanasis placed his cup on the table. His eyes squinted with suspicion. Kate pushed the words out. "He wanted to warn me about being with you. With you and your friends. He said he had been *protecting* me." She stopped. "Whatever that means."

"*Ti einai auta ta haza pou les?*" His shoulders raised, and he spread his hands as he asked, "What is that craziness you're saying?" Thanasis's eyes widened.

Kate didn't want this to be happening, but she couldn't stop now. Her words tripped over themselves. "He said that . . . he said that his protection was coming to an end. And . . . and that I could end up in a very bad situation." Kate knew she had just lobbed a grenade into the quiet of their summer idyll.

"*Gamo teen* . . ." Thanasis began a typical Greek curse but didn't finish. He stood up and paced back and forth on the narrow balcony, head down and his hands clenching and unclenching. Kate found her hand covering her mouth, almost as if trying to stuff the words back inside.

Finally, he came to stand directly in front of her and squatted. "What did you say to him?" Switching back to English, he seemed to be working hard to control his voice.

"Nothing really. I mostly listened. I guess they must have seen us at Leftheris's house, and he wanted to warn me." She wasn't afraid of Thanasis's barely-suppressed anger, but a tightness still filled her chest.

"We do not do anything illegal. They cannot arrest us for *tipota*," emphasizing the Greek word for "nothing" with his voice and a sweep of his hand. He stood up and moved back to his chair. "What is the interest in you? Did you tell him about the hotel or Stelios?"

Kate flushed and answered quickly. "I know better than that, Thanasi." Her own anger now sparked. They were like boxers in their respective corners in the ring. Their eyes stayed away from each other. Silence sat between them like an unwanted guest. Gradually, his face softened, and he placed his hand gently on her knee.

Kate took a deep breath. "It's strange," she offered. "I think maybe he has a soft spot."

"Soft spot! A security policeman?" Thanasis scoffed at the idea. His hand was back into his own lap.

"No, really," Kate protested. "Both times we met, he talked about the children at ELEPAAP."

Thanasis's expression remained unchanged. He shook his head. "Koukla mou . . . you do not understand Greece."

Kate knew this much was true. How many times was she like an outsider peeking in through a frosted glass window? She didn't want tension, especially since this would be their last day together. "I don't want to get trapped in something that isn't really my fight. Do you understand?" Her voice was raw, like it was torn from somewhere deep inside.

A young boy's melodic voice drifted up from the street, hawking cherries. Usually, Thanasis would have rushed down and brought back a paper bag of sweet bounty to share. Kate implored him. "You do understand, don't you?"

Just below the balcony, the village was coming to life after siesta.

"*Laheia!*" A baritone voice offered lottery tickets. A bicycle bell dinged. Afternoon greetings were exchanged. The wheel of life turned, indifferent to Kate and Thanasis's struggles.

He placed both hands on her knees. "I thank you for waiting this long. For giving us more time." His eyes clouded with tears. He reached out and put his arm around her shoulder and their heads touched. With no words spoken, they stood and went inside to their bed.

An hour later, folded in his arms, Kate wasn't sure if he suspected this had been their final lovemaking. It was longer than usual, with an intensity from both of them. Their bodies moved together in wave after wave of passion. She nuzzled into his neck. The softness. The security. The sense of no boundary between where she ended and where he began.

Too soon, Thanasis kissed the top of her head, then reached for a cigarette to share. She watched the lit match spotlight his profile, and she understood political struggle would always inhabit his soul. She wanted to throw a net over him and steal him away from his ideals and make him be an ordinary person.

"Nikos and Marika came in last night. I need to do some things before meeting them. You will come later to the taverna?"

Kate admired his nakedness as he left the bed and headed for the bathroom.

"I like Marika," Kate said, avoiding an answer. She slipped a T-shirt over her head and retrieved her unfinished coffee from the balcony.

The last sip of cold Nescafe was gone by the time Thanasis came from the shower, toweling his hair, and jeans hugging his slim waist. The scar from the night of the fire was more visible at times like these, the accordion webbing of the skin on one arm. It always brought a brief chill inside her.

"You go on," Kate told Thanasis after he was dressed. She met him at the door, and they embraced. Kate held on a second longer. She wanted to remember how it felt—how he felt. The curve of his shoulders. His scent. The sweet softness of his neck. Thanasis kissed her again, long and deeply. His finger brushed her cheek and lingered. He kissed the top of her head, and she closed her eyes.

The door shut. This time she was out of tears. Tapping a cig-arette from the pack lying on the table, she lit it and sat on a chair, her feet propped on the bed.

She would miss his sweetness the most. His way of making sure she got the first cup of coffee. It was the surprises—appearing at her door with a smile and a box of bright red strawberries hiding behind his back. It was his far-away expression when he talked about the world that needed to change. It was the kindness. And the handsomeness. And the sex. And the gateway into a part of her that had not existed before.

Staying any longer, she risked being swept once again into his magnetic force. She stubbed her cigarette until it extinguished.

sixty-four ✿

Resting the inside of her wrist on her lips, Kate traced the touch of Thanasis's last kiss. Her head leaned against the window of the bus headed for Thessaloniki. She moved her hands back and forth on her face, searching for any lasting scents—the soap he used, a hint of smoke.

Beside her, the small traveling bag was crammed with her bathing suit, jeans, tops, and all the necessities she'd carried the past few weeks, from Thanasis's apartment to the beach house multiple times, once to Metamorphosis, and back to the city. She fingered the leather straps of her bag that had dug into her shoulder as it banged against her back down stairways and across paths and along sidewalks. There was a sense of relief, but it was momentary.

Thanasis. When, she wondered, in the midst of conversation with friends at the taverna, would he realize fully she was not coming to join him? There was farewell in his sweet, final kiss. He did not look back as he went out the door.

Kate pictured him returning to their empty room and seeing the bed with the pillows she'd fluffed and the covers she'd smoothed. He would go out on the balcony, light a cigarette, and stare out into the night. She desperately hoped they both could finally find peace. Neither would have to work so terribly hard at chasing the hopeless dream of being together.

With legs propped against the seat in front of her, Kate's knees pressed against the smooth metal. Through the window, she contemplated the stretches of sea and sand. Beachgoers folded umbrellas and packed away belongings. Their figures were shadows against the fading light, calling up memories of lazy afternoons with Thanasis, swimming in the clearest blue she'd ever seen.

A police car sped around the bus on the curving two-lane road, reminding Kate of Captain Hercules. Fear hijacked her thoughts as she recalled the recent newspaper headline of a bombing in Athens claimed by the 17th of November.

"Thanasis," she whispered and shook her head. He was filled with a zeal for life, both in politics and in love. "That's who he is, and that's why I loved him," she whispered. Kate would have to abandon her passion for him, just as she was abandoning this beautiful scenery fading into the distance.

The bus left the highway and threaded through the streets of a village to pick up passengers at a local stop. It was evening, and the marketplace was bustling. A young woman headed into a butcher's shop with a straw basket slung over her shoulder. Last week she could have been that woman. Feathery green tops of carrots and stalks of leeks peeked out over the edge of her basket. Even the leather sandals and long skirt were the fashion Kate had adopted, just as she had adopted a way of life. Or tried to adopt it.

"*Paraligo.* Almost."

Straining her neck, Kate followed the woman until she disappeared into the shop. For the first time she wondered about Thanasis and his next love. *Will she be someone like this? A Greek woman he won't have to fight with to reach common understanding?* The thought of another woman in his arms stung. Kate refocused attention to the sidewalk, hoping to imprint memories of this village scene, but mostly trying to shake off this last thought.

The bus stopped near a coffee shop to pick up a few more passengers. Inside, men sat with their friends around small tables, with the ever-present demitasse cups of coffee and drifting cigarette smoke, fingers throwing dice onto backgammon boards. These scenes, which had become commonplace in her daily life, would soon disappear.

Back on the highway, the bus jerked into high gear and skirted an expanse of perfectly still sea. Clouds on the horizon reflected the colors of a disappearing sunset. This beauty and her sadness melted together, filling her with a magnitude of loss.

With each mile being eaten by the bus speeding toward the city, Kate reluctantly acknowledged the end of a love and a way of life. She would need to bury both of them deep within.

sixty-five

Kate stepped down onto the black asphalt and watched the bus as it trailed fumes into the night air and vanished into the darkness. Crossing the highway, she entered the metal gates leading to the Stylianou farm. She put her bag on the gravel and admired the view. The moment was perfect in its symmetry. Her first and her last evenings were here, in this place that had embraced her so fully.

Windows from the house glowed with lights and energy. Quiet blanketed the landscape, absent the daytime sounds of peacocks, sheep, and chickens. In the space of less than one year, Time the Magician had transformed this setting from an unknown place into her second home. Kate slipped the bag back on her shoulder.

"No tears," she whispered, determined to make this last evening with her Greek family a happy one.

Climbing the wooden stairs to the kitchen, Kate heard the clatter of pots and pans. As she paused on the steps, memories flooded in. She gazed at the few lights twinkling on the hill in the distance and remembered her walks. Down below, the outline of the gazebo brought to mind the awful pig slaughter at Christmas. Rows of trees stood silently in the fields, and Kate could almost hear the laughter of family and friends seated on the ground in the afternoons, sorting through mounds of almonds to send through a shelling machine. The poignancy of these recollections threatened her resolve to keep her emotions in check. She steadied herself.

Through the open window, Soto's voice explained something to his mother in his slow cadence and labored pronunciation. She visualized Lena moving from task to task while still concentrating on what her son struggled to say. Although his speech had improved, Kate wished she could have done more to help him. Kate sighed deeply, hoping her efforts had made at least a small difference. She knocked on the wooden kitchen door and opened it.

"*Kalos tin.*" Lena welcomed her with a broad smile. Soto's lips puckered to one side with the overflow of excitement, and Kate reached out to give him a hug. Lena kissed her on each cheek and brought her close. Against Lena's shoulder, she kept her eyes shut, commanding her tears to stay inside.

Kate regained her composure and forced a smile. "*Mepos eeparhei krevati yia xena?*" Asking if perhaps there was a bed available for a stranger.

Lena answered with a mock seriousness. "*Vevaios, alla yia polla thollaria.*" Her reply indicated, "Certainly, but it would cost many dollars."

"*Eho. Eho.*" Kate repeated she had the money. Soto, following the conversation, squealed with his usual laugh that ranged from high to low notes.

Kate heard footsteps coming from the living room, and Yiannis peeked around the corner. "Cheerio!"

"*Manolis!*" Kate answered without hesitation. It was one of his favorite jokes. A Greek named Manolis is in London. The Greek word for "mister" is *kurios* and is often used in Greece to ask, "What is your name?" Manolis mistakes the British greeting, "cheerio," for that question and replies, "Manolis!"

"Katina." He gave her a bear hug.

"Teliosame." Kate struggled to keep her voice firm, saying they had come to the end.

"Fevyes?" Yiannis asked if she was leaving.

"Tomorrow." Kate nodded and her voice broke.

Lena, summoning her usual stoicism, deflected the emotions that threatened and said, *"Autoi zousan kala kai emeis kalitera."* It was the ending in Greek fairy tales that, "They lived well, and we lived even better."

Kate grabbed her bag and headed down the hallway. In the familiar bedroom that had been her nest, she turned on the light. Her yellow suitcase waited on the other twin bed. Kate had brought it to the farm when she'd changed her ticket to stay longer in Greece. Slumping on the bed as the enormity of the events of the day flooded in all at once, she shook with quiet sobs, wondering what Thanasis was doing at this moment. It would be too early for him to leave the taverna, but by now he would realize she would not be joining him. He would lift glass after glass of retsina, her absence noticed by his group of friends but most likely not mentioned. Kate let her tears have their way down her cheeks. He would be okay. Just as she would be okay. Eventually. But not yet.

"Katina, ela na fame!" Lena's invitation to "Come and eat" reached down the hallway. Kate washed her face in the bathroom, the place that always smelled of the pure white *Karavaki* soap, with the little boat on the package.

Before taking her place at the table, Kate sought out Aris and gave him kisses on each cheek. He cocked his head and greeted her. *"Mas eleipes polee?"* asking if she had missed them very much, even though she had seen them less than one week before in Metamorphosis.

"*Then boreis na fantastees poso mou leipete.*" He couldn't even fantasize how much she had missed them, she told him. Aris grinned.

"*Kai . . . eme . . . eme . . . emena?*" Soto struggled to ask, "And me too?"

"*Akoma pio polee, agape mou.* Even more, my love," bringing another cackle from him.

Yiannis pulled a bottle of beer from the refrigerator. "And now we drink to our Katina. Steen ygeia mas," which they all repeated.

Kate crunched through the layers of Lena's homemade tyropita. After they brought her up to date with family news, the conversation switched to English. The boys were accustomed to this change of language for topics their parents didn't want them to hear. They kept eating, with Soto stabbing the food in his bowl and swerving his fork to his mouth.

Yiannis, always her protector and confidant, charged ahead. "What happened, Katina?"

"Well," she said, "you may be surprised to learn that the Greek security police take good care of their imported labor." She tried to couch the story of Captain Hercules in humor. As she told her story, Yiannis listened intently and Lena clicked her tongue, shaking her head back and forth in disapproval. Both expressed surprise with the extent of his interest in her and agreed she had no choice but to take him seriously.

"And with the man?" Lena was careful not to use Thanasis's name, since it was obvious both boys were trying to eavesdrop.

Kate brought her napkin to her mouth, pretending to wipe it, but actually trying to keep herself from bursting into tears. "I told him about the conversation and that I couldn't stay any longer." She reached for her glass and finished the remaining beer. "It wasn't easy. I didn't tell him directly that I was leaving, but he understood. I know he understood."

"Katina, Katina." Yiannis regarded her with both sympathy and love. "Your grand Greek adventure became something that you did not expect. The final twist of the cinema." Of course, Yiannis would liken it to a movie.

Kate sighed and with her fork gathered up the last remnants of tyropita still on her plate. They changed the conversation to school starting soon and news from ELEPAAP. They spoke of future plans when she would come back to Greece to visit, and she hoped they might come see her someday in America.

Reluctantly, she said goodnight to all of them and headed for her room. After the light was out, Kate struggled to stay awake as long as she could, listening to the distant noises of trucks on the highway traveling back and forth between Thessaloniki and Yugoslavia. For as long as possible, she wanted to be a part of this place, this exotic and lovely place that had become her home.

When the morning sunlight and the cries of roosters found her, Kate listened for sounds of the household waking up. Already, she dreaded her last hug from Yiannis before he left for work. The final scenes unfolded in her mind.

She'd lug her suitcase down the backstairs with Lena, while the boys played soccer on the grass. Aris would return temporarily to the shy boy she first met, his way of hiding his feelings. Emotions would hijack Soto, as he flung his arms around Kate, unable to get out any words.

Lena would drive to the airport, a reversal of her first trip to the farm not quite one year ago. Bidding her farewell would be the hardest of all. After their final embrace, Kate would walk into the airport and eventually head toward the waiting plane, the heat steaming from the tarmac. The plane would bump down the runway and launch into the air, as it hovered over the sprawling city and the sparkling Aegean. And then it would all disappear.

sixty-six 🌿

$\mathcal{S}$hutting off the car engine, Kate studied the scene out the windshield for a few moments. Layers of snow surrounded the gracious two-story home in the Boston suburbs. She relished the opportunity to shift from the busyness of her life in Cambridge to an afternoon and dinner in this Greek American home. It had been six months since she had left Greece, but a yearning for her adopted country remained strong.

Once back in America, she had chosen Boston as her next place to live at the urging of her younger brother who was studying there. It seemed a good decision, offering a connection to family and also a cosmopolitan city to explore.

Kate slipped on her coat and left the warmth of her car to meet the brisk winter air. She walked along the well-shoveled walkway, rang the doorbell, and listened for a shuffle of steps. The door opened. Kate exchanged a kiss on each cheek with her friend Irenie, a lovely dark-haired woman near her own age.

Once her coat was stowed in the closet, they headed for the kitchen. Both the living room to the left, and the dining room to the right were impeccably maintained. The Greek aesthetic of finely woven tapestries and oriental rugs were combined with elegant American furniture and crystal lighting fixtures. Kate was learning firsthand that Greek American housewives took as great a pride in their homes as did their counterparts in Greece.

As they approached the kitchen door, Kate was reminded that, even more than the invitation to join Irenie's family for dinner, she loved participating in the meal preparations.

"*Dolmathes.*" Irenie announced the day's cooking project. Merely the mention of the word for stuffed grape leaves made Kate's mouth water. As in previous visits, the warmth of this room with its multitude of aromas brought a deep feeling of pleasure, albeit tinged with nostalgia.

"Yeia sas." Kate greeted Irenie's mother, aunt, and cousin, whose hands were busy as they worked in an assembly line to make the evening meal.

"Kalos tin." They welcomed her with broad smiles.

"Dolmathes?" Kate asked, as she slid into an empty chair around the table alongside Irenie.

"*Laxano* dolmathes." Irenie's Aunt Aliki emphasized these were made with cabbage rather than grape leaves. Her fingers kneaded pink ground beef in a large bowl. She puckered her lips and blew a kiss toward Kate, then used the back of her hand to push her wayward glasses back up the bridge of her nose. Aunt Aliki's face danced with liveliness, reminding Kate how her friends in Greece conveyed more information with one facial expression than their American counterparts did with a half dozen words.

Kate had met Irenie by chance. One Saturday morning, two months after her move to Boston, they both stood in line at a small Greek market in Cambridge where Kate shopped for imported Greek products. She was making a concerted effort to hold on, in any way possible, to the life she missed.

"Excuse me, but which feta do you buy?" Kate had asked Irenie as they waited at a counter displaying several containers with blocks of the white cheese submerged in salty water.

"We actually like the French," she'd told Kate, then lowered her voice. "But don't let the Greek Consulate know."

"Siopee!" Kate used the Greek word for "silence," then zipped her lips with her fingers. They both laughed. Poignantly, in Irenie's face, Kate found a mosaic from friends in Greece she was missing.

After answering Irenie's questions about her connection to Greece, Kate took a chance. *"Mepos theleis na pame yia café?"* shakily asking if maybe she'd like to go for coffee. It was one of her first chances to speak Greek in America, other than a few words with the storekeeper or brief calls to her friends in Greece.

Irenie responded with the characteristic head movement of assent, and they both headed for the cash register before moving outside onto the sidewalk.

The two women quickly developed a close friendship. There was the added bonus that Irenie's mother had been born in Thessaloniki. Much to Kate's delight, Irenie invited her to meet her family, which led Kate into this circle of Greek hospitality, something she had sorely missed.

Aunt Aliki spoke up again. "Come—come. You ate the cabbage dolmathes of Greece. And now you must learn to make them for the husband you will find any day now!" Kate and Irenie exchanged glances. Irenie's relatives may have left Greece long ago, but their village ways lived on. Aunt Aliki threw back her head and laughed, the rows of brush hair curlers kept in place by pink plastic piks.

Late-afternoon sun streamed in from the kitchen window. Fortunately, these visits kept Greece alive for Kate, something she had desperately tried to do since leaving. She stayed in touch with the Stylianou family and Georyia with phone calls on holidays and name-day celebrations. But not Thanasis. He had not tried to find her, nor had she tried to contact him.

The cabbage, trapped in a slow boil in the large pot on the stove, released its scent, a most distinctive aroma. Irenie's mother, Antigone, rose to attend to what was cooking. Her dark hair was also wrapped in curlers. She stabbed and punched tomatoes in a pan on the stove, on their way to becoming the red pulp of tomato sauce for the dolmathes.

"*Ti kaneis koritsi mou?*" Antigone's smiling eyes searched Kate's face, asking how she was.

Kate was comforted by endearments such as "my girl," echoes of words once part of her everyday life.

"*Kala. Eftiaksa ta koulourakia sou, alla then petihan.*" Kate responded that she'd tried making Antigone's sweet cookies with sesame seeds but had not succeeded.

"*Then peirazei. Tha ta kanoume mazi pali.*" No matter. They would make them together again. Antigone busied herself at the stove, bracelets jangling as she stirred the pot in time to the Greek music from the radio on the counter.

Glancing at the wall clock, Antigone called, "*Koristia,*" to the "girls." She brought a bowl of freshly washed parsley atop a cutting board to the table. "Here's for one of you." Retrieving two small onions, she offered a knife and another cutting board. "And here's for whoever needs to cry and blame it on the onions."

Kate rose and took the onions. "I didn't live in Greece without bringing back some very special kitchen skills. I may look American, but just wait until you see how I chop my *kremeithia.*" She moved to the counter, distancing herself from the beehive of chatter around the table. At times on these visits, she was overtaken by a strong melancholy, missing so much of her life in Greece.

As Kate began slicing through the parchment outer skin of the onion, she listened to the melody of bouzouki music from the Greek American program on the radio. As the song ended, a recording of the sounds of a shepherd's pipes came on, accompanied by the clanging bells of goats being herded on a hillside. It was the introduction to the national news broadcast from Greece, dispatched to expatriates on Greek radio stations around the world.

Familiar words opened the program, wishing a good evening to all. Kate struggled to understand what she could from the rapid pace of the announcer's recounting of the news, including a report of marches in Athens and Thessaloniki. Thousands of people in the streets. Kate couldn't make out what they were protesting, but she knew it was something important.

Kate stopped chopping. Thanasis. She was sure he was there. Or hoped he was able to be. She could see the leather jacket, his arms helping to hold a banner. She imagined the intensity of his eyes and the ragged anger in his voice. Kate knew Thanasis was at home in his world. It was a world now very far away from hers.

Just as quickly as she had conjured him, the image of Thanasis melted away. The aching in her heart lingered a few moments more. Wiping her cheek with the back of her hand, she blinked the remaining tears back inside. *"Oriste,"* saying, "Here you go," as she presented the onions. Aunt Aliki scraped them into the bowl with the ground meat.

Irenie caught Kate's attention, signaled, and they moved through a small pantry and out onto the screened back porch. There was still a touch of sunlight amid the chilly air. "What were you thinking about a few minutes ago?" Irenie had come to know her well. "Thanasis?"

Kate nodded. "The news reported protest marches in Athens and Thessaloniki. I'm sure he was there. I pictured him in the huge crowd." A tinge of sadness crept in with a flood of memories of their time together. Her recollections were like fireworks that brightened the sky and brought a thrill with swirls and designs and an explosion of colors, before ending when the last bits of light died, and ash fell to earth.

She stared into the dusk, wondering what direction her life would take next. Every workday, Kate headed to a school for severely disabled children, enthusiastic about her students and grateful for her solid commitment to a professional life. She delighted in going sleeveless so the underarm hair she'd grown as a badge of 1970s feminism could be seen by everyone, even her conservative family. This person could flaunt convention, pleased at the thought of lovers visiting her bed on the third-floor apartment in Cambridge.

Yet somewhere inside was also the skinny little girl who loved spending time at home, following her mother around. She longed for that place of peace and security, to get married, and have children.

Kate and Irenie stood together in the evening quiet. "You aren't done with him yet?" Irenie prodded her out of her silence.

Moving to the other side of the porch, Kate plucked a few dead leaves from an abandoned rosemary plant. She rubbed them between her fingers and brought a faint scent to her nose. It was a habit she'd brought from Greece. "I am. But I admit there are still fantasies every now and then. He was a very handsome lover, you know." She laughed at this last comment. "And there was a kindness about him. Even with everything that happened. I don't think there was a mean bone in his body."

Irenie was skeptical. She'd heard the Thanasis stories several times.

"No, really," Kate said. "There were lies, and politics was a huge part of who he was. But there were reasons I fell so hard for him and kept letting him back in my life." She ran her fingers over the dried leaves once more. "It would never have worked out." Kate let out a long breath.

Irenie struck a pose, imitating her aunt, "And you'll meet some nice Greek boy . . ."

Kate briefly considered the prospect before shaking her head to dismiss it. "I can't imagine that ever happening." She knew married life with a typical Greek American would be too confining for the person she had become.

Irenie approached and touched her cheek. "You'll meet someone else. Don't worry, *Kaitaki*." Here was yet another name for her. Little Kate. She loved being in this world of sweet nicknames and delicious food and genuine hospitality. Greek culture at its finest. She watched Irenie disappear through the door.

Despite the cold, Kate lingered, settled on a stool, and considered yet again what she'd brought back with her. Her commitment to children like Soto, Demetraki, Giorgos, and the others. Yiannis was never too far away, as she imagined him sitting beside her at the independent movie theater, watching French New Wave movies or Italian films. Memories of dancing with Georyia always resurfaced when she listened to Greek albums on her stereo.

On weekends, Kate worked shifts at the Cambridge Food Co-Op, making friends with the leftists there. One night at a party, she'd even met a young man from the Black Panther Party in Oakland, complete with black beret, which brought back memories of coffee with Fotini in the upstairs apartment where she'd first learned about the Black militant George Jackson. On her bookshelf was his memoir purchased at Molhos, her beloved bookstore in Thessaloniki. She continually attempted to weave together what she'd experienced in Greece with her new life in Boston.

Kate sighed and shifted her feet from the rung of the stool, readying to go back inside. Just then, a whiff of something in the air ignited another memory. Smoke from a fireplace in the neighborhood. She watched as the sun cast an orange glow on the snow layered in the backyard, reminiscent of light from the bonfire that evening in Langathas. Dusk. Orange. Smoke. The trio of those elements whisked her back to the Fire Walking ceremony.

Closing her eyes, Thanasis's hands were on her shoulders, shortly before he had abandoned her. Kate hadn't been able to consider fully what she'd experienced during the ritual; the trauma of the evening had eclipsed any chance to do so. With everything which had happened now part of the past, she could finally reflect on that night.

Kate remembered the Fire Walkers as they approached the circle of embers. Until this moment, she had forgotten about a woman who captured her attention, the one who had twirled her red scarf with lively insistence. Middle-aged, hair pulled back, she was someone who would be passed on the street with no reason to register her face or anything else about her. She stood at the edge of the burning coals, her mouth set in a thin line of determination.

The woman began tentatively, then gradually quickened her pace as she skipped across the glowing embers, kicking up sparks with her bare feet. She moved with a decided purpose on her next round. As the woman began a third and final trip back across the coals, Kate recalled the almost beatific expression on her face, her head held high. She had been transformed.

The clatter of kitchen noise interrupted her reverie. Rising to rejoin the group, she hesitated. Kate now pictured herself on the edge of a circle, glowing with challenges stretching out before her. She had gone to a country hostile to Americans, not knowing anyone and understanding only a few words of Greek. She'd created strong bonds of friendship and had been reasonably successful with her work. She'd been schooled in politics and European culture. She'd fallen in love with a man who had betrayed her, yet she'd taken a second ride with him on a fast-moving carousel. And, in the end, she'd known when it was time to get off and come back home.

Gradually, a radiating strength and confidence arose in her chest, infusing her with a deep sense of well-being. She, too, had been transformed.

Surveying the gathering twilight with its smattering of stars rising to populate the sky, she moved her head in affirmation, a gesture she had brought from Greece.

Kate smiled into the evening, her future ready to unfold.

acknowledgments

Deepest gratitude to those who helped bring *Walking on Fire* to life. I've written thousands of words in classes and groups since my own Greek experience, and writing teachers Sean Murphy and Tania Caselle of "Write to the Finish" were instrumental in giving form to this present version. This endeavor would not have succeeded without the collaboration and assistance of my brother Charles Crawley and sister-in-law Libby Slappey; they are the best! My Thursday night writing group of Jane Hart, Jay Boyle, Lenora Shatkin, and Alan Brickman have provided countless opportunities for exploring the writing process. Debora Seidman and Dianne Vonna of my Write to the Finish critique group have been welcome companions on this ride and added many invaluable suggestions over the past six years. My friend Gretchen Lutz has cheered me on every step of the way.

Great thanks to Brooke Warner, Shannon Green, copyeditor Lorraine White, and the team at She Writes Press for the opportunity to be part of an amazing publishing house.

Family and friends, both in the US and in Greece, have been a constant source of support and love. I could never have walked through the fire of writing and publishing without them.

ABOUT THE AUTHOR

Photo credit: Paula Passi McCue

Kathryn Crawley was born of pioneer stock and raised in the small West Texas cotton town of Lamesa. She received undergraduate and graduate degrees in speech pathology from Baylor University. Unforeseen events and an adventurous spirit led her to Casper, Wyoming, Colorado Springs, Colorado, and Thessaloniki, Greece, where she worked in a center for Greek children with cerebral palsy from 1974 to 1976. She went on to establish roots in Boston, where she continued her career as a speech pathologist. Today, she enjoys life with her partner, Tom, daughter, Emilia, and two dogs in a Boston suburb.

SELECTED TITLES FROM SHE WRITES PRESS

She Writes Press is an independent publishing company founded to serve women writers everywhere. Visit us at www.shewritespress.com.

Pieces by Maria Kostaki. $16.95, 978-1-63152-966-5. After five years of living with her grandparents in Cold War-era Moscow, Sasha finds herself suddenly living in Athens, Greece—caught between her psychologically abusive mother and violent stepfather.

The Greek Persuasion by Kimberly K. Robeson. $16.95, 978-1-63152-565-0. During a summer in Greece, Greek American professor Thair Mylopoulos-Wright begins writing about her mother and grandmother's early-life experiences—an exercise that starts her on a quest for wholeness, and ultimately inspires her to forge a path for herself that goes beyond the traditional.

Cleans Up Nicely by Linda Dahl. $16.95, 978-1-93831-438-4. The story of one gifted young woman's path from self-destruction to self-knowledge, set in mid-1970s Manhattan.

Split-Level by Sande Boritz Berger. $16.95, 978-1-63152-555-1. For twenty-nine-year-old wife and mother Alex Pearl, the post-Nixon 1970s offer suburban pot parties, tie-dyed fashions, and the lure of the open marriage her husband wants for the two of them. Yearning for greater adventure and intimacy, yet fearful of losing it all, Alex must determine the truth of love and fidelity—at a pivotal point in an American marriage.

Just the Facts by Ellen Sherman. $16.95, 978-1-63152-993-1. The seventies come alive in this poignant and humorous story of a fearful rookie reporter at a small-town newspaper who uncovers a big-time scandal.

Estelle by Linda Stewart Henley. $16.95, 978-1-63152-791-3. From 1872 to '73, renowned artist Edgar Degas called New Orleans home. Here, the narratives of two women—Estelle, his Creole cousin and sister-in-law, and Anne Gautier, who in 1970 finds a journal written by a relative who knew Degas—intersect . . . and a painting Degas made of Estelle spells trouble.